PRAISE FOR THE AMISH OF SWAN CREEK SERIES

"In a world that has gotten so cold these books are just what I needed. I will take values anywhere I can get them and I certainly got them in this series. There are no "issues" just respect for each other. **A must read.**" — *Amazon Reviewer*

"Very **positive, uplifting books.** I really like this author!" —*Amazon Reviewer*

"I read a little, and then I **couldn't put it down.** I have now read 10 of Tattie's books back to back." —*Amazon Reviewer*

D1541555

THE AMISH OF SWAN CREEK COLLECTION

TATTIE MAGGARD

FIVE PORCHES PRESS

SWEET COMPETITION

"Dearly beloved, avenge not yourselves, but rather give place unto wrath: for it is written, Vengeance is mine; I will repay, saith the Lord."
Romans 12:19 KJV

CHAPTER 1

The barn door remained open as the young ladies in their best dark blue dresses and black "goin' out" *kapps* and young men in their Sunday suspenders and black polished boots filed in.

"He's cute," Miriam Wittmer whispered loudly to her sister with a giggle. They strolled through the barn, arm in arm.

"Not him, and keep your voice down. Listen, I don't have much time to teach you what you need to know before I join church so you're going to have to pay attention."

"Emma, you may be my big sister but I can handle things myself. I'm sixteen now, practically an adult."

Emma stopped walking. "Choosin' a life mate is no silly matter. Do you want to be stuck with someone like Ebby your whole life?" Emma thumbed in the direction of a plump man in a black felt hat sitting on a hay bale in the corner of the barn. He spewed out a line of tobacco, wiping his mouth with his sleeve, then looked up in their direction. He gave a crooked grin. Miriam's eyes grew as large as saucers.

"I didn't think so." Emma shook her head softly. "Take this seriously and don't do anything dumb. Whatever happens at this singin' tonight will be known by every unmarried person in the community before sunup. Now, take Abram over there. He's a handsome man with a future. I hear he's ready to take over his *vater's* whole cabinetry business."

"I still don't know why you can't come to the singin's after you get baptized. Isn't everyone invited?" Miriam walked with her sister to a series of long benches set up in the dusty barn.

"Well, of course I could, if I wanted to, but singin's are mostly for those who haven't matured enough to want to join church yet. I figure when I get baptized I won't have any need for singin's. Luke can come and ask to court me openly, instead of all this secretiveness that goes on after dark on Sunday nights." She and Luke had been together for over two years and the only thing standing in the way of a marriage proposal was for them both to join church in the fall.

"Are you sure you're ready to join church? I mean, isn't there anything wild you want to do first? Just once in your life, sister, don't you want to just let go and see what happens?" Miriam's eyes were filled with excitement. Excitement that scared Emma.

"*Nay*. I'm a grown woman and have no need of such silliness." She hoped to persuade her sister to also hurry through *Rumspringa*, the time when Amish teenagers must decide for themselves whether or not to reject the trappings of the modern world. *Rumspringa* usually ended with the youth joining the church and being accepted by the community as an adult church member. Some just took a lot more time to decide than others, and occasionally one would do something stupid. Emma hoped Miriam wouldn't do something she'd regret, or worse, something to disgrace the whole family. She'd heard tell of a few people over the years who had taken it too far.

Miriam let out a sigh. "You're eighteen, but by listenin' at ya I'd swear you were pushin' forty."

"Nothin' wrong with puttin' away childish things, sister. In fact, I'd of joined church a year ago if I hadn't been waiting for you to turn sixteen. I couldn't let you out the first time on your own."

"And why not?"

"You're my baby sister and I want you to know I'm here for you, that's all." Emma tucked an unruly strand of Miriam's blonde hair back into her black *kapp*.

"*Vater* made you, didn't he?" Miriam's face held a knowing grin.

"That's irrelevant." Emma's father had only asked her to make sure Miriam made it back home safely. He knew whatever else happened was out of his hands, but Emma was the responsible one. As the elder sister, it was her job to take care of Miriam.

After the singing was done, some of the young ladies brought out snacks and placed them on a long table by the barn's open double doors. It was nearly ten at night and Missouri's late summer air hung heavy across the lot, where, with plates and drinks in hand, the young Swiss Amish paired off to socialize.

"*Vie gatz*, ladies." Luke Graber's brown eyes shone in the battery-operated lights spilling from the barn. "Emma, would you care to keep company with me tonight?" He handed her a Mason jar of sweet tea and then took a sip of his own.

"I think I should stay with Miriam tonight, Luke."

"Don't be silly, sister. I'll be just fine." Miriam smiled at her sister, warmly.

"But this is your first singin'." Emma took hold of her sister's arm with her free hand. "I can't just leave you here with no one to talk to. What kind of sister would I be?"

Jeb Lengacher was suddenly at Miriam's side. "*Vie gatz*," he said.

"Hello, Jeb. How are you?" Miriam smoothed her black apron with her hands and stood a little straighter.

"*Guete, danki.* Would you do me the pleasure of accompanying me this night?" Jeb's large frame cast a shadow on Miriam that swallowed her up.

"*Ja*," Miriam said, and without another word disappeared into the night with Jeb, leaving Emma's mouth agape.

"How could she just leave me standing here like that?" Emma asked after a moment.

Luke fought back a smile. "Does it surprise you so much that your little sister doesn't need your help?"

"She does need my help, Luke."

"She seems fine to me. Come on, we'll sit and talk a while and then we can go check on her." After a few seconds of waiting, Luke pulled at Emma's shoulder to get her to turn away from the direction Jeb and Miriam had disappeared into the night.

Emma remembered her first singing and how scared she was. Being the oldest child, she didn't have the benefit of a sister's help. She remembered being shy and following her cousins for the longest time. Miriam was different. Much more confident and sure of herself than Emma had been at sixteen. Maybe she *would* be all right for a while. Still, the thought of her little *schweshta* alone with Jeb Lengacher ate at Emma.

CHAPTER 2

*E*mma carried a large bowl, her bare feet dusty and calloused from the summer's work, always careful not to surprise a copperhead hidden in the tall grass behind the house. She reached the garden and knelt down beside Miriam who had loosened a plant with a hand rake. Together they dug in the rich soil with their hands till dirt caked under their fingernails. Emma dropped the first potato in the bowl. She wanted to ask her sister about the night before but couldn't find the right words. As she opened her mouth to speak Miriam began to sing.

> *"Yodel ay I ee, my beau sings to me*
> *Yodel ay, yodel ay, yodel ay hee*
> *Yodel ay I ee, when thy word comes to me*
> *We'll marry and live on the hill*
> *Yodel ay, yodel o, yodel ay, yodel o,*
> *Yodel ay, hee hee, yodel ay hee"*

"You're certainly in a good mood." Emma rubbed the dirt off the small potato and placed it in the bowl. Yodeling was a part of their heritage often forgotten by most of the youth in the community, but Miriam seemed to be an exception. She always yodeled when she was happy.

Miriam let out a breathy sigh. "It's a different world now for sure, sister. Full of promise of good things to come, *ja?*" Her face shone with vibrant youth.

"*Ja*, I suppose. Each new day holds the promise of something new, but what has you thinkin' on it today with the tater diggin'?"

Miriam laughed and peeked over her shoulder at their two-story, white farmhouse.

"No one is about," Emma reassured her. "*Mam* took Hannah, Ada, and Jonas to the quilting bee and *Dat* is in the barn. We can have our words," she said softly.

Miriam let out an anxious breath. "It's Jeb. He's a sight to behold, ain't he? He's tall and handsome. His straw-colored hair that curls around his ears and eyes the color of the noontime sky. And his muscles..."

"Miriam! Don't be naughty." Emma blushed but she knew Miriam was right. Jeb was nice enough looking to make any young girl's knees wobble when he was around, but he was also pig-headed and had an ornery streak like a coon. "*Ja*, he's a sight all right, but not really the sight I want to see holdin' your hand every other Sunday night."

Miriam frowned. "Tell me, *schweshta*. Just what is it you have against Jeb?"

Emma grabbed the hand rake and began loosening the next potato plant.

"Well, he's a mite...competitive for one thing. Bishop says competitiveness leads to pride. We had a whole lesson on it at our last baptismal class."

Miriam's mouth turned up on one side slyly. "And if I remember correctly it's *you* findin' it so important to win when Jeb is around." She pointed her finger straight at Emma. "I see how hard you played volleyball, trying to make him look bad."

"I did no such thing." Emma refused to look up and meet

Miriam's eyes. "Jeb needs no help from me or anyone else to make him look bad." Emma thought back to all the times in the schoolyard when she and Jeb were made to sit out of games because of their competitiveness and "poor sportsmanship" the teacher called it. Emma wondered why she had always found it so important to beat Jeb at everything. It wasn't something she was proud of and she certainly wasn't about to admit it out loud.

Miriam lifted her chin. "Sister, I'm surprised. I figured those classes would have done you more good than that."

Emma's face grew hot. She took a deep breath, remembering the scriptures she'd learned about anger. "It's just...I know you can do better. Promise me you'll not get too serious until you've given the others a chance and I'll leave you be. There's a string of fine young men waiting to get better acquainted with you."

Miriam took the spent potato plant in her hand. *"Ja, Mueter,"* she said and threw the wilting plant at her sister, the dirt from the roots exploding as it hit Emma's apron.

"Hey!" Emma squealed, brushing the dirt from her lap. "I'm not trying to be your *mueter*, so stop calling me that!" Emma laughed. She thought again of Jeb and the last conversation they'd had in school before she graduated at the end of eighth grade. He had talked about their people as if he didn't understand their own ways, the ways he'd been raised in since birth. Maybe he really wouldn't join church. It saddened Emma to think of losing even one of their own to the world. Maybe it bothered her more because he lived just down the road.

"Emma?" Miriam tilted her head. "I was only fooling."

"What? Oh, I know. We'd better get these potatoes in." There was still much to do before supper.

"Race you to the house?" Miriam raised one eyebrow playfully.

"Now who's the competitive one?" Emma asked, handing Miriam the bowl. She bolted for the kitchen door. "You're on!" she called behind her.

A SOFT BREEZE blew through the open window above the sink in the Wittmer's kitchen. Emma dried the last plate from the dinner dishes and placed it in the cupboard.

"Do you hear something?" Miriam called from the sitting room. Emma and *Mam* walked in, Emma still holding onto a dishtowel. "Sounds like music," *Mam* said.

Miriam sat in the rocking chair, mending *Dat's* trousers. She set them on the side table and stood.

All three of them crowded at the window to investigate. A few seconds later a horse appeared down the road pulling an open black buggy. A man in a straw hat sat up front.

"Ain't that the Lengacher's boy? Jeb?" *Mam's* eyes narrowed.

"There must be at least six different instruments playing all at the same time," Miriam marveled. "And it's so loud."

"It ain't right," Emma said. "What would the bishop say if he heard?"

"Not a thing." *Mam* turned from the window. "He ain't joined church yet. Still exploring all the trappings of the world, I suppose. He knows right from wrong; he'll come round, eventually."

Emma huffed. "Well, he shouldn't try to trap us along with him." She took her dishtowel back into the kitchen and hung it on the cabinet handle.

"I think it's kind of pretty." Her sister's voice carried softly through the house.

Emma winced. Didn't Miriam know how things like radios were just another way of letting the world straight into your heart? Emma removed her work apron and hung it on the hook. "I'm going to check the mail," she called out to no one in particular and hurried out the back door. The grass was cool on her bare feet, her medium blue dress and dark "everyday" *kapp* instantly warming in the bright sunshine. She passed her three younger siblings, the two youngest were sitting in a dirt pile playing horse and buggy with wooden toys and stones.

"Did you see that buggy that just went by?" Hannah asked. She was keeping an eye on Ada and Jonas playing in the yard.

"We did."

"Can you believe Jeb would be so disrespectful as that?" Hannah asked, her face scrunched with disgust.

Emma just shook her head. At twelve years old, Hannah seemed to have more sense than Miriam.

She reached the white mailbox by the dirt road, the sound of Jeb's music still lingering, though he was no longer in sight. She touched the mailbox and said a silent prayer before opening it. Inside lay a stack of glossy papers, fire mail as they called it, because it was kept for use when they needed to keep a fire. No one in the house dared to read any of it except *Dat*, though he said it was nothing more than coupons and advertisements.

Emma quickly thumbed through them all, and just as she was about to give up hope, an envelope appeared with her name on the front. Luke had written her. The last Sunday singing felt like ages ago. How she longed to hear from him and know the things on his heart. But not here. She would soak up every word, but she'd do it someplace private. She ran into the house and put the fire mail in the stack by the cook stove under a stick of wood and, hiding her letter in the folds of her dress, she slipped back out unnoticed. Past the pond, through the field, and down into the deepest holler she ran. It was cool down there and the runoff from yesterday's rain made what looked like a creekbed to cross. Emma sat on a big rock and let her feet dangle, her toes at times touching the muddy water below. She opened the letter, careful not to tear the envelope too badly, knowing she would keep it for all times hidden away in the bottom of her hope chest in her room. Removing the paper inside, she held it close to her heart for a moment knowing Luke had held it last.

Emma,

I did enjoy the pleasure of your company Sunday last. I do think of you always when I'm working and when I'm sitting. You have become a source of much joy in my life. It is often that I wonder just how much you think of me. I look forward to the next singing time and especially the long drive to take you home. I wish I had better words to give you as you deserve so much more.

Luke

Emma's eyes were misty. Luke never wrote much, but she didn't care. He had poured his heart into his letter and it was his heart she wanted. As soon as they both took their baptismal vows they'd be able to be married, and just in time for the wedding season in late fall.

CHAPTER 3

*A*da Hilty's kitchen was set up much like the Wittmers'. Emma pumped the handle of the water pump repeatedly and waited for the glass to fill.

"Do you have the drinks ready, Emma?" Emma's *mueter* called from the doorway.

"*Ja*, Mam. I'm pouring the last one now." The screen door let in a welcomed gust of wind, cooling Emma's face.

"*Guete*. I'm sure the men will be powerful thirsty. It's not easy, barn building. We must help them any way we can." *Mam* loaded the drinks onto a large tray. She had some gray showing from under her *kapp*, but it made her look wise, dignified. In a year or two she could be a *gruszmueter*.

The thought put an exciting shiver all through Emma. She wanted so badly to marry Luke and keep house for her own. One day, she too would have gray hairs peeking. She hoped when she did they would look as lovely as her *mueter's* did now.

"Ada said there was another tray somewhere in that cabinet over there." *Mam* nodded her head in the direction of the other side of the room.

"I'll find it," Emma said, holding open the screen door for her *mueter*.

Mam smiled and carried the tray out.

Miriam entered with a grim expression. "Need some help?" she asked.

"*Ja.* I'm looking for Ada's tray. Here it is." Emma pulled the wide tray from beneath the cabinet and shut the door. "You can help me load more drinks."

Miriam quickly placed cups full of water and sweet tea evenly on the tray. "Well, the dangerous part is over. It scares me just to watch. I keep imagining what would happen if one of those beams should fall." Miriam's face twisted.

"You mustn't think that way, *schweshta*. You must ponder the *guete*."

"I know, but it makes me wonder. The *Englishers* have ways to do these things—easier ways. Less dangerous, perhaps."

Emma stopped. "Miriam, where did you hear that?"

"Jeb and I were talking about it outside. They use cranes to lift many heavy things." Miriam picked up the tray.

"Miriam," Emma took hold of her arm, "Jeb is just trying to scare you outta joinin' church. There ain't no one who can raise a barn without some kind of danger. I'm sure of it."

"But Jeb says…"

"Jeb's lettin' the devil use him as his instrument. Now I know you think he's *guete* looking and all, but is that the kind of man you want as a life mate? A man who can't even trust God enough to help us raise a barn?"

Miriam stood silently, slowly shaking her head.

"I didn't think so. Do you know how disappointed *Vater* would be if he heard the words that's been comin' from your mouth? Jeb Lengacher is not a person you need to be keepin' company with and you know it. Now, I thought you promised me you'd give some other young men a chance." Emma held the door open for her. "Take these drinks out there and find a thirsty one."

Miriam exited without a word, but as the metal screen door slammed shut she heard her speak. "Care for a drink, Jeb?"

Emma peeked through the screen to see Jeb just outside the door. His light blue eyes pierced hers.

"Emma," he said, tipping his hat.

How much had he heard? Emma blushed. She gave him a slight nod and watched him take a drink from Miriam's tray.

"We need more cheese and crackers out this way," Ada Hilty called as she swept by Jeb and Miriam on her way to the kitchen.

The things Emma said had been true from her heart, but still she knew she shouldn't have said them. Not in that way, and for sure not in Ada Hilty's kitchen. What if Jeb had heard what she said? Emma took a deep breath.

So what if he did? Maybe it would do him some good to know the truth about himself. How any self respectin' Amish woman would run from him and his loud radio blaring all across the county. *Ja*, maybe it would be a *guete* thing for him to have heard.

"WHOAH, PRINNY." Emma pulled the reins and the buggy came to a full stop at the side of the dirt road. Luke's buggy stopped on the other side. He tipped his hat. "*Goota morga, miss.*"

"Good morning to you, too. What brings you this way?"

"An errand for my *mueter*. You?"

"An errand for my *vater*." Emma laughed.

"It's *guete* to see you, Emma." Luke's brown eyes held hers. "Listen, there's something I need to talk to you about."

"*Ja?*"

Luke looked away in silence.

"What is it, Luke?"

"It's Jeb."

"Jeb?"

"He's saying things, not nice things, about you, Emma. He said you weren't as perfect as everyone thinks you are and that I should keep my eyes open. I think he was suggesting you weren't faithful. I don't care for gossip and I told him so. He reeked of alcohol."

"Luke, I would never—"

"Emma, don't think for a second that I believe any of that. I'm just telling you because he's your closest neighbor and it's important for you to know what he's up to. He had this pocket phone he said was really smart. He kept asking it questions and it answered him in a woman's voice."

"Who was he on the phone with?"

"No one. It was the phone talking to him."

"A girl phone? That's so...creepy."

"He's letting *Rumspringa* go to his head. He'll come out of it soon."

"What if he doesn't, Luke? What if he doesn't ever join church?"

"Then that's his decision." Luke stared at Emma for a moment. "I've got to get going, but I'll see you at church Sunday?"

"*Ja.*"

Luke smiled, then made a clicking noise from his cheek and the horse trotted off.

So Jeb *had* heard what Emma said and he wanted to get back at her. *Not to worry.* It wasn't like anyone was going to believe Jeb no matter what he said. Not with his latest behavior.

DARKNESS FELL on the Hilty's new barn lot. Emma, Miriam, and Luke stood together just outside the barn door.

"That was a very nice singing," Miriam commented. She took a cup of sweet tea from the table.

"*Ja*, it was," Emma said.

Jeb walked up to where they stood and stopped between Emma and Miriam. Even in the dark Emma could see Luke's hands ball into fists.

"Hello, Jeb." Miriam smiled.

"Emma, Miriam, Luke." Jeb nodded to each of them respectively.

Miriam stood straight and gave Emma a defiant look. "Would you want to take a walk with me, Jeb?"

"I don't think your *schweshta* would want you to be seen with the likes of me, Miriam. Maybe you should ride home with Emma and Luke tonight." He tipped his black felt hat and turned to walk away.

"Why do you have to be that way, Jeb?" Luke asked.

"Keep your eyes open, Luke." Jeb never turned back around.

Emma and Luke exchanged glances.

"Jeb, wait," Miriam called, but he kept walking.

"Let him go, Miriam," Luke said to her. "He'll simmer down eventually."

Miriam's chin jutted out, eyes narrowed. "Now look what you've done. Why can't you just mind your own affairs instead of always pushin' yourself into other people's business?"

Emma shook her head. "Miriam—"

"*Nay.* It ain't right, sister. I've been quiet long enough. This is my life that needs livin', not yours. You act like you're being so holy. Do you think this is what the Lord wants? Talking about people the way you do? Meddling? Those ain't our ways and you know it."

"I know things you don't, Miriam." Emma crossed her arms in front of her.

"She's right, Miriam," Luke said.

"Not you, too! What has my *schweshta* done to you? I'll find my own way home, *danki*."

"Miriam, wait." Emma started after her, but Luke grabbed her arm.

"Maybe a brisk walk will do her some good. It's only a couple miles if she doesn't get a ride, and it's a nice enough evening for it."

Emma rubbed her face with her hands. Why did her sister have to be so stubborn?

Luke led Emma through the barnyard to the place where the buggies were hitched. "Tell me, Emma, what's going on between you and Jeb?"

"What do you mean?" she asked.

"Why do the two of you...clash so? I thought I understood it years ago in the schoolhouse, but now that we're all grown it doesn't make much sense. Do you have hatred for him in your heart?"

"*Nay.*" At least Emma didn't think so.

"Or maybe it's something else?"

Emma stopped walking. Just what was he implying? "What else, Luke?"

"I don't know. That's what I'm asking you." Luke's eyes scanned Emma's.

"I should go home and wait for Miriam. Will you take me now, Luke? I'm so sorry to have ruined your evening."

"It's fine. We can go." The pleasant tone of his voice didn't match the look of disappointment on his face.

Emma watched the roadside from Luke's buggy all the way home, but there was no sign of Miriam. It must have been an hour, maybe two, before she heard soft music and horse hooves on gravel. It was Jeb—had to be. Who else dared to have their own music player they carried with them everywhere? Emma hurried outside and hid behind the tree as the buggy approached. It slowed to a stop in front of the house just on the other side of the mailbox. Jeb got out and helped someone down out of the buggy.

Miriam.

In the light of the moon Emma made out the shadow of Miriam's hand. Jeb kissed it and then let go. Miriam swept by Emma and into the house through the back door. Emma followed at a safe distance. She had thought hard about what to say to Miriam. Convincing her that staying away from Jeb was in her own best interest wouldn't be easy, but now what she'd planned didn't seem to fit. She would give Miriam a few moments to find her way upstairs then she'd slip off to bed herself.

CHAPTER 4

The Wittmer family stood by the buggy parked in front of the house. Everyone but Emma and Miriam were headed to a wedding in Gawson's Branch. "Are you sure you'll be okay here alone? We could still get someone to do the chores and you two could come along with us," *Vater* said.

"*Nay, Vater.* There's no need. Miriam and I can manage for two days."

He bit his lip as he glanced at them both. "I've asked the Lengachers to look in on you."

"You didn't have to do that, *Vater.*" Emma wished he hadn't. "We'll be just fine. We'll take care of everything while you're gone. You'll see."

"The Lengachers are our closest neighbors and that's what neighbors do for each other. If you need anything just ride Prinny over and ask, day or night. Promise me."

"I promise, *Vater.* Now go so you can reach Uncle Josiah's before dark. It's a long trip."

"*Ja.* That it is."

Mam kissed Emma and Miriam on the cheek and tucked a bag of snacks under the bench seat in the family's buggy.

The two eldest sisters could have gone too, if they'd wanted, but long rides in the family's open buggy weren't as exciting as they used to be. Besides, someone had to do the chores.

That night Emma cooked up ham and fried potatoes for supper and Miriam made doughnuts for dessert.

"We'll never be able to eat all these," Miriam said. "I forgot we usually have seven mouths instead of two."

"No matter." Emma licked the powdered sugar from her thumb. "We'll wrap the rest up and eat them for breakfast."

"Doughnuts for breakfast?"

Emma raised one eyebrow. "Who's to know, *schweshta*? Who's to know?"

Miriam laughed. "Maybe the extra chores will prove to be worth it."

It was good to hear her laugh. She had been so upset with Emma and they'd not spoken much at all for days. Maybe they just needed time to let it fade naturally. Emma hoped all was well between them. She was done trying to help her sister. If Miriam wanted to be with Jeb, that was her business. *Mueter* and *Vater* wouldn't like it one bit and they could let Miriam know about it once they found out, but Emma had decided the moment she heard Miriam laugh that it wasn't worth the trouble. Her sister's friendship meant so much more to her than being right.

After supper and Bible reading by lantern at the kitchen table, Miriam and Emma climbed the stairs to their rooms. Emma's was the first, by the stairs, and Miriam's the last door down the hall with another bedroom and a washroom in between.

Emma couldn't have slept long when she heard a sound downstairs. Was it Miriam? What would she be doing this late after the lanterns were all out? It was completely dark in her room. She felt for the lantern, but thought better of it. She knew how to navigate the house after dark and there was no time to waste fumbling with lighting a lantern. Emma tiptoed to the staircase. Someone with a light walked by the foot of the stairs but it wasn't a lantern and it wasn't Miriam. Emma's breath caught in her throat. She'd seen that glow before. It was a pocket phone. Every *Englisher* in town had one and they never ceased to stop looking at them. *Englishers* rarely spoke to each other anymore, but they were very busy looking at their phones. Who was this person in Emma's house and what did they want? Emma froze. The figure moved to the front door and hesitated. It was definitely a man. What was he doing? He waited with his hand on the door. The light from his cell phone stopped abruptly. The house was deadly silent. Emma breathed carefully, hoping to remain unnoticed. She squatted down in the middle of the staircase and stared into the dark living room. What was he waiting for? From outside came a familiar whistling. Luke's brother, John.

It was Wednesday. John went past the house in his buggy every Wednesday night around the same time. *It must be just after ten.* Emma considered calling out to him. She'd have to make a run for the back door, but he drove slowly enough, maybe she could catch him and tell him there was a stranger lurking about. The whistling grew louder. Horse hooves on rocks. Quietly, the *Englisher* opened the door and peeked his head out. In the light of the moon Emma made out his face.

Jeb Lengacher.

The sight scared and relieved her at the same time. It wasn't an *Englisher* at all, only Jeb, wearing blue jeans and a tee-shirt just like the *Englishers* wear. Jeb was put out with her and Emma understood why. She shouldn't have said the things she did for him to hear. She doubted Jeb would hurt her, although men given to too much alcohol were sometimes known to do peculiar things, but he wasn't an *Englisher*. An *Englisher* in the house without permission probably did mean harm, but Jeb, he was just here to see Miriam after dark. And since he was leaving, Emma supposed he must have already done just that.

So he'd taken to wearing *Englisher* clothes now? Did he really think to win Miriam's heart dressing that way? Surely Miriam was smarter than that. Emma truly hoped so. It wasn't for her to say anymore, she was leaving it be. Jeb shut the door behind him and Emma watched him slip away through the yard from the window in the living room. She only hoped John hadn't seen him leave. The shame for poor Miriam. Emma gritted her teeth, remembering the promise she'd made to herself to stay out of Miriam's business. Did her sister not realize how important her reputation was?

EMMA SQUIRMED in the wooden pew, trying hard to pay attention to the bishop as he droned on and on.

Just a few baptismal classes left before I can join church, Emma thought to herself. She straightened her *kapp.* Everything was falling into place. Soon she'd be a church member and eligible to marry just in time for Luke to propose and their names to be published in the upcoming weddings. They'd marry by Christmas, and start a house of their very own by spring. It was all Emma could do to pay attention, but she knew she must. Joining church was serious business. She'd finally be seen as an adult. The ladies would sew a quilt at the quilting bee for her and Luke.

"Emma," the bishop said. "I need to speak with you privately."

Her face grew hot as she followed him to the back of the room. Had he noticed her daydreaming? Oh, what was she thinking, letting her mind wander so?

"Emma, there's been talk of a person that claims to have seen an *Englisher* leaving your home late at night when your parents were away. Is this true?"

Emma put her head down.

"Emma?"

"Well, *ja.*"

"Who was this man, Emma? Do you know him?"

"*Ja.*"

"Who is he and what business did he have in your home after lights out?"

It wasn't her place to tell the community about Miriam and Jeb, and besides, what would people think of Miriam if they knew she was entertaining Jeb, of all people, without her parents present?

"I can't say."

"But you know him?"

She couldn't lie. Certainly not to the bishop. "*Ja.*"

"Emma, each of us has to search our own heart to decide whether or not to reject the world and take a vow to be completely faithful to the ways of the *Ordnung.* It's apparent to me that you're still undecided. Take another year to think on it. You're still young. No one is forcing you to be baptized yet."

What? Wait a year? She couldn't. Her heart sped. What about Luke? "Oh, please, I'm ready. I really am."

"Then who?"

"Who what?"

"Who was this *Englisher?*"

She loved Luke and would do anything for him, but she couldn't betray her own sister. "I…I can't say."

"If you can't follow the *Ordnung,* you aren't ready to take the vow."

"But—"

"I don't want to see you take a vow and then break it. It would mean *shunning,* Emma. You don't want that. You're too young to remember the last time it happened, but it's very painful for the entire community. We will avoid it if we possibly can, but for you I see no other way. You may begin baptismal classes again next fall. You are excused." With that the bishop walked away, leaving Emma's plan for her life torn in pieces. A whole year? Would Luke wait for her?

～

EMMA STAYED in her room instead of attending the singing that night. She couldn't bear to see Luke. What would she tell him? If Bishop Amos knew, then everyone else would know soon enough. Why was she the one in trouble? Was it the price she paid for being the eldest? Was it her fault because it happened when she was in charge?

"You missed a *guete* singing," Miriam said when she finally came in. "Jonas Hilty gave me a ride home. He's such a nice young man. Did you know he can lift the back end of a wagon all by himself?"

Emma stared up at Miriam blankly from where she laid on the bed. "What about Jeb?"

"What about him?" Miriam said as if she didn't have a care in the world.

"I thought you were sweet on him, that's what."

Miriam turned her palms up casually. "Oh, he's nice and all but Jonas... Jonas is dreamy."

Emma gritted her teeth at her sister's indecisiveness.

Had she not heard the news going about yet? Would she make everything right when she knew? It was Miriam's shame, not hers. "I thought you and Jeb were getting...pretty serious."

"Oh we were. He kissed my hand, Emma." Miriam squealed. "But then Jonas came along and asked if he could give me a ride home." Her eyes widened. "And of course I said *ja*."

"Miriam," Emma stopped her, sitting upright. "There's something you need to know."

Miriam sat beside Emma on the bed and untied her *kapp*. "What's that?"

Emma took a deep breath, not sure where to begin. "When a young man and a young woman decide to visit each other late at night..."

"*Ja*, like a singing night?"

"*Nay.* Like at her parent's house when her parents are not home."

Miriam's eyes widened. "Oh."

"You see how that might look to passers by?"

"*Ja,* that might not look so *guete.*" Miriam's eyebrows wrinkled.

"So you see how that might affect the way people see those two in the community, right?"

"*Ja.*" Miriam's face was solemn.

"And even if it was innocent enough, it would be important to not let people think that evil was occurring, right?"

"Oh, *Ja.*"

"*Guete.* I'm glad we have an understanding."

"We do?"

"Well, don't we?"

"I guess, *schweshta.* I still don't know why you didn't want to come tonight. Luke was there."

Emma's heart skipped a beat. "Did he ask about me?"

"*Ja.*"

"What'd he say?"

"He just asked where you were, was all. I told him you weren't feelin' well, like you said."

"*Danki.*"

Miriam had acted like she didn't know what Emma was talking about. It wouldn't take long before Miriam heard the rumors. Then she'd know her shame was being shared with everyone. Emma felt sorry for her. She was so...naive.

"*Goot nacht,* Miriam."

"*Goot nacht, schweshta.*"

*E*mma's arms were crossed in front of her. She had finished her morning chores quickly and walked the mile and a half down the road to the Lengachers. She found Jeb still milking the cows in his *vater's* barn.

"Hello, Jeb."

"Emma." Jeb's blue eyes were bloodshot, and his forehead wrinkled.

She tapped her foot. "I guess you know why I'm here."

"*Nay.* Why are you here, Emma? Have you decided I'm not *guete* enough for the cows here, as well as your *schweshta?*"

Emma wondered what Miriam saw in him. Beyond his *guete* looks he had no desirable traits.

"I saw you. Dressed in *Englisher* clothes. I don't know what you and Miriam had going on, but I want no part of it."

"That makes the two of us. She's riding with Jonas now."

Emma sensed a bit of jealousy. "Well, your little visit left the bishop with a lot of questions."

"And what did you tell him?"

Emma shifted her weight to one side. "What was I supposed to say?"

He paused. "And Luke? What did he say?" Did he enjoy hearing of her trouble?

"I haven't spoken with him yet." It pained Emma to think about it. She'd hoped to resolve this before she saw him again.

"Afraid he won't find you so *perfect* anymore?" Jeb smirked.

Emma took a deep breath to calm herself. "Just tell the bishop you came to see Miriam and that she asked you to leave. It's not like you care what he thinks of you anyway."

"And since when are you an expert on all my cares?" The stream of milk slanted into the bucket noisily.

"Come on, Jeb. It's not right and you know it."

"A lot about the world isn't right, Emma." He didn't even look at her when he spoke.

"Will you speak with the bishop or not?"

"You're right. It's nothing to me what the bishop thinks."

Emma gritted her teeth. How could he do this to her? She let out a huff. Of all the low-down things to do to a body. Out the door she went, slamming it behind her. She stomped all the way back through the barn lot and to the road. There sat Jeb's buggy.

Him and his fancy pocket phone and blaring music.

Who did he think he was anyway? A thought stopped Emma. The whole community was tired of hearing him drive around with it, blaring everywhere he went. So disrespectful. Emma would do what each of them wanted to do. She looked around. No one was watching. She quickly hopped up into Jeb's buggy. His radio sat in the floor next to a bag of chewing tobacco. So this was the source of the forbidden sounds. How did the stupid thing work, anyway? She pushed each button in order. There were so many.

Nothing happened.

She twisted the knob—nothing. She looked around, still no one in sight. She needed to hurry though. Was there no way to destroy this thing?

In her frustration, she hit the knob with her fist and a light came on. She pushed another button and it made a noise. A disk, the shape of a flat donut came out. She took it in her hand. The picture on the top of it was of several people holding instruments. Jeb knew musical instruments were not permitted, but neither were radios.

She broke it in half. It snapped so suddenly it made her jump. She dropped one piece and shoved the other into the slot. The radio pulled it in like it was eating it. Emma drew her fingers back quickly, afraid they might get eaten, too. She pushed a few more buttons. Nothing happened. She quickly climbed down from the buggy and ran home without looking back.

CHAPTER 6

*E*mma had tossed half the night. Why had she done that horrible thing to Jeb's radio? Jeb was in the wrong for what he'd said to Luke. Now that people believed she'd been keeping company with an *Englisher*, well, she almost hated him, but she knew that wasn't their ways. The bishop saw her as immature, and not ready to take the *Ordnung* seriously. And then she had done a foolhardy thing like breaking his music "donut." Perhaps the bishop was right about her. There had always been something about Jeb that made her forget right and wrong and simply try to out do him. Was that any way for her to act?

Nay.

She would apologize to him. Today. After morning chores. She would convince him to go to the bishop and then she'd be allowed to finish her classes. There was no way she was going to wait another year to marry Luke.

Emma dressed quickly and tied her everyday *kapp* under her chin. First stop was the outhouse, then breakfast, which *Mam* would have ready any time, and morning chores. When she had a moment free, she'd slip away and find Jeb.

Emma opened the back door to the kitchen and then stumbled out into the morning sunshine. She rubbed her tired eyes with the backs of her thumbs and when she opened them she realized she was being watched.

At least a dozen of the family's goats were grazing in the yard. One was in the garden, munching on the okra, and another was between her and the outhouse, staring at her.

How in the world?

Emma stepped around the side of the house. The gate was wide open, and a goat stood in the buggy, digging under the bench seat with its nose.

How, indeed. Gates didn't just open themselves.

Those strong schoolyard feelings rose up in Emma. Jeb had messed with the wrong gal. She knew she should go to Bishop Amos and tell him everything, but then he'd find out she destroyed the radio player. That wouldn't help her case to get back into baptismal classes. It was too late for that. She could tell Luke, but he may get so mad he'd only make matters worse. She would have to settle this by herself. Emma went inside and got Miriam. Together they spent half the morning herding goats, and they still had to do their regular morning chores. By the time all the goats were safely back inside the gate, their eggs were cold and their toast stale. The whole time Emma was planning, plotting.

THAT AFTERNOON EMMA pulled a baking sheet from the oven.

"Just what are you up to, Emma?" *Mueter* asked as she entered the kitchen.

"Nothing, *Mam*. Just making something special for a friend."

"Well, you're going to *kill* your friend with that much habanero. Roasting it intensifies the heat, dear. You'll want to add several bell peppers to that and only use a little per jar. You are making salsa, right?"

"Um, something like that. This person really likes it hot."

Mueter raised an eyebrow.

"But…I'll only use a little."

"*Guete*," *Mueter* said before strolling out of the kitchen.

This time when Emma paid a visit to Jeb she cut through the field by the Lengacher's house. Jeb's buggy was parked by the fence, allowing Emma to sneak up to it, unnoticed. She climbed inside, keeping her head down. Where was it?

The radio was lying in a heap of parts. Jeb had taken it completely apart trying to fix it.

There it was. Emma quickly opened the tobacco bag, the strong smell hitting her in the face unexpectedly. With gloved hands, she added the habanero paste made from roasted habanero peppers from their garden. She worked the paste evenly into every bit of it, then sealed the bag and set it exactly how she'd found it. Emma smiled. That would teach him to let all her goats out.

SINCE THE TOBACCO INCIDENT, Emma awoke each morning with the same knot in her stomach. She wondered how many tobacco plants were ruined with her last stunt. It was a sin to waste things so. It was a mean trick, but so was letting all the goats out. Jeb knew the goats were her responsibility. Still, it wasn't right, stooping to his level, and she knew it. It just burned her inside. It was the same force that made her want to get the last word in an argument. Why did she have to be so…competitive? It was wrong —so wrong.

Emma dressed quickly and tied on her *kapp*. Today would be different. She would reflect on the situation and pray earnestly about it. Then maybe she'd know how to handle things. Emma stepped out the kitchen door and into the sunshine. She looked about. Nothing. Just to be sure, she ran around the side of the house to check the gate. The goats all stood inside their fence as they were supposed to, chewing their grass without a care. Emma hurried into the outhouse and shut the door. What could she say to Jeb to make all this right? It was getting rather complicated.

Emma turned to face the wooden bench with a toilet seat bolted over the hole, but from the side of the tiny structure were two eyes looking at her. A solid white stripe appeared as the animal turned its back to her and lifted its tail.

Skunk!

Emma threw her hands out in front of her, but it was too late. She'd been sprayed. She quickly threw open the door and ran out screaming. She thought she heard someone laughing behind the outhouse, but saw no one.

Emma bathed in tomato juice, vinegar, baking soda, peroxide, and lye. The smell finally lessened from her body, but her dress still reeked of burning rubber. She hung it on the clothesline to dry, hoping the sun's rays would cook out the rest of the smell.

"This just hasn't been your week, has it, Emma?" *Mueter* said, her tone quizzical.

"*Nay.* It hasn't." Emma ground her teeth as she spoke. Jeb was an unbelievably callous person. A skunk? What a horrible thing to do to someone. What if it had been someone else in her family, like her *vater*? The realization dawned upon Emma.

Jeb knew she was about to go in, because he'd waited for *Mam* and *Dat* to use the outhouse first. He was probably standing there the whole time, listening to her scream. Then she recalled the laughing she'd heard. Emma's blood boiled.

Jeb was going to get it now. But how?

A plan began to form in Emma's mind. She waited a couple hours, then went outside and felt the dress on the clothesline. It was dry enough. She certainly wouldn't wear her good clothes for this deed. She only had three dresses and she couldn't risk ruining another one.

She changed quickly and found her gloves and an old sack.

Last night they'd had chicken for supper. Hannah was in charge of taking out scraps. Chicken bones and unusable organs were usually taken far away from the house so they didn't draw critters.

Throwing the sack on the other side of the fence, Emma hiked up her dress, wadding the excess material into a ball she held with one hand, and pushing down hard on the barbed wire with the other. She carefully made her way over without snagging her clothes.

Now where was that scrap pile?

EMMA DREADED the day as soon as her eyes opened. What would she find when she went out the kitchen door this time? Then again, Jeb wouldn't notice the stench coming from his buggy until later in the day. If she were lucky, he wouldn't need to drive it until church tomorrow when the mess she left under his bench seat would have time to percolate in the sun. She laughed quietly to herself. It served him right. Still, she wondered when this bitter feud would end.

She'd miss her baptismal class tomorrow. Sometimes people missed class for one reason or another and Bishop Amos always let them make it up. If she could get Jeb to see reason, maybe she could make up the class when he confessed all his wrongdoings.

After checking the goats and the outhouse, her new morning ritual, Emma hurried in for breakfast.

"You're smelling much better today." Emma's *vater* smiled big and took a sip of coffee.

Jonas held his little hand over his face and faked a cough. "I think I got the smell trapped in my nose."

"Eat your breakfast, Jonas," *Mueter* warned, unsuccessfully trying to hold back a smile. "We'll leave as soon as we get morning chores done." It was Saturday, the day the Wittmer family went into town.

"Can we get some candy when we go to the store?" Jonas asked.

"That's up to your *vater*," she said. "Miriam, Emma, are you riding with us today?"

"*Nay*." Emma took a big bite of scrambled eggs. She didn't feel like talking to anyone in the community yet.

"I'll go," Miriam said eagerly. "I want to look in the dollar shop. Can we go there today, *Dat?*"

"*Ja*," he said. "If we have the time. It depends on how fast everyone can get their chores done."

Miriam shoved the last bite of egg in her mouth as she stood. She washed it down with goat's milk and ran out the door. Emma knew Miriam would finish her chores in record time and even help the others with theirs to get to stop at the dollar shop. She figured Miriam was after tinted chapstick to make her lips look blushed and shiny. She'd seen one of the girls at the singing put on some and had been talking about it since. Like *Mueter* would ever let her out of the store with it.

The dollar shop, the Amish open market, and an occasional stop at a grocery store or Wal-Mart was all the shopping they ever did in the small town of Asheville, the town nearest to the Swan Creek Amish settlement. Some of the plain folk could be seen on a Saturday, eating in the local restaurants, but *Dat* preferred not to. Not unless they were out all day for some reason, and he didn't like staying in town that long. Emma would miss out on a trip to the dollar shop, but it was better than running into anyone she knew. But *Mueter* and *Vater* would be talking to people from the community, and so would Miriam. What would they say when they returned?

CHAPTER 7

A few hours later, Emma hung her head, staring at the kitchen floor.

"Emma, how could you? We trusted you." *Mueter's* voice was stern.

"Who was this *Englisher* the whole community is jabberin' about?" *Vater* asked.

"I just can't believe it," Miriam whispered.

"Miriam," *Mueter* said, "take your brother and sisters upstairs please, while we talk with Emma."

Emma raised her head and watched Miriam pick up their baby sister, Ada, who had been crawling on the floor.

Why was Miriam not in trouble?

"I think you should ask Miriam," Emma said. "I believe she knows more about this than I do." She hated for it to come down to this but enough was enough.

Miriam's face turned white as a sheet. "What do you mean?"

Mueter's head cocked to one side. "Miriam, what do you know about the visitor that was here the night your *vater* and I were away?" She waited for an answer.

"I first heard of it today, same as you. I never pictured my sister doing such a thing, though. Is it true, Emma?"

"Miriam! This has gone on long enough," Emma huffed. "Tell them the truth!"

"I don't know what you're gettin' at, sister, but I don't know any *Englishers* personal. Not enough to have them over as visitors."

How dare she claim innocence in all of this? It was rare that Miriam got into trouble with *Mueter* and *Vater* and it usually had to do with something silly she had done not even realizing it when it did happen. But telling an outright lie? It wasn't like Miriam at all. Jeb had been a bad influence on her, indeed.

"All right," *Mam* said. "Upstairs, Miriam, and take the younger ones with you."

Emma couldn't believe her ears. "*Mam*, I..."

Vater stepped in front of her. "Who was it? And what were they doin' here?" he demanded to know, not in a completely angry way but more of a disappointed one.

Silence.

Emma was confused. What was Miriam hiding? Why would she be so cold as to let Emma take all the blame for what she had done?

"I didn't do anything wrong," Emma said finally.

Vater raised his chin. "You didn't tell us when we returned that anything was amiss. That's wrong enough. If you won't tell us, you can go to your room and we'll decide what to do with you later."

Emma was eighteen years old, every bit a woman, old enough to marry and have a home of her own, but when her *vater* sent her to her room she went without a word.

LUKE WAS WAITING for Emma as the Wittmer family buggy came

to a stop in the Byler's yard. "Emma, could we have a quick word?" He held up his hand, helping her down.

She waited beside him as the rest of the family hurried into the Byler's barn where the services would be held.

As soon as they were out of earshot, Luke began to speak. "Who was the *Englisher?*" His tone had changed, becoming almost hostile as soon as no one else could hear.

There would be no way around it. Emma would have to tell him. "It wasn't an *Englisher* at all, Luke. It was Jeb."

"Jeb? How could it have been Jeb?" His demeanor changed as the realization dawned. "Everyone is saying it was some *Englisher* from town."

"It was Jeb. I saw him with my own two eyes. You know how he hates me."

Luke shook his head. "He doesn't hate you."

"Oh, I believe he does."

"Well, then why didn't you tell everyone it was Jeb in the first place?"

Was he angry with her? "I should have."

"It just doesn't add up, Emma." Luke's eyebrows pushed closer together.

"Are you doubting me, Luke?"

"Well, *nay,* but it does sound a little off, don't you think?"

Off? Emma couldn't believe she was hearing this. "Jeb. The one with the music box and pocket phone?" She spoke slowly. "The one who's given to alcohol?"

"I saw Jeb the other day. He's turning away from those things. In fact, he'd torn his radio player to pieces. I told you he'd come round."

Emma's mouth dropped open. "Are you seriously taking his side on this?" Emma could feel her throat getting tight as her voice became higher pitched.

"There are no sides, Emma. Come on. We can talk more later, we'll be late for our baptismal class."

Emma hesitated. "I can't."

"What do you mean you can't?"

"The bishop is excluding me from classes, at least until I can get the proper people to come forward."

"The bishop told you not to come to class?" He hesitated.

"Then how will you join church?"

"I can't. Not this year, anyway."

"And why would he do that?"

"Because I wouldn't tell him who the *Englisher* was." Emma was starting to see how wrong she'd been in not telling on Jeb and Miriam from the beginning.

"Then why don't you tell him?" he growled.

"Who would believe me now?" The words came out louder than Emma had intended.

Emma and Luke stood face to face as a moment of silence threatened them. This wasn't going well. Why wouldn't he believe that she was doing everything she could?

Finally, Luke spoke. "Emma, I don't think we should see each other for a while."

One of the Byler's sons arrived in his buggy and the young family hopped out. Emma lowered her voice. "You're breaking ties with me?"

"I just need time to think." Luke looked over his shoulder at the people walking by.

Realization dawned on Emma. "You mean you don't want to be seen with me because everyone is talking about me."

Luke stood straighter with her comment. "Well, it's a horrible thing my brother witnessed, and you're not exactly denying that there was someone there."

"It was Jeb, I told you!" her voice a mad whisper.

"I don't know what's going on between you and Jeb, but I have a feeling whatever it is, it didn't start just recently." Luke took a step toward the barn.

What on earth was he implying? "Luke, wait."

He turned to her. "Some of us still have plans to join church this fall. I've got to go or I'll be late."

"Can't we talk about this?" Tears threatened.

"Some other time."

Emma watched Luke walk through the side door of the barn where the baptismal classes were to be held that day. She stood there, not sure what to do. Everyone inside thought the worst of her, and standing before them and giving a true account of everything she knew wouldn't do any good now. It would be her word against Jeb's.

EMMA BURIED her face in her pillow. Another singing night had came and gone without her. The hurt she was left with in the barnyard at church that day had now morphed into anger. How could Luke take Jeb's side on this? And Miriam, her own *schweshta*.

And what about Jeb? They'd competed in everything from foot races, to fishing, to schoolwork when they were young, but it had never turned to hatred.

She gasped. Did he hate her? Was that why he had started all this in the first place?

Did she hate him? Emma was convicted by the thought. She didn't want to hate anyone. But maybe this was hate. If it was, how did she turn it around? She tried to remember what she had learned in the baptismal classes she'd attended. She knew they were to love their enemies and do *guete* to those who meant them harm. Emma hadn't done that. She'd broken Jeb's music donut instead. If only she'd have done as the Bible said she wouldn't have a dress that still reeked of burned rubber.

Ja, she could have stopped all this, but she hadn't. She'd let her need to win keep her from doing the right thing. But no more. She sat up and grabbed the Bible from her side table. She opened it and began reading, hoping it would reveal an answer to her problems. After a while, Proverbs 25:21 and 22 caught her attention.

"If thine enemy be hungry, give him bread to eat; and if he be thirsty, give him water to drink:
For thou shalt heap coals of fire upon his head, and the Lord shall reward thee."

That was it. That was exactly what Emma wanted to do to Jeb, heap coals of fire on his head. If being nice to someone who hates you could torture them like that, she was going to be as nice to him as she possibly could. In fact, she doubted there would ever be anyone as nice to Jeb as she was going to be.

CHAPTER 8

"*A*re those chocolate crinkle cookies?" Hannah asked as Emma pulled a sheet out of the oven, the sweet smell of butter and cocoa rolling toward them.

"They're not for you." Emma wiped the sweat off her forehead with the sleeve of her dress.

"Well, *Mam* won't be too happy you're heating the whole house up using the wood stove again. You nearly baked us all roasting peppers the other day."

Emma rolled her eyes at her younger sister. "All right. One cookie."

"Two."

"Two, and you'll not mention it when *Mueter* gets back from the quilting bee."

"Deal."

Emma carefully lifted each cookie onto the cooling rack. The powdered sugar had crackled, making a lovely design on top. "There. They're perfect."

"I'll be the judge of that," Hannah said, taking two. She took a bite.

"Well, how are they? Are they as *guete* as *Mueter's*?" Emma waited anxiously for her response. Hannah just bobbed her head up and down, still chewing.

"All right, then. Don't let the others see you with those and remember our deal."

Emma cleaned up the kitchen quickly. She hadn't said many words to Miriam or *Mam* and *Dat*, and she wasn't sure she wanted to, not with a batch of cookies she couldn't explain. Everyone seemed eager to hear her apologize for something she hadn't done. The sooner she left the house, the better. She loaded up the cookies carefully in one of *Mam's* old pass-around containers, hung her apron on the hook, and hurried out the kitchen door.

Emma walked through the field to Jeb's house. It was a mile and a half by road, and only a bit shorter cutting through the fields, but it gave her time to think about what to say to him. She would have to apologize. It would be difficult, seeing as how he'd done the most to be sorry for, but she knew she'd also done wrong. She would just have to forget everything he'd done and focus on the wrong she did. Taking a deep breath, she crossed the fence.

Jeb came out of the barn carrying a bale of hay.

"*Vie gatz*, Jeb. May I have a word?"

Jeb dropped the hay bale on the ground in front of him and took off his straw hat. He wiped the sweat from his forehead with his shirt sleeve, but didn't speak.

Emma stepped forward, straight and tall. "Jeb, I'm sorry for sayin' the things I did to Miriam. It was wrong and mean-spirited. I'm also sorry if I ruined your music player. If you tell me where you got it, maybe I can work to replace it for you."

"You're sorry?" Jeb's blue eyes squinted in the bright sunshine.

"*Ja*. I made you some crinkle cookies. I hope you like them." She held out the container.

"Did you bake them with dirt?" Jeb asked, a slight smile on his sweaty face, his dirty blond hair sticking to the side of his neck.

"*Nay.* I said I was sorry. I've come here to call a truce."

"So little Miss Perfect finally did wrong? Well, that *is* occasion to celebrate." Jeb took the container from Emma's hand. "Is that all you came for or are you gonna burn my buggy on the way out?"

"I truly am sorry, Jeb. You'll see." Emma smiled a little at the thought and turned back the way she'd come. She crossed the fence and looked back once more at Jeb, wondering if he would like the cookies she'd made, but instead she saw Jeb emptying the container into the pigs' trough. It should have hurt Emma's feelings. She'd worked hard on those cookies, but instead it made her laugh. She laughed the whole way home. He really believed they were made of dirt. The irony of it all. The coals of fire were already starting to come down. What nice thing could she do for Jeb next?

THE NEXT DAY Emma visited Jeb again. "I brought you cinnamon bread." She handed a foil wrapped bundle to him. He propped his shovel against the fence. He looked ready for a break but he didn't speak, only took the bread from Emma's hands.

Silence followed.

"Well, my morning trip to the outhouse was uneventful. Thank you for that," Emma said, not sure how to start a conversation with Jeb.

"I do aim to please," he grumbled, taking off his gloves. He threw them on the grass beside the propped up shovel, standing there awkwardly, bread in hand.

"How were the crinkle cookies?" Emma cocked her head to one side, trying to gauge his emotions.

"Oh, I've got your *mueter's* container." Jeb jogged to the barn, grabbed it from a high shelf just inside the door, then jogged back to where Emma was standing.

"And?" she probed.

"And what?"

"How were they?" Emma widened her eyes in anticipation, trying hard not to smile.

Jeb's look told Emma he wasn't sure what to say.

"I saw you throw them out," Emma said finally. "I don't blame you, you know."

Jeb let out a breath and leaned on the green metal fence post with his hand.

"They really were *guete* cookies. I told you I was done feuding with you."

Jeb unwrapped the bread and smelled it. "I don't buy it. The day Emma Wittmer doesn't get the last word is the day the pigs put on a party in the barnyard." He gave the bread a toss over the fence and wadded the foil into a ball. He slipped it in his pocket and leaned on the fence post again. It was exactly what Emma expected him to do. She let out a little laugh.

"Are you saying I'm argumentative?" Emma crossed her arms in front of her.

"Well, aren't you?"

"Maybe. But those aren't our ways and I'm turning from them. You'll see in time. Maybe you'll even turn, too."

"Our ways? You sound like my *vater*. Always talking like we live in some fairytale land where everything is perfect if only you follow *our ways*."

"Well, what's so wrong with *our ways*?"

"Let's see. Where to begin? Oh, I forgot. I have work to do. Maybe some other time." Jeb picked up his gloves and put them back on.

"What's the hole for?" Emma asked, looking down at his work.

"Next year's apple trees. *Mam* wants six, or eight, or ten, she really can't make up her mind. I'm digging up the holes and going to fill them with straw and manure, so they'll be ready for spring."

"Where's your *vater* and *brooda*? Don't they help?"

"They're all busy with other things. I do my chores, run errands for *Vater*, and take care of my *mueter's* whims."

"A *sehr-gut booup.*" *A very good boy.* Jeb certainly was a hard worker. That was a trait more desirable than looks to most Amish women, and Jeb had both. It was a shame he was so hard to get along with. Emma let out a sigh. "Tomorrow, then. I'll go see what else I can cook up for you to throw out."

Jeb shook his head and grabbed his shovel.

THE HEAT in the house was unbearable with the oven so hot. "What are you making?" Miriam asked as she entered the kitchen.

"Sugar cookies," Emma said reluctantly.

"Can I help?"

"Oh, I think you've been enough help, *danki.*" Emma mixed the contents of the bowl with added vigor.

"I know you've been in a bad mood lately because of all the rumors going on about you and I've been trying to give you your space but..."

"That's exactly what I need from you, Miriam—space. *Danki.* For understanding."

"*E feshtay nit.*"

Of course she *didn't understand.* No one did.

"You've been holed up in your room or out in the field every day." Miriam's voice was soft.

"Well, what do you expect from me?"

"I just wondered when things would go back to normal between us, *schweshta.*"

Emma winced at the word sister. She couldn't believe Miriam

was so empty-headed. If she weren't so angry she'd feel sorry for her. She hated it that she still carried the anger in her heart and knew it was time to let it go—and she was trying—but it was just so hard. She really didn't know where to start. Would it always be this hard or would she wake up one day and be able to forgive *and* forget?

"Maybe another day, Miriam, but not today."

~

JEB WAS NEAR THE FENCE, when Emma came up to him. Jeb leaned the shovel against the fence and held out his hand without a word.

"*Guete* afternoon, Jeb." Emma handed him the container. "So you were going to tell me what is so wrong with our ways today?"

"Ah, you mean you haven't figured it out for yourself yet?" Jeb opened the container lid as he pretended to think. He flung the contents over the fence close to where Emma stood. She hopped back so she wouldn't get hit, and he replaced the lid, handing the container back to her. Then he pulled his phone out of his pocket.

"Do you see this?"

Emma nodded. "*Ja.*"

He held the phone out to Emma. She put the empty cookie container under her arm and took the device.

"I can carry this anywhere I go. With the push of a few buttons I can talk to someone on the other side of the world."

All those buttons. She didn't even know how to turn it on. It reminded her of the music player she'd destroyed. For a second, she wanted to destroy the phone, too—with Jeb's shovel. Emma thought a moment. "Do you speak Chinese?"

"*Nay.*" His forehead wrinkled.

"They why would you need to call China?"

"You're missing the point." He took his phone and put it back in his pocket.

"We have a phone shed at the end of our road, Jeb. You can use it anytime you want. I bet it'll even call China if that's so important to you." They were lucky to have it. It was only permitted because one of the local kids had some pretty frightening seizures from time to time. The boy's parents had decided to leave the community until Bishop Amos suggested it. Every family who lived on the road had a key and shared the bill, using it for work and emergencies only.

"You just don't get it, do you?" Jeb shook his head.

"Get what?" Emma asked.

"What's so wrong with having a phone in your pocket?"

"You're carrying the world around with you. Is that what you really want?"

"Maybe. Is that so bad?"

"You don't mean it."

"You know, you're just as closed-minded as everyone else around here. I used to think you were different, a free-thinker. Someone who couldn't be made to just line up and take the brainwashing. I guess I was wrong about you." Jeb picked up his shovel and started to dig.

"Jeb, come on." Emma's voice was soft. She wished she could replay the conversation. He had opened himself up to her and she could have used the opportunity to convince him to do the right thing and confess to the bishop, only she'd missed her chance.

"*Nay*, come back when you have some ideas of your own, not just what you've repeated from the bishop's sermons."

Emma was unsure what to say. She hadn't realized Jeb's feelings of resentment for her and for the church ran so deep.

*E*mma stared at the recipe card, trying to picture where in the cabinet all the ingredients were located.

"Emma, what are you up to?" *Mueter* asked.

Emma jumped. "I…" She didn't know *Mam* was still in the house.

"It's okay. I do the same thing." *Mueter* looked at the recipe Emma had in her hand along with the mixing bowl and spoon on the kitchen counter.

"You do?"

"*Ja*, I always bake when I'm angry or when I'm thinkin' something out. I know you have a lot on your mind, but you're heating the house up somethin' awful with all this baking in the hottest part of the day. The old wood stove…well, she needs a rest now and then."

Emma frowned. How would she make cinnamon rolls without heating the oven?

Mam read her thoughts. "How 'bout some of my famous potato candy?"

"Oh, potato candy? I love potato candy. Is it hard to make?"

"*Nay*. Easy as pie. Well, even easier than that really. I've got just enough left over mashed potatoes from dinner." *Mam* took a bowl from the refrigerator.

"I thought you were going to make potato cakes with those for supper."

"Well, I'll just have to find something else for supper, now won't I?"

"*Danki, Mam.*"

"Don't thank me. You're the one who's going to do all the work. Now measure out half a cup of those mashed potatoes and use that bowl to mix it all up in."

Emma plopped the mashed potatoes in the bowl and scraped out the measuring cup.

"Now you add in enough powdered sugar to make a thick dough."

Emma reached for the powdered sugar jar shaker in the cabinet.

"Oh, no, you'll need a whole bag for this. It takes a lot."

"Two pounds?"

"*Ja*, sometimes a little more, depending on how wet the potatoes are. Just work it in a little at a time." *Mam* watched Emma stir the mixture with a large spoon. Then she dropped in a capful of vanilla extract from the little glass bottle. "That's for flavoring."

Emma stirred till her hand hurt.

"Now you roll it all out flat like a pie crust and then spread a half cup of peanut butter on top."

Emma was glad to stop stirring. She plopped the mound onto the counter dusted with powdered sugar. When it was rolled out and the peanut butter was spread, *Mam* showed her how to roll the whole thing up like a cinnamon roll. Then, with a piece of white thread, Emma sliced the roll into half-inch pieces and set them on a platter.

"And there you are," *Mam* said when the last one was cut. "Easier than pie." She smiled at Emma and removed her apron. "You'll be back in time to go to Ada's for peach jam-making, I hope." *Mueter* didn't turn around as she placed her apron on the hook.

"Yes, *Mam*." Emma vaguely wondered where her *mueter* thought she was headed. She must have noticed Emma leaving the property recently, but she was thankful that she hadn't asked.

~

EMMA CLIMBED over the Lengacher's barbed-wire fence just as she had done almost every day that week. Jeb had made some progress on the massive holes, which were evenly spaced in the small lot by the fence. Jeb was leaning against the rail of the pig pen watching her walk toward him. He held out his hand to receive the container Emma was carrying today.

"Oh, no," Emma said, taking a step back. "I worked very hard making all this potato candy."

"Potato candy?" he asked, suddenly viewing the container with interest.

"*Ja*, it's my *mueter's* recipe. She even helped me make it. It would be a terrible waste to throw it all out. Couldn't I have a piece first?"

Jeb raised an eyebrow. "Be my guest."

She opened the container and took out a small roll and popped the whole thing in her mouth at once. "I just love potato candy," she said.

Jeb had watched the small piece go from the container to her mouth; she knew she had his attention. Sitting down on the hay bale next to Jeb, she looked up at him. "I was thinkin' 'bout what you said about pocket phones, and I think you may be onto something."

"What's that?" He put his hand up to cup his ear. "I thought I just heard Emma Wittmer say I was right about something."

"*Ja*. If you really have a legitimate reason to have a phone—I mean, if you need it to make money or something, why shouldn't you keep it in your pocket instead of at the end of the road?"

"Really?" Jeb watched Emma put in another piece of candy. She chewed several seconds before continuing. "Sure. And I've heard if you get bored you can play games with it. And if you don't have any friends, it will talk to you—keep you company. Maybe it will even keep you warm and snuggle up with you on cold winter nights." Emma shoved two more candies in then stood to her feet and quickly flung the contents of the rest of the candy over the fence rail. Jeb's eyes watched it travel through the air and down to the pigs' trough. Emma sat back down. "I wonder if I can get one that will do the dishes and hang out the wash for me." She licked her fingers one by one. "I'm gonna go home right now and pen a letter to the bishop asking for permission to get one."

"You do beat all, do you know that? Here I thought you were finally being open-minded." He looked again at the empty container and then at the pigs, happily eating at their trough.

Emma wiped the growing smile off her face. "Seriously, Jeb, do you really need a pocket phone or do you just like having one?"

"This ain't just about cell phones."

"Then what's it about?"

Jeb paused a moment. "Doesn't it make you feel like a fool sometimes?" he said quietly.

"What do you mean?"

"Like when it takes you all day to do the wash? The *Englishers* can throw it in the machine and come back in an hour when it's done."

"Machines can break, and the power could be down."

"I didn't say it was perfect."

"And neither are our ways, but they're still *guete* ways, Jeb."

"I suppose, for some." His voice was calmer now, more like a pouting child.

She was beginning to get into that thick skull of his. He would see reason soon enough. "Listen, I promised my *mueter* I'd be back in time to go with her to Miss Ada's jam makin' frolic. But we'll talk more tomorrow, all right?"

"No one's stopping you, I guess," he mumbled.

"See you then." Emma jumped to her feet. She crossed the barnyard, careful not to step in any of Jeb's holes, and climbed over the fence, where she allowed her smile to return. She promised herself on the way home that as long as she lived she'd never forget the look on Jeb's face when she threw the rest of his potato candy to the pigs.

THE SUN SHONE hot in the field next to the Lengacher's house the following afternoon. "You're here early," Jeb commented without looking up, as Emma clumsily crossed the fence wearing her work apron and gloves, a large shovel in hand.

He was digging holes again. From the looks of it he'd been working all morning.

"What have you cooked up for the pigs today?" he said, sweat dripping from the end of his nose.

"Nothing. I don't want to spoil them. I came to help." She proudly displayed her shovel at her side.

"You? Help? With what?" Jeb asked.

"With these holes, silly." Emma gestured to the holes Jeb had been working on all week.

"There must be a hole already in your head. *Froe* don't dig holes in the hot Missouri sun."

Emma's mouth dropped open. "My only *brooda*, Jonas, is just six years old. Who do you think helps with all the hard work around our place? Hmm? I've dug my share of holes."

Jeb just shook his head and continued working. "You're not digging and that's final."

"You don't think I can dig a hole, is that it?"

"*Nay.* I *know* you can't dig a hole." Jeb looked nearly out of breath already. With his hat in hand, he wiped his forehead with the sleeve from his upper arm. He could use her help, only he didn't think she was able.

Emma felt her strength come alive. "Where does the next hole go, about here?" She pointed to the ground with her shovel. Jeb didn't say a word. She pierced the grass with her shovel, putting all the force of her anger into it. Her perfect life had been turned upside down and it was all because of this one man who didn't think she was as capable as he was at anything. Emma had a little trouble breaking through the grass, but once she got below that she dug at a steady pace.

Jeb began digging faster as she made quick progress. Emma picked up her pace. It didn't take long to get a good hole started, but all too soon, Emma began seeing stars. She would throw out a shovelful of dirt, then Jeb, then Emma, as quickly as they both could. Several minutes passed. Finally Jeb threw down his shovel in exhaustion, but Emma kept on going.

"All right, stop. You're pretty strong for a girl," Jeb said between huffs. "No need in killing yourself over it."

"I'm not a *mately*. I'm a grown woman." Emma dropped her shovel and plopped herself on the ground, panting. She wished she could jump head-first into Swan Creek to cool off.

"Well, anyway, you're pretty helpful for someone who hates me. Why is that?"

"I don't hate you, Jeb." She stared up at him, still trying to catch her breath, glad the sun had hidden itself behind a cloud. "I mean. I did. But then. I started being all nice. And…it's hard to be so nice to someone. And hold contempt for them. In your heart."

Miriam rose up in her thoughts. She still held contempt for her *schweshta.* Maybe it was time to heap a few "coals of fire" her way. Emma sat silent for a moment, letting the stars dissipate while Jeb was still bringing his breathing back to a normal speed.

"We could have had a machine come in that would have dug all these holes in minutes," Jeb said, waving his hand angrily at the large holes he'd been working on all week.

Emma finally realized the problem. He resented his work because he believed there were easier ways not permitted by the Plain Folk.

"Well, *ja*, if we were lazy *Englishers*. But then I would have missed showing you up in a hole-digging competition. Our way was much more fun, *ja?*" Emma smiled, then stretched out on the cool ground and took in a deep breath.

Jeb laughed and plopped down beside her. She looked up at him and began to laugh, too. He was so much different than the boy she knew in school. His voice was deeper and didn't squawk when he was angry and the lines on his face were more defined. Aside from that, he was so much more serious. It was good to see him laugh again. Maybe now she could get him to go to the bishop and confess the truth, clearing her name.

Finally the laughing died down and their eyes met. She propped herself up on one elbow as he moved closer, his expression more serious. Her gaze dropped to his mouth and her heart sped at the closeness of his body. She wondered at the new feelings inside her. Did he feel it, too?

A loud, several note melody came from Jeb's pocket. He stopped suddenly, pulled his phone out of his pocket and pushed a button. Swallowing hard, Emma pushed aside an unexpected sense of disappointment. What would have happened if they hadn't been interrupted?

"What's that?" she asked, turning her attention to the phone in his hand.

Jeb stared at the screen. "You'd better head home."

"What's wrong?"

"It's going to rain in about thirty minutes." Jeb looked up at the sky.

Emma examined the clouds. They were a little dark but it didn't look like rain. "Did your phone tell you that?"

"*Ja.*"

"And you believe everything it tells you?"

"*Ja*, it's an app."

"What's an app?" Emma sat upright.

"An application."

"Like for a job?" Now she was really confused.

"*Nay.* Here, look." He leaned close to show her the screen, his arm brushing hers, sending a tingle up her spine. "It will tell me when it's going to rain within half an hour. I've never seen it wrong, either."

"But how does it know?"

"It knows the exact location of the phone and looks it up on the weather map."

Heavy rain starting in twenty-eight minutes, the screen said.

"You don't really think it's going to rain in exactly twenty-eight minutes, do you?"

"Close enough to it, *ja.* If you hurry, you'll make it home just before it starts."

Emma wanted to argue about how wrong he was about the rain, but that was conversation for another day. He was still certain rain was coming, and she couldn't prove to him yet that it wasn't.

"Well, I better hurry, then." Emma grabbed her shovel. She climbed over the fence and started home, slowly. She had worked too hard, too fast, digging that hole, and had no intention of losing her breath again by running all the way there, shovel in hand, because some pocket phone told her so.

She was about halfway there when the heavens opened and the rain came pouring down. She was soaked through when she returned home, but at least it had cooled her off.

*M*iriam yodeled as she and Emma hung the wash on the clothesline in the backyard. Emma clenched her jaw. It was hard for Emma to be nice to Miriam. She wondered why it was so easy to do nice things for Jeb when he was the one who had displayed the anger toward her. Miriam was just lying to keep herself out of trouble. Perhaps it was harder to forgive family because you expect more from them.

"The next singing is coming up," Emma said in between tunes. She didn't really want to start a conversation with her sister, but it was preferable to her yodeling.

"Oh, Emma, are you coming with me this time?"

"Thinkin' on it." Emma stuck a clothespin on the corner of a dishtowel, anchoring it to the line. She was still upset Luke had dismissed her so easily. She hated more than anything for him to think she was hiding in her room, pining away for him on a Sunday singing night. It burned her insides just thinking on it.

"We'll be hosting the church service after this one." Miriam shook out a towel and draped it over the line.

"Are you sure?" Emma let go of the line.

Miriam's face lit up. "*Ja*, won't that be fun?"

"I suppose." Usually Emma would be thrilled about her family hosting church, but not this time. Luke's family had always helped hers to set up and serve, and they, in turn, helped out at the Graber's house when it was their turn. Emma couldn't bear being in the same kitchen with Luke's *mueter* and sisters. What if they asked her why she and Luke broke ties? Emma's face burned hot. What if Jeb never told the truth? Would she always be known as the girl who entertained *Englisher* men after dark?

AFTER SUNDAY SERVICES and dinner it was time for youth games. Miriam followed Emma across the barnyard to the grassy lot where a large volleyball net was set up.

"Hey, look." Miriam elbowed Emma in the side. "There's Luke. Hi, Luke," she yelled and gave a little half wave. Emma was starting to think coming to the singing was a bad idea. She put her head down, trying to hide her face from Luke's stare with the edge of her *kapp*.

"We should play," Miriam said, pulling on Emma's arm.

"I don't know, Miriam," Emma said as they walked toward the sidelines. She wanted to just sit and watch, but Becca Lengacher was giving her the evil-eye beside the only empty chairs. Becca never was one to pretend niceties, always giving her true opinion with her facial expressions.

"We'll play," Miriam called. "Is there room for both of us?"

"Come on in," one of them said, but as soon as the sisters stepped in, several of the players on that side left without a word, leaving the teams awkwardly unbalanced. Some of the players would have to come over to their team to make it fair, but as the players realized this, more of them left.

Jeb walked toward them. He bent over and stepped under the net. A game that started with nine or ten players on each team had quickly dwindled down to four against four. Since they were the only two girls, Miriam went under the net to the opposing side, leaving Emma with Jeb and two other young men.

Emma knew this wasn't anything like a true *shunning*, where the whole community pretended you're not even there and wouldn't let you eat or do business with them, but she was starting to understand what that must feel like. Maybe Jeb was right to question their ways.

What was she thinking? It was his fault people were treating her this way in the first place.

The ball was served and it came her way. All those angry feelings bubbled up inside her and she hit the ball as hard as she could with her double fist. Miriam hit it back to Emma's side and Emma nearly ran into Jeb trying to get to it first.

"Whoa, there, little red," Jeb said to her quietly.

Emma hadn't heard that name in years, not since they were in primary school and he would tease her about her anger. She'd get so worked up she'd turn red in the face. Jeb's teasing had only made it worse.

"We're on the same team, remember?" he said, his eyes soft. Was he just talking about volleyball or was he letting her know he was finally ready to trust her?

Could she trust *him*?

She'd trusted Luke. Emma glanced at Luke, standing smugly with his arms crossed in disapproval of her on the sidelines. How could she have been so wrong about him?

Jeb nodded to her from his position by the net. The ball came to Emma. She hit it into the air just above Jeb. With his height it wasn't hard for him to spike it straight down, just over the net. He gave her a look that said, *guete job*.

After that, their team dominated the volleyball game. Jeb and Emma were in it to win, and working together they won, ten to three.

~

AFTER THE SINGING, the young people paired off in the darkness of the barn lot. Emma hadn't thought about how she'd get home. She'd been with Luke since she was sixteen and he'd always made sure she got home okay. He hadn't so much as spoken to her in weeks. As far as she knew he wasn't riding with any other girl, but it was only a matter of time before he did. Not that she'd have him back after the way he'd treated her, but still. Emma gritted her teeth at the thought. Now she'd have to find Miriam and whoever she was visiting with tonight, and beg them to let her tag along. It was supposed to be the other way around. Emma had always imagined Miriam being the socially awkward one who needed someone to tag along with. Now she was trying out boys like *Mam* tried out recipes, a new one each week, and Emma had been the one left without a way home.

"Need a ride?" The voice seemed to come from out of nowhere.

Emma turned around to find Jeb sitting in the grass, sipping a plastic cup of sweet tea.

"That's okay. I can find Miriam and ride home with her." Emma wrung her hands together.

"It's on my way. I live next door, you know." He got up, dusting off the back of his pants with his hand.

"*Nay*, really, Jeb, it's okay."

"No, it's not. If I know you at all, I know you're too stubborn to ask anyone for a ride. You'd walk the four miles home first. Then tomorrow morning I'd have to hear my *mueter* at breakfast talking about how horrible it was that the pretty little Wittmer girl got eaten by a bear last night. If only *someone* would have driven her home." He stepped closer to her, the side of his face now bathed in moonlight.

Emma's breath caught and before she could think about it she asked, "Would she really call me pretty?"

Jeb paused. "Umm, *ja*, actually. My *mueter* has always spoken kindly of you."

Emma tried to catch his gaze but he avoided her. She cocked her head to the side, forcing his eyes to meet hers. "And how do you speak of me?"

"Well, not too highly as of late, but I guess it's time to get over that. *If* you're done trying to kill me with baked goods, that is."

Emma smiled, pleased with his playful answer. "I'm a fine baker, Jeb Lengacher."

A laugh escaped his lips quickly. "I pity your husband, if ever he should cross you."

"And your poor wife. I'll send her regular sympathy letters." Together they walked across the barnyard to where a dozen topless buggies were parked.

Jeb helped Emma up into his buggy. She sat down, wondering how on earth she ever ended up riding home with Jeb, of all people. Of all the things that could happen, she never would have imagined it. Then, all at once, something entered her nose.

"What is that awful stench?" she said before she could think better of it.

Jeb plopped down next to her and gave her a pointed look.

"Oh…sorry about that," she said in a tiny voice.

He took the reins and made a clicking sound, jogging the horses into motion.

The air circulating through the buggy dissolved the smell, so Jeb kept the horse at a steady pace. The miles went by quickly.

Jeb was smarter than Emma had ever given him credit for. He spoke of his plans for the future, never mentioning any desire to leave the Amish community. She secretly hoped he had changed his mind and wouldn't mention all the ways plain living was more burdensome than the way the *Englishers* lived. She found herself enjoying his company much more than she expected. She was pleased to find there was more to him than a handsome face with a boyish grin.

Jeb soon brought the horse to a stop, jumping down and hurrying to the other side of the buggy to help her. Emma took his outstretched hand, made silvery by the light of the moon. With a little hop she landed just next to where he stood with only mere inches between them. Warmth from his strong hand awakened the curious feelings Emma held for him and she made no attempt to let it go.

"Emma, there's something I need to tell you." Jeb's eyes landed on Emma's lips, somehow drawing her forward.

"Then you should say it," she said slowly.

His eyes found hers again. "I'm sorry."

They were the words she'd waited to hear for so long, only now they didn't seem so important. He leaned in. Did he mean to kiss her? He pulled her hand close to his chest and held it there. Her heart sped in anticipation. She drew in a sharp breath, hoping he would and yet surprised by the thought. Suddenly his lips introduced themselves to hers, a most pleasurable and exciting how-do-you-do.

CHAPTER 11

*E*mma was finally starting to see the fruit of her labors. Jeb was sorry for what he'd done to her. She had expected him to crack eventually, with all the nice deeds she'd been doing for him. What she didn't expect was to fall for him. He'd kissed her on the last singing night, and now she was wearing a hole in her bedroom floor with all the pacing she did, trying to figure out what she was supposed to do next. She had been going to his house to get him to forgive her, and he obviously had. But going over there now would just be her wanting to see him, and since they had kissed, it might seem desperate. But she wanted to see him, if for no other reason than to help sort out these new feelings she was having for him.

Emma recalled Jeb's soft lips meeting hers and the way her chest tightened when he pulled away. She'd said *goot nacht* and hurried quickly inside, not knowing what else to say. What if he regretted kissing her? What if it were all some big mistake? Jeb was in the *Englisher* ways pretty deep. She'd heard about how *Englishers* shared kisses like the Amish shared sweet breads. And shouldn't *he* be the one to come visit *her*? But she'd avoided him many days already—so long that maybe he would think she wasn't interested in seeing him. Or worse, that she was somehow upset with him. She couldn't have him thinking that—*nay*, not if she wanted a peaceful trip to the outhouse each morning. She would have to see him.

Today.

THE WALK to Jeb's house took twice as long as usual. Emma poked along, kicking at rocks as she went. What would she say when she arrived? That she'd been thinking of him? *Nay.* Maybe that she was just checking on him? Did he need checking in on? All too soon, she was climbing over a familiar barbed-wire fence. She walked around the holes Jeb had been working on and into the barn lot, but she didn't spy Jeb. She peeked inside the hay barn door. Jeb had his back to her, lifting a bale of hay. She started to call out to him but heard a voice.

"It ain't right, Jeb." It was Becca, Jeb's oldest sister who was two years younger than Jeb. She sounded put out. Were they arguing? "You shouldn't be keeping company with her. I know you like trouble and she's trouble all right. Didn't you hear what's going around about her? Keeping company with *Englishers* after dark. When her *vater* wasn't even home. It's shameful, I tell ya'."

Emma held her breath to hear more.

"You can't believe everything you hear, Becca." Jeb cut the bale of hay loose with his pocket knife and pulled a chunk off for each horse stall.

"I can believe it just fine. That Emma Wittmer has always been a goody-two-shoes. She's always thought she was better than everybody else. Well, now look at her."

Jeb knew Emma was innocent. Would he tell her?

"I'm sure people are saying all kinds of evil about me and you ain't mad about that. What does it matter what people say?"

"Because you're just horsin' around before you join church

and everybody knows it. You ain't never hurt anybody having a phone. And everybody knows you just carry it around to feel important. But Emma, she's no *guete*. And you're disgracing the family name by driving her home in your buggy."

Emma had heard enough. She certainly didn't want to add to her shame by being caught eavesdropping. She backed away from the door silently, then ran as fast as she could for the fence. Her eyes were starting to blur as she neared it. She had to get out of view. Jeb or his sister could walk out that barn door any second and see her. Emma ran faster and suddenly fell hard to the ground. She had stepped into a shallow hole. She stood quickly, but her ankle hurt. She laid down on the ground parallel to the fence and rolled under, not caring if she ruined her dress or not. She got away as fast as her ankle would let her, and as soon as she was safely on Wittmer land she sat down and cried. Her reddened, swelling ankle hurt, but the pain was insignificant compared to the burning in her heart.

Why did people have to be so mean? Saying things that hurt so? Then she remembered the time in Ada's kitchen, when Jeb overheard *her*. The words she'd said ran through her head and pierced her heart. She, too, had said some pretty hurtful things. Emma decided right then to work at guarding her words. She had a lot of time to think as she limped her way home. Finally, she crawled under her own fence and Emma stopped at the garden to rest. She watched Miriam run out of the house and toward her.

"Are you all right, *schweshta*?"

"*Nay*," was all Emma could say as new tears began to fall.

Miriam took her by the arm and helped her to the house.

"Where's *Mam*?" Emma asked, when Miriam finally got her into the living room. She sat down in *Mam's* rocking chair and Miriam helped prop her foot up on the side table.

"She's at the quilting bee. Should I hitch up Prinny and fetch her?"

"*Nay*. I'll be all right."

"*Vater* won't be home for a while, either. He's helping David at the Schwartz's today."

Now that Emma was safely at home it felt like a gate inside her opened and all the sadness just ran out all at once, the tears flowing freely.

"You're worrying me something awful, *schweshta*. I can go get help."

Emma felt Miriam's hand on her shoulder. She wiped her eyes with the sleeves of her dress.

"*Nay*. It's not that." She looked into Miriam's eyes, so full of concern. All the anger she'd had toward her began to melt away.

"Well, I certainly hope you're all fixed up in time for Sunday's services. It'll be a busy day and we'll sure need you." It would be the Wittmer's turn to host. Emma dreaded it something awful, trapped in a kitchen with a bunch of folks who thought she was pure evil wasn't her idea of a *guete* time. At least it wasn't Becca. How she would ever face her again, Emma didn't know.

"How did you hurt yourself?" Miriam asked.

"I fell in a hole," she said finally.

"What kind of hole?" Miriam sat down in the floor beside Emma's chair.

"I was at Jeb's."

"What in the world for?"

"I know. After the way he ruined my life it must seem strange for you to hear this, but I've been going there a lot lately. When I've been leaving through the field, I've been visiting Jeb."

"You have? I've been wondering what you've been up to. You've been keeping everything so secret lately. So, how did he ruin your life?"

"You know, all the rumors going around about me."

"'Bout...you and the *Englisher*?" Miriam hesitated to say it, no doubt afraid of angering Emma.

"*Ja*, when I got the blame for you and Jeb sneaking around, I was so mad at the both of you. I wanted to kill Jeb and never speak to you again, but I've since learned how to let go." Emma smiled weakly.

"What do you mean, *sneaking around?* And what's this got to do with the *Englisher?*"

"Jeb was the *Englisher.* When you two were doing..." Emma shook her head. "I don't want to know what you were doing—I got the blame for it. And it hurt me that you would lie like that, but I forgive you."

"Jeb's an *Englisher?*" Miriam's face was scrunched up tight.

Must I always explain everything out for Miriam? Emma took a deep breath and began slowly, "When Jeb visited you the night *Mueter* and *Vater* were away, he was wearing *Englisher* clothes, don't you remember?" Was her sister that dense, that she hadn't put this together on her own yet?

"I didn't visit with Jeb that night."

"What? You mean when he was here, in this house, you didn't even see him?"

"Jeb was in the house? What for?"

Miriam had no reason to lie to Emma now. Jeb hadn't been in her home on business with her sister, he'd staged the whole thing on purpose, just to ruin her reputation, which he'd managed to do quite well. Her blood ran hot, her ankle the only thing keeping her from marching back to the Lengacher's barn right that instant and giving Jeb a piece of her mind.

CHAPTER 12

*S*eeing Jeb enter the barn for Sunday service sent a jolt
through Emma. The warm tingly feelings were back,
but Emma shook them off. How dare he come here after what
he'd done? The whole community was talking about her and it
was all Jeb's fault. He'd set her up. How could anyone be so mean?
And the feelings she had for him—what was wrong with her?

Bishop Amos cleared his throat loudly, indicating the service
was about to begin. Emma walked to the side of the barn where
the women were seated, but Jeb grabbed her dress sleeve first
before she could find a seat. She defensively pulled her arm back
and moved away from him. Hurt flashed in his eyes, his head
tilted to one side quizzically.

Jeb turned to face the crowd, standing at the front of the
room. "I have something to say." Nearly everyone was seated now
and he had their full attention. "I'm the one who John saw leaving
the Wittmer house dressed in *Englisher* clothes." Gasps came from
the crowd, but no one spoke. "I knew he'd be happening by to
see. I did it 'cause I was tired of everyone talkin' about how
perfect Emma was, wanting to join church so soon." He hung his
head. "Maybe I was also hoping if I did something bad enough I'd

be asked to leave, and then I wouldn't have to decide if I was going to join church or not. It was wrong and I apologize, Bishop. Emma." He turned to face her. "I'm sorry. I know all you ever wanted to do from the time we were little was to join church and marry, and I ruined that for you. I saw you were happy and I wasn't, and it made me envious of you. And for that I'm powerful sorry."

Bishop Amos stood beside Jeb. "Well, I'm surprised at you, Jeb," he said. "Bearing false witness against your neighbor and keeping it a secret all this time, but you did the right thing to confess." He turned to address the crowd, "There's not a sin so great that a man can't own up to it and seek forgiveness." He reached out and shook Jeb's hand. "You all heard what Jeb said. Emma is innocent. Let's let the idle gossip stop." The bishop motioned for Jeb to take his seat.

Emma spied Luke across the room, scowling at Jeb. She supposed now he would believe her, but he was far too late. She turned back to Jeb, her conscience nudging her. She was wrong about him. He wasn't at all what she had thought. Sure he liked to joke around and talk tough, but on the inside he was smart and warm, and he needed to know she was sorry, too. "But I'm not innocent, Bishop." Emma turned to face the crowd. The women all gasped again.

"What's that?" Bishop Amos asked.

"What Jeb said was true. He was in my house when my parents weren't home and I knew it was him, even though I didn't know what he was doing. I should have told you the truth when you asked, but instead I went to Jeb's…and broke his radio player."

"Emma!" *Mam* said, her face held disbelief. Some of the women had crowded around to hear better.

Jeb spoke up. "But I let all the Wittmer's goats out to get back at Emma." Suddenly Jeb was getting all the attention again.

"And I put habanero pepper paste in his chewing tobacco."
Everyone stared at Emma now.

"Well, I put a skunk in the outhouse when I knew Emma was coming."

"That was you?" Emma's *vater* said, instinctively putting his fingers under his nose. "She stunk for a week!"

"*Dat!*" Emma's cheeks flushed.

"I can't believe you'd do such a thing," Jeb's *mueter* wailed.

"I put chicken innards in Jeb's buggy," Emma blurted, "and then I made him chocolate crinkle cookies."

"Will you both settle down?" Bishop held his hands out to try to quiet the crowd. Then he paused. "What's so bad about crinkle cookies?"

"They was made of dirt," Jeb offered with wide eyes.

"They were not! I told you they were *guete* cookies. It was a peace offering. But I was trying to heap coals of fire on his head like the Bible says. I was being nice out of spite!" Emma put her head in her hands.

The bishop started to speak but then stopped. Emma glanced up at Jeb.

He opened his mouth to say more, but Bishop Amos held up his hand to stop him. "That's enough. I'm sure there is more, but I'm going to assume you are *both* equally to blame *and* equally sorry."

Emma and Jeb looked at each other. "We're sorry, Bishop," Jeb said.

"*Ja*, we're sorry." Emma clasped her hands together.

"Well, you should be. I know your parents raised you both better than that. We don't repay evil for evil, but since neither one of you are church members yet we will let it go and speak of it no more. Did everyone present hear that?"

No one made a sound.

"*Guete.* Now you two have interrupted long enough. I want to see both of you privately after services."

Jeb and Emma both took their seats on opposite sides of the room and immediately order was restored.

After services, everyone exited the barn except for Emma, Jeb, and the bishop.

"I've heard complaints about the two of you since...well, since you were both in primary school." The bishop stood over Jeb and Emma where they sat on the front bench. "Now, I've had a lot of time to ponder this situation, why normal correction hasn't worked for either of you, and to tell you the truth I'm still not sure." He lowered his voice. "You asked me to forgive you and I think everyone here has, but it's up to each of you to seek forgiveness from the Lord. If you haven't asked Him into your heart, you'll always feel that need to compete your way into Heaven, and with each other. Does any of this ring true?"

Jeb and Emma looked at each other. "Yes, sir," they said in unison. Emma knew then why he'd saved these words for private. Not everyone in the congregation believed you didn't have to work your way into Heaven. Emma remembered her *vater* saying it had been only by the grace of God that the lot fell on Amos, making him their bishop.

"*Guete.* Now I think it goes without saying that there'll be no more lying. Let's have a few moments of silent prayer together and I'll pray that the Lord look down on you and give you both strength."

MIRIAM AND EMMA showed some of the young men where to set up the volleyball net for the before-singing games. Emma found Jeb sitting in the barn on one of the wooden benches they'd set up for church earlier. His black felt hat lay next to him on the seat, his head down.

"Why'd you do it?" Emma asked.

Jeb turned to face her. "Do what?"

"Confess."

He picked up his hat and fumbled with the small metal buckle that held the band on. "I was wrong."

"Of course you were," Emma said, "but why now? What made you confess today?" She hoped it was because he was developing feelings for her, feelings like the ones she was having.

He stopped fumbling with his hat and looked her right in the eye. "I heard tell Luke's getting serious about courting Edna Byler. You two were getting along right fine till I came along and I aim to make it right."

"What do you mean?" Emma watched him put his hat firmly on his head and stand.

"You'll see." Jeb stomped through the barn, a determined look upon his face. Emma saw him heading straight for Luke who was standing just beyond the open barn doors.

"Jeb, wait," she called, but he kept going.

She followed behind him.

"Luke, I'm sorry for what I done," he said. "You and Emma had somethin' real special and I'm sorry I ruined it."

Luke's jaw was set. "It's not right, Jeb. Emma was my girl. She tried to tell me how deceptive you were, but I didn't listen. I *defended* you. And you just wanted to ruin her *guete* name. Now you got her all confused, thinking *she* was the one in the wrong."

Emma stepped up beside them. "I was, Luke. We both were."

"Actually," Jeb said, "we all three were. That's what you're really mad about, isn't it? That she told you the truth and you still didn't believe it. You're mad at yourself."

Luke's eyes flashed fire as he drew back a fist and planted it right in Jeb's face with a smack. Emma jumped as a scream escaped. The strike had thrown Jeb off balance, causing him to stumble a step. He righted himself and stepped forward. Luke drew back again, but Jeb pointed to the side of his face, the side that wasn't turning red.

A crowd had gathered but no one spoke. The Bible said to

turn the other cheek, but Emma had never seen it illustrated so literally. Luke was breathing hard. He gave Jeb a long stare, then he said, "Come on, Emma." He motioned for her to come to him.

Did he honestly think to win her back now? *"Nay."*

"What?" Confusion was knitted into all his facial features.

"Nay," Emma said again, more pronounced this time. She narrowed her eyes.

"We need to talk," Luke said between clenched teeth.

"I think everything that needed sayin' just got said. You can see if Edna Byler needs a ride home tonight."

Luke huffed. Then he walked away, flexing and shaking his right hand.

"Are you okay, Jeb?" Emma asked, glad the event was over.

"Ja. Much better now." He lightly touched his right eye. "I guess I deserved that."

"Maybe so, but never again." The people who had gathered began to clear out. Emma lowered her voice to just a whisper. "You're indebted to no one now, Jeb, 'cept the Lord. Pity the man who can't forgive you, 'cause anyone can see you truly are sorry." Emma took hold of his light blue shirt sleeve and turned him the direction of the house. "Come on, we'd better get something cold on that. You're starting to swell."

"I am sorry I ruined things with you and Luke."

Emma stopped to make sure she had his full attention. "And God saw fit for us to not be together. My perfect plan for my life wasn't so perfect, I guess." She thought a second and then pulled again at his sleeve till he began to walk with her.

"Emma, can I take you home tonight?" His hand covered his eye.

"Nay." She glanced over at him, hiding a sly smile already forming.

"Why not?"

"'Cause this is my house. You, on the other hand, may need

some help gettin' home. Don't worry, I can hitch up Prinny and take you in my *vater's* buggy."

"Or I could just let you take my buggy."

"Oh, dear no. Your buggy smells like something died in it." Emma scrunched up her nose at the very thought.

"And whose fault is that?" his voice raised a little.

"Both of ours. *Equally.*" She stopped him and pointed a finger in his face. "Bishop said so."

He started to laugh but then winced, holding his eye once more. "I'm sure glad we're friends."

"Why is that?"

"Because you are a worthy opponent, Emma Wittmer, and I'm not sure I could ever of beaten you."

"Ha, well there's a first. Are you conceding?" She tugged him along to get him walking again.

"*Nay.* I have another proposition."

"What's that?"

"I propose from here on out we always agree to be on the same team."

"Hmmm. We'd be unstoppable, that's for certain." She nodded her head. "I agree."

"*Danki*, Emma."

"For what?"

He'd stopped walking again. "For helping me to see plainly. Our ways aren't perfect and other ways can be *guete* too, but our ways are still good, *ja?*"

Her heart leapt for joy at those words. "*Ja.* That they are. But what about your pocket phone? Won't you miss it? You may need to call China suddenly, and who will alert you when it's going to rain?"

"I don't speak Chinese and the rain doesn't scare me."

"Well," she thought out loud. "What if you need a girl phone to talk to you and keep you company?" Emma raised one eyebrow.

"Maybe I could just walk through the field and visit a neighbor instead," he said softly.

Her heart skipped a beat at his words. "Mrs. Schwartz?" Emma teased.

"I don't know, does Mrs. Schwartz make potato candy?"

"Maybe." Emma leaned in closer to Jeb's face with a crooked smile and whispered, "But ours is better."

REDEEMING RUTH

"Let no man despise thy youth; but be thou an example of the believers, in word, in conversation, in charity, in spirit, in faith, in purity." 1 Timothy 4:12 KJV

CHAPTER 1

*T*he leaves had turned color overnight, or at least it seemed that way to Sydney since she hadn't noticed them yesterday at her little apartment in the city. The trees there were lonely statues fading into the background, nothing like the acres and acres of forest she was seeing now, riding in the car with her mother through the southern Missouri hills.

"Why are we doing this again?" Sydney reached toward the floorboard for her purse.

"Doing what?" her mother put on her right signal.

"When you said we were going on a weekend getaway, I wasn't expecting to tour hillbilly Amish country." Sydney pulled out a tube of dark-red lipstick and flipped down the visor.

"Sydney Ruth Glynn." Her mother peered over at her with a scolding glare in her eyes. Sydney hated her full name and her mother knew it.

When she opened the hinged mirror cover, the lights beside the mirror illuminated her fair skin and deep brown, almost black hair. She wiped at a bit of unruly mascara at the corner of her hazelnut eyes and then generously applied the color to her lips.

"Would you rather have stayed at home by yourself?" Her mother turned her head both ways before driving onto a gravel road.

"No," Sydney said reluctantly. She hated being alone. She hated it almost as much as school, but she went to school to keep from being alone—that and to get a free meal. The free meals she received for breakfast and lunch were hardly enough to keep her going all day, especially with all the calorie and fat restrictions now in place to fight childhood obesity, but when her mother was away for weeks at a time—doing God only knew what and with whom—it was much preferred to the empty pantry at home. She'd dropped five pounds the last time her mother went away. That was when her mother first met Mitch, but he was old news now. She had moved on to another love interest named Dan, a man Sydney had mysteriously not heard much about. Sydney closed the visor and dropped her lipstick back into her purse. The afternoon sun was warm on her face. She lowered her window halfway, tugging at the tank top that clung to her chest. She brushed her long hair back with her fingers in the soft breeze.

"Hand me my phone," her mother said.

Sydney dug in her mother's purse and pulled out the cell phone. Her mother took it and began pushing buttons.

"Come on," her mother whined, then pushed a few more.

"Maybe it's just a bad signal," Sydney offered.

"No. It's junk. It's been acting strange for a while now. I knew it could die any day." She finally tossed the phone to the backseat floorboard. "Let me see yours." She wiggled her fingers in anticipation.

Sydney dug her phone out of her purse and checked the screen. "There's no signal here, not even one bar."

"Figures. That's just how the Amish like it."

"Is that why you left?" Sydney knew she was pushing it. Her mother didn't like to talk about her past, but coming back to see her family like this must mean she was finally ready to deal with it.

"Look, there." Her mother pointed ahead of them at a buggy. It was a large open wagon with huge wooden wheels, drawn by a horse. A young man in a black hat and blue long-sleeve shirt and suspenders sat beside a slightly rounded woman wearing a dark blue dress with a black apron and a black bonnet on her head. The only indication that they hadn't just stepped back in time a hundred years was the orange reflector triangle hanging in the back. Sydney had seen Amish people a time or two in her life, but never in a buggy.

Why would anyone choose to live this way on purpose?

"Do you know them?" she asked her mother.

"Maybe." She shrugged.

"How much farther to your family's house?"

"It's just up the road."

"So we're almost there?"

Her mother just nodded, unusually silent.

Sydney wasn't sure if the excitement she was experiencing was the curiosity of meeting real Amish people or the relief of finally getting out of the car after the five hour drive to get there. She had taken turns with her mother, driving the easier parts of the trip, but it had still been long and boring. They watched as the buggy pulled into a long driveway leading to a large two-story farmhouse complete with a windmill and several outbuildings.

"How many people do you think live here?"

"Anywhere from two to twenty is my guess." The car slowed at the driveway where the Amish buggy had just turned. Sydney examined the mailbox from her open window. It was black with white hand-painted lettering that read *Jeremiah J. Schwartz*. The car came to a complete stop.

"Is this it?" Sydney asked, but her mother didn't answer. She was pale and her large brown eyes protruded more than usual.

The ever-present darkness under her eyes seemed worse than before they'd left. No amount of makeup could hide it now, although her mother had certainly tried. Her mid-length frosted dark hair, set in place perfectly with hairspray, looked like it belonged to a different face—one that wasn't so tired and worn.

"No," her mother said, never taking her eyes off the buggy heading up the lane. She turned the car and followed it slowly up the hill to the farmhouse.

Sydney's stomach turned. If this wasn't her family's house, why were they stopping? And how many uncomfortable meetings would they have to endure before this nightmare weekend ended?

The car stopped close to the house, but her mother had left enough room not to scare the horse, still hitched up to the buggy. The people were standing in the yard watching them. Sydney stepped out of the car at the same time her mother did. The young man's stare bore into her, and with the gentle breeze against her bare arms, she suddenly felt naked. Somehow the white tank top and faded jean shorts didn't cover as much as they had back in the city. Sydney held her arms against her chest.

"*Vie gatz!*" Sydney's mother called out.

She'd never once heard her mother speak Swiss German, although it would make sense that she knew it. She hadn't left Amish country until she was fully grown.

"*Vie gatz,*" the young man said, though not as enthusiastically. He stepped toward them. He was long and lean, clean shaven with high cheekbones and a sharp jawline. He couldn't have been much older than Sydney, his jet-black hair barely long enough to wave slightly under his straw hat. "May I help you?" he said slowly, deliberately.

"I was wondering if the Hiltys still live around here."

"The next road down on your left will take you to Hilty's Circle."

"JoHannah," the woman beside him said. She was probably in

her early to mid fifties. She set down a yellow Dollar General bag where she stood and came over to stand next to Sydney's mother. "Is that you, JoHannah?" she asked, her eyes bright. Sydney's mother went by JoAnn. No one called her JoHannah.

"How are you, Naomi?"

"JoHannah, we thought we'd never see you again. Come into the house. You must stay a while." She took "JoHannah" by the hand and walked with her into the house, leaving Sydney and the young man to follow behind. They entered the house through the kitchen. A wood cookstove sat on the opposite side between the kitchen and a living room beyond it, and in the middle of the room a large wooden table with matching wooden chairs, one with a dark blue cushion tied to the seat.

"Come. Sit. This is my youngest son, David. The rest of the *chinda* have all grown up and left me, I'm afraid."

"And Jeremiah?"

"My husband went to be with the *guete* Lord, a little more than a year ago."

"I'm sorry to hear that," JoHannah said.

"And this must be your *chind*?" Naomi sat down on the cushioned seat and motioned for everyone else to sit at the table with her.

"This is my Sydney." Mom smiled as she sat.

"Nice to meet you," Sydney said, taking a seat at the table.

"It's a pleasure to meet you, Sydney." Naomi extended her hand and, after shaking Sydney's, she held onto it for a moment on the table top. Sydney glanced at her mother, who gave her a tight smile. It was a warning to be nice no matter what, just like when her mom would bring a new man home.

"Well, have you met with your kin yet?"

"No. We just got into the neighborhood and happened to see you going up the drive."

"Well, the Hilty houses are all full up right now and my poor house stands here empty. You're welcome to stay here for as long as you're visiting. You will be staying a few days, won't you, dear?"

"Yes, we're planning on being here at least overnight. That would be very nice of you, Naomi."

"Well, then it's settled. David, help them get their things and unload the goods we bought in town. I'll get the spare rooms ready, then we can visit some more." She smiled and then got up and left the room quickly, leaving the other three to do as the lady of the house had instructed. David held the door as Sydney crossed the threshhold, her mother followed, clicking the remote to open the trunk of the car. She handed David their bags and closed the trunk. David didn't speak, only took the bags into the house and carried them upstairs.

In the living room, every sound, even their soft footsteps, seemed to echo on the wooden floors. The furniture was hard wood, beautifully handcrafted, with hand sewn pillows here and there. A large rug offered the only softness about the room other than the solid white curtains and a single knitted afghan draped over the back of a rocking chair. Sydney wondered if they considered soft furniture to be too fancy. She tried to imagine growing up in a house like Naomi's. To think, she was almost Amish. If her mother hadn't left she would be living in a home just like this one right now, maybe even engaged to an Amish boy like David Schwartz.

David came back downstairs a moment later. He hung his hat by the front door on a long row of empty hooks. His mother stopped halfway down the staircase. "Your rooms are ready," she said. Sydney and her mother followed her back up the stairs. David nodded to Sydney as she walked past him. Her pulse sped. If she were Amish, she would say he was hot. Then again, if she were Amish she probably wouldn't be allowed to say that.

As Sydney put away her things in the guest room down the hall from the stairs, she overheard a voice outside the door. It was Naomi. "David, I want you to ride over to the Hilty's. Tell them JoHannah has come back to us and that we'll bring her by later this evening."

"Do you expect a *guete* meeting?" His voice held concern.

"I don't know. They'll be surprised, that's for sure. Go quickly."

Sydney listened to the footsteps growing quieter. She guessed it would be a big surprise. Her mother's family hadn't seen her in over sixteen years. Would they be happy she'd come? Sydney got the feeling her mother didn't leave on the best of terms. What if they weren't welcome? That was hard to imagine after meeting Naomi. Such a kind woman. And so friendly. For a second she was jealous of David. His mother would never have left him alone to fend for himself the way her own mother had. She shook the thought from her head. Jealous of the Amish. It was laughable, really.

She checked her cell phone. Still no signal. She supposed there was no use looking for a plug-in, her mother had already told her not to expect any electricity. She set it on the side table next to her purse then pulled a red knit sweater from her bag and slipped it over her head. Its wide neck still showed the straps of her tank top, but covered much more than the tank alone. Rummaging through her bag she found one pair of jeans. They were torn at the knees and in a few places in the back, but they still hid more skin than the super short shorts she was wearing. She changed quickly and headed back downstairs.

"May I use the restroom?" Sydney asked Naomi.

"Sure thing." Naomi walked through the living room into the kitchen. Sydney followed, curious. Naomi stopped at the back door and pointed outside the screen window to a small gray shed on the other side of the yard. "Outhouse is just out back. The paper's in a coffee can. It keeps the critters out of it." Naomi winked then walked back into the living room without another word.

The screen door creaked precariously as Sydney opened it.

She closed it carefully behind her and made her way to the outhouse.

Sydney cringed. It smelled like a gas station restroom with a deep earthy smell mixed in. She hovered over a toilet seat bolted over a hole in a covered bench, the draft making it difficult to concentrate. She opened the plastic coffee can lid, afraid of what she might find inside. She was overjoyed not to find a corncob, but instead a rather thick, cushy brand of toilet paper. So not everything was plain.

"The washroom is right this way, dear," Naomi said as Sydney re-entered the house wondering how the Amish women survived without electricity.

Naomi showed her how to use the hand pump to wash her hands. Sydney figured the soap must have been handmade. It was a creamy brown color and too soft for a regular bar of soap you'd buy in the store, but it washed off clean and smelled like lemons.

How much extra time did it take to do things like making your own soap? And why did they even bother? It wasn't like soap was expensive.

After a long visit with Naomi and David over sweet bread and tea, Naomi instructed David to ready the buggy. They were all going together to the Hilty's. It made Sydney feel a little less anxious knowing her new friends were coming, too.

David helped his mother into the buggy, then Mom, and finally he gave his hand to Sydney. An eagerness flashed in his eyes as they touched, the electricity coming from his warm, heavy hand a pleasant surprise. She stepped up into the buggy, which was much higher than she'd expected, and took a seat on the back bench.

"*Mam?*" he asked when it was his turn to board.

Naomi was sitting in the front bench beside Mom with the reins in hand. "If I don't drive once in a while I'll forget how. Besides, it won't be your face they'll be looking to see coming around the corner. You just sit back with Miss Sydney."

Sydney swallowed tightly as he dropped down next to her, his nearness causing her pulse to quicken. It didn't take long to arrive at Hilty Circle. David had explained that the Hilty's driveway cut into a half-moon, making a huge circle drive that connected to the main road. This allowed the driveways of all three Hilty properties to connect while creating a privacy screen with the joining of trees between the houses and the main road. There were several buggies already in the yard as they came to a stop at another two-story farmhouse with weathered paint in the shade of dove gray. People spilled from the door of the house onto the porch and into the yard, all dressed the same, like little tin soldiers in black and blue.

"Why are all these people here?" Sydney whispered to David.

"It's just the Hiltys. You should see it when we have church." His words came out slow, like he had to perfect them before speaking them. He jumped from the buggy and held his hand out for Sydney, then her mother and, lastly, Naomi.

Suddenly a throng of people surrounded them.

"Give them some air," a stern-looking man said with some authority. Everyone immediately took a step back. He held his hand out to Mom and she took it.

"Hello, *Dat*," she said. He pulled her to himself and hugged her tightly for several seconds before pushing her back to get a better look at her. He let out a short breath, but didn't speak.

"This is my daughter, Sydney."

Sydney held her hand out to her grandfather and he pulled her firmly to himself just as he had her mother. When he finally let go he said, "Come inside," and the mass of people moved toward the house all at once. Some were young and some old, men and women. The children were playing in the distance, a large group of them kicking a ball around in the grass. Sydney wondered how they would all fit inside the house. As they were ushered in, it was as if the walls around Sydney constricted. She looked around for David, but he wasn't in sight. The prodigal daughter was answering questions posed by several people at once and Sydney strained to hear her mother's answers. Why she left, why she'd never come back until now, why she chose now to visit.

Sydney had to answer questions of her own.

"How old are you, dear?"

"Sixteen."

"Do you live far away?"

"About five hours north of here."

"Will you be staying long?"

"Just for the weekend."

Everyone gave their names, but as one name went into her ears, it seemed to push the last one out. She'd only made it as far as the kitchen. Now her mother was in the living room with her grandfather. Someone handed Sydney a glass of sweet tea. Her chest felt tight. There were too many people taking her air.

"Thank you. Excuse me," she said and turned around for the door. Not to be rude, but she thought she might explode if she didn't get out of the room immediately. As she stepped through the door, the air washed over her. It was much too hot in there for her red knit sweater.

Leave it on and chance a heat stroke, or take it off and chance giving someone else a stroke?

The people standing around on the porch looked surprised to see her. She found a rocking chair and sat down. When she looked up, David was in the chair next to her.

"You okay?" he asked.

Sydney's chest loosened at the sight of him. "Yeah, I am now. I just needed some air."

David nodded slowly. A moment later the crowd swarmed again.

"Are you all right?" one of the women asked.

"Can I get you anything?" said another.

David glanced at Sydney, then stood. "This is just very overwhelming for her, meeting all her family for the first time." He held his hands out in front of him; a subtle gesture to give her some space. Just then, a man marched up the walkway with a woman and several children struggling to keep up behind him. When the people saw him coming, they parted and let him through. Even David took a step to the side. The man stopped in front of Sydney, still sitting in the chair. His beard was full and bushy but no mustache, his eyes a hazel brown.

"Are you JoHannah's daughter?" he asked firmly. His tone made Sydney shrink.

"Yes," she said nervously. Who was this man? Sydney held her breath, unsure of the man's intentions. He took off his hat, knelt down on one knee, and said, "I'm your *vater*."

Sydney stood. "I'm sorry, you must have me confused for someone else." The tightness in her chest returned.

He stood, his eyes narrowed in on hers. "You're JoHannah's daughter? Her only daughter? And you're sixteen?"

"Yes."

"I'm your *vater*. What did JoHannah tell you about me?" The man's eyes were pleading.

"You're not my father. My father is Roger Glynn. He was from Oklahoma."

"Is that what the witch told you?" Hatred ignited in his eyes.

Sydney sidestepped away from the man.

"Simmer down, Samuel." David's jaw was set. His eyes narrowed and hardened.

The man took a deep breath and let it out with a huff. "I'm sorry. I shouldn't have said that about your *mueter*."

Sydney held her hands out in front of her. There was no way this man was her father. "This is all just a big misunderstanding. My mother is inside. Talk to her if you don't believe me. If you can get in there."

"Oh, I'll get in there all right," he muttered as he placed his hat back on his head and started for the door. The people parted as he neared and he didn't slow down even as he disappeared inside the door. He left the woman and children staring at Sydney. She supposed the woman was his wife, who clearly didn't know what to say. She just stood there, avoiding any eye contact with Sydney; the children, who all looked younger than Sydney, rushed to her as their father left.

"You're our *schweshta*, sure as the world. Just look at that hair, Sarah," one of the teenaged girls said, "it's just like yours."

Sydney could barely see any of their hair with the full black bonnets they wore, but their eyes, they were familiar. The realization washed over her and Sydney's mouth dropped open. How could her mother have lied to her like that?

Angry German shouts spilled from beyond the screen door. Sydney turned back to the teenaged girls. "What is he saying?" she whispered.

One of them hung her head and shook it softly. The other leaned in. "We can't repeat that for you, miss."

Samuel burst out the door and stamped over to them. "Get in the buggy," he told his family and they all scattered. He turned to Sydney. "You are my daughter and always will be. Come to my house. David will bring you." He pointed at David. "We have a lot to say, but not here. Not with that woman around." He spat out "woman" like it was a curse word and pointed to the kitchen door.

"Samuel..." David warned, not looking the least bit intimidated by Samuel's temper.

The man took a deep breath. "Not with your *mueter* around. Know this, daughter of mine, I love you and I have always loved you. Don't believe everything she tells you." With those words said, he stomped away to his buggy.

Sydney flopped back into the rocking chair. She struggled to breathe even in the open air of the porch. The heat was overwhelming. Throwing modesty to the wind, she lifted the red knit sweater over her head and threw it down over the porch rail behind her. She heard one of the women gasp. The white tank top clung to her chest. She pulled at it, letting the soft breeze cool her. David shifted his weight uncomfortably, his eyes wide. Then he moved to stand with his back to her, shielding her from unwanted company.

She waited a long time before her mother finally came out, bringing with her aunts and cousins, left and right. Sydney shook many hands and took in many names. It seemed everyone wanted to talk to her, but the accusing look she shot at her mother spoke volumes. After that, her mother's eyes studiously avoided hers. Sydney had pictures back home in a photo album on the shelf of her and her father, Roger Glynn, the man she had been named after. Who was he if not her father? And why make her look like an idiot in front of all these people by not telling her sooner? Her mother had done many questionable things over the years, but this one beat all. But Sydney held it all in. She would remember her manners and be a good girl, not giving into the temptation to scream at her mother. For now, anyway. And she wouldn't dare fight in front of Naomi and David. Oh, but the ride home would be a loud one.

*S*ydney couldn't sleep that night. She was too busy envisioning the conversation she would have with her mother, what she would say, what her mother would counter with, and the exact words that would ultimately crush her defense. Her mother was wrong, so very wrong, to have hid this from her, and why? What did it matter that her father was Amish? Sydney was curious about his side of things, but no, she didn't really want to get in the middle of their argument—whatever it was about. She'd lived most of her life without a father and unlike her mother, she didn't need a man to take care of her. She'd proven time and time again she could take care of herself. Sydney glanced at her cell phone. It was after two when she finally rolled over and went to sleep.

SYDNEY AWOKE, startled. She was in a different bed, a different room. How had she gotten there? Then without warning, the previous day's events swept over her and shrouded her with darkness. She rubbed her eyes. All she could think of was using the restroom until she remembered there wasn't one. She dressed quickly in the other tank top she'd packed, pink with matching shorts. They were way too short for Amish country, but it was still too hot for jeans. What did it matter? They were leaving later in the day, never to see these people again. Sydney doubted she could offend them that much with her clothing in only a few hours. She tied on her tennis shoes and went downstairs.

Naomi stood at the stove. David sat at the table with no hat, shirt, or shoes, only his black pants on, suspender straps hanging at his sides, eating fried eggs and bacon. She hadn't expected to see him this way, not with all the emphasis the Amish put on modesty, but maybe that only applied to the women.

"Good morning," Sydney said, trying to sound cheery.

David jumped up, his chair scrubbing the floor loudly, wiping his mouth on his arm. He turned to face her, his biceps large and defined. "What are you doing here?" he mumbled with his mouth full. He looked Sydney up and down, his dark eyes a contrast to his light colored skin.

Sydney couldn't bear to wear that hot sweater again today, but David's look of shock made her wonder if she should reconsider.

Naomi looked at her the same way. "*E feshtay nit,*" she exclaimed with a spatula in her hand, looking as if she'd just seen a ghost.

"What's wrong?" Sydney asked, looking down at her outfit. Was it that bad? It was short, but it didn't have any offensive writing on it or anything. She twisted around to catch a glimpse of her backside, still not understanding the big deal.

David shot into the other room.

"I don't understand," Naomi said to her.

"What do you mean?" Sydney spied the outhouse through the window.

"Sydney, did your *mueter* run into town this morning?"

"Not that I know of, why?"

David reappeared quickly with a shirt on and his suspenders up.

Naomi and David exchanged tense glances.

Silence except for the sizzle of eggs in the skillet on the woodstove. The smell of the eggs beginning to burn made Sydney's stomach roll.

"Sorry, *Mam*." David sat back down, scooting his chair up to the table, scraping the hardwood floor. His cheeks were rosy and his head hung low. He took another big bite of egg.

"Well, haven't I told you to put your shirt on before breakfast, company or not?" she scolded, waving the spatula at him.

"*Ja*," he said quietly, not looking up again.

"Wash up, Sydney. Your breakfast will be ready in a few minutes...if I haven't burned it already." Naomi turned her attention back to the skillet on the stove.

Sydney used the outhouse and washed up in the washroom with the pump just as Naomi had showed her. The smell of the lemon soap made her hungry. She peeked in the kitchen doorway. "I'll go wake my mom," she said.

"Sydney, wait." Naomi motioned toward the table with both hands. "Sit down, dear, and we'll sort this all out."

Sort what out?

Naomi put out some bacon and two fried eggs on a plate and handed it to Sydney. Sydney sat down.

Naomi opened a drawer. "Your mother had a pretty *guete* visit yesterday, *ja*?" She pulled out a fork and handed it to Sydney, closing the drawer with a swing of her hips.

"Yes, I think so. She seemed to have had a good time."

"And did she say anything to you last night, before bed?"

Sydney thought back to the night before. "No." She hadn't wanted to speak to her mother, so she had closed the bedroom door.

"Sydney, I don't know how to tell you this, but your *mueter* isn't here. When I saw her car gone this morning, I went upstairs to her room. All her things were gone and her bed made up. I didn't check your room. I just assumed..."

She'd assumed.

Like any reasonable person, she couldn't believe that anyone could just leave their daughter, but it happened.

Naomi laughed, but Sydney sensed it was strained. "Surely she'll be back soon. She probably just made a trip into town."

But Naomi didn't know Sydney's mother—not anymore. Sydney ate her eggs in silence, trying to reassure herself it would all be okay. She didn't want to tell David and Naomi the truth—that her mother often left without saying goodbye anytime things got heated between them or when she got a new boyfriend, or even when she simply got bored. How would she break the news to them and what would they want to do with her? She hoped Naomi was right, that her mother had simply gone into town and would return shortly.

After breakfast, Sydney excused herself and went up to her mother's room. She had to see it for herself. All her mother's things were gone and the bed was made just like when they'd arrived. She went back to her room and sat down on the bed. When had her mother left? She reached for her cell phone on the nightstand to check the time, but it wasn't there.

"No," she said out loud. "No, no, no." She rummaged through her purse and her bag, but the cell phone was gone. Her mother had taken it and she wasn't coming back.

Sydney descended the stairs. As she reached the bottom she heard whispering in German, but it stopped abruptly as David and Naomi came into view.

"Are you ready?" David asked.

"For what?"

"To go see your *vater*. It's Sunday. There's no church today, so it's a *guete* day to visit."

"I don't know if I can handle all those people at once." Sydney's cheeks got hot just thinking about yesterday's crowd, and the possibility of speaking with her father again didn't sound much more pleasant.

David thought a moment. "How about I ride over to the Byler's and invite your *vater* over here to visit with you in private?" He looked at his mother and she agreed.

Sydney hesitated. What would they think of her if she refused? Finally, she nodded.

"*Guete.* I'll be back shortly." His warm smile was reassuring.

It wasn't long before the buggy came rumbling up the long drive. Sydney peered through the curtains. It was just the two of them. She breathed a sigh of relief.

Samuel Byler sat in a hard chair across from Sydney in the living room. David and Naomi were in the kitchen at the table. Other than the occasional coffee refill for Samuel or an offer of pie, they steered clear of the living room. Sydney was glad for the privacy, but at times wished they could help her fill in the gaps in conversation.

"So what do you like to do?" Samuel asked.

"I don't know. Just hang out," she said, unable to concentrate on small talk.

"Do you have a boyfriend?"

"No." Sydney bit at the side of her fingernail, her hands beginning to shake.

Silence.

"What is it you want to do with your life?"

"I don't know." Sydney wondered if Amish teenagers had answers for all these questions. She knew he was trying to be nice, but all his questioning was intrusive and it made Sydney increasingly insecure about herself. She was quickly becoming aware of how pathetic her life was, but this was no time to deal with those issues. Her mother had left her with no way home. Of course, it wouldn't matter soon anyway. Overdue notices had cluttered the apartment counter before they'd left. There might not be a "home" to come back to anymore.

Did she plan on dumping me here from the very beginning?

Her father's words ran together in her ears, causing her to tremble. She put her head into her hands and began to sob.

Naomi was soon at her side, her hand gently rubbing her upper back.

"Did I say something wrong?" Samuel asked gruffly.

Sydney shook her head and stood. She started to speak, but couldn't find her words. She ran up the stairs to her room, closing the door behind her.

It was evening before she dared peek her head out. The smell of grease and corn reached the top of the stairs. First she visited the washroom. She scrubbed her face with lemon soap, hoping the mascara would wash off cleanly with it. She considered going back upstairs for more makeup, but what did it matter what she looked like? David and Naomi would tire of her eventually and she would need to venture out on her own. She would be seventeen before long, maybe someone would give her a job in exchange for a place to stay. She certainly couldn't stay here forever.

Naomi was in the kitchen, setting the table. "Ah, Sydney. I was just about to call you for supper. Do you like beans and fried cornbread? I've also made fried potatoes. We'll put some meat on your bones yet." Naomi laughed as if nothing in the world were wrong.

Sydney's stomach growled. "That sounds really good. Thank you."

"Sit here," she said, setting a plate on the table. "You must be starving. David," she called loudly over her shoulder. "Food's gonna be all gone before you get in here."

"I'm here, *Mam,*" he called before appearing in the doorway.

"You know I wouldn't start without you. Now sit down so our guest can eat."

Naomi and David sat and David said a blessing. Sydney closed her eyes and bowed her head just like they did until it was over. Then David passed a plate of fried potatoes over to Sydney first. She took some and then passed the plate over to Naomi.

The meal was filled with endless chatter about how many eggs the chickens had been laying and how it was more than what they'd heard about the neighbors' chickens laying this time of year, and church, and the words to a song Naomi couldn't quite remember. But all Sydney could think of was how happy the two of them looked. It didn't matter what they talked about. She had never been able to talk to her mother that way and the conversation with her father earlier in the day had ended very badly. What made these two different?

"We've discussed it, Sydney," Naomi said when she'd finally pushed her plate forward to show she was finished. "We want you to stay here with us for a while. Isn't that right, David?"

"We have plenty of room," David said. "And *Mam* could sure use some help around here."

"I don't know." The question took Sydney by surprise. Her living in Amish country? How would that even work? "I should really be getting back to school."

"We discussed it with your *vater*, he thinks you should study to get your school certificate. What did he call it? Your GED." Naomi put her hand on Sydney's. "He said he'd pay for any books you needed and whatever it took to get the test."

It sounded too good to be true. Sydney sipped her tea nervously. "Then what?"

David's eyes danced. "Then you can go wherever your heart leads."

After supper dishes were done, Naomi got out a cloth bag and sat down in her rocking chair. She pulled out two long knitting needles with a blue baby booty attached. She began to knit. David and Sydney sat in the living room with her, awkwardly staring at the floor.

"David, I think it's time to make a visit to the game closet."

Naomi pulled at the long string of yarn in the cloth bag by her chair.

"What's that?" Sydney asked.

"Before all my *chinda* left home they'd play games before bed each night."

"Did you play, too?"

"*Nay*. My knitting keeps me occupied." She rocked in the rocking chair, her fingers working the yarn quickly.

David stood. "Well, let's go see what we can find," he said stiffly.

Sydney followed David upstairs to the room where her mother had stayed, the reminder of her betrayal cutting open a fresh wound. The sun was starting to set outside the window. They would soon need a lantern to see. In the closet they found a stack of board games. It was odd to even be thinking of playing board games at their age, but Sydney figured without television they had to do something.

"Do you play chess?" he asked.

Sydney shook her head. "I'm not smart enough for chess."

"Why would you say something like that about yourself?" He meant it literally, sounding genuinely curious.

Did she really want David to know she wasn't passing half her classes?

He stepped inside the closet and Sydney craned her neck over his shoulder to see, his dark hair inches from her face. "Well, it's complicated, isn't it?"

David pulled the box out from the middle of the stack. "You have to know how the pieces move, but it's not complicated. I could teach you." He turned around, game in hand, suddenly very close to Sydney. "If...you wanted."

She took two steps back, pretending not to be affected by his intense closeness, and let him out of the closet. He stepped around her awkwardly, clearing his throat.

They took the game back downstairs to the kitchen table and

David set it up along with a lantern for when it got too dark to see.

"The object of the game is to capture the opponent's king. Each of the pieces moves in a different way. Here's the king." He handed her the white game piece. "This one is yours." He set it in the appropriate square in front of Sydney. "The king is weak and slow, but the game cannot go on without him. Every other piece is used to either protect the king or defend his honor. He can only move one space at a time, but in any direction. Then there's the queen." He held up Sydney's queen. "She's fast and cunning, zipping across the entire length of the board in a single turn to ward off attackers."

Sydney raised her eyebrows. "So the woman is the hero in this game?"

"I suppose you could say that, she seems to have most of the power."

"I'm surprised you're allowed to play it."

David laughed, lightening Sydney's mood. It had been a very difficult day.

"What ideas do you have about our people?"

The way he said "our people" bit at Sydney. Her mother and father were both Amish, the same blood as David's, but they weren't her people. She didn't know anything about them.

Sydney bit at the side of her fingernail. "I figured you to be a bit more boring than you are."

"Is that *Englisher* talk for a compliment?" He sounded amused.

"I'm sorry." She put both hands on the table. "No, that came out all wrong. I just didn't picture the Amish playing board games."

"What did you think we did for fun?"

Sydney thought a second. "Stare at the wall?" Sydney didn't know why she was being so rude to him, he wasn't the source of her anger.

The questioning look from David, along with the stress of the day, made Sydney surrender to a laugh. He smiled back, eyes glistening.

Sydney let out a tired sigh. "What did you think I'd be like when you first saw me?" She ran her fingers through the length of her hair, trying to loosen up a little.

David's eyes wandered downward, away from Sydney. She sensed his reserve and dropped her arms, sliding her fingers under her legs.

"I try to keep from making snap judgments about people," he said, still not making eye contact.

"What's this piece?" Sydney picked up the white pointed piece in front of her, trying to change the subject.

"That's the bishop."

"Don't the Amish have a bishop?"

"*Ja*. Our bishop is Amos, but he's not a typical bishop."

"What do you mean?"

He hesitated. "*Mam* has instructed me not to talk about matters of the church with outsiders."

Sydney's lips pressed together in a frown.

"But you're not a real outsider, are you?" David waited for her to respond.

"I suppose not."

"A bishop is chosen by the casting of the lot."

"You mean they draw straws or something?" That would certainly be a strange way to get a job.

"Something like that, *ja*. Only this bishop believes a little differently. It's caused some friction, to be sure."

"What happens then?"

"Well, the lot is the will of God, so if someone doesn't like it the only thing they can do is move to another district. Some have."

"You would move just because your preacher doesn't believe exactly like you do?"

"*Ja*. Aren't some things important enough to move for?"

Sydney had moved when she left for this weekend trip and hadn't even known it. "Yeah, I suppose."

"How about we practice playing with only a few pieces till you know how they move?" David slid the pieces into a pile carefully with his arm. Then he took out the king, queen, and bishop of each color from the pile and set them on the board. "I'll go first." He took his bishop and slid it diagonally across the board. "Now you go."

Sydney touched her bishop and slid it diagonally, looking to David for acceptance of her move.

"*Guete.*" He moved his bishop again in another direction, taking out her king. "And I win," he said casually. He reset the pieces. "You go first this time."

She moved her king one space then he picked up his queen and sent it across the board. Sydney moved her queen across to his side. "How long has it been since you played games like this?"

"Hmm, my last brother moved out about a year ago, not long after my *vater* died."

Sydney was sorry she'd asked.

"We played games every night, back then." He moved his king one space.

"Well, what do you do every night now?" she asked, moving her queen.

"Just stare at the wall." He faked seriousness until he got a laugh out of Sydney, then he joined her. She was thankful for it. The stress of the day had exhausted her. With each laugh she shared with David at the kitchen table she drew strength.

CHAPTER 3

*S*ydney slept fitfully. It had been a life-changing day. So many things to think about, the father and siblings she had just found out about, wondering where in the world her mother was, whether or not she could ever pass a GED test, and David... She rolled over in her sleep. She could see her mother drifting further and further away. Sydney reached out her hand to catch her, but couldn't. Darkness surrounded her and she was all alone.

The piercing sound of her own scream woke Sydney. It was pitch black. Where was she? She jumped forward and her feet hit the floor. She screamed again and began to run. Her knee hit something hard and she fell to the floor. A beam of light moving in all directions came at her accompanied by loud thumps and she screamed again, throwing her hands over her head.

"Sydney," a man's stern voice called out. "What is it?" Rapid-fire words were shot out in Swiss German, but Sydney understood none of them. David knelt down where Sydney was heaped on the floor. She gasped, panting in terror, and then grabbed his arm, trying to catch her breath.

She'd done it again.

It only happened when her mother was away. The times when she was alone. She'd never told anyone about them before, how she often woke up in another room, but now she would have to explain. "I…"

"It was a night terror, wasn't it?" David asked.

"How did you know?" her voice a broken whisper.

Naomi came bounding up the stairs. "What on earth?" she said.

"She's got the night terrors." David stood and handed his flashlight to his mother then backed away into the darkness.

Naomi examined the situation, shining the light in Sydney's eyes. "Come, let's get you back into bed. Have you hurt yourself?"

"No."

"*Guete.*" Naomi took Sydney's still shaking arm and pulled her to standing, then led her back into her room. "Are you all right?"

"Yes. I'm sorry."

"For what, dear?"

"For scaring you." Her arms and legs trembled as tears of relief threatened.

"Don't worry about it, just get some sleep. Here. You take the flashlight, in case you need it."

"Thank you."

"Are you sure you're all right?"

"Yeah. I think so. Thank you."

Naomi turned, a never ending ponytail tapered down her back. She closed the door behind her. Sydney wished the door was still open, but she was too exhausted to get up and open it. There she sat on the bed, in nothing but her underwear and a long night shirt. Her new friends had seen too much of her, inside and out. She found the button on the flashlight and switched it off, but it was too dark. Switching it back on, she decided to leave it pointing up on the night stand, just for a little while, until she was sleepy.

Morning came. The sun shone bright in her window, waking

her gently. She saw the flashlight and remembered everything that had happened the night before. She switched it off but it was too late, the batteries were already dead. Why did she have to go and embarrass herself in front of David and Naomi like that? They'd been so kind to her and she'd probably scared them half to death with her screaming in the night.

No one mentioned a word about it at breakfast and Sydney was thankful. It was Monday and Sydney wondered what David and Naomi did all day with no television, radio, or electricity.

She watched Naomi make a sandwich and wrap it up. Then she handed it to David and hugged him quickly. He nodded to Sydney before he left the house.

"Where's he going?"

"He's working at the shop today with his brothers. I expect you've got some wash that needs done up?" Naomi said. "Go fetch it and I'll show you how it's done. I figure it'll be a little different than what you're used to." She smiled a crooked smile.

A few minutes later, Naomi led Sydney outside the kitchen door into the backyard, each carrying a basket of dirty clothes under their arm. Naomi set out two large tubs and filled them with water. She built a small fire under the first.

"Now what?" Sydney wondered out loud.

"Now we sweep."

"I thought we were doing laundry?"

"Have to let the water get hot first." Naomi led the way back into the house. Sydney shook the rugs over the front porch rail. She wondered why they never used the front door, the view of the hills in varying shades of autumn was so beautiful this time of year. Naomi swept all the floors upstairs and down.

Then they returned to the huge wash tubs. Naomi threw in Sydney's clothes, added some homemade soap from a white jug then "swooshed" it around. The sun was warmer now, almost hot, but the warm water from the tub felt nice on her bare arms. They soon formed an assembly line of washing, rinsing, and running the clothes through the wringer to squeeze all the excess water out. The wet clothes were then dropped into a basket at the end of the line to be hung up when they'd finished them all. After Sydney's clothes were done they washed Naomi's, then the towels and sheets, lastly David's clothes went through. Sydney helped hang the wet clothes on the long clothesline. Her pink tank top hanging next to David's long-sleeve shirt seemed so out of place, just like she felt. Still, looking at all the clothes flapping in the warm fall breeze, she felt a sense of accomplishment. She couldn't imagine how long it must take the Hilty families to do all their wash.

Naomi cocked her head at the view of the clothesline. "How about a hot bath while we wait for the clothes to dry, *ja?*" she asked.

"That would be wonderful," Sydney said. It had been days since she'd bathed and she was starting to feel sticky. "How do you…"

"Easy as pie," Naomi said with a wink. Back in the kitchen, Naomi pulled out a huge stainless steel pan and used the hand pump to fill it with water. She placed the pan on the cookstove and began to heat the water for Sydney's bath. There was also a reservoir built into the cookstove for heating water and Naomi filled it, too. In a back room on the first floor was a bathtub. It would take quite a while to pump and carry enough water to fill the tub, but Sydney didn't care. She hauled as much water into the tub as she thought could be heated by the water on the stove.

As she soaked in the tub, made almost luxurious by the drops of lavender oil Naomi had added, Sydney wondered at the Amish ways. Why would anyone want to spend all day to just get a bath and wash some clothes? It seemed like such a waste of time, yet what else did they have to do? It was the same for Sydney. She had nothing else to do, no one else who cared about her. Just a handful of friends who weren't really friends at all and a mother who didn't even say goodbye. Sydney pretended the feeling of not belonging anywhere was only because she'd learned to be independent. Yes, she would stay with Naomi and David a while, but she didn't like being a charity case. She would have to earn her keep.

DAVID RETURNED LATER in the day, though he hardly ever stepped foot inside. Sydney found him mending the chicken house door. No one told him how or even that it needed done, he just came home from the woodworking shop where he and his brothers made furniture to sell in town and began repairing the door that was coming off its hinges.

"How old are you?" Sydney asked him as she held a glass of water his mother had sent.

He pulled the nail from between his lips and began to hammer it in the door. "Seventeen. You?" his voice low and even.

"Sixteen." She watched him with the door, wishing she knew how to do something useful. Anything at all.

"What about school?" she asked.

"What about it?" He took the water from her hand as she offered it to him.

"Are you homeschooled?"

"*Nay*, we have our own school, but it only goes to eighth grade."

Sydney wondered how an eighth grade education could get you through life, but apparently the answer was right in front of her. He didn't need to know calculus to fix a chicken coop or to build furniture. What good had it been for her to learn the capitals of foreign countries when she didn't even know how to start a fire by herself?

He handed her the empty glass. "*Viel dank.*"

"What does that mean?"

"Sorry. It means, much thanks."

Sydney held his gaze a few seconds beyond what was comfortable. "You're welcome." She walked toward the house with the empty glass, the sound of a hammer tapping behind her, then an angry word she couldn't quite make out. She turned to see David had dropped the hammer. He shook his hand through the air.

AFTER SUPPER DISHES were done Naomi grabbed the empty laundry baskets. "Clothes should be dry now," she said.

"I'll get them for you." Sydney took the empty baskets from her.

"I'll help." David's hair was flat in places where his hat sat all day. He took one of the baskets out of the stack in her hands.

"You do laundry?" Sydney questioned.

"And dishes, but with you here maybe I can get out of dishes." David smiled playfully and walked out to the line. He quickly started unpinning his pants. He gave them a good shake and then dropped them into the basket at his feet. Sydney followed his example, but started from the other side. She quickly learned why he shook them out so hard, a spider ran across Naomi's dress as she was unpinning it and hid inside the collar. Sydney shivered. That didn't happen with the clothes dried in the basement dryer at the apartment complex.

They were nearing the middle of the line at Sydney's clothes. She unpinned her pink tank top and turned to find David blushing.

"I...think you can handle the rest," he said.

Sydney looked down the line at her pink lace bikini underwear. She hurried down the line and snatched them off quickly, her cheeks burning instantly. David was already heading back into the house with his basket. She followed close behind.

"So what do we do with them now?" Sydney asked.

David set the basket down in an open room off from the kitchen, beside the washroom. It had a long countertop in it with cabinets above and beneath. Sydney set her basket next to David's.

"*Mam* will iron them all tomorrow, whether they need it or not." David's head was down.

"I take it you don't iron?" Sydney tried to catch David's eyes.

"*Nay*, I don't really see the point." He was still avoiding looking at her.

"I'm sorry." Sydney tried not to laugh at his bashfulness, but it was too tempting.

"I don't know what you're talking about," he said as he tried to leave, but Sydney stopped him with her hand on his chest, forcing him to look at her.

"Do I intimidate you?" Sydney asked, almost proud of herself.

"You're very forward but no, you...distract me." He finally met her gaze, his eyes sharp, almost accusing. It took Sydney by surprise.

"How?" She removed her hand, more serious now.

"Surely you know." His eyes made a complete up and down of her. Sydney felt the same naked feeling she had the day he'd first laid eyes on her.

"I don't...have anything else to wear." She crossed her arms in front of her, sheepishly.

He gave her a half grin. "Are you up for a little night shopping?"

SYDNEY SAT NEXT to David in the buggy on the trip into town. The sun was just starting to set, so she wore her sweater over her clean pink tank top and ripped blue jeans. She wished she'd brought more clothes with her. She hadn't even brought her coat. She wondered what her mother had done with all her things, not that she had much. They'd been evicted before and had lost almost everything then. The buggy moved slowly. Cars would pass, more as they drew nearer to town, but hardly any compared to where Sydney had lived. Up ahead, another open black buggy just like the one they were riding in.

"Do you know them?" she asked David.

"Of course." Was he calm about everything?

"Well who are they?" she asked.

"I can't see them yet to tell."

"Then how do you know you know them?" She laughed.

"I know about everyone in Swan Creek Settlement."

"Really?"

"Well, maybe not personally, but I can probably tell you which family they're from."

The buggy, much closer now, carried a young couple not much older than Sydney and David. The girl waved to them as they passed and as soon as they were out of view the guy gave a loud whoop.

"What was that about?" Sydney turned to look behind them.

"They think we're courting." David never took his eyes off the road.

The Wal-Mart in the tiny town closest to the Swiss Amish community wasn't even a supercenter. It had clothes and all kinds of other things but not a grocery store. Sydney hadn't seen one that small in several years. She thumbed through some of the long-sleeve tops in a rack at the front of the women's department and chose a deep purple one. She held it up to herself then peered down the sleeve at the price tag.

"I've been instructed to buy anything you need," David said.

"By?"

"Your *vater*."

Sydney frowned.

"But if it hadn't of been your *vater* it would have been my *mueter* and if not her than me. Go, try it on." He crossed his arms over his chest, his voice slow but authoritative.

Sydney was in no position to argue. She had less than twenty dollars in her purse and the clothing she had been wearing was obviously offensive. But she still had no idea what to buy.

Grabbing several tops and a new pair of jeans she headed to the dressing room. David followed close behind.

When she stepped out of the dressing room door wearing a v-neck sweater and dark colored jeans she paid close attention to David's expressions. She waited for him to speak but he remained quiet.

"Well?"

"Well what?" His arms were folded and his finger was under his chin.

"Is this...distracting?" Sydney did a little half turn and back.

He looked both ways around him then back to Sydney, where his eyes raked boldly over her. Then he nodded in a tight little up and down fashion.

Sydney looked down at the v-neck of the sweater then shut the door again. This was going to be harder than she thought.

Two hours later David loaded the white plastic sacks into the dark buggy, and gave Sydney a hand to help her up. She'd settled on some pretty drab items, but David seemed to like them so she knew everyone else would approve. It was better than the looks of shock she'd been getting from everyone.

"Thank you," she said as they began the road home.

"No, thank you," he was trying not to smile and only looking at the road.

Sydney laughed. "What's the big deal anyway? It's just clothes and our bodies are just...bodies. What does it matter what we wear?"

He turned to her, the streetlights becoming more and more scarce as they left the little town of Asheville behind them. "Don't you care for your husband?" His words were thought out, as usual, but the darkness made it difficult to see his expression.

"I'm not married." Sydney laughed.

"*Ja*, but you will be. One day. And he's out there somewhere right now. And when he sees you wearing that…that…" he motioned his hand toward Sydney's mid-section like there were something wrong with it, "what you've been wearing, he's going to be mighty jealous that you're sharing what's his with the rest of the men out there." He turned his attention back to the road.

Sydney took a moment. "Well, I've never thought about it like that before. I guess your wife will have to be mad at you for running around with your shirt off." She peeked at him from the corner of her eye, waiting for his response.

"That was an accident." He sounded genuinely hurt by her remark.

She laughed until he finally laughed along with her. Whoever his future wife happened to be was one lucky girl.

The house was completely dark when they finally returned. "I guess your mother went to bed already?" Sydney said.

"*Ja*, she's very trusting."

The reply took Sydney by surprise. She hadn't meant anything by the question, it was simply an observation.

"How do you find your way in the dark?"

"You get used to it. I know every stump and rock and how to avoid them." David jumped down from the buggy.

"Well, I don't," Sydney said.

"Wait here. When I return I'll walk you in."

David unhitched the horse from the buggy. Sydney watched him disappear with the horse into the darkness. He returned several minutes later.

He held a hand out to her, his touch sending shivers down her spine. With a hop she was down on the ground beside him. He reached into the buggy and threaded the shopping bags with his arm.

"This way," he said, taking her arm. She held onto it tightly, savoring the closeness. He led her in the kitchen door and helped her find a chair at the table. "I'll light a lantern," he said. She could hear the bags being set down on the floor. He fumbled with the lantern on the kitchen table. A few seconds later the whole room glowed. A Bible lay in front of them.

"We've missed Bible reading."

"Will your mother be mad?"

"*Nay*, but it's a family tradition. As far back as I can remember our family has read the Bible at the kitchen table in the evening, often by lamplight." He removed his hat, laying it on the other side of the table and sat down in a chair beside Sydney's.

"I didn't know that."

"We miss days here and there, like when company comes calling." He opened the Bible and read a chapter of John out loud.

"Now what do you do?" Sydney asked.

"Now we have a silent prayer." He bowed his head and Sydney did, too. A moment later he closed the Bible and laid it back where he found it, by the lantern. The reflection of the light glittered in his eyes, then all at once he shifted about uncomfortably. "It's getting late," he said. "We should probably go to bed. I mean, I can walk you to your room."

Ordinarily that would sound really lame, but as dark as the house was it was kind of a necessity. He gathered the bags up on one arm and stood with the lantern. Sydney followed him through the living room and up the staircase to her room at the end of the hallway. Inside, David set down the bags on the bed.

"*Mam* will need this lantern in the morning, sometimes she gets up before daylight. But I can wait for you to put these things away before I go."

She went to the bed and shook out the contents of the bags. David set the lantern on the side table and sat down on the edge of the bed. She picked up the items one by one and began to fold them into a nice stack. David helped. She picked up the stack and put the clothes in the side table drawer, where the lantern sat. "Wait," she said to herself, digging out the long nightgown she'd bought out of the stack they'd just folded. She closed the drawer and held the garment with both hands. "Thank you," she said to him when she'd finished.

He turned to her, his intense brown eyes flickering in the lantern light. "Is there anything else you need?" His voice no more than a hoarse whisper.

She sensed a drawing power, some unknown force, pulling them together, like a magnet pulls at metal. Was it his eyes? Each time she held his gaze became more intense, more powerful. He took a step toward her. Did he feel it, too? She drew in a deep breath. He reached around her and picked up the lantern. "*Goot nacht*, Miss Sydney."

"Good night."

She watched the light from the lantern cast huge moving shadows on the wall as it followed David out the door, leaving her to change for bed in total darkness.

*I*t was finally starting to feel like fall. The air had a thinness to it, much easier to take in, and it left Sydney anticipating good things to come. David had a blue wire egg basket in his hand. He opened the chicken house door elaborately, showing Sydney it was no longer in a state of disrepair. Inside, only one hen sat solemnly on a nest made from wooden boards nailed together into a long tray, six, on one side of the small shed. The boxes were filled with wood shavings. In the corner of the room sat a silver metal trashcan with a matching lid. David opened the trashcan and pulled out an old pan with a broken handle he used to scoop up the chicken feed with. He threw the feed outside the coop on a bare place on the ground, chickens flocking to it from out of nowhere. He motioned for Sydney to step inside. It was cramped, but there was enough room for them both. "All the eggs are right under that hen." He slowly lifted his hand up to the chicken and before he could touch her she jumped up and flapped her brown wings as she sank to the floor of the hen house and ran out a tiny back door and into the yard. He gathered the eggs into the basket and handed it to Sydney. She counted them. Thirteen. They stepped back outside and David latched the door shut.

"We let them out the back door every morning and shut them up about dark."

"Do you ever eat them?"

"Not usually. These are laying hens, we keep them just for the eggs."

"Are they tame?"

"Some wouldn't care if you picked them up and petted them and some would flog you. A little advice though, never turn your back on a rooster."

Sydney committed that to memory. The rooster, whose name was Red, jumped on one of the hen's backs and dug at her neck with his sharp beak. Sydney cringed at the sight.

She brought the eggs into the house to Naomi who was making lunch, or "dinner" as they called it, for David to take to the woodshop. He came in and grabbed his sandwich. Naomi hugged him tight, like she did every morning before he left. He opened the kitchen door, "I'll take you to see your *vater* when I get home."

Sydney nodded and then he shut the door behind him. He was a grown man at only seventeen. Was it because all his siblings had already grown up and he thought he had to as well? Or was it because his father died and left him in charge? Sydney couldn't decide if it was sad or just noble, but either way she admired him heavily for it.

It was ironing day. Sydney watched as Naomi heated a heavy iron on the stove and ironed out the wrinkles in the dresses they'd washed the day before. After a while, Naomi pulled out one of David's long blue shirts and handed it to Sydney. "You try," she said.

Sydney shook out the shirt and laid it down flat on the ironing board Naomi had set up in the middle of the kitchen. She took hold of the iron carefully and set it down on the sky blue fabric.

"Now remember, you must keep it moving and don't stay in one place too long or it will burn."

Sydney rubbed the iron all around the back of the shirt. She was determined to do it right and make herself useful for once. She put the iron back on the stove while she tried to get the sleeve flat on the board.

"*Goota morga!*" Someone called and knocked at the kitchen door.

Naomi rushed over and opened it, a young woman in Amish dress holding a gallon jar of milk stood on the other side. Her feet were dirty and bare. "Brought your goat milk." Her eyes fell on Sydney. "Oh, your company is still here. How wonderful."

"Sydney," Naomi shut the door as the young woman walked toward the middle of the room, "this is Emma Wittmer. She lives just around the corner a ways."

"Nice to meet you," Sydney said, extending her hand.

Emma shook it and then exclaimed, "Wow, are you Samuel's daughter? You don't look anything like they said." She shook her head. "I'm sorry, I didn't mean it like that. You look lovely."

"It's okay," Sydney stood up straight in her jean skirt that fell to below her knees and long-sleeve cotton tee shirt in a soft pumpkin color. She felt it was very plain and somewhat warm even, but she knew it wasn't the kind of clothes people talked that much about and she was done making a scene. It was time to start fitting in, or at least fading into the background some.

"Well, I brought your milk." Emma handed the jar to Naomi.

"And I've got your eggs." Naomi picked up a wicker basket of eggs from the counter and handed them to Emma.

"Won't you stay? I'll make some tea," Naomi said.

"Oh, no, I've got to be getting back. Miriam will be starting the ironing soon and I promised to help. It was nice meeting you,

Sydney." Emma nodded to them both and then exited the kitchen door.

"I didn't even hear a buggy," Sydney commented.

"She walked. How's that ironing coming?"

"Good but I think I need to be on the other side to get this sleeve." Sydney stood the iron upright on the board and walked around to the other side, bumping it as she went. The board upset and the hot iron tumbled down with a heavy knock-thud on the hardwood floor.

"Oh, I'm sorry!" Sydney's hands went up to her mouth. The iron landed on its side and she knew it was too hot to touch, but the edge was burning the floor. "What do I do?"

Naomi grabbed a dish towel off the counter and ran to the hot iron. Using the towel like an oven mitt she knocked the iron over flat so she could grab the handle. She put the iron back safely on the stove. Sydney sank to the floor. It had burned a black mark the length of the iron into the hardwood. She touched the mark with her fingertips, feeling a slight roughness in the still hot wood. It crossed two boards and a third had a dent in it where the iron must have landed first, right on its tip. Couldn't she do anything right?

SYDNEY HELPED DRY the last of the supper dishes as she watched David carry an armload of wood inside the kitchen door and arrange it neatly in a rack beside the stove. It was evening, the time of day when all the chores were finished up and there was nothing left to do but visit and rest. Next he would visit the washroom to wash his face and arms. He'd return shortly, minus the woodshavings, smelling like lemons.

"Are you ready to use all the pieces tonight?" David asked Sydney as they sat down at the table with the chess set and a big bowl of popcorn.

"I can try," she said.

"You're learning very quickly for someone who thought she wasn't smart enough to play." David arranged the pieces on the board.

Sydney admired the way David rolled his "r's" when he spoke, his accent hardly noticeable otherwise, unless you were listening for it. David wasn't nearly as bashful now. Sydney wondered if he was getting used to her or if the clothes made all the difference, but now he was able to look at her with confidence and she didn't catch him staring at her quite as much. Still, she thought it strange that a teenaged boy would want a girl to cover up, while most spent all their time trying to sneak a peek at the opposite.

"You must be a better teacher than the ones I had in school."

David had something that most didn't. Was it maturity or just a knowing of what he wanted in life? Either way, Sydney craved to have some of it for herself—her life was a mess.

"You go first," he said.

She pushed a piece across the board. "Do you think Amish kids grow up faster than English ones?"

"I don't pretend to know anything about *Englishers*." He slid a pawn ahead two spaces.

"Aren't you curious about them? They're curious about you."

"Don't I know it. Everywhere we go people stop and stare, some point or ask us strange questions."

"What's the strangest thing anyone's ever asked you?" Sydney daintily picked up a single piece of popcorn and sampled it, still full from supper.

"Someone asked me once if I thought it would steal my soul to let them take my picture."

"What did you say?"

"I said, 'No, Miss, not with the new digital models. I just don't want my face all over the internet.'"

"You didn't!"

"I did. *Mam* pulled my ear when she heard it but I'd do it again."

"How old were you?"

"I believe it was just last year."

Sydney erupted in laughter. "Did you ever see that movie about the man whose mother followed him everywhere, even on his honeymoon? I can't remember what it was called."

"Amish don't watch TV." He smiled.

"Oh, right. How stupid." She shook her head and felt heat rise to her cheeks. "I know, I just totally forgot."

"It's okay. I'm starting to forget you're an *Englisher* sometimes." The dim light in the house was fading as the sun set. David lit the lantern on the table. "So is that what you did at night? Watched television?"

"Yeah, mostly."

"It must have been lonely with no brothers or sisters."

Sydney remembered the emptiness she'd felt being home alone and the times she'd worn out her welcome on friends' couches to keep from it. "Yeah, it was."

"Did your mother watch television with you?"

"No." Sydney shook her head.

"Don't tell me she knit baby booties all night in a rocking chair."

"No, she didn't do that, either. A lot of nights she didn't even come home."

"Did you know she wasn't coming?"

"No. She just didn't show up for the rest of the week."

David fidgeted with one of the chess pieces. "How old were you?"

"The first time I was eleven."

David frowned. "What about your *vater*, or the man you thought was your *vater*?"

"Roger Glynn? He was only around a few years when I was little. I barely remember him."

"I'm sorry, Sydney. I can't imagine a *fro* who could leave their *chind,* or a man who could ever walk away from you."

Sydney avoided his gaze. "Well, that's what's happened with every man who's ever been in my life."

"You mean you had a *beau?*"

"Something like that. I think my life was a little too complicated for him."

"And he left you, too?"

Sydney nodded.

"You deserve better."

"It is what it is. My life, I mean. I just take it one day at a time anymore."

"I couldn't imagine not having my family."

"Yeah, I can tell family is really important around here."

"What else is there besides the people you care about? I'm glad you're here with your family now. You have so many people who love you." David took a handful of popcorn from the bowl.

What she had was a bunch of people who shared her DNA, not people that cared. Sydney figured David would never understand that difference though. Not from his point of view.

*S*ydney rose early with hope in her heart. On ironing day she had ruined Naomi's kitchen floor. Neither Naomi nor David had said a word to her about it but she knew it was bad. Each time she crossed the kitchen to go outside the mark told her she wasn't good enough to be there. That she should just give up and leave and not embarrass herself any further. She tried to ignore it but each time it was still there, accusing her. Today would be different. She'd work twice as hard, and soon the mark would be something they'd all laugh at over supper.

She dressed quickly in another long-sleeve tee made exactly the same as the other only in light tan instead of light pumpkin. At least it was comfortable. She put on the other long jean skirt she'd purchased, the same as the first only a bit lighter shade of denim. She struggled to put on her tennis shoes which didn't match her new outfit at all. It was the only pair of shoes she had, but she was convinced they made her look dumpy. Sydney remembered Emma's visit the day before. She had walked the whole way there, barefooted. It seemed like none of the women in the community wore shoes. Sydney had ran barefoot a lot when she was a kid, sometimes going all the way down the block and back if the sun wasn't too hot on the pavement. She kicked the tennis shoes off and removed her socks, wiggling her toes around.

That was better.

Her feet felt cool on the grass outside. A sharp rock poked her heel and she winced. Sydney carried the egg basket to the hen house. She could feed them and gather eggs before breakfast. She unlatched the door and as soon as it opened a dozen or more chickens came flying out at her. She put up her hands to protect herself. That was when she remembered she was supposed to let them out the back door first. Leaving the door swinging open she ran around to the back door and fastened it up so it would stay open all day, leaving the chickens the option to come in or run around outside. Then she came back to the front and stepped inside. There sat the one rusty-brown chicken who still didn't want to leave the nest. She opened the metal trashcan lid and scooped out a pan of feed like David had showed her yesterday. Sydney spilled it out onto the bare ground. Now for the eggs. They were under the chicken. How could she get her to move?

"Aren't you hungry, little chicken?" Sydney whispered to her. "Don't you want to go outside and play with your friends?" She slowly lifted her hand up to the chicken, hoping it was enough to scare it away, but it didn't move. The hen just gave a tired blink, not intimidated the slightest bit. Sydney lunged forward at the hen, but still she didn't budge or even flinch. She would need to be bold. Sydney steadied herself, took a deep breath, and reached for the hen. Her intent was to push her off the nest quickly, but she hoped it would scare her enough she'd jump down before actually making any physical contact. The hen jumped up and flapped her wings a couple times, then lurched at her, pecking her hand. Sydney drew her hand back quickly, but the hen jumped from the nest, flapping her wings wide. The hen came right at her in a cloud of dust. Sydney screamed, dropping the egg basket, and running out of the hen house. She stumbled and fell forward into something—someone.

"What are you doing?" David held her up to keep her from falling.

"I was trying to take care of the chickens for you."

He looked down. "Barefooted? You're lucky I just cleaned the chicken house. And you could have stepped on a rusty wire or something." He let go of her arms as she stood up straight.

"None of the girls I've seen wear any shoes." She pushed her hair out of her eyes and stood in the shadow of his straw hat.

"And they haven't their whole lives. Did you often run barefooted in the city?" His voice was deep and authoritative.

"No."

He towered over her. Why did she feel like a child being scolded?

He took hold of her arms again sending a shiver through her. He leaned down to communicate clearly, "You don't have to try so hard."

She didn't? Her eyes met his lips and she wanted to kiss them. A week ago she would have, without question, without thinking of the consequences or what it would mean in regards to a relationship. But now she valued his opinion of her and his friendship.

His eyes darted around her face and then he released her gently. "Come, *Mam* will be getting breakfast."

He motioned for her to walk in front of him, his eyes avoiding hers.

IT WAS WEDNESDAY, sewing or mending day, as Naomi called it. After Sydney poked her finger with the needle learning to sew a simple hole in her sock, she was sent to the kitchen to study for her GED test. Her father had provided several books, but they were all outdated. The person he had talked to said she could start with those and move to computer practice whenever she felt she was ready. At that point she'd need to go into town to the library, and often. It was both liberating and confining at the same time. She sat at the table with books and notebooks scattered about, a pen in one hand, gently rubbing her thumb against her sore forefinger with the other. It was ironic that her father even wanted her to get a GED since their own people, including his own children, weren't permitted to go past the eighth grade. It was as if he was pointing out what she already knew deep down, that she could never stay. It wasn't that she'd decided that was what she wanted, she really didn't know. But not having the option nagged at her. It wasn't like she was some regular outsider. She was born of Amish parents, just raised differently. Very differently.

Her brothers and sisters, who shared nothing in common with her other than looks, were overjoyed when she'd visited. It was still odd to even think of having a sibling at all, let alone a house full of them. They'd wanted her to move in, but the looks she'd received from Martha, her father's wife, held anything but invitation. Sydney didn't blame her. She wouldn't want to live with her husband's *other* child either. It was too weird for anyone. She still couldn't help being jealous of her father's children. She never had a father. Roger Glynn, the man her mother said was her father, was only in her life a few short years, then he disappeared as quickly as her mother had.

JoHannah.

Why had she come back and why had she left again so suddenly? Sydney had watched as her grandfather had welcomed her mother back. No one was forcing her to be Amish, but she could have visited before now. The only person that Sydney could think of that stood in her way was Samuel Byler, her real father. He used her mother's name like it were a curse word. But he was nice enough to Sydney. He'd sent money to Naomi and

David to help take care of her and bought her all these school books she was supposed to be studying, but was he just trying to pay her off? When she turned eighteen he'd be free from his responsibilities for her, they all would. No one would need to feel guilty for turning her away then, especially with an education. She re-read the last paragraph in her book, determined to pass the test.

SYDNEY HEARD the buggy come to a stop outside the kitchen window late that afternoon. She was glad it was time for a break from her work and maybe some time to visit with David. Outside, she watched him unhitch the horse and walk it to toward the pasture. Sydney followed.

"How was work?" she asked when she finally caught up to him.

"*Guete*. How did you get along sewing with my *mueter* today?"

"How did you know we did sewing today?"

"It's Wednesday."

"So that's a weekly thing?" Sydney scrunched her face up.

David laughed. "Don't you like to sew?"

"I don't know how."

"How can that be? You're old enough to marry." They stopped at a gate while David unlatched it.

"Sixteen is old enough to marry?" Had she heard that right?

"For some."

Sydney wondered about the people who married at sixteen. She suspected the only reason someone would marry that young was if they were forced to. She opened her eyes wide at the thought.

"Don't worry, my *mueter* will teach you all the sewing you need to know." The gate swung wide as they walked through it.

"So you're telling me you can sew?"

"I can mend."

Sydney just stared at him.

"My *mueter* believed even the boys should learn how to do basic things, in case they find themselves bachelors at some point or have to care for their wives. So we can all cook and clean and mend a little." He took the rope off the horse and let the horse go. It took off in a trot.

"Do you have sisters?" Sydney asked.

"*Ja*, but most of them grew up first, so I was still young when they all married away." They walked back out of the gate and David pulled it to and latched it.

Sydney was quiet a moment.

"What's the matter?" he asked.

"Nothing, why?"

"Because you stopped asking questions. I figured that to mean there's something wrong with you."

"I'm sorry."

"*Nay*, I'm the one who should be sorry. I was only teasing, but now I think I was onto something. Is there something bothering you?"

Sydney turned away from him, folding her arms over the top of the gate. "I'm just…not good at anything."

"That's not true."

"Yes. Yes, it is." She nodded her head.

"Maybe you never learned to sew because your *mueter* wasn't around to teach you. How is that your fault?"

"It's not."

He folded his arms over the gate beside her. They stood a long while watching the horse graze about in the open field beyond the gate, the cool wind wrapping Sydney's long skirt around her legs.

"Come," David said finally. "If you can't sew I'll teach you to chop wood like a man."

Sydney raised her eyebrows.

"Or, I can chop wood and you can stack it up by the house, it's really up to you." He raised his shoulders and then dropped them with a soft smile.

Sydney followed him to the wood pile. David handed her a pair of gloves, his own hands thick with calluses. He pushed his hat down tighter upon his head then grabbed the chopping ax with both hands and swung it hard, into the air and back down, the wood instantly falling into two pieces on the ground on both sides of the stump.

"What do you do at the woodworking shop?" she asked, unable to look away.

"We make furniture." He set another large piece of wood onto the stump.

She watched him a few more moments before asking, "I know you make furniture, but what do *you* do?"

"Whatever needs done." He grunted, swinging the ax again and again, his broad shoulders heaving. Then he stopped, noticing her as if for the first time.

"Oh." Sydney took the pieces he'd cut and stacked them on the wall of wood against the house then returned to the chopping stump for more, the whole time wondering if he'd caught her staring.

"Well, you could come see the shop sometime if you wanted, but it might be a little boring."

"That'd be nice." She smiled as she took another armload of wood to the stack.

CHAPTER 6

*D*avid took Thursdays off work to take his mother to the market and catch up on things around the house. Naomi had said that "the market" was the name for the Amish farmer's market, a time set aside each week for the Amish to gather and buy and trade the goods they produced. It was open to the public and there were some non-Amish who had stands there as well, but it was mainly the Amish people who ran it. They would continue to meet each week until the end of September when most of the harvest was already in and most put their gardens to rest until early spring.

Sydney stayed close to Naomi's side as they walked down the beaten paths made between rows of long tables outside in the grassy lot just outside of town. David had disappeared as soon as they'd arrived, almost as soon as they got out of the buggy. They passed tables stacked with jams and jars of pickles; some sold eggs, others honey. At the end of the aisle Sydney spied her oldest sisters, Sarah and Katy, selling apples at their table.

"Come, stay with us," they begged her as soon as they noticed her standing there. Naomi encouraged her to stay while she shopped. It seemed to be a place to socialize as much as it was to buy food.

Sydney stepped behind the table to stand with them. "Have you sold much?"

Katy giggled. "We're too busy looking at boys," she whispered from behind the hand covering her mouth.

"Katy! Shush up," Sarah warned.

Sydney smiled. "And I thought you two were here to sell apples."

"Well, don't you think there are a lot of cute boys here to look at?" Katy asked.

Sydney scanned the open lot. Some of the tables had colorful tablecloths waving in the breeze. Being plain didn't apply as much when you were trying to sell something to the public, she guessed. There were many straw hats in the crowd but they seemed to look alike from where Sydney stood. The girls only had slight differences from this distance, some wore sunglasses and others didn't. Some had fair skin and others had fairer skin, she noted as they filed past. Occasionally one would carry herself differently, with poise, like she was someone important and knew it, like the girl walking up the next aisle from them. She was laughing and talking with David. He was laughing, too. It was a precious thing, to make David laugh. Sydney often went out of her way to try to do it at home. How had this girl made it look so easy?

When Naomi returned, Sydney was relieved to be on their way. Meeting and greeting every person that stopped at the apple stand was exhausting.

"It was nice visiting with you both," Sydney said.

"We'll have to do it again," Sarah said and Katy nodded.

"Well, how about tonight?" Naomi offered. "You can see if your *vater* will let you stay overnight with us. That way you two can get better acquainted with Sydney."

The girls' faces lit up brightly. *An Amish slumber party?* Sydney just smiled politely.

~

ABOUT THE SAME time that Sydney and David usually started their nightly chess game, her sisters arrived. Samuel stayed in the buggy as the girls climbed out with one bag between them. They ran up to the back porch to greet Naomi.

"I know you'll have a *guete* time," Samuel said confidently. "I'll pick them up tomorrow after chores. I have to run into town anyway."

"See you tomorrow then," Sydney said and her father tipped his hat to her.

Inside, David went straight into his room and shut the door. Sydney didn't blame him. The oldest girl, Sarah, had already expressed to Sydney how much she liked David. The girls would sleep upstairs with Sydney. She led them up to her room. "So," Sydney said once her bedroom door was shut. "What would you ladies like to do now? We have a whole closet full of board games. David's been teaching me how to play chess."

They looked at each other and erupted into giggles. Immediately *kapps* started coming off, hair came down, and soon their aprons lay in heaps upon the floor.

"Don't those have straight pins in them?" Sydney asked. She picked them up and folded them carefully, setting them on her side table.

"Do you have any makeup?" Katy whispered loudly.

"I…"

"We saw you wearin' makeup the first day we met you." Sarah's brown eyes were pleading.

"What about your father—our father? Won't he kill all three of us?"

"How would he know if you don't tell him?" Katy asked.

135

Sydney could see the sun setting. Soon it would be dark and no one would be able to see them anyway. "All right," she said hesitantly.

The girls squealed. Sydney got out her purse and sat with it on the bed. Sarah took it from her and started rummaging through it. Katy pulled it from the other direction and they finally settled on just dumping it out onto the bed.

"I found lipstick," Sarah said, holding it up.

"And I found a set of keys," Katy said. "Do you drive a car?"

"I can. Here's my license." Sydney pulled the card from her wallet.

Katy held it up. "Wow."

"Sydney, can you do up my hair?"

"Mine too," Katy said.

"How?"

"Just something pretty. Can you make a french braid?"

"I guess I could try."

Sarah turned her back to Sydney, giving her full reign of her hair. It was long and beautiful, the same dark color as Sydney's. She didn't know where to start with it, though. It hung past where she sat, cascading onto the bed.

"Do you two do this kind of thing often?" Sydney asked.

They both giggled.

"I thought you had to wear your *kapps* all the time."

"Well, we do wear them all the time, except in our bedroom at night. And when *Mam* and *Dat* leave us home alone."

Sydney stopped. "They leave you home alone? For how long?"

"Just a few hours while they go into town."

Sydney let out the breath she didn't know she had been holding. She tried to separate the Rapunzel-like hair into sections for braiding. "What else do you two do while your parents are away?"

They both giggled again. "Katy sews up her underwear."

Katy punched Sarah in the arm and Sarah pushed her back.

"Well, you do."

"You mean you make your own?" Sydney asked.

"*Nay, Mam* makes them, but they're so bunchy up top," Katy said.

"So she takes 'em in at the waist to make her look skinnier," Sarah offered.

"Well," Katy said. "At least I wear underwear!"

"Don't tell her that!" Sarah wailed.

"Hey, can I try on your clothes?" Katy asked.

Sydney wondered if they'd each had an energy drink on the buggy ride over. "I don't think they'd fit you." Katy was thirteen and tiny.

"They would probably fit me." Sarah, fourteen and a half, might fit into her clothes.

"Only if you're wearing underwear," Sydney said.

Sarah frowned.

Sydney couldn't believe she was having this conversation.

Sarah's eyes flew open with a gasp. She turned quickly, causing Sydney to drop the sections of hair she'd just separated. Sarah grabbed Sydney's wrist and held onto it tight. "Do you have any cigarettes?"

"Nooo," Sydney said slowly. This was going to be a long night.

CHAPTER 7

avid could scarcely be found until the Byler sisters were gone the next day. Late into the night Sydney had sneaked them both downstairs to scrub their makeup-caked faces with lemon soap in the washroom. When morning came they were dressed prim and proper before Sydney was even fully awake. Well, all but Sarah, who Sydney knew wasn't wearing any underwear, a fact she could have lived a long happy life without ever knowing. Their father had picked them up and Sydney was exhausted.

"Did you have a *guete* time?" David asked, his eyes twinkling. He must have known what a handful they were.

"Uh, it was very interesting," Sydney said as they sat at the kitchen table, afraid to say more.

"Well, are you ready to go?"

"Go where?"

"It's Saturday, town day. *Mam* will want to do some shopping and I'm taking you both out to eat for dinner, my treat."

"No dishes?" Sydney asked.

"No dishes."

In town, Sydney marveled at the people who would openly stare at them, some pointing, as they drove by in the open buggy. Sydney still felt self conscious wearing her new modest clothing, but that was nothing like wearing a *kapp* and apron everywhere you went. She tried to picture herself in a *kapp* and surprisingly the image came to her. She'd use the edge to hide herself when she wanted some distance from people. But with David beside her what did she have to fear?

It was a silly thought. She could never be Amish, even though her parents had been. It made her wonder though, how long she'd be allowed to stay in Amish country. David had told her that when the youth reached a certain age they would join church or leave the community. They could still visit but they wouldn't stay because they weren't allowed to marry if they weren't a member of the church. She knew her presence as an *Englisher* had only been tolerated as long as it had because of simple charity, and because of Samuel. Hot-headed or not, her father was a respected member of the community. Still, Sydney knew it couldn't last forever. She just hoped she was smart enough to make it on her own before that time came.

The buggy pulled into a small restaurant with a hitching post outside for the Amish to tie their horses. Sydney wondered how many other local businesses were as accommodating. Inside was an oriental buffet, southern Missouri style. The Springfield area was famous for their cashew chicken and fried rice, but up north, where Sydney was from, the same dish looked quite different. "So this is the *real* cashew chicken?" she asked David as they each took a clean plate from the end of the buffet. "I've heard about it."

"You mean to tell me you've never had cashew chicken?" David asked.

Sydney shook her head.

"And I thought our people were shut off from the world," he

muttered. "Here, this is how it's done." He put the small, crispy fried chicken pieces in a small pile on one side of the plate and fried rice on the other side. Then he put gravy over the chicken pieces and topped it with green onions and cashews. "Trade me." He gave the plate to Sydney and she gave him her clean plate. She carried it to an empty booth and sat, waiting for David and Naomi to join her. When they all sat they paused for a silent prayer over their food. David shuffled his feet to indicate the prayer time was finished, then the waitress came over and set down their drinks in front of them.

She didn't stare awkwardly, so Sydney figured a lot of community members ate there from time to time.

Sydney watched Naomi stuff herself with lo mein noodles and egg rolls. She loved Naomi's cooking but it was nice to have something different once in a while. The friendly conversation was missing though; David and Naomi were very reserved in public, not talking unless they really needed to. It was unusual to eat with them in so much silence, but the noises all around compensated. The soft murmur of other diners, the clanking of dishes when the waitress cleaned a table, and the ding of the door as someone came in or left. All sounds, so common to Sydney before, yet now, so very far removed from her usual.

When they returned home, after the goods from town had been put away, and before Sydney could even sit down, Naomi got out the mixing bowls and spoons, getting ready to bake. It was a busy afternoon that ended in a few dozen cookies, a few pies, and one large two-layer cake. Sydney was glad when evening came and Bible reading was over and she could rest at the table with David and a friendly game of chess by lantern light.

"You look beat," he said as soon as Naomi went on to bed.

"Well, this pie didn't bake itself." Sydney let out a tired laugh and cut into the pie, placing a piece on each of the two dessert plates in front of her at the counter. "What have you done all afternoon?"

"The barn roof needed patched."

"Well, I bet you're tired, too." Sydney handed him a plate of pie and sat down by David at the corner of the kitchen table. She picked up her fork and took a big bite. Pecan, her favorite. So much better than the store bought kind.

"Are you too tired to play?" she asked. "We don't have to if you don't want to," she said.

"*Nay*, I enjoy our games."

She caught a glimpse of his eyes before he took a bite of pie. Had he meant something more by that? Sydney shifted in her chair. She set down her fork and opened the chess box. She removed the board, unfolding it onto the table between them. She took another bite of her pie before she removed the pieces. She was just now able to set up a chess board all by herself, having memorized where each piece belonged at the beginning of the game.

"Now that you know the basics, it's time to move onto strategy," he said.

"Okay, how do I do that?"

"You're the white side, so try moving the pawn in front of your king ahead two spaces."

Sydney moved the piece where David said.

He quickly moved one of his pieces and it was her turn again.

"Now move your knight."

Sydney reached for her knight.

"*Nay*, not that one."

She touched the other one. "Which way does it go?"

He put his hand on hers, guiding the move. Her pulse sped and suddenly their eyes met. He cleared his throat. "I think you can take it from there." Letting go of her hand he shifted in his chair, the warmth of his touch lingering.

CHAPTER 8

*S*unday finally rolled around and Sydney was amazed
she'd made it so long without electricity. She hadn't
been bored, like she thought she'd be. There was always so much
work to do, even a bath in Amish country could be considered
work because of the effort it took.

"I could stay here," David said as Sydney walked into the
kitchen for breakfast.

"*Nay*," Naomi said, "how would that look? I'll stay, you go."

"Go where?" Sydney asked as she sat down.

"Today is a church day," Naomi said hesitantly.

"Could I come?" Sydney took a sip of milk.

David's eyes went from Sydney to his mother and finally back
to Sydney again. "We'd need to talk to Bishop Amos about it
first."

"Oh," Sydney looked down at the eggs in her plate. "Well,
don't miss out on my account. I'm pretty tired from yesterday."
She tried to hold her voice steady, not wanting them to know
about the sudden disappointment that had washed over her.

"I'm sorry, Sydney," Naomi said. "We should have thought it
out beforehand."

"No, really, it's okay. You both go. I'll be fine," her voice was high-pitched. Sydney knew she'd let it out that she was disappointed and now she regretted it. It wasn't their fault, she knew how closed off the community was to anyone they viewed as an outsider, but now they knew she wanted to go and that she was hurt. "I can't promise there will be any pie left when you get back, though." She took a big bite of her eggs and smiled as she chewed, trying to lighten the mood. They'd baked so much food yesterday, pies and cookies, and a large two-layer carrot cake. All that food would be tempting to stay out of if she were there alone, but she'd only said it for their benefit.

"I'll take the carrot cake to the church dinner and some of the cookies. I'll leave you the pies since you fancy them, and I'll bring you a plate when we return."

"How long does church last?"

"Oh, it'll be late in the afternoon before I get back. David will likely bring me on home and then go back for the singing."

"Singing?"

"It's more of a youth social than anything," she said.

"Ah." Sydney pretended it wasn't that interesting. "Well, I think I'll rest a while and maybe do a little studying. Is there anything you need me to do while you're gone?"

"It's the Lord's day. There will be no work done other than what's necessary," Naomi said.

It was nice to have a day where they could rest. Sydney was beat. She wouldn't even think of doing any studying except she couldn't figure anything else to do while David and Naomi would be gone so long.

After breakfast dishes were done, Sydney set out her books on the table. It was awkward, knowing David and Naomi would soon be leaving without her, but she kept reading her study book, pretending not to notice when they carried the food out to the buggy. They came back in the house to say goodbye.

"We'll be back before you know it," Naomi said and gave

Sydney a side hug where she sat in the kitchen chair. She wore her good "going out" *kapp* and the dress she wore looked a little brighter than the one she wore for yesterday's baking. Sydney caught the smell of lemons as Naomi let go. When she went through the door, the screen creaked and clanked as it shut.

David pulled out the chair beside her and straddled it, sitting towards its back, peering over with his black felt hat in hand, to gaze intently at Sydney. His shirt was crisp and his hair combed neatly. "I really am sorry," his voice smooth with compassion.

"What? No. It's not a big deal." Sydney set her book down.

"I'll talk to the bishop myself."

"It really is okay, David."

"I know, but I'll make it up to you anyway. I'll take you to see your *vater* tomorrow evening, and get you out of the house."

"I don't really want to," Sydney said quietly.

"Oh. Well. I guess we'll just have to think of something else, then."

Sydney liked the idea of David making it up to her. Once again she felt his drawing power. He was like a magnet, always pulling at her when she got within his reach. He cleared his throat, stood and pushed the chair back in. He put his hat on his head, tipping it downward in one motion in a final nod to Sydney, then with another creak-clank of the screen door he was gone.

"Popcorn for supper?" Sydney didn't know what had gotten into Naomi when the idea of it came about.

"Of course," Naomi said as she measured out the popcorn kernels that sat in a glass jar on the kitchen counter. "We always have a snacky supper on church nights. I guess since we eat so well at church—that and it's less work to cook."

Popcorn for supper was fine with Sydney, but she still couldn't believe a woman like Naomi, who worked constantly and hardly ever sat, wouldn't make a big meal for once. It was a surprising side of Naomi she rather enjoyed seeing.

"Well, I guess since you're our guest we should at least have something to go with it. How about an apple bowl?"

"Sounds interesting. Can I help?"

"Of course." Naomi shook the popcorn pan vigorously on the stove. "Get out two bowls and dice an apple into each."

Sydney washed the bright colored apples they'd purchased from her sisters' stand at the market. Then she sectioned them off and cut away the core, making it easy to dice them.

"Now what?"

"Now you add a few raisins from the canister over there, a spoon of apple butter, and a spoon of peanut butter and you're done."

Sydney did as she said and as the popping on the stove slowed to a stop she had two beautiful dessert bowls in her hand. Naomi poured the popcorn into a brown paper bag that she carefully cut away the top of, making the bag easier to reach into and carried it into the living room.

"When will David be home?" Sydney asked, stirring her apple bowl with a fork as she sat down on the wooden bench.

"Sometime after I'm asleep, I reckon. That's the way it's supposed to be anyway."

"What do you mean?"

"Well, I told you singings were mainly for the youth to socialize. It's not for us parents to know who they're socializing with or how late they stay out. Oh, some would really like to know, but it's up to the youth if they want to share or not."

"So you don't know if David is dating anyone or not?"

"Courting," she corrected. "No. We're close, but some things a boy has to keep to himself."

"I saw him with a girl at the market."

Naomi leaned in closer. "What did she look like?"

"I don't know. Tall and pretty?"

"Hmm, well. I'll sure hate to see him go. He's my very last baby. Fine boy, that one is. Oh, all of my *chinda* were wonderful, but David, he's different. He became a man the day his *vater* died. He's hard-working *and* responsible. There aren't many like him his age. But now I have you around to keep me company and I have to say I've missed having another *fro* in the house." Naomi got up and lit two lanterns; the sun was setting and the darkness of night was well on its way.

Sydney thought of David as she ate her snacky supper. Was he out on a date at this very moment? It bothered Sydney much more than she wanted it to. She was getting too close, not at all what she was used to doing. She did a good job until now of keeping everyone at a distance, not letting them in, not letting them see what was inside her. But David and Naomi had begun to let her see what was inside of them. Could it be that this was the time she could finally let her guard down? She dared to hope.

Naomi went to bed not long after, and Sydney knew she would stay in bed and not pry when David returned. But there was no rule that Sydney couldn't.

IT WAS midnight before David finally returned. Sydney sat in the lantern light of the living room, waiting as he came through the kitchen door. He walked in, added a few sticks of wood to the fire in the woodstove and peered into the living room at Sydney.

"Everything all right?" he asked quietly, his voice breaking the long silence.

"Yes, everything all right with you?" Sydney pulled softly at the ends of her hair.

"*Ja.*" He took off his hat and walked it over to the stairs, hanging it on a hook on the wall.

"Well, *goot nacht*," he said and then started off through the living room toward the back hall where his room was.

"Night," Sydney said, still sitting on the living room bench.

She heard him take another step, then he turned around. "You're up awful late. Couldn't you sleep?"

"No." Sydney had forgotten to come up with an excuse for waiting for him but that would do nice enough.

"Was it the night terrors?"

"No."

David came back and sat down beside Sydney. He pulled his arms through his suspenders, letting the straps hang at his waist, then he sunk down into the long bench.

"Tired?" she asked, suddenly more awake now that he was beside her.

David only grunted. He ran his hands back and forth through his hair, loosening it all the way to the roots. Then he ran his fingers through it like a comb once more to settle it back down. He was wearing cologne. Sydney had never known him to wear it before, a scent somewhere between the earth and pine needles. He sat close enough to her that she felt the warmth of his body next to hers, a bold move, or perhaps he was beginning to look at her like a sister. He could have sat anywhere in the room. What did it mean? She refused to be the next to speak. He'd sat down next to *her*, after all. Eventually he would say something and Sydney promised herself she'd wait for it, no matter how long it took. He stretched his arms out wide and rested them over the back of the pillow-lined bench, one of them landing behind her head. He let out a tired breath and cocked his head toward her.

Silence.

She met his gaze, smiled lightly, then looked away. Sydney squirmed in the seat, repositioning herself a bit. Another quick glance told her he hadn't looked away. She held onto his eyes with her own, waiting, so patiently waiting. She dropped her head down and drew in a massive breath, letting the air out of her lungs slowly. She lifted her head up toward him, boldly now, determined not to look away again until he first spoke.

David shifted his body and drew closer. Her heart sped, closer still, until he was so close his mouth was touching hers, ever so softly at first, then more and more. It was a relief to her system to know he had felt the pull drawing them together, too. She reached an arm around him, her hand landing on the back of his neck, the warmth of his skin sending exciting shivers within her. They were calmed by his hand, caressing her back. She wondered where someone so quiet, so reserved, stored such strong feelings. With her eyes still closed she felt the fingertips of his other hand sweep across her cheek. They kept going until they met her hair. He ended the kiss gently and drew back. She placed a hand upon his chest, feeling it move up and down, the soft panting of his breath the only sound. He watched as his own fingers, still in her hair, combed it slowly as they traveled the length. The strand finally fell through them and back down onto her shoulder, his attention still on it alone. Finally he looked into her eyes again, only now they held regret. Sydney reached and felt for the strand of hair in question, wondering what she had done wrong.

David stood, rubbed his hands over his face and started again for his room.

"Wait," Sydney said.

He stopped but didn't turn around.

What could she say to make him come back, to explain himself? How could she ever sleep again wondering what just went on inside him? "What's wrong...with my hair?" She winced at the lameness of her own question.

He shook his head, his back still facing her. "It wasn't mine to touch." Then he disappeared into the darkness.

Sydney knew who he believed it belonged to, her future husband. It was silly though, wasn't it? To worry about someone you may not even know yet. She wondered if he'd kissed the pretty market girl and worried over her hair. Then it came to Sydney, Amish girls always wore a *kapp*.

CHAPTER 9

*S*ydney tried hard to see her dark hair in the tiny mirror she kept in her purse. She didn't know what to do with it, but since the Missouri weather changed so very often from warm to cold and back to warm again she decided to put it up if she could, that because of the changing temperature maybe no one would notice the sudden change in her. She wished she knew how to make it into a lovely braided bun, though she doubted her Amish friends would like that either, as that might be too fancy. She pulled it into a tight ponytail and then looped it around one more time, letting the ends stay in the top under the band.

There.

Now her hair was out of the way at least. It would have to do.

She went downstairs for breakfast and Naomi and David were already seated at the table. "I was just about to call for you," Naomi said.

Sydney skillfully avoided David's gaze as she sat. "So, what do we do today?" she asked.

David opened his mouth but his mother spoke first. "Monday is always wash day. And after that you have some studying to do. How's it coming, getting ready for that test?"

"Oh, good. The math section I think will be the hardest."

David opened his mouth again. "I think you should go live with your *vater*."

"David?" his mother chided.

"It's okay, Naomi," Sydney said.

Naomi blinked with bafflement. "What's this all about, David?"

"It's my fault," Sydney began. "Last night, after David came in, we talked a while in the living room and I kissed him goodnight. I shouldn't have done it and it won't happen again. I'm sorry, Naomi." It was only a half-truth, but surely when he saw that she knew of his regret he'd go along with it and he could forget the whole thing if that's what he really wanted. Sydney's eyes begged David to let her stay. She waited for his response.

"I'll ride over and get Samuel and bring him back to discuss this." His voice was even and emotionless.

His words stabbed Sydney's heart. How could he go through with this? What had she done wrong? All this trouble over hair? She'd put it back, didn't he see she was trying?

David stood.

"Now?" Naomi took hold of David's arm but he wouldn't budge. "You haven't even had your breakfast yet."

"I'll be back soon." He stepped into the living room and came back through with his hat on this time and out the kitchen door he went, leaving Naomi speechless and Sydney near to tears.

It wasn't long before David returned with Samuel.

"Now, what's this all about?" Samuel stepped inside the kitchen but didn't attempt to sit down.

"I think it's time for Sydney to move in with you," David said.

"David, please, don't do this." Sydney stood and grabbed his arm, "Please."

Samuel's head tilted sharply when he saw Sydney's hands on David's arm.

"What's this? Are you two gettin' familiar?" His eyes narrowed.

David bristled as she released him.

"What's that mean?" Sydney asked, apprehension in her voice. She studied them both.

Samuel stepped forward and put his finger up sharply to David's face. "Have you defiled her? Speak!" His voice echoed off the hardwood floor.

David wasn't intimidated by Samuel but Sydney wondered if maybe he should be.

"You mean like you defiled her *mueter*?" His voice was strong and firm. "*Nay*, I did not." He pushed Samuel's accusing finger down and away from his face.

"Tell him, Sydney," Naomi said quietly, not making eye contact with the men.

Sydney didn't know what to say. "I..."

"*I* kissed Sydney," David said.

"*You* did?" Naomi asked.

"*I* did," David said clearly, "and I will not dishonor her again."

"Very well," Samuel said. "She can share a room with Sarah and Katy. I'll go home and arrange things with Martha and we'll move her tomorrow, first thing after morning chores. You think you can keep your hands off her till then?" he growled.

David's eyes narrowed, his jaw tight.

"What about me?" Sydney cried. "Am I like a stray dog you just pass around?" She ran out of the kitchen and up to her room, slamming the door behind her.

SYDNEY WAITED for darkness to fall from her bedroom window. It wouldn't be long now. She didn't know where she would go, but it would need to be far from here. She would miss Naomi, maybe the most. She'd been more of a mother to her in the short time she stayed with the Schwartz family than her own mother had ever been. And David. He, she couldn't understand. He had been the one to kiss her and now he was throwing her out into the street. He'd tried to talk to her about it, but all he could say was that she needed to spend time with her "*vater*" while she could, and that living with her was just too tempting. She packed her things into her bag carefully. They barely fit with the new clothes her father had given her money for.

She remembered the buggy ride with David in the dark to buy them. That must have been what it felt like when the young couples rode home together after singings. Sydney didn't realize until just then she'd been hoping for the day she would hitch a ride home in some handsome young man's buggy. Had she really thought she could just walk right in and become Amish like they were? She'd at least hoped she could stay with Naomi a while, she'd learned so much from her already. At supper, Naomi had tried to tell her that she'd love living in her father's house with all her siblings. Sydney's breathing became labored just thinking about it.

She took a little trip to the kitchen and back with her flashlight and closed her bedroom door behind her. Everyone was in bed, it wouldn't be long now. She'd wait an hour, maybe two just to be sure, then she'd leave the house and walk the three and a half miles into town. She'd hitch a ride and be long gone before breakfast. She sat on the edge of her bed and waited. She'd already cleaned the bedroom, even made the bed. It looked just like the day she'd first entered it. The emptiness of it reminded her of her mother's room when she found it the day after her mother left her. Sydney would take the flashlight, she hated to, as it really wasn't hers. David had bought fresh batteries for it on their trip into town and gave them to her to use.

They would all be happier tomorrow. Sure they'd be sad a day, maybe two, that they couldn't help the poor girl left on their doorstep, but they'd soon be their happy selves again and could go on with their lives without further disruption. Only a few more minutes and she could go. Sydney took a moment to scratch out a note of thanks to the Schwartz family for their kindness and hospitality, signed it, and folded it neatly to be found in the morning on her nightstand. There was nothing left to do now but go.

She hoisted her heavy bag over her shoulder and peeked out the bedroom door. She tiptoed down the stairs, avoiding all the creaky places she already knew too well. She felt the warmth radiating from the woodstove as she passed it in the kitchen. Quietly, she opened the heavy door that led to the outside. Knowing the screen could give her trouble, and that David's room was close by, she opened it ever so slowly and just enough for her to slip through. She carefully closed the doors behind her and, still on tiptoe, pulled the flashlight from the pocket on her bag. There was just enough moonlight to get to the beginning of the driveway before the shadows were so heavy she couldn't see a thing. She switched the light on and began walking, at a normal pace.

Behind her, the familiar sound she had hoped not to hear, the creak-clang of the screen being let go by someone exiting the house.

"Sydney," David called out.

"Let me go, David."

"I will not." He started toward her.

She quickly memorized the path lit in front of her then turned off the flashlight she carried, the total absence of light a jolt to her, but she kept walking. There was nothing for her to run into, she told herself...yet. She walked faster. She could hear his footsteps behind her, coming closer. His arms around her with the heavy bag on her shoulder threw her off balance and they both fell to the ground. She wrestled with him, but it was no use with the bag she carried and his massive size. He instantly had her pinned down to the ground, his body on top of hers. She felt the flaps of his open shirt on her face as he held her wrists tightly with his hands. "Where would you go, Sydney? To your *mueter*? Do you even know where she is?" His voice was low but commanding.

"Get off me!"

He grunted in frustration but rolled them both to the side, not letting loose of her. She raised her leg to kick him away and he threw his legs up and clamped them around hers, stopping all movement. Sydney was breathing hard now and his grip hurt.

"So you're just going to run away, like your *mueter* did? You, of all people, should know how much that hurts others." His face was hidden in darkness, his words she didn't want to hear, they cut her deep. She hadn't really thought it would matter that much to him whether or not she stayed.

"You didn't want me!" she cried.

"That's not true," he raised his voice.

She was in tears now. She was angry at them for coming, but they were there anyway so she let them go. "Then why won't you let me stay?" her voice a shivering whimper.

He let go of his hold on her. "It's too cold out here on the ground. Let's get you back inside."

"No. Answer me!"

He huffed and sat up. An awkward silence passed. Finally, David spoke. "We can't stay in this house together and stay blameless, it doesn't work and you know it. Can't you feel it, each time our paths cross? Is that what you want? A smart girl like you, to end up disgraced just like your *mueter*, forced to marry someone you hardly even know? I want a *fro* who loves me, not one that was stuck with me."

Sydney's mind went in all different directions. "What do you know about my mother?"

"Come in the house. Promise me you'll not leave without telling me, and I'll tell you everything I know about her."

Sydney thought about it a moment.

"Do I have your oath?" his voice rose again.

"Yes," she said finally.

David stood and pulled her to her feet. He ushered her inside the kitchen and told her to sit down while he lit the lantern on the table. Sydney set her things down by the table leg and sat in the chair. The soft light reflected off the walls and she could see David's bare feet as he put more wood in the stove. His shirt, dirty in the back, still hung open. He closed the stove door with a squeak and began snapping his shirt from the top down. When he finished he sat down at the table with Sydney.

"What do you know about my mother?" she asked.

"First, I need to know why you despise your *vater* so."

"I don't despise him. I just don't know how to talk to him."

"That's why you should live in his house. You're his daughter, you must learn to talk to him. Do you know what I'd give to be able to talk to my *vater*, even once more?" David's father had died not too long ago. Sydney had forgotten.

"You don't understand. I don't *know* them. And all those people at once, I don't know if I could handle it."

He thought a second. "You mean people make you nervous?"

Sydney bit at her fingernail and nodded at the same time.

"I'd forgotten that was a problem for you." He rubbed both his temples with one hand.

"Yes, and now I have to go live there and share a room with two other people. And I really don't think Martha likes me being around."

"I hadn't thought about that either," David said. "I'm sorry."

Sydney bit her fingernail again. "And I'm trying to get my GED. How am I supposed to ever study in a house like that? And what about Naomi?"

"What about her?"

"Well, believe it or not, David, she would miss my help around here, she said so herself."

"All right. You've convinced me. I'll figure this all out."

"You mean you'll let me stay?" Sydney dropped her hand to the table.

"Well, we'll have to figure it out with Samuel somehow. But I'll think of something. Just don't worry yourself about it."

"What about my mother?"

"I'll tell you everything I've heard about your *mueter*, but I don't know how much of it is true. Your *mueter* and her best friend were both after Samuel, your *vater*. It seems that JoHannah got to him first and her friend went missing. She was found face down in Swan Creek three days later. Your *mueter* ran off and no one saw or heard from her until you showed up on our doorstep."

Sydney hadn't expected that, the weight of it falling on her like a ton of bricks. They sat in silence several moments. "Thank you," she whispered.

He nodded. "Now, we better get to bed before we wake *Mam*." David stood and pushed his chair back under the table.

Sydney picked up her things from the floor and started for her room.

"Sydney," David said. "My *mueter* isn't the only one who would have missed you."

Sydney gave a tight smile and went on to bed, wondering if David would be able to fix the mess she was in.

SYDNEY LAY AWAKE, thinking about her mother's friend. Who was she and what happened to her? It scared her to think her mother might have had something to do with her death. What a horrible thing to happen. She wondered what tomorrow would bring and if she would indeed have to move into her father's house. David wasn't afraid of him but Sydney was. He wasn't the kind of man you crossed and got away with it. And what would happen with David? Would he never kiss her again? This, and many more things, went through her head as she slowly slipped away.

The darkness choked her. The sound of rushing water—

Sydney struggled to breathe.

Her eyes flew open with a scream. The sensation that someone was holding their hands around her throat was so real. She screamed again and as soon as she was free from the covers, she leapt from the bed and hit the wall with a thud. Sydney shook her head and screamed once more, her whole body shaking uncontrollably. She felt around on the floor, not knowing which way was which. She heard the door open, "Sydney, it's me, it's David."

Silence.

"Sydney?"

"I'm over here, on the floor."

She heard David get down on the floor beside her, his hand hitting her leg when he finally reached her.

"Where's the flashlight and I'll get it for you."

"It's still in my backpack. I'm not sure now where I set it."

"Are you okay?"

"I am now." Her breathing was still heavy.

"Are you sure?"

"Yes, thank you." Sydney's tiny voice cracked and squeaked.

"Don't cry. It's going to be okay," he whispered.

"I know. I'm just so…nervous."

"I shouldn't be here in your room like this. Can you find your way back to bed?"

The sound of muffled cries.

She could feel him put his arms around her then he scooped her up and carried her to the bed. For a moment she felt safe. A calmness came over her as he set her down gently.

"How can you see in here in the dark?" her voice a broken whisper.

"I can't. Are you going to be okay? I can get *Mam* to come in if you want."

"No, I'm okay. You can go."

She could sense his presence leaving her then the click of the door latch shutting. Outside her door she heard soft whispers in Swiss German.

~

MORNING CAME. Sydney was exhausted but her eyes opened at the same time as always, no need for an alarm clock anymore. She dressed quickly, worrying all the more about her fate. She put her hair up and tore up the note she'd left the Schwartzs the night before.

When she opened her bedroom door, David's slumped-over body fell at her feet. She took a step back to keep him from seeing up her skirt. What was he doing on the floor beside her bedroom door? He shook his head and massaged his eyes with his fingertips. Sydney sat down on her floor beside him. "I promised I wouldn't leave again but you didn't believe me."

"I believed you. I just wasn't sure you wouldn't fall down the stairs to your death in one of your screaming fits. You don't belong on the second floor. I should have insisted you moved the first time it happened."

"Well, that won't matter after today, now will it?"

David stopped. "Do you smell that?" he asked.

"What?"

"I think it's bacon. Let's go eat some."

Sydney shook her head and walked carefully around him to the other side and reached down for his arm. He took hold and she pulled as he rose, finally up to standing position. His eyes were red, his shirt dirty, and his hair shaggy.

"You might want to clean up a bit before my father gets here."

"I'm not scared of your *vater*," he grumbled, brushing off his backside.

They ate breakfast in silence. Sydney knew it was just a matter of time before her father would be there to take her back with him.

David ate quickly. "Are you done with that?" he asked her, eyeing a piece of her bacon.

Sydney wasn't hungry. How could she eat at a time like this? She handed him her whole plate.

"Sydney, you really must eat, dear." Naomi frowned.

"You're finished?" David asked.

Sydney nodded a yes.

"Then let's go." David shoved one last piece of bacon in his mouth, tucked in his shirt, raised his suspenders and took off out of the kitchen. A minute later he was back with his hat and boots on and headed for the kitchen door.

"Where are we going?" Sydney asked.

"To the doctor."

"The doctor? Are you sick?"

Naomi put her hand on Sydney's. "Do exactly as he says. Now hurry. There isn't much time. Your *vater* will be here in a few hours."

Sydney stood, still not sure how the doctor was supposed to help.

THE OFFICE WAS unlike any doctor's office Sydney had ever been to. "Are you sure he's a real doctor?" Sydney whispered.

"*Ja*. There's only one person Samuel won't argue with. A doctor." David sat with his hat in his lap, waiting for Sydney's name to be called.

"How's that going to help?"

A door opened from the back of the room and a woman appeared with a clipboard. She was wearing what looked like shoes with individual toe sections built in them. "Sydney Glynn?" she called.

David and Sydney stood.

They were left alone in the examining room for only a few minutes when the "doctor" came in.

"Sydney, right?"

"Yes."

"I hear you have been having trouble with sleep terrors, is that correct?"

"Yes, I've had them off and on for a few years."

"Well, I'm afraid there's not really a cure for that. Have you been under a lot of stress lately?"

"Well, yes." When wasn't she stressed?

"We don't really know why some people have them, but it seems stress makes them worse. Have you tried lavender in your bathwater?"

"Yes," David said. "We tried that."

Sydney looked at him. How did he know what was in her bathwater?

"I take it you're not up late with any electronic devices?"

Sydney and David both shook their heads.

"Good. Well, I'd say just try to reduce your stress level a bit and try to make sure you're in a safe place in case it happens."

"So," David said, "she shouldn't be sleeping upstairs?"

"No, that probably wouldn't be the best place for her if she's doing any running with disorientation."

"So, when you say to reduce stress, you mean she probably shouldn't move to a new house?"

"Not if she can help it at all. There are medications you can take for stress but the best thing is to try to manage it yourself first by meditation, taking a walk, and just not taking on too many new things at once. Does that make sense?"

"Yes, Doctor. We appreciate your time."

"Sydney, is there anything else you'd like to talk about?"

"No, that makes a lot of sense. Thank you."

"Glad to be of help." The doctor left the room and David smiled to Sydney.

"Let's get you home," he said.

THE BUGGY ARRIVED BACK at the Schwartz house just as Samuel's buggy was pulling up the driveway. David helped Sydney down and they stood there in the yard waiting for Samuel to get out. Sydney's stomach turned as Samuel's buggy came to a full stop.

"Are you ready to go?" Samuel asked first thing, hopping down.

"There's been a change of plans," David began. He squinted at the sun, shining brightly now. "She's staying here."

Sydney braced herself. Finally David was on her side, a force she knew stood a chance, but her father was also a hard man and Sydney thought for a second yesterday that their encounter might end with one fist plowing into another's.

"Now, you look here. What do you mean by telling me she's stayin' after just yesterday you said you couldn't keep your dirty hands off her? She's too young to be marryin' if that's what you're gettin' at, David Schwartz, so you'd best think better of it. Ain't no daughter of mine gonna' go out thatta way. She'll be married right and proper, when she's *guete* and ready."

David raised a hand to silence Samuel. "I'm moving out."

Sydney's heart sank to the ground.

Samuel let go of his thought. "Oh. Well, that's all fine and *guete*, but she's my daughter and she'll be livin' with me from here on out."

"We just got back from the doctor's office." David shifted his weight where he stood.

"Doctor? You never said nothin' about no doctor." Samuel's whole manner softened. "What's ailin' ya, girl?"

Sydney saw her chance. "I have night terrors, sometimes they're pretty scary." She raised her skirt up before she thought better of it and showed Samuel a huge bruise on her knee. "This is where I hit the wall, just last night."

"I've heard of those," Samuel said. "But Martha and the girls will know how to handle it."

David started again. "The doctor said it is brought on by stress and that she should try to keep a low stress environment or she may have to have pills to help her manage it. He said she shouldn't move or make any big changes any time soon."

"I see." Samuel removed his hat, his eyes downcast. Suddenly Sydney felt sorry for him. He was genuinely worried about her.

"Well, if you want to stay here I guess it's up to you, but you're welcome to change your mind any time. There will always be room for you in our house, even if we have to build on."

"Thank you," Sydney said. "I was thinking we should get together more, maybe on Sundays when you're not at church."

"Well, you could come to church, too," he said.

Sydney looked to David for the answer to that.

"*Ja*, I spoke with Bishop Amos and he said it would be fine. You'll have to sit in the back and you may not understand any of it since it's in Swiss German, but you're welcome to come."

"Really?" Sydney asked.

"*Ja*." David smiled.

"Thank you, David."

David tipped his hat to her then went into the house, leaving Sydney alone with her father.

"This stress he's talking about, is it as bad as all that?"

Sydney leaned against the side of Samuel's buggy. "I ran away last night but David caught me and wouldn't let me leave."

"David did?" He sounded surprised.

Samuel's face slowly twisted and it made Sydney regret saying anything.

"I guess I owe the boy one, then." Samuel dug into his pocket and pulled out his billfold. He opened it and dug out a folded piece of paper and handed it to Sydney.

"What's this?"

"Read it. It's a letter from your *mueter* to me, telling me she was leaving. This letter proves that I didn't leave your *mueter*, she left me. She left me the same way she left you, sad and hurting with no explanation and no thought to anyone but herself." He put his billfold back in his pocket then he took both of Sydney's hands and tilted his head downward to meet her eyes. "Stay here. You are my daughter and always will be. I'll help you get an education if that's what you want, and you'll always be taken care of. You can come and go as you please, just...don't leave me the same way your *mueter* did."

Sydney nodded in agreement. He truly did care for her. "What happened between you two?" she asked.

Samuel winced. He leaned against the back of his buggy. "What happened to us should never have happened to any couple, but we were so young. We hadn't joined church yet and thought we knew better than our parents. I had two girls on the line, your *mueter* and her best friend. I knew I had to choose one or the other and I chose your *mueter*. We were in the barn one day, doing things we knew we shouldn't be doing. Your *mueter's* friend caught us. She was very hurt and accused your mother of deceit. They got into a huge argument, her friend ran away and no one saw her for days. Everyone in the community got out and looked for her, but it was no use. We found her, drowned, in Swan Creek three days later. I tried to marry JoHannah but she wouldn't. She disappeared, leaving only a note, and I didn't hear from her again for seven years. Then she found me one day, said she needed money and showed me a beautiful little girl she said was mine. I gave her the money she asked for and made her promise to meet with me again but she never came. I tried to find where she was living but she didn't want to be found. I never should have done what I did. I was wrong and I'll always regret it, but what JoHannah did—keeping you from me—was a bitter, heartless act. Now here you are, nearly a grown woman, and you'll have nothing to do with me and I don't blame you because you don't even know who I am."

Sydney had no idea they had so much in common. She silently stepped forward and put her arms around her father. He held her close. She heard a low whimper in her ear and then a sniffle.

～

"I'LL BE JUST down the road if you need anything," David said as he loaded the last of his things into the buggy.

"You'll be back for supper every night," Naomi said in a tone that didn't leave room for argument.

"I will, *Mam*."

"And Saturday evening?" she asked.

"I wouldn't miss it for the world."

"What's Saturday evening?" Sydney asked.

"It's David's birthday. He'll be eighteen." Naomi bit her lip.

"It's just another day, *Mam*, but if it'll get you to make me a chocolate pie I'll let you make a big deal of it." He hugged his mother and then watched her quickly disappear into the house. David waited until the door shut completely. "I want you to take my room."

"What for?" Sydney asked.

"So you won't fall to your death down the stairs in the night, that's what. And to be closer to my *mueter*. Take care of her, Sydney. Please." His eyebrows were scrunched together.

"I will." Sydney owed him everything, giving up his own home and mother just so she could stay. It pained her to think about but it was already done. Now how would they live without him?

He climbed up into the buggy, tipped his hat to her and took down the long driveway.

CHAPTER 10

The mid-November winds nipped sharply at Sydney as she brought in an armload of wood and set it in the stack by the woodstove. She returned outdoors for another as David pulled up in his buggy. He jumped down quickly and strode over to her as she reached down to pick up the first stick.

"Let me get that for you," he said. "Get in the house." The wind blew at his straw hat, threatening to remove it from his head. On her head, a solid blue handkerchief, the same color as all Naomi's dresses, folded in half to form a triangle, and tied under her hair in the back, preventing her hair from blowing into her face.

"I can help," she said, putting another stick into her arms. Her black, fleece-lined leggings offered warmth as the strong wind pushed against her denim skirt. He set two more sticks into her arms.

"That's plenty," David said. "Now go."

She hurried her stack inside and opened the door for David as he came in with his armload. She helped him stack it by the woodstove. He dusted himself off and then returned outside, this time to care for the horse that had brought him there. When he returned, he strode past her and into in the living room to hang his hat on the hook. Sydney waited where she stood by the stove, her hands hovering over it, trying to relieve the aching cold lingering in her fingers. As he came back and opened his mouth she said, "Only one."

"One? Well, they're about to quit laying then. Has the rooster been playing nice?"

"Yes, mostly."

"*Guete.* Don't worry, there will be plenty of eggs when warm weather comes back, many more than we can eat. You're doing a *guete* job caring for them."

Sydney smiled. David seemed to have a way of always making her feel capable. It was when he wasn't around that she struggled with feeling inadequate.

Naomi came out of the washroom. "There you are, finally," she said when she saw him, as if he were late. In reality, he came home at the same time each evening, but she'd always say something like that each day. "Well, sit down. Supper is just about to come out of the oven." Naomi walked to the counter and put on her oven mitts.

"Let me wash up first," he said.

Sydney set the table the same as she had every evening for the last two months. David would sit at the head of the table and Naomi and herself sat opposite each other on the long sides. The only time it was different was on off Sundays when they had company, usually some of Naomi's children, David's brothers and sisters, who took turns visiting, along with their families. Sydney poured some milk in David's glass and Naomi pulled the casserole out of the oven, making the kitchen the most comfortable room in the house to escape the cold. Sydney threw down a potholder on the table just before Naomi set the hot dish down on it. They had kitchen duty down like clockwork. David returned and they all sat and bowed their heads, David saying grace, then Naomi cut into the casserole with a stainless-steel spatula and scooped out a large section and laid it on David's plate. She waited for him to taste it before helping herself to some. He was the head of the household, and they strived to treat him as such. His income provided for their needs. Sure, his brothers chipped in when needed, but David had taken on full responsibility for his mother's care, and now Sydney's, and he did it without ever once complaining. For that, they were grateful.

"How's the studying coming?" David asked between bites. Sydney hated that question. The test was important to her and she had tried, but without computer access it was difficult to make any progress. She only had an hour each week in which David would drop her off at the library in town while he and Naomi had shopping to do and come back to get her after. At this rate, she wondered if she'd ever be ready.

She took a deep breath, thinking on how to answer. "Slow."

"Have you had any visitors?"

Sydney took a sip of water from the glass in front of her. "Just Emma Wittmer. She brought us some goat milk even though we had no eggs to trade with." She had drove her family's buggy over and stayed for hot chocolate so she could warm up some before heading back home.

"They're *guete* neighbors." David took another bite of casserole then scrunched his eyebrows together. "This is new." He pointed to the food on his plate with his fork. "I don't believe I've tasted it before." He seemed to think on it a second then took another bite.

"Well, do you like it?" Naomi asked. Sydney remained silent.

"*Ja*, it's tip top. What is it?"

Sydney smiled. "It's winter squash and farro," she said quietly, trying to contain her excitement. "I came up with it all on my own."

"There's something else in there." David took another bite.

"Leeks."

"It's *sehr-gut*, Sydney. I believe I'll have some more."

Sydney scooped up another serving with the spatula and care-fully shook it onto his plate then turned her attention to her own.

"We'll make a fine *hoosefro* out of you yet," Naomi said with a wink. She had worked hard teaching Sydney practical skills they both knew she desperately needed, but never had she mentioned she was training her to be a *housewife*. Sydney wondered if there was any deeper meaning behind that statement. She shifted in her chair.

David cleared his throat. "Well, things are really picking up at the shop. People are putting in orders for Christmas gifts, I guess."

Sydney hadn't realized Christmas was even coming yet. Last Christmas immediately came to mind. She had been left alone again. Sydney remembered how hard she'd tried to pretend it was just another day, that it didn't mean anything. But it had, hadn't it? All the Bible readings she and David and Naomi had shared told her so. Even then, the aching hole in her heart had told her so.

"We need to be thinking about where we'll spend second Christmas," David said.

The unfamiliar term brought Sydney back to the table. "What's that?"

"First Christmas," Naomi said, "is with your immediate family, those in your *hoose*. Second Christmas is when the extended family gets together to celebrate."

Sydney nodded an understanding.

"Will you be celebrating second Christmas with your *vater*, then?" David asked.

"I probably should." She'd come to enjoy spending time with her father and his large family. She had even grown to love her mother's father, her *gruszvater*, as David and Naomi would say. They were far from catching up on all the years lost but they'd made a good start.

"Tell them all we'll have second Christmas here," Naomi said to David. She was talking about his many brothers and sisters and their families. Sydney had wondered how they would all fit in the house, but after seeing how church services were conducted she figured they'd find a way somehow, even if they had to have second Christmas in the barn. She admired their dedication to family.

"So, are you up for chess tonight?" David asked Sydney.

"Aren't you tired?"

"I am. But it relaxes me."

"I don't know, David. You should probably get back before it gets even colder." Sydney hated to see David leave when it was so cold. She knew how miserable it could be to ride in the buggy in freezing temperatures.

"A quick game then."

Sydney nodded. She wouldn't be able to talk him out of it.

They began Bible reading as soon as supper was finished, leaving the dishes to be done after David left. The time spent with him was more important. Sydney cleared the table and wiped it down, then she dried it well with a white dishtowel. David retrieved the Bible from the shelf and opened it up on the table. Sydney hung the towel on the cabinet handle and took her seat again, eager to hear what would happen next.

Yesterday evening they had begun reading about Ruth. Sydney remembered that she had been from another land, marrying into Naomi's family, God's chosen people. And when her husband died, Ruth wouldn't leave Naomi, her mother-in-law. Sydney understood that. Her Naomi had become like family to her as well. He read that Boaz, who didn't even know Ruth, had been so kind to her anyway. Sydney listened intently to David, who had already begun reading aloud.

"'Then she fell on her face, and bowed herself to the
ground, and said unto him, Why have I found

grace in thine eyes, that thou shouldest take
knowledge of me, seeing I am a stranger?
And Boaz answered and said unto her, It hath fully
been shewed me, all that thou hast done unto thy
mother in law since the death of thine husband:
and how thou hast left thy father and thy mother,
and the land of thy nativity, and art come unto a
people which thou knewest not heretofore.'"

Sydney had come as a stranger unto a people she didn't know
of before.

"'The Lord recompense thy work, and a full reward
be given thee of the Lord God of Israel, under
whose wings thou art come to trust.'"

Sydney had worked so hard. *I trust in you, God.*

"'Then she said, Let me find favour in thy sight, my
lord; for that thou hast comforted me, and for
that thou hast spoken friendly unto thine
handmaid, though I be not like unto one of thine
handmaidens.'"

Oh, how different she was from all the others. *Will you accept
me, too, God?* A tear rolled down unexpectedly, marking the seriousness of her thoughts. Her shoulders shook.

David stopped reading. "Are you okay, Sydney?"

She hesitated then nodded, not meeting his eyes. Then all at
once the tears came and Sydney shook her head. She wasn't all
right. There was something very wrong, deep within her. She
heard chairs scoot and scrape across the hardwood floor. Soon
both David and Naomi were seated on both sides of her, each

with a hand upon one of her shoulders, silently. She knew what they were doing there—praying. For her. She bowed her head and closed her eyes, determined not to stop praying until she'd settled things between her and the Lord.

IT WAS FINALLY CHRISTMAS. Everyone would be home today, celebrating with their immediate family. There would be plenty of time for visiting extended family during Second Christmas. Sydney helped Naomi most of the morning in the kitchen, preparing dinner. They had made lots of candy the day before. Naomi had strung Christmas cards all across the living room, and tonight they would light a candle in each of the living room and kitchen windows in addition to their lanterns.

Sydney could feel the spirit of Christmas bubbling up within her, just like a child waiting on a new toy would. This was the day to celebrate the birth of the Lord, *her Lord,* and she was going to do it with family.

Sydney poured a pan of gravy into a bowl and set it on the table. "Is that everything?" she asked Naomi.

"I believe so. David," she hollered. David appeared quickly. He'd been waiting in the living room since he'd arrived about an hour earlier. He sat down and the prayer was said.

Just as they were about to dig in, David said, "I've got a surprise."

Naomi was holding out a dish of cheesy potatoes for him but he was ignoring her. "Can't it wait until after dinner?" she asked.

"It's snowing. Look." He pointed to the kitchen window.

Naomi put down the dish and they all went to the window. Big snowflakes, soft and white, fell to the ground outside. "We didn't even see snow last winter," David said. "Just an inch or two of ice."

"We had a foot up north, all at once, and then no more," Sydney said.

"Down here we're lucky for one good snow a year, and it never happens on Christmas."

"I didn't know the Amish wished for a white Christmas, too," Sydney said.

"They don't," Naomi said, sitting back down. "Just David. He's always loved snow." They ate dinner and talked at the table until everyone said how full they were, then Naomi started to clean up the table, preparing for the many dishes ahead.

"How about you let me do the dishes, Naomi? I'll clean all this up while you rest."

"Oh, no, I couldn't do that. You're our guest here, Sydney. I couldn't let you do all the work."

Sydney's heart fell at the word guest, she pressed her lips together. She'd come to think of this place like her own home. She shared in the chores each day, trying her best to be useful. She didn't want to be thought of as a guest.

David glanced her way. "No, *Mam*, Sydney's right. You go rest a bit and we'll clean this up."

Sydney knew Naomi would do whatever David said. He ushered her into the living room and came back in the kitchen and started pumping water.

"You really don't have to help," Sydney said. "It's Christmas. You should be spending time with your mom."

"I haven't helped with any dishes around here in months. And you're my family, too."

Sydney smiled at that and began washing dishes. "Well, I guess I could let you help."

"You should. You and my *mueter* really outdid yourselves. That was a lot of food. And all those desserts—we'll be eating candy for a month."

Sydney laughed. He wasn't exaggerating. "I wish I could have gotten you both a present. You've been so kind to me, taking me in like you did, and I still feel bad that you have to live over at the woodshop." It was something she'd meant to say for a long while but hadn't.

"I still live here. I only sleep there, and I already told you, no one around here is expecting a gift."

"I know. At least I was able to let your mother rest after all that cooking. That's sort of a gift. Is there nothing I can do for you?"

David rinsed a plate and dried it with a white dishtowel. "You are my gift, Sydney. You've been a gift to the whole family." Those were nice words to hear, but Sydney wondered how much meaning was behind them.

When they finally finished the dishes, David took the dishtowel she was drying her hands with and set it down on the counter. "I have a surprise for you," he said, turning her around by her shoulders. He was behind her now, with his hands over her eyes.

"Is this necessary?" Sydney asked. What was he up to?

"*Ja*. Now walk." He nudged her forward into the living room and then removed his hands. She opened her eyes and saw Naomi sitting in her rocking chair, knitting. Next to her was another rocker, polished and new, with a slightly curved back and softly molded seat. "Do you like it?" he asked.

"Is this for me?" Sydney asked.

"*Ja*. I made it for you, at the woodshop. We sell a lot like it, but I tried to make yours extra special."

"Thank you." Sydney fingered the arm of it, running across the curve of the wood. "It's beautiful."

"Well, sit down, try it out."

She sat. "It's wonderful. I can't believe you made this for me."

"Well, every lady needs a comfortable sewing chair."

She laughed. Cooking, Sydney had down. Sewing was another story. She leaned back in her chair and rocked, hoping the chair would indeed make the difference.

hey met at Emma Wittmer's house to go on an "outing". David had brought Sydney, and Emma's friend Jeb was already waiting at Emma's when they arrived. A few minutes later they got into the car. It was a Honda Pilot with a third row seat and a strong heating system. David and Sydney got in first, all the way in the back, and Jeb and Emma took the middle row. Only the paid driver sat up front. They had commissioned him to take them into the city of Springfield for the day. Emma had called it an "outing," but to Sydney it sounded a lot like a double date.

"I haven't been in a car in months," Sydney commented. "It's so strange to be in one now."

"I know," David said. "They go so smooth it makes me want to go to sleep." His arm stretched out on the top of the seat behind Sydney.

"I could never sleep in a car," Jeb said. "Too dangerous. Would you want to be asleep if we ran off the road?"

The driver peeked at him from the rear view mirror.

"I'm sorry," Jeb said. "I didn't mean it like that. I'm sure you're a *guete* driver."

The man laughed and kept on driving. His name was Wayne Stevens. He'd been David and Naomi's driver for years. He was called on whenever they needed to go further than just a few miles. Today his money would come from David and Jeb as they were going to split the cost.

"Where are we going first?" Sydney asked David.

"Jeb and I have a full day planned. First, a little shopping."

Sydney wondered where the Amish shopped when they came to the city, but decided to allow herself to be surprised.

It was cozy in the third row by themselves. The seats were smaller back there, forcing them to sit closer together. Sydney had worn her dark denim skirt, as she thought it to be the most formal of the two, and she had on her old red knit sweater with a tee shirt beneath along with her heavy coat. Winter was upon them, and the bitter Missouri winds whipped at the car as it sped up, having finally reached the highway.

David stretched his arm upward and then dropped it slowly to his side, taking Sydney's hand as it fell. This sent an exciting jolt through Sydney, the warmth from his strong hand traveling up her arm and all the way through her. He'd not been so forward since the night he'd kissed her, just before he moved into the woodshop apartment. She had worried maybe he had stopped viewing her in a desiresome way because of all the negativity it had brought.

She'd worn her hair back in a simple braid, always careful to keep it away from David's attention. Holding her hand was a bold move, but they were on a date with friends, and no one could see from where they were sitting. Sydney wondered when this transition in their relationship had taken place. He'd been attentive, but not affectionate. She lightly placed her other hand in the crook of his arm, holding onto it just above his elbow, then looked up to him for permission to keep it there. His eyes held desire. He wanted to kiss her. Sydney looked away, hoping no one else could see what was clearly written on David's face.

"This is going to be so much fun," Emma said.

Sydney agreed.

Their first stop was Bass Pro Shops Outdoor World, a sporting goods store, or so Sydney was told. She wondered how sporting goods could be considered date-like, then again, she still wasn't sure if an "outing" really was a date, but as they entered the building she understood the appeal.

Just through the doors they were met with the sound of rushing water. In front of them was a wooden bridge with water running below it. Above the bridge, a waterfall, the source of all the noise. Sydney looked out across the water. Real fish swam in a large indoor aquarium and there were pennies in the bottom below. They crossed to the other side of the bridge and stopped. "We'll meet back in an hour, does that sound *guete?*" Jeb asked as they clustered together.

"*Ja,*" David said and led Sydney away, up a flight of stairs, to a set of double doors. Sydney gave a little wave to Emma as she went.

"What's up here?" Sydney asked.

"A museum." David's smile held a secret. They walked into the museum, a long room with guns from every time period in cases along the walls.

"Where is everybody?" Sydney asked. There were plenty of people downstairs but no one upstairs.

David shrugged his shoulders. "It's a weekday." He grabbed her hand and held it again as they strolled the length of the museum. David's hands were rough and calloused and warm. All the hard work he did was evidenced by his hands and it made Sydney proud to know him. They had become close friends, but, until today, she hadn't noticed his desire to be more than that, not since he'd kissed her. He had obviously wanted to cool things down between them, but she'd begun to wonder if the spark had been put out altogether. So the question burned within her, threatening to ruin the moment, the whole day even, but she couldn't contain it.

"How is today…different?" They turned the corner and found a new hall of gun cases, this one also empty of people.

"What do you mean by that?"

"You're just so…forward today."

He let go of her hand.

"No, I didn't mean it like that." She grabbed his hand again and held it with both of hers. "It's just, you've never wanted to hold my hand before."

"I've wanted to."

"You have? When?"

"Every evening when you're chatting away at the supper table. Each time you sit next to me in the living room. When I take you and my *mueter* to church on Sundays. On Thursdays, when we stroll the open market." He stopped her from walking further, turning her to meet him, face to face.

"The open market's been closed since late fall," Sydney said.

"I know."

He'd been thinking of her romantically for months?

"Now do you want to know all the times I've wanted to kiss you?" David rubbed her hand with his thumb.

She nodded. Of course she did.

"Right now."

"But you won't?"

"Let's see, we're miles away from the community, so no one to see us, except Jeb and Emma, and they won't tell. We're not *really* alone together as there are at least hundreds of people shopping in this building at the moment, my *mueter* and your *vater* certainly aren't going to catch us. I suppose all that is left is to ask if you're willing."

"I can see you've thought this through."

"Most every day I think it through again."

Sydney held onto his hand and drew closer to David. From

over his shoulder she could see an elderly couple, arm in arm, coming through the double doors at the opposite side of the room. Sydney dropped her head and cleared her throat. David turned around, now knowing what Sydney already knew. They pretended to look at the long glass gun cases as they strolled through the museum, her arm linked in his.

~

"So, how long have you two been together, now?" Sydney asked Jeb and Emma as she twisted fettuccine alfredo onto her fork during dinner.

"A few months," Jeb said between bites of ravioli.

"How did you two meet?" Sydney asked.

"We've known each other our whole lives." Emma bumped shoulders lovingly with Jeb, seated next to her.

"Well, how did you come together then. Was it a singing thing?" Sydney immediately wished she hadn't said anything at all. Maybe she wasn't supposed to ask these kinds of questions. She had really only meant to make small talk.

Jeb nearly choked on his ravioli to tell the story first. "She tried to kill me."

Emma laughed. "Will you please stop telling people that? I didn't try to kill him." She took a sip of soda, her mouth and eyes serious now. "*He* tried to kill *me*."

"I did not," Jeb said, wiping his mouth.

"Skunks can be dangerous, Jeb. Some carry rabies." Emma had her pointer finger up for emphasis.

"Skunks?" Sydney asked.

"It's a long story. I'll tell you later," Emma said quietly, then forked in a bite of salad.

"And then you can come ask me, and I'll tell you what *really* happened," Jeb said. Emma elbowed him and he winced playfully.

Sydney didn't know they were such an outgoing couple. David just sat beside her, so very reserved.

"So," Jeb said, his blond hair curling toward his ears, "David tells me you're trying to get your GED. Is it very hard to do?"

"*I* think so." She laughed. "I plan on taking it in the spring. The study materials are all on the computer now, and I only get to town once a week to study. That's been the most difficult part."

"What will you do with all that education?" Jeb asked between bites of ravioli.

"I hadn't really thought about it."

"Well, spring is right around the corner," Emma's lovely voice chimed in. "I saw the first of the crocus flowers had bloomed out by the house this morning."

"Are you going on to college after your GED?" Jeb asked, ignoring Emma altogether.

"I don't know," Sydney said. "It depends."

"On what?" David finally spoke up.

Emma stood. "If you'll all excuse me, I need to use the ladies' room. Sydney?"

"Yeah, me too. Excuse me."

In the ladies' room Emma apologized for Jeb. "I'm sorry. He doesn't know when to stop with the questions sometimes."

"It's okay," Sydney said.

"You don't know, do you?" Emma stared at Sydney's reflection in the mirror.

"Know what?"

"If you're gonna stay or not. It's okay. A lot of us don't know at your age. No one would expect you to decide any time soon," Emma said.

"And David?" Sydney stared at the reflection of herself and Emma, noting the many differences between them and their worlds. Emma was born and raised in the community, and knew what she wanted out of life. Sydney had always just lived from day to day, hoping to survive life's punches.

"He'll stay," she said softly.

Of course he would. Sydney couldn't imagine him ever leaving the community for any reason, even for the woman he loved.

"He's a *guete* man, hard working, too. Just try not to get too close, if you know what I mean, until you know for sure. It hurts us all when someone leaves, but it would kill David. He's completely taken with you, I can see it in the way he looks at ya."

Completely taken. Sydney had never heard the expression but could easily guess the meaning. She was completely taken with David as well.

Back at the table the men spoke openly in their Swiss German dialect, knowing perfectly well no one else in the room could understand them. They switched seamlessly over to English as soon as the ladies sat back down. Sydney realized then that they wouldn't ordinarily speak English in public. They did it for her. She felt cheated. *It must be nice having a second language.* It was just one more thing her mother neglected to give her growing up.

THE CAR TOOK them back to Emma's house late in the day. David and Jeb went to get their horses hitched back up to their buggies and soon they were going their separate ways. Sydney sat closer to David than she usually did, although she knew now that they were back amongst the community it wouldn't do to let anyone see her sit that close. Sydney was wrapped up in a blanket and could see her breath in the air from the deep cold of winter. It would be dark soon. The later they stayed out, the colder it would get. They were halfway between the Wittmer house and Naomi's when David stopped the buggy suddenly. He turned his body far around to see all the way behind them, nothing but the sun setting in the west, then back to the front. No one was on the lonely dirt road but the two of them.

She wanted badly to kiss him. She knew he'd tried all day to arrange a private moment for that very purpose. This was the last chance, or so it seemed, before David might hide his feelings again, pretending like he wasn't attracted to her. It could be months before Sydney would get another chance like this.

"Are you still willing?" he whispered, his warm breath freezing in the cold air as he leaned toward her.

She met him more than halfway, and drank in the sweet tenderness of his kiss. Her hand reached out of the blanket and into the cold in front of her, settling on David's coat. She fingered the zipper, finding it open halfway down and slid her fingers just inside.

Warmth.

She made out the shape of a shirt snap, but dared not disturb it, lest she anger him again. Oh, but she wanted to. The tip of one finger slid between snaps and made it inside, something she hadn't meant to do. She pulled back.

He took hold of her hand and held it to his chest, ending the kiss. "Marry me, Sydney."

She opened her eyes wide. "What did you say?"

"Marry me." His eyes brimmed with passion.

"Because I touched your bare chest?" Was this some Swiss Amish custom she hadn't yet heard of?

"No. Because I want you to be my wife."

"You mean someday, right?"

"No."

"We can't just marry to avoid temptation."

"Our people do. The Bible says it is better to marry than to burn with passion."

He looked her over seductively, causing her heart to do a somersault. By the looks of it, he was on fire. The magnetic energy he projected drew her forward. He took her mouth again, and she melted in his warm embrace.

She pushed him back and took a deep breath, causing an

aching hole deep within her. "The bishop won't marry us, you know that. Neither of us are church members."

"I wasn't talking about joining church," he said as he tried to kiss her again.

"David?" Sydney shook her head in disbelief. Emma had just said how David would never leave. Sydney knew it as well. What was going on? "Why would you want to leave your people, your mother, what about your brothers and the woodshop? You love your work."

His eyes were intense. He would never leave, unless...

"You don't think they'll ever allow me in, do you?"

"It would take time, a lot of time. You'll have to learn Swiss German to even begin to study for baptismal classes."

"Then what is it?"

"They'll want to know you're serious."

"Maybe I am."

"They may require a waiting period, to prove it."

"And you don't think I could wait that long?"

"You're a smart girl. What would you do? Wait around here forever?" There was an edge to his voice. "No, you'll probably go off to college, find yourself a career in the big city and marry someone else. Just as soon as you pass that test of yours."

"Is that what you're afraid of? Is that why you haven't offered to take me to the library more?"

He shook his head, sighing in exasperation.

"You're right. That's not it. You said it yourself, it's better to marry than to burn. You wouldn't wait for me."

"I would," David said with his mouth, but his eyes said he *hoped* he would.

A SHINY RED car sat in the Schwartz driveway as David pulled the horse to a stop.

"Is my *mueter* expecting company?" David asked.

"Not that I know of."

They opened the door and walked inside the kitchen.

"You'd better stand next to the stove and warm up," David said.

Voices came from the living room. Who was Naomi visiting with? Sydney walked on in. There she found her mother, sitting with Naomi in her rocking chair, having tea and sweetbread. It was a cinnamon bread Sydney had made herself the day before. She'd bought the tea the day Naomi wasn't feeling well and David had taken her to the market, just the two of them. The lanterns were already lit, though it wasn't quite dark yet.

Her mother's presence in the room seemed so out of place. JoHannah, wearing a fancy pantsuit, her nails manicured, and hair-sprayed hair, who'd left without saying goodbye months ago.

Naomi's home was simple and plain, and for a while it had been Sydney's home, too.

"Sydney! There you are. I've been waiting for you most of the day." Her mother rushed over and hugged Sydney.

All the words Sydney had rehearsed in her mind to say to her if she ever came back fell out of her mind and onto the floor. She longed to pick up just a few of them and cram them down her mother's throat. "Umm, we were in the city."

"Yes, Naomi told me all about it. I've come bearing good news. You have a new step-dad. Remember Dan I told you about?" She flashed an expensive looking ring at Sydney. "Well, we flew to Vegas and got married. Isn't that exciting? We've got a charming two-story house in the country. Well, it's not like this kind of country, it's five wooded acres just outside of the city, but it's beautiful. You're going to love it."

Sydney didn't say a thing. Instead, she slowly turned around, walked across the floor toward her bedroom, feeling everyone's eyes on her as she left.

"I'll talk to her," she heard David say behind her.

Sydney removed her coat and laid it on her bed as she entered. She did a turn, taking in the things in the room, the small lot of possessions she'd come to own: her clothes, a lantern of her own, the quilt blocks she'd started sewing but hadn't finished yet. She plopped down onto the bed, then fell the rest of the way backward landing hard on the mattress, staring at the ceiling, blankly. She could see the blurred image of David standing in the doorway from the corner of her eye, arms folded.

"Just be firm," David said in a low voice.

"What's that supposed to mean?" she said without moving.

"Just tell her nicely and firmly that you're staying here."

"I wish I could."

"What do you mean?"

Silence.

"You can't be serious." He stepped inside the door, closing it behind him. "The woman isn't fit to own a cat, much less a daughter."

Oh, how she would miss how he rolled those "r's." "I'm seventeen. I can take care of myself." Sydney sprang out of the bed and began to pack her things.

"*This* is your home now. You belong here." He pointed to the floor for emphasis.

He meant that. Sydney pulled some clothes out of the drawer.

"You can't go. What about your *vater* and your sisters?"

Sydney stuffed the clothes into her bag. "I'll write them."

"What about us?" he whispered.

"You said you'd wait." She held his stare, daring him to go back on his word, but he remained quiet. "I'm going back with my mother. I can get my GED in just a few weeks if I have computer access, then I'll be back. If I stay here it will take months, if it ever happened at all."

"Will you come back?"

"Yes."

"Then why is this test so important to you? People don't take this test for the fun of it. They take it so they can get a job or go to college."

"Maybe I need to pass so I'll know I'm not a failure at everything I try to do, did you think of that?" The words out of Sydney's mouth surprised her. She hadn't realized it until just then herself.

He rubbed his temples with one hand, a growl of frustration escaping his throat.

She gave a loud sigh and turned from him, pulling a skirt out of the drawer. "Aren't you the least bit concerned with what your mother will think of you and me in the bedroom with the door shut?"

David stepped forward and grabbed Sydney's elbow, causing her to drop the skirt she had just picked up. It fell into a heap on the floor. He pulled her in, grabbing her around the waist, pressing his mouth to hers. She gave in to him instantly, letting her arms tuck under his and wrap around to his back, the warmth of his body removing the last of the chill from the buggy ride home. His kiss was urgent and persuasive. Any longer and she would have changed her mind.

"Come back to me, Sydney." His eyes begged her. "I know you're not ready to marry and you're not done with the world yet, but when you grow tired of it, please come back to me."

The two-story house in the country was all her mother said it was. It had a huge fridge with an ice maker built in the door, all new furniture in the living room, an exercise room, she would have her own bedroom and she even saw a pool table upstairs, though she couldn't remember now exactly where.

She wondered what Dan, her new step-dad she'd heard so little about, did for a living to be able to afford this set-up. It was more house than they needed, than anyone needed really. But it didn't matter to Sydney. She didn't plan on staying that long. She hadn't told her mother yet. In fact, she'd barely spoken to her on the five and a half hour drive back to the city. Sydney had always imagined the confrontation she'd have with her but now, after everything she'd been through, everything she'd learned, it hardly seemed worth it. She couldn't change her mother, she could only strive to forgive her, and that was much harder than winning any argument.

"Come on, Sydney. I'll show you *my* bedroom. There's a hot tub in there." She scrunched up her nose along with a smile.

"I'm kind of tired, Mom." The words fell out of her mouth like a rock. It was so hard to call her mom after what she'd done. "I think I just want to go to bed."

"Sure." Her mother's voice was high-pitched. She was putting on a big show, trying to convince herself she was a good mother. Or maybe it was all for Dan. Only time would tell.

Sydney went straight to bed, beat from the long day.

SYDNEY AWOKE IN A STRANGE PLACE. It took her a second to get her bearings straight as to where she was. Then the day before came flooding back to her. David had kissed her, more than once, and he'd asked her to marry him, an unbelievable request coming from him. And yet, it was she who didn't want to leave the community. She didn't know it for sure until that very moment, when he'd suggested they leave the Swan Creek Settlement and marry, that she didn't ever want to leave the people. *Her* people. She knew it in her heart, if not yesterday when David had asked, then right now as she lay awake, staring at the ceiling in her mother's house.

JoHannah's house.

She knew she wanted to live among her brothers and sisters, her father and grandparents. She knew she wanted to be Amish and accept their faith. So what was she doing in northern Missouri?

She knew.

It was the GED test. The test that stood in her way for months. The test that kept telling her she wasn't good enough. Not smart enough. She had to conquer this test before she could go home and join church. She was going to pass that test if it killed her.

She would need to study, but first she'd promised to write her father and David.

She dressed quickly in her denim skirt and long-sleeve shirt and then got out her notebook. She really wasn't sure what to say just yet, except that she'd made the trip okay and that she would definitely be back after she took her test. When she was done, she noticed the letter to David sounded much like the letter to her father, and although she already regretted it, she decided to just mail them as they were and write something more next time. She would just need an envelope and a stamp.

Her bedroom door opened without a knock. "Good morning." Her mother stood with her face lit up like Christmas. "Ready for a little shopping spree?" she asked.

Sydney tried to ignore her enthusiasm. "Do you have a stamp and an envelope?" she asked.

"Why do you want a stamp and an envelope?" Sydney's mother watched her tear out two pages in her notebook and fold them both in thirds.

"I barely got to say goodbye to anyone and I'd like to send them a letter." She lifted her chin, meeting her mother's look of disgust straight on.

Her face softened into a small tentative smile. "All right. Maybe we can swing by the post office on the way back."

"Why not on the way?" she challenged.

"Okay, on the way. Listen, Sydney, I know you're still upset with me and I'm sorry. I'm going to make it up to you. This is our big chance to make it in the world, to finally *be* somebody. I had to leave you a while. I needed to make sure this was going to work out between me and Dan."

Sydney sat up straight, her temper threatening. "Who is this Dan person anyway? If it weren't for all this expensive stuff I'd say he was imaginary." Sydney motioned around the room with her hand.

"I'll tell you all about it. While we shop. Get dressed." Her mother turned to leave.

"I am dressed."

Her mother turned once more and gave Sydney a full up and

down. "Oh, Sydney, you poor dear. I figured your father would take better care of you than that."

Sydney's insides burned. She thought back to the day her father had called her mother a witch. Sydney took a deep breath. She wanted this to work—no, it *had* to work. Sydney finally knew what she wanted in life. Family. And it was waiting for her, back home. She would count down the days until it was so.

IN TOWN, her mother had her trying on tons of clothes with insane price tags. "Try this one." Her mother took a dress off the rack, black with spaghetti straps. She held it up to Sydney. It came way above her knee.

"Mom, I don't wear clothes like that anymore. Besides, it's still winter."

"Well, it's not for everyday, Sydney." She laughed. "It's a party dress for when your father's clients come over."

Sydney stared at her blankly. When her mother finally noticed she said, "When *Dan's* clients come over. The point is, we both need to look the part so he can keep making money and we can keep buying whatever we want. Does that make sense?"

It was now perfectly clear why her mother had come back for her. She needed her to look the part of a happy family. It hurt. It wasn't as if she thought she suddenly cared, but a little remorse would have been a nice gesture. Apparently, even that was too much to ask.

Her mother hounded her until she finally tried the dress on. It fit perfectly, if you could call anything that leaves you that exposed a perfect fit. She felt naked. Now she knew exactly what David saw in her those first few days.

"I'm not wearing this, it's too short." She handed the garment back to her mother.

"You'll get used to it," her mother whispered and threw it over her arm.

Her mother seemed to have an endless supply of money, either that or it was all credit card debt, but it gave Sydney an idea. "What I really need is a computer."

Her mother's face brightened. "We'll buy you one. Today. Top of the line. How does that sound?"

She gave her mother a sweet smile. If JoHannah could be fake, so could she.

$\mathcal{E}$very minute she could, Sydney studied for the GED exam. She felt like one of those reality TV stars working at some crummy job for a chance at a million dollars. Only this was her life at stake. The thought crossed her mind daily to just give up and hitch a ride back to her father's house. She knew he'd take her in and not say a word. In fact, he'd be thrilled when she told him she wanted to join church—overjoyed even. But this was something she had to do. She refused to be like her mother, dependent upon a man for everything. She needed to know she was smart enough to make it on her own if she wanted to. It was well into the night before she stopped studying and went to bed. At least if she slept late she could avoid her mother.

Days passed before she met Dan. He appeared one evening in a black BMW, Mom was waiting for him at the front door. "So you must be Sydney," he said as he walked across the living room. "I've heard so much about you." He shook her hand like he was closing a business deal. Dan was a well dressed man in his early fifties, clean cut, average build, not too heavy or skinny. His eyes were dark, like the hair on his head that looked to be getting thin on top. He certainly wasn't her mother's usual type. The men she usually dragged home were handsome, sometimes brainless, usually lazy and pigheaded, but always very handsome. So her mother had decided to find someone with money for a change. Well, Sydney hoped he had better character and judgement than her mother had. He had to have some brains to make all the money he did, unless he was into something illegal, but by the looks of him she figured he'd made it honestly.

"I've not heard that much about you, sir. What is it you do for a living?"

Sydney could see her mother from the corner of her eye, shaking her head subtly. Her mother didn't want her asking too many questions, which made Sydney want to ask more.

"I'm a Business Development Manager." His voice was loud and strong like someone trying to sell something to an audience.

"That sounds...fascinating. Tell me about it." Sydney smiled at him politely.

"Ah, I'm glad to see a young person interested in business. You see, it all comes down to one thing. In business, you must find a need and fill it. And if there's not a need, create one. That's really all there is to it. If you can just remember that, you're ahead of three quarters of the employees the agency has sent over to me in the last year. These kids with their fancy degrees don't know beans about anything, much less business." He took off his coat and Mom hung it in the coat closet.

"Don't you have a degree?" Sydney asked.

"Actually, I have an associate's degree from a community college. But I was determined. If you're determined enough, you'll make it."

Mom linked his arm into hers. "But all your children attended Ivy League colleges, didn't they?"

"Yes, you're right about that. And when you're ready for college, Sydney, we'll send you to the very best school as well."

"That's very generous of you, sir," Sydney said, knowing good and well she wouldn't be around long enough for that. Still, it was nice of him. She'd heard the horror stories about step-children, about how they didn't always get treated well, but she had no reason to believe Dan was anything like that. She breathed a little easier having met him, and knowing he wasn't an international drug smuggler or anything.

"So, Sydney. How is your aunt Ida getting along?" Dan sat on the long, plushy couch.

"My aunt?" Sydney asked.

"Yes. Your mother told me you'd been living with her while she was ill."

"Yes. Aunt Ida. She's...much better now." Sydney gave her mom a peculiar look.

"Well," her mother said, "I think we should all go out to dinner to celebrate our new family. What do you say, Dan?"

"That's a great idea," Dan said. "Just let me freshen up a minute and I'll be ready." Sydney watched Dan disappear into the hallway.

"Sydney, go change your clothes," Mom said. "We're going out."

Sydney rolled her eyes, went into her room and shut the door. It took her a few minutes, but she found a nice top that looked almost dressy, and one of the nicer skirts she'd picked out when they went shopping. The only reason her mother bought it was because it was sold as a set with a low-cut satin blouse.

It was pretty late when they got home from supper at an upscale restaurant in the city. Sydney shut the door to her room and changed into her long nightgown. Then she took out her computer and spent the next several hours taking practice tests. She didn't do half bad. Only the math kept her from a passing score. Just another few weeks and she wouldn't need to stay here with her mother anymore. Sydney lay her head down on the pillow as the sun rose through her bedroom window.

What felt like two minutes later her mother was in her room shaking her awake. "Rise and shine!"

"Why are you doing this?" was all Sydney could manage to mumble out that made any sense.

"Today's a big day for you. If you hurry, we can grab a bite to eat on the way." Her mother started to step out of the room.

"Wait. Where are we going?" Sydney rubbed her eyes.

"To get you enrolled in private school, silly. Now get dressed, and no jean skirt! I swear if I see that thing on you again I'm going to burn it," she mumbled as she walked away.

Sydney got up and stumbled into the living room where her mother sat holding a home fashion magazine.

"Umm, Mom. I don't need to go to school."

"Of course you do, Sydney. How will you ever get in college if you don't?"

"Well, I was thinking about getting my GED instead."

"Oh, no. That would never work." She thumbed through the magazine, barely glancing at each page.

"Why not?"

"Because all the rich kids go to a private school. They don't homeschool. Remember what I said about playing along and impressing clients? This is part of it."

"You want me to go to school to impress Dan's clients?"

"Well, don't think of it like that. You'll make a ton of friends and you can use those friends later on as contacts, you know, networking? That's how you do business, Sydney. It's all about who you know, you know? Ha. That sounded funny. But you get the point, honey. Now get dressed so we won't be late."

Sydney swallowed hard, trying not to reveal her anger. The woman was impossible but the Internet connection was good there, so Sydney got dressed and met her mother in the living room. "Do you have any coffee?" Sydney asked, still sleepy-eyed.

"You're a coffee drinker now?" Her mother shook her head. "All right, we'll get some on the way." She stepped into the kitchen at the bar and grabbed her purse and a large manilla envelope and they headed out the door.

Ms. Crissip, the principal at J. Henderson Academy, showed Sydney and her mother where all Sydney's classes would be. It was a much smaller school than the last one Sydney had attended, and much nicer. Ms. Crissip was a pencil-thin woman in her late forties with medium length brown hair and a skirt shorter than the little black dress Sydney's mother had bought for her. Back in Ms. Crissip's office, her mother had paperwork to sign.

"It will be difficult coming in so late in the year, Sydney, but if you work hard at it you'll do fine." She smiled as she handed her mother a pen. "Now I just need Sydney's transcripts." Ms. Crissip held her hand out. Sydney watched her mother open the manilla envelope she'd been hanging onto all this time. Out came Sydney's records. All of them. Her birth certificate, social security card, shot records, and school transcripts.

"It looks like there's a gap here where Sydney wasn't in school." Ms. Crissip pushed her glasses further up on her nose.

"That's a mistake," Mom said. "We pulled her out to home-school, but somehow it didn't make it into her file. We have her homeschool transcript right...here." She pulled out another paper from the stack on her lap and handed it to her.

Sydney wondered what on earth it was she was supposed to have been learning when her mother was "homeschooling" her the last five months, especially since she hadn't seen or heard from her during that time, but Sydney kept quiet.

After copies of all the documents were made, her mother slid them back inside the manilla envelope.

When they finally arrived back home Sydney was exhausted. Mom threw her purse and the manilla envelope back on the bar. "Well, my work's done for the day. I'll be in the hot tub if you need me."

Sydney watched her mother disappear down the hall. She

desperately craved sleep, but the envelope was too tempting. Sydney took it back to her room and took out its contents. Seeing her social security card, she remembered a time once, when her mother had used Sydney's social security number to get the utilities turned on in their apartment. She wondered how many times she'd entered Sydney's numbers when she knew her own wouldn't work, having not paid the bills too many times. These documents were Sydney's. She ripped paper out of her notebook and slid it into the envelope, weighing it out with her hands, adding more till it felt the same as the papers she'd removed. Then she put the envelope back by her mother's purse, hoping it appeared undisturbed. Now she just needed to hide the documents. Under the mattress? No. She needed someplace her mother would never find them. But where? Sydney stepped into her walk-in closet. It was still mostly empty. Sydney's meager amount of clothes could never hope to fill a closet so big. Even all the clothes her mom had purchased for her could never fill it. She finally pulled up the carpet in the corner of her closet and shoved the documents beneath it.

Sydney thought back to another time she had pulled up the carpet. She was twelve and had been given twenty dollars to feed the neighbor's cat while its owner was away. She had hidden it from her mother, beneath the carpet in the corner of the living room behind a chair. The furniture didn't come with them when they were evicted. Mom had moved them out quickly while Sydney was still at school. Sydney figured the landlord eventually found her twenty dollars, either that or it was still there, rotting away.

Sydney carefully tucked the carpet edges back under the trim with the end of a wire hanger. Was she getting a little paranoid? It was possible. But her mother would have no more control over her soon. She rested that afternoon and into the evening.

"Wake up," Mom shook her. "Dinner time."

Dinner?

Sydney jumped. Had she slept that long? But her room was dark. Only the hall light from the open door spilled in. So it was supper time.

She followed Mom into the dining room, two Styrofoam containers and two cans of soda awaited them. Plastic forks, white napkins, and fortune cookies littered the table. So she had gone into the city for Chinese food. Sydney wondered if Dan cared that her mother didn't cook. It wasn't that she couldn't. There had been times when she had prepared all kinds of home cooked dishes but it wasn't often. If she had the money she would eat out, if not, it was microwave or box dinners.

"Where's Dan?" Sydney asked.

"He had to work late."

Sydney sat at the table, sleepy-eyed, trying to force herself to be hungry. Finally she took a bite. It was supposed to be cashew chicken. She'd had it from the same restaurant before, only now she knew it wasn't the *real* cashew chicken like in southern Missouri, where the dish originated.

She thought back to all the meals she shared with David and Naomi and how they always talked at the table at home. She missed them all so much, especially David. The way he'd kissed her the day she left was something she'd never forget. Her insides tingled just thinking about it. She said a silent prayer to bless the food and to give her strength. Her mother was still her mother and she needed to try to give it another chance.

"Mom, is there anything you want to say to me?"

"Like what?" Mom opened her soda can with a pop and it gave a slight spewing sound.

"I don't know. Is there anything you think I should know? Maybe about you, or about my dad?" Sydney took a hefty bite and forced herself to chew.

"You think because I lied about your father that I'm lying about other things?" She took a drink.

She tried to structure her words carefully. "If you were, this would be a good time to come clean."

"I was just trying to protect you, Sydney."

"How?"

"I couldn't have Samuel sticking his nose into our business, that's all."

"So you lied to him."

"I didn't lie. I just didn't tell him about you." She took a bite.

Too often, Sydney would back down when conversations got heated. Her mother had a way of making her feel guilty for even asking. This time, Sydney ventured further. "He said you promised to meet with him again and you didn't show up."

Mom's eyes flashed a subtle warning. "It wouldn't have changed anything."

"What do you mean?"

She took a deep breath. "They talk about forgiveness, Sydney, but they're not as forgiving as they seem to be."

"You mean, about your friend?"

"I don't know what you're talking about." Mom shook her head.

"Your best friend, that died. It wasn't your fault, was it?"

She was quiet a moment. "No," she said finally, "but they made me feel like it was."

They finished eating in silence. Sydney was afraid to ask any other questions. It was a start anyway. Sydney wondered if she would ever understand her mother and if her mother ever really loved her at all, or if she had only kept her so she wouldn't have to face the world alone.

CHAPTER 14

"*H*ere's some money for lunch," Mom said, handing Sydney fifty dollars. She set her purse back on the floorboard.

"Is the food there that good?" Sydney asked, exhausted from less than four hours sleep. She'd stayed up most of the night studying, and dreaming of home.

"It's for the whole week. If you have any left you can keep it."

Sydney got out of the car in front of the school building and walked halfway up the sidewalk, watching for her mother to stop at the stop sign down the street and then make a left hand turn out of sight. Sydney adjusted the bag on her shoulder. She then walked down the sidewalk past the school.

Down three blocks she found a Starbucks, ordered a large Frappuccino and parked herself at a corner table. She could make a lot of progress toward the test today. She pulled the computer and power cord from her bag and powered it up.

Six and a half hours later she started moseying down the street toward the school. She waited until she saw the flood of people coming out of the double doors, going random directions before she walked up closer. A few minutes later her mother drove up.

"How was it?" she asked.

"I...learned a lot today," she said, wondering if she'd told a lie or not.

The next day went pretty much the same. She had spent the day at Starbucks studying online for her GED and walked back to catch a ride home. She got into the car.

"How was school?" Her mother's eyes blazed like fire.

"Bad day?" she asked, sheepishly.

"When the principal calls to ask when your child will be coming to school and you know you just left her there, yeah. It's a bad day. How could you do that, Sydney?"

"I'm sorry." Sydney wasn't sorry, but she knew that was what she was supposed to say.

"What were you doing? I went to the mall and all the stores on the strip. Where were you?"

"I was at the coffee shop."

"All day?"

"Yes."

"Tomorrow you will be in school if I have to drag you there and sit on you to make you stay. Do you understand?"

Sydney nodded her head. She wasn't intimidated by her mother—not anymore. If her mom kicked her out on the street it couldn't be as bad as staying with her. But she was so close to being ready for this test, so close that it wasn't worth arguing about.

THE NEXT DAY, Sydney went into her first class and sat down in the back. The teacher gave a lecture on microbiology that made her sleepy, but Sydney had slept well the night before. She wondered why she hadn't had a night terror since she'd arrived, especially sleeping at such weird hours and sometimes not much at all. The whole thing had been so stressful, but for some reason when she slept it was sound. She was thankful for that. Since she'd been able to study at Starbucks for two days she'd gotten some sleep at night, making everything so much easier. Only now she had to go to school. Her mother saw to it, walking her to her first class.

Everyone had a computer opened in front of them, which gave Sydney an idea. She logged onto her GED prep website and studied, too. During study hall in the library she did the same thing. Pretty soon it was the last class of the day, Algebra. There weren't computers in this class, so Sydney did the assignment in the book. She completed it with no trouble and had some time to spare. It was the math portion of the practice tests she had always scored the lowest on. Sydney bravely got up and took her notebook to the teacher's desk. If she was going to pass the GED exam, she was going to need help.

"May I help you, Sydney?" Ms. Allen asked.

"What do you know about linear and quadratic functions?" Sydney smiled sheepishly.

Soon the bell rang and all the students filed out of the room, except Sydney. "Thank you for clearing that up for me. I know it wasn't part of today's lesson," Sydney said.

"No," Mrs. Allen said. "It isn't often a student is genuinely interested in mathematics. It's quite refreshing." She smiled.

"See you tomorrow, Ms. Allen."

CHAPTER 15

One Thursday afternoon, it finally happened. The computer showed passing scores on all Sydney's practice tests. She was worried it was an error and did them again the next day. They weren't the best grades in the world but she knew she could pass. It was time for her to go home to Swan Creek. It had been weeks since she'd left. She missed everyone so much.

After Mom picked Sydney up from school, she informed her it was time to get ready for a party. She was instructed to clean up and put on the little black dress.

"I told you I'm not wearing that." Sydney waited for her mother to unlock the front door.

"You have to." Mom walked inside and set her purse on the bar in the kitchen.

"It's against my religion," Sydney said firmly.

"Don't start that with me. So, you spent a little time on the Amish farm, you're not some backwards hick."

Her mother's words stung. Is that what she thought of the community? Her own relatives? Sydney went into her room to change, only she found all her clothes were missing. Everything was gone except the skimpy black dress laid out neatly on the bed.

"Where are all my clothes?" Sydney stood firm with her arms crossed in front of her.

"They're in a safe place. Put on the dress, Sydney. If you ever want to see them again, put on the dress."

Sydney thought about her choices. "If I wear this for you tonight, you'll give me my clothes back?"

"Yes."

"All of them?"

"Yes."

"*Tomorrow?*" Her voice rose.

"Yes, now go get dressed. We'll have guests arriving soon."

Sydney put on the dress. It didn't really match her braided hair, so she took it down and combed through it with her fingers. Maybe if her hair sat on her shoulders it would cover her body more.

Just a few more days, she told herself.

She met her mother in the living room.

"You still look...plain," her mother told her. Mom dug in her purse and pulled out some lipstick. She rubbed some on Sydney's lips and Sydney pressed them together to smooth it out like she'd done so many times before, but not in a long time. What must she look like? She was afraid to look in the mirror. She couldn't imagine what David would think if he saw her dressing this way again.

"All right," Mom said, "I'll be busy most of the night making sure everyone is comfortable and socializing. You just be polite and look pretty, okay?"

"I can't believe you're doing this."

"What?"

"Selling us both for some act just to get money. You don't love Dan. I feel sorry for that poor man. You've lied to him just like you've lied to me." Sydney made for her bedroom door.

"Sydney! Get back here."

"Don't worry, Mother, I'll play the part tonight, but not forever." Sydney went into her room and slammed the door.

She was leaving. Soon. She wasn't sure how or exactly when, but she knew she couldn't stay with her mother any longer. Maybe on Monday when her mother would give her more lunch money she could use it to hire a driver. Only fifty dollars wouldn't get her that far. She could hitchhike, but her father would kill her—if David didn't first. How would she ever get home? It wasn't like she could just call her dad to come get her. They didn't have phones in their houses and didn't even venture out this far from home, not without a driver. Sydney remembered David and Naomi's driver. Wayne Stevens. The man David and Naomi always hired to come and get them. He would come and get her if she could only find his name and number. Maybe he would understand and let her father pay when she got there. She wondered how many Wayne Stevens there were in the Asheville area. A quick Internet search brought up only two. She wrote the numbers down in her notebook.

"Guests are here," her mother called from the living room. Sydney could see the headlights coming up the drive from her window. She stepped out of her room and into the living room, standing up straight and tall, ready to greet the guests. More and more arrived, every few minutes until the living room was mostly full. Sydney shook hands and gave her name and smiled her best, but it wasn't long before the room started feeling stuffy and small, the walls pressing closer and closer in on her. Too many people she didn't know and she felt naked before them in the too-short dress her mother had forced her to wear.

When her mother was busy, Sydney slipped out the front door, onto the porch. The blast of cold was like walking into a freezer but at least she could breathe. She held her arms close to her chest, daring herself to stay out as long as possible.

Then, up the driveway, came the headlights of another car.

She had thought this would be all of them by now but no. Sydney watched someone step out of the passenger side door. Sydney took a step closer, trying to get a better view. The man walked forward, coming into the lights from the porch now.

It couldn't be. "David?"

Sydney could hardly believe her eyes. David stopped at his name and observed her.

"David, I can't believe you're here." She rushed down the porch steps to where he stood, frozen.

His eyes held hurt. "Maybe I shouldn't have come," he said and turned to go.

What? He'd come all the way from home to tell her that? Then she looked down at the dress, what there was of it, and all the bare skin beyond it.

"David, my mother made me wear this dress."

"She *made* you?" His voice held disbelief.

"She took all my clothes," she said in a small voice.

He stopped but didn't turn around.

"Please, David. Take me home. I was just looking for Wayne's phone number so I could call and ask him to come get me. I want to go home, forever."

He turned around and stepped toward her. She was shivering now.

"Then let's go home," he said.

"I have to go get my things."

"Do you want me to come with you?"

"No. I'll be just a minute."

Sydney slipped back inside, the warmth from the house not curing her shivers of excitement. She snuck into her room, closing her door behind her. She would need to take as little as possible to get away without her mother seeing her. She grabbed her notebook, scribbling a note to her mother. *Gone back home with David.* She tore the page out and left it on the bed, then shoved her notebook into the bag. She looked around the room.

Her computer. She stuffed it in the bag, too. But how would she get the bag outside without her mother seeing? Did she really even need all this stuff? Her coat was in the closet by the front door. She couldn't risk that. Her computer was just to study for the test. But she'd proved she could pass the test. Did she really need a certificate saying so? She thought about her birth certificate and social security card. Would she even need those things? She dug them out from under the carpet in her closet and slipped them in her Bible, leaving her transcripts that wouldn't fit. It wasn't right to let her mother use her social security number, she was taking them. Her mother had all her clothes. The only thing she really needed from this room was her Bible. David had given it to her and she wouldn't leave it. She hugged it to her. Then she walked back into the party like nothing happened. She was just about to dart for the door when Dan caught her.

"Sydney, I'd like you to meet Mr. and Mrs. Crumb."

"Nice to meet you," Sydney said, shaking hands.

"You certainly are a lovely young lady," Mrs. Crumb said.

"Thank you." Sydney hid the Bible behind her back.

"And I love your dress," Mrs. Crumb said.

"Thank you. My mother picked it out." Sydney gritted her teeth. When would the woman stop talking?

"Your father tells me you attend private school?"

Her father? She wanted to tell the woman that her father was an Amish hillbilly, rough and tumble, with hands thick and worn from years of hard labor, but also the kindest and most sensitive man she'd ever met. Sydney felt a tear starting to form and she quickly blinked it away.

"Yes. That's correct."

"Do you like it there?"

"I...have learned a lot of valuable information there." Sydney tried to be as honest as possible. The math teacher had helped her with the things she'd struggled the most with and it was because of her that Sydney finally knew she could pass the test if she wanted to take it.

"I bet you're already thinking about what college you want to go to."

"I'm thinking about going into business for myself, so we'll see what happens."

Sydney spied David outside the living room window, peeping in. "It was very nice meeting you, Mrs. Crumb, if you'll excuse me." Sydney walked away and seeing her mother and Dan both had their backs turned, she slipped out the door again. She walked fast past David and down the steps, and hurried over to the same car they'd rode in for their "outing" with Jeb and Emma. She got in the middle row of seats and slid all the way over for David. He got in and shut the door and the car turned around in the driveway. Sydney held her breath until they hit the main road.

"Where is your coat?" he asked, still shaking his head at her.

"I couldn't get it," she said quickly, feeling like a fugitive running from the law.

"Your mother took your *coat*?" His eyes were wide.

"No. I didn't want her to see I was leaving."

"You didn't tell her?" David raised his voice.

"You don't understand, David. She wouldn't have let me leave."

David stared.

"I left her a note. That's a lot more than she ever left me. She'll know soon enough. She just wanted me here to help them present a family image for clients. She didn't want to be with me."

"You knew that before you left," he said, his voice a little softer now.

"I've worked hard the whole time I've been here. And now it's finished."

"What's finished?"

"I can pass the test."

David closed his eyes. "The test again."

"It was always about the test."

"Why?" he asked.

"Do you remember the mark I made in your mother's floor with the iron?"

"That was an accident."

"I know that, but it was because I didn't know what I was doing. I'm tired of always feeling like I don't know what I'm doing. I want to accomplish something. And now I know what."

"What?"

"You'll see." Sydney shivered.

"We've got to get you something to put on."

"I can stop in town," Wayne said.

"No. Get me closer to home." Sydney wasn't going to risk being caught.

"I think there's a blanket in the very back," Wayne suggested. "I can stop and see."

"No. No stopping. Just get us down the road," Sydney insisted.

"Was it that bad?" David asked.

Sydney nodded.

"I could tell from your last letter it was bad."

Sydney had tried not to write too many details. She didn't want anyone to worry. "Why did you choose today to come?"

"That was my fault, Miss Sydney," Wayne said. "He wanted to come sooner but I couldn't come till the weekend."

"And what did you expect when you got here?" she asked David.

"I didn't know. I just wanted to make sure you were all right."

David climbed over the seat and into the third row then leaned over and pulled a blanket back with him.

"Thank you," Sydney said. "Thank you both."

It was a long night. Sometime, pretty late, they went through an all-night drive-through and each ate a burger and had a soda. After that, Sydney fell asleep on David's shoulder, listening to him chat away with Wayne, and holding his hand in the dark.

David woke her and the dome light from the car hurt her eyes. She looked through her window but saw nothing but darkness. "Where are we?" she asked.

"Home." David held his hand out for her, with her Bible in his other hand. She took it and he pulled her out of the car. She stumbled the first step. David took her arm into his and thanked Wayne as they headed for the dark kitchen door.

CHAPTER 16

*S*ydney awoke in her own bed, under the covers Naomi had made for David, still in a party dress, the smell of bacon with each breath she took. She'd made it home. David had came for her and she was so thankful.

David. Where was he?

Sydney climbed out of bed and ran her fingers through her tangled hair. She found David and Naomi in the kitchen, sitting at the table eating breakfast. He must have slept upstairs.

"Oh my," Naomi said when she saw her. "David said JoHannah took all your clothes. Is that true?"

Sydney nodded.

"We were going to go buy her some, but the store in town was closed when we came back through," David said.

"Well, she can't wear *that* to town. She'd freeze. Not to mention embarrass herself."

Sydney wondered what Naomi thought of the way she dressed when she first came. Short shorts, skimpy tank tops, lots of makeup.

Sydney didn't say anything, she just walked back into her room sleepily and removed the soft quilt from the bed and wrapped it around her. Then she came back to the breakfast table and sat down. "Any bacon left?" she asked quietly.

After breakfast, David disappeared a while and came back with a dress and *kapp*. It wasn't new and didn't smell the best, but David said Emma wanted her to have it.

"I hadn't thought to borrow a dress from Emma, but you did." She smiled at David for being so thoughtful.

"It's just till we can get to town and buy you more clothes."

"*Fabric*, you mean?"

He gave her a questioning look.

"I'm sewing my own clothes, *viel dank*."

He raised his eyebrows.

"And I'm talking to the bishop tomorrow about joining church."

"What about the test?"

"I didn't really need the test. I just needed to know I could pass it."

"So you're not going to college?"

"I never had plans of that, David." She shook her head softly.

"So it really was just for you, then?"

She nodded.

He let out a sigh. "I'm sorry I didn't try harder to help you study. If I had, you wouldn't have left with your *mueter*."

"It's okay, David. I learned a lot more on that trip than I ever expected to."

SYDNEY STOOD before the church in Emma's dress and *kapp*. The people murmured softly.

Then the bishop spoke. "Samuel Byler's daughter would like to be considered for baptism into the church. This meeting will be to discuss, and vote on, whether or not to accept her. Sydney, please state your full name."

She took a deep breath. "Sydney Ruth Glynn."

The room erupted in voices, murmuring to each other, some gasping.

"Silence," Bishop Amos said, and the room was instantly quiet again.

"Your middle name is Ruth?"

"Yes, sir." Sydney nodded.

"And your mother gave you this name at birth?"

Sydney nodded again. What was he getting at? Why was her name such a big deal?

"What did your mother tell you about the name she gave you?" His voice was so much less formal now.

"She didn't."

Sydney could hear sobbing from a woman in the back.

"Is there something wrong with my name?" Sydney thought back to all the times she hated her middle name, hiding it from everyone, but how her feelings had changed when the Lord entered her heart as she read the book of Ruth. She thought of it now as her spiritual name, though she hadn't told anyone that. Now it seemed like the name was a source of discontentment among the people.

No one spoke.

"What's wrong with my name?" she asked again.

"It's not your name they don't accept, it's me." Her mother stood at the back of the room, which was once again filled with voices. She strode toward the front, eyes locking with Sydney's.

"This people you want to be a part of, they will accept you and love you until one day when something happens that's out of your control they won't anymore. Like when they found Ruth and all eyes were on me. Every time I showed my face in the community people would whisper. I knew they blamed me. No one ever thought about my feelings. How I'd lost my best friend over a mistake made during *Rumspringa*. How every time I looked at my baby girl I could see Ruth's face and the children she'd never have." Tears were forming in her eyes. "I waited sixteen years to return, but it's still just the same. I will always be blamed for what happened to Ruth. You don't want to stay here, Sydney. Let's go home."

"I am home." Sydney stood firm.

Her mother laughed. "You can't be serious. You're never going to be able to join church. You couldn't even pass the tenth grade. I had to lie just to get you into private school. Do you really think you can learn Swiss German?"

"I do." Sydney fought back tears. She held herself straight and tall, never wavering. She wouldn't let her mother get the best of her. She wasn't stupid and it wasn't her fault she'd done poorly in school. She could learn the language, she knew she could.

Samuel stood. "If my daughter wants to join church, she's going to join church," he said firmly. "Just because you didn't accept our ways, doesn't mean our daughter won't." He stood there like a rock, unmoving, strong.

Her mother, looking around at the faces against her, shook her head and started to leave.

"Wait," Bishop Amos said. Her mother stopped.

"This is Ruth's family and none of them blame you for her death," Bishop Amos said, pointing to the back.

The crowd gave forth a family. They came forward and hugged her, one at a time, in a line.

"Leave if you want, but the anger you carry is your own. Ruth's death was ruled an accident by the police and by the people. She slipped and hit her head, just like anyone could have, had it been God's will that their time had come."

Sydney watched her mother wipe tears from her eyes but when they had finished she walked out the door without looking back. Sydney debated about whether or not to go after her. She finally decided not to. It was her mother's decision and the power of forgiveness had already been at work. If nothing else, it would give her mother something to think about for a while. Sydney's place was here and her fate hadn't been determined by the congregation yet. What would they decide?

One man stood. "Bishop, I make a motion that we accept Sydney as a candidate for baptism."

"I second that motion," said another.

"Then we'll vote. By agreeing to this, Sydney will be treated like any of our youth, allowed to take the baptismal classes and join church if she so chooses. She has spent her whole life in *Rumspringa*. However, she has spent very little time learning *our* ways. Because of the seriousness of the life-long, unchangeable decision of joining this church we will require two full years from now, living among us, before she will be allowed to take the vow. She will spend the time learning our ways, and the language." He looked to Sydney.

Sydney nodded. "I understand."

"All in favor, raise your right hand." Many hands went up. "All opposed, raise your right hand."

No hands went up.

"We are agreed."

Sydney drew in a cleansing breath. She really was home at last.

CHAPTER 17

That night Sydney attended her first singing. In the past she'd sat in the back during services and left when Naomi did. Now that she was no longer an outsider, she sat with Naomi, and when it got dark, she'd catch a ride home with David in his buggy, and experience what it was really like to be an Amish youth. She didn't understand all the songs, since some of them were in their Swiss German dialect, but in time she knew she would. If she could pass her GED test, she could learn their language.

She sat with Emma Wittmer and Emma's sister, Miriam, and when the singing was over, and the youth spilled from the barn onto the dark property, David was waiting for her. There was little socializing going on because of the bitter cold; most paired off and headed straight for their buggies.

"Would you do me the pleasure of accompanying me this night?" David held out his arm for her.

"I'd love to," she said, taking his arm with hers. She straightened the *kapp* on her head, wondering when it would stop feeling awkward.

They walked in darkness to David's buggy. He helped her up

then covered her with a thick, soft blanket. They rode together down the road toward Naomi's, a burdensome heaviness hanging in the freezing air between them.

"This has been quite a day for you," he said.

"Yes, it has." The sound of wagon wheels on gravel filled in the gaps in conversation. She needed to just say what was on her heart.

"The day you left..." David began.

"David," she stopped him.

"What is it?"

Sydney brought forth her confidence. "I want a man who loves me, not one that's just stuck with me. And the Bible tells me that true love waits. Jacob waited for Rachel for seven long years, but if you can't wait for two and a half then I'll find another." It had came out just as she'd rehearsed. Now she would wait for his reply.

David stopped the buggy on the side of the dirt road and turned to her. He took her hands into his. "It's a lucky man who's offered a first place in line to wait for *you*, Sydney Glynn."

"Do you mean that?" She was still unsure. She hoped to settle the matter and get these butterflies out of her stomach once and for all.

"*Ja*." He lifted her chin with his forefinger and kissed her on the lips gently, then he pressed his forehead to hers. "I don't believe Jacob ever regretted waiting for his Rachel and I won't either."

Sydney reached her arms around him, pulling him into a hug. He held her there with his chin upon her *kapp*. "I love you, Sydney," he said.

She pulled back and looked up at him. "I love you, too, David, but I think I'd rather be called Ruth."

∾

IT FELT like spring had arrived overnight. The Easter lilies beside Naomi's house had bloomed and Ruth stopped to smell one in the yard on her way out.

"Take some with you, if you'd like," Naomi said.

Ruth smiled. She quickly picked a handful of them and then strode across the yard to the shop. She opened the door and went inside, a bell jingling on the doorknob. She set the flowers down on the counter next to the receipt pad she used to add up order totals. She had a fire built in the woodstove in no time, then she set about straightening up the goods on the shelves. It was a Saturday, many buggies would be going in and out of the long driveway to visit her shop. Some of the women would be needing fabric to sew new dresses and the men would need rubber boots for keeping their feet dry from the spring rains. The children would eye the candy and board games, all appropriate in nature, unlike those found at the stores in town. Naomi would come in and visit later in the day and bring her a cup of coffee and a kind word. She would miss riding into town with David and Naomi, but she would help Naomi to bake up some pies for tomorrow's church gathering. She would just need to keep an eye on the window at all times for customers to arrive during the day. The shop brought in more than enough money for Ruth and Naomi to live on but David wouldn't allow her to use it for that. Her father had built the shop for her and wouldn't take a dime of it back, calling it an early wedding present. So she saved the money she made, only giving some away for charitable purposes, when the collection came round in church to help someone that needed it.

It had been difficult, at first, finding all the items to fill her store without a computer or even easy access to a telephone, but she'd managed to find some companies willing to work with her by mail. She turned a circle in her store, with arms outstretched, amazed she'd been able to accomplish so much in such little time.

"Do you sell your sunshine in this store as well? I'd like to purchase some, if that's the case." David stood at the front of the store with his hat in his hand.

"You're here early," she said.

"I wanted to see my *fro* before I took *Mam* into town."

His woman. He only said it when they were alone but Ruth didn't mind the term. She'd thought of him now as her man, though she'd never say such a forward thing out loud. It wouldn't really be official for another two and a half years.

"Well, here I am." She stepped in front of him.

"You could close up the shop and come with us."

"*Nay*," she said. "There's much to do here."

"I'm so glad for you."

"For what?"

"I've watched you change from a lost little girl into a grown woman, smart, confident, and hardworking, now running your own business."

"Well, I had good teachers."

"Speaking of which, how are your Swiss German lessons with Emma coming along?"

"Very well. She's going to start walking over when it's a little warmer. I told her she could hang out here anytime."

"Well, then you'll learn it in no time. As fast as you two speak to each other, I'd say in…just a few weeks."

Ruth laughed. She and Emma had become great friends.

David brushed her cheek with the back of his fingertips. She took hold of his hand and lowered it, holding it out in front of her. "You'd better get *Mam* into town."

His mouth turned up on one side, giving a half smile. He lifted her hand to his mouth and kissed it while holding onto her gaze. "I'll see you at supper."

She nodded, then watched him step out into the yard, the sun shining brightly now, putting his hat back on his head as he went. She watched the man she would one day marry climb up into the buggy with his mother. They drove away as another buggy pulled in. Ruth said a silent prayer for her family, all of them, for their health and safety. Lastly, she said a special prayer for her mother. That one day she would be able to forgive herself and return again, if not to dwell with them, then to visit, and one day see her wed.

ABIGAIL'S LETTERS

"Whoso findeth a wife findeth a good thing, and obtaineth favour of the Lord."

Proverbs 18:22 KJV

CHAPTER 1

*A*bigail Lengacher scratched out the order on her notepad. "So you want the whole set, right? The long bench, the short bench, two chairs *and* a rocker?"

"*Ja,*" the man said.

Abigail supposed he must be furnishing a new house. According to their Swiss Amish custom, he probably married last fall and spent the rest of the winter with relatives. Abigail forced a smile. "We'll have them ready for you in about three weeks." She watched the man walk out the door, the bell ringing behind him.

Another marrying season had come and gone without her. She hadn't expected the years to fly by so quickly. It'd been twelve now, since she'd joined church at twenty, six since she came to work at the woodshop for the Schwartzs. Jeremiah himself had hired her, before he died, leaving the business to his sons. She'd kept the books, took orders, and helped the customers choose furniture, especially picky *Englishers* who came through often, just to "browse."

It was a *guete* job, but Abigail only stayed to escape the confinement of her mother's house, where her newest baby sister needed lots of care and attention—attention Abigail couldn't bear to give. With each new child born into the home, she secretly wished it would be the last, that maybe, when the babies stopped coming, the longing for one of her own would finally go away.

It was impossible to get any privacy in a house full of people where she shared a room with two of her sisters. Mountain Woodworks had become a sanctuary to her. When no one was in the storefront, and the Schwartz brothers were in the back working, Abigail could dream. It was a foolish game she played in her mind, pretending that some of the furniture there on display was hers, in her own home, that she shared with her own husband. She imagined herself mending socks in the rocker after the baby was asleep, setting dinner down on the beautiful oak hardwood table, and letting her hair down at night before she crawled into a huge bed. She tried to picture her future husband's face, waiting for her, but the image wouldn't come.

Was it finally time to face what was probably her God-given fate, to be an old maid forever? Her friend Bertha, from the settlement to the north, would tell her not to give up hope. They wrote to each other often, encouraging one another, although Bertha had been the only one doing any encouraging lately. She had married late in life and lived many happy years with her husband before he died.

Bertha had arranged for Abigail to correspond with a man from her community named John. Close to Abigail's age, he too never married. At first, Abigail sat at her place inside the storefront, watching out the large windows each day for the mail to arrive. But as the letters came, and she wrote back, she realized any relationship-building done on paper would be slow as molasses. It had been months already, and he was still content to ask her how much rain her district had received in each letter— hardly anything Abigail could call romantic. Early on it had seemed he would get right down to business, but then there was a break in his letters, and she'd not heard from him for a while.

Abigail decided not to get her hopes up. She'd been hurt

before. Like when she was in her early twenties and the *beau* she'd had for years decided to marry another. She was so devastated she didn't attend a Sunday night singing for a whole year. After that it seemed like all the eligible young men avoided her. But the worst part came a few years later, when the people started calling her an old maid. She could hear them whispering behind her back. It was difficult to even make friends because she had nothing in common with any of the women her age in the community. She had stopped going to the jam frolics and quilting bees. It was just too difficult to relate to anyone there. She felt most at home with the Schwartz brothers, even though they didn't say much. Sometimes she ate her dinner with David, in the front of the shop, at one of the table and chair sets they were trying to sell.

Abigail glanced outside the window, still much too early for the mailman. Romantic or not, it was exciting just to open a letter, knowing a man was thinking of her when he wrote it. She hated to admit it to herself, but she knew if he'd just ask her, she'd say yes. Even in his first letter to her she would have. That was how badly she wanted to be married. She had given the woodshop's address to keep it a secret from her family. If they knew she was writing letters to a man, her sisters would tease her relentlessly, and her mother would pry. And besides that, if it didn't work out, at least this way she could suffer the shame of it in private.

Abigail had finally caught up at work after taking a few days off to help her mother get the garden ready for spring planting. The Schwartz brothers hated it when she went away, as she often had to, when her help was needed for frolics. They too, would be away from time to time, helping someone to build a barn, or bring a harvest in. It only bothered them because none of the Schwartz brothers liked to do paperwork. Each of the four men were smart enough, they just didn't want to do it. Of course, they'd rather be shaping wood pieces into furniture than figuring payroll. Even Abigail had watched them longingly at times, wishing for something different than the storefront chair that sat behind the counter.

The bells jingled, indicating someone was opening the door. In stepped David's Ruth. It was odd that people had already begun referring to her as David's. People should call her Samuel's Ruth, since she was Samuel Byler's daughter, and wouldn't be married for at least two more years. But ever since she'd come into the community she was only seen with David.

She was prettier than an *English* picture, and even more so now that she was plain. Abigail wished she were half as pretty. She hated her own dirty-blonde hair and the freckles on her face made her feel like she wasn't a grown woman, but a *mately*.

"*Goota morga*, Abigail." Ruth's use of the Swiss Amish dialect still needed a little practice.

Bless her heart. She's trying so hard to fit in. Abigail knew what it was to feel like an outsider. She would remember her in her prayers. "*Goota morga*, Ruth. I'll go tell David you're here."

Through the door to the woodshop, Abigail was met with a blast of fresh wood scent. She was glad for it. Later in the day it would reek of varnish. "David, someone's here to see you." Abigail raised one eyebrow and smiled.

He stopped what he was doing and laid down the hammer on the worktable with a clank, his expression of delight not well hidden. For such a reserved person, he was an open book when it came to his Ruth. He followed Abigail back to the front.

Abigail sat back down in her chair and pretended interest in the order she'd just taken down.

"Everything all right, Ruth?" David asked.

"*Ja*. I just had to come to town to pick up an order for the shop and I thought I'd drop by. Is that okay?"

"Of course," he said.

Abigail watched them from the corner of her *kapp* as they stood there, saying more with their eyes than with their mouths.

She wanted to be angry with them. Sometimes she was angry when she saw couple after couple find love and happiness, but these two belonged together. It would be two and a half years before they could marry, and at the end of that time they would deserve all the happiness in the world.

"Why don't you run your errands in town and stop back by for dinner?" he said quietly.

"I didn't bring any dinner." She laughed.

"Well, then I'll make up something for you in my apartment. It won't be anything like you and my *mueter* make, but it just might do."

David lived in the tiny apartment at the very back of the woodshop. He'd moved out of his *mueter's* house to let Ruth live there until they could be married.

Abigail watched as David walked Ruth out the front door, the bell jangling as it shut behind them. *What a man.* If only she were younger she would have done her best to grab that boy up. There weren't many men who would offer to cook for their gal on their dinner break from work, just to spend a little time together. At this point she'd settle for the more traditional type, like her *vater*, who would surely starve if *Mueter* was away for a whole week and no one was there to cook for him. Lucky for him, *Mueter* never went anywhere, and he had a house full of daughters for backup.

Abigail picked up the broom in the corner and began to sweep the floor. The spring rains had brought in mud that had dried into little brown patches, but she was thankful for something to do that didn't require sitting in the chair up front. Again the bell jangled and Abigail didn't look up, supposing it was David coming back inside.

"How are you, *schweshta*?"

Abigail turned, almost dropping her broom. She quickly propped it up against the front counter. "Jesse!" She rushed to where her brother stood with his hat in hand. He was a widower now, his *fro* having died of a rare brain cancer several months ago. He looked like he'd aged another ten years since they'd put her in the grave.

"Are you thinking of moving back into the district?" Abigail asked. Jesse was one of her closest siblings in age, maybe that was why they had always got along the best.

"I'm thinking about it. Maybe a fresh start would be *guete* for all of us." His wife had left him with four children to take care of, the youngest was only two.

"I think that would be a wonderful idea, Jesse. Maybe if you moved you could find a *guete* woman to help you with your *chinda.*"

The bell jangled again. A man entered, but Abigail hardly noticed.

Jesse nodded solemnly. "Keep us in your prayers," he said and held onto her arm.

The intensity in his eyes broke Abigail's heart. He was still in a lot of pain. So maybe she wasn't the only one who wouldn't get a happily ever after to their story.

"Always," she said, as tears began to form in her own eyes.

"I've got some business to do in town, but I'll drop by the house later and we can visit when you aren't so busy." He replaced his hat and walked out the door as David came back inside.

"Are you being helped?" David asked. Abigail turned her attention to the man who, she supposed now, had been waiting on her while she spoke with her brother. He looked to be in his thirties. Abigail had never seen an Amish man that old without a beard. He was tall and well built with dark brown hair and eyes. Every married man she knew had a beard and no mustache, even the widowers, like her brother Jesse. His hat and suspenders didn't look like what men in her district wore. *Perhaps they have different customs for widowers where he is from.*

"I'm looking for Abigail Lengacher," the man said.

"Well, you're in luck. She's right here." David motioned toward Abigail and then disappeared into the workroom.

"What can I help you with, sir?" Abigail walked behind the counter and stood.

"You're Abigail?"

"*Ja.*"

"Abigail Lengacher?"

"*Ja.* Do you have an order with us?" Abigail picked up the notepad, ready to thumb through it.

"No. I was told..." He stopped with a look of confusion.

"*Ja?*" She sat her notepad down again.

"I was told you may have work available here. I'm looking to relocate from Gawson's Branch. I'll be in the area a couple weeks to decide."

"There have been several families to move here from Gawson. It seems we have the only land available for a hundred miles. Do you have a large family?" Abigail couldn't help but ask. He was a handsome man and the practice of nosing when she had the chance had become routine for her. She wasn't really looking for a widower; she would much prefer to have her own children as to have half a dozen of them thrown on her all at once, but for him she may have to think twice.

"No, ma'am, I'm the only one."

Her breath caught in her throat. "I'm... I'm so sorry for your loss. It's heart wrenching enough when a man loses his wife, but to lose all his *chinda* as well? What a terrible tragedy."

"No, ma'am, you misunderstand. I'm not a widower. I've... never been married."

Abigail's mouth dropped open. "I do apologize, sir. I...I shouldn't have pried. I..." She thought quickly. She couldn't just say she'd never been married either. *Nay*, that would be much too forward. "I think we may have a job opening." She cleared her throat. "Wait here. I'll go get David."

Abigail hurried herself to the woodshop. Had the Lord

Almighty finally saw fit to answer her prayers? She knew the decision would need to go through Atlee, Asa, and Joe, but she hoped to plead with David first. Of all the Schwartz brothers, David was the easiest to talk to. As embarrassing as it was, she hoped David would understand the situation as soon as she mentioned he'd never been married, because she wouldn't dare to explain her fascination with the man further.

Abigail sat biting her nails in the chair up front for what felt like hours. She glanced up at the clock on the wall. The man had been in the woodshop with the Schwartz brothers for forty-five minutes.

Just relax.

What was she worried about? If they didn't want to hire him for a two-week job, wouldn't they have sent him away by now?

The sound of the shop door made Abigail jump. She watched David shake the man's hand.

"Thank you," the visitor said. David shut the door behind him, and suddenly Abigail was alone with an eligible man.

She stood and smoothed her apron with her hands. "Was David able to help you?"

"Yes, thank you, Abigail." The way he said her name was so personal, but he was avoiding eye contact.

"I didn't catch your name, sir."

"Reuben, Reuben Miller." He stepped forward and shook her hand.

Miller. Just like her penpal, John Miller, who was also from Gawson's Branch. Abigail wondered if they were related, but Miller was such a common name it was hardly worth asking. "It's nice to meet you. So you'll be working here for a few weeks?" She hoped.

"I was told to take an hour for dinner and come right back."

"Oh, that's wonderful. I'm...so glad we could help."

The bell jangled and in came Ruth with a bag from McDonald's.

"I think they just quit for dinner break," Abigail said to her. "You can go on back."

"*Danki*," Ruth said.

Abigail waited until Ruth closed the door behind her before speaking again. "Would you like to get some dinner?" Wait. Did she just ask him to have dinner with her? What was she, some *Englisher* woman? How terribly forward. "I mean...or I could bring you something back from town. The guys usually bring something with them or go home, but my house, my *vater's* house, it's too far away for that." Oh, how she wished she hadn't said all that. What kind of a fool would he think she was? She opened her mouth to say more but then closed it again tight. This was a problem that could only be fixed with silence. It was his turn to speak. She pressed her lips together, trying to wait patiently, her stomach lurching in ways hunger couldn't cause.

"You won't be having lunch with your *beau?*"

Lunch? Who says that? And what beau?

"I don't have a *beau*. Or a husband. I'm not married, is...is what I mean." She cleared her throat.

He tilted his head and gave her a long stare. "I guess we could get some lunch together, then." Reuben walked to the front door and held it open for Abigail, its jingle a merry sound.

CHAPTER 2

*A*bigail arrived for work early with a bounce in her step. She'd brought an extra large dinner today, enough for two. The day before, she'd met Reuben, a very nice man who, like herself, was in his thirties and still not married. She hoped he was a gift from the *guete* Lord, an answer to her prayers at last. She unlocked the door and stood leaning on the edge of the tall counter, watching out the large windows.

A few minutes later a buggy rolled in. He would lead his horse to the stall out back and soon be jangling the door.

Abigail paced. She grabbed the broom and swept the floor. It couldn't be dirty. The very last thing she'd done before locking the doors the afternoon before was sweep. Still, she couldn't just sit. Not when there was a handsome, eligible man her own age nearby. Abigail prayed for God's will in her life and to help her hold her tongue, so she wouldn't make a fool of herself like yesterday.

Finally the bell jangled and Reuben walked in. He removed his hat. "It's beautiful weather for this time of year, isn't it?"

Abigail nodded. "*Ja*. It is." She clenched her jaw against the awkward silence that followed. "Were you able to find any properties yet?"

"What's that?" He turned his ear slightly toward her.

"I thought you were looking for land to buy so you could move into the district."

"Yes. I am. But there are other things I'm looking for as well." He caught her gaze.

Was he implying... Of course he was. Why wouldn't he be? They were both unmarried. Abigail's heart thumped wildly.

The door jangled again and Asa and Joe walked in. "Well, Reuben, are you ready for another hard day's work?" Asa slapped Reuben on the back.

"Yes, sir." Reuben smiled. It was odd that he had called Asa sir. Asa was probably six or eight years younger than Reuben and it just wasn't the usual manner in which men talked. Abigail watched them all disappear into the woodshop and close the door.

Dinner break was hours away and Abigail forced herself to stay busy. It wasn't time to do payroll, but she got everything in order for it to be done later in the week. She caught up all the books and started cleaning things that hadn't been cleaned in years. She went through boxes of paperwork, throwing out what was obviously unimportant, then arranging what was left into organized piles and eventually stacked it all back neatly where she found it. Then she'd hunt for another stack somewhere and do the same.

Behind her chair in the corner was a tall bookshelf. Abigail wasn't nearly as tall as any of the Schwartz men were, and had to stand on a chair to reach the high shelves. She organized each one and dusted it before returning the items. She found old hinges, a spray paint can, a small paintbrush, a handful of screws, and a few dust bunnies mixed in with papers, some that looked rather important, such as the store's business license.

Wasn't that supposed to be hung up for everyone to see?

Abigail shook her head. She pulled another stack of papers from the shelf and hopped down from the chair, hovering over the trash can. On the top was a sale ad for a local business. She dropped that into the trash. Next was a glossy cardstock that said it could save the business a lot of money on their Internet service. She dropped that one, too. Then she was just holding a letter with her name on it. It was from her penpal, John. She read the date. It had been sent over a month ago. Abigail's cheeks flashed hot.

Was it really that hard for the Schwartz brothers to manage when she was away, tucking the mail in any old crevice, rather than just leaving it in a stack behind the counter where she could find it? She wanted to kick Asa. She knew it was him. The other three had much better sense—and weren't quite as tall.

Dear Abigail,

I know this is very sudden of me after only a few letters, but after much prayer I've decided to take the chance. I think God has allowed us to find each other for a reason. I know from talking with your friend Bertha that you are an honest, God-fearing woman who would make a guete wife. With your permission, I'd like to come visit you so I can ask for your hand in marriage in person. With your acceptance, I promise to be faithful and to love and serve you the rest of my days.

I anxiously await your response,

John

Abigail rushed herself over to her chair and sat, taking in large gulps of air and almost missing the chair completely. She caught herself and slid all the way back in its seat, letting herself digest this new information. Somewhere out there was a man who wanted to marry her.

But the date.

She looked at the mail stamp again. Oh, how she wanted to

kick Asa. If her chances for marriage were ruined she would do more than just kick him.

Oh, merciful heavens!

She prayed that the Lord would forgive her for her anger. But now what was she to do about the letter? He was waiting for a response. And she'd written to him since and said nothing of his proposal. What must he think of her? She had to write him.

Today.

Before the mail went out. She put the letter away and grabbed a pen and paper, staring at it long and hard. She was still staring at it when Reuben walked into the store front.

"Would you like to go to lunch with me today, Abigail?" he asked.

She put her hand over her mouth and held it there. She had to keep her words in until she'd organized them properly. It certainly wouldn't do for her to blurt out what was on her mind at the very moment. He stepped forward and held out his hand to her.

How incredibly forward. Does he mean to sweep me off my feet in only two weeks? She took his hand and stood, leaving the blank piece of paper and pen behind.

He let go of her hand, his brown eyes twinkling. "We could walk to the restaurant down the street or I could hitch up and we could go somewhere further into town."

"I brought dinner today," she somehow managed to get out.

"Oh." His face fell at her words.

"But I brought enough for both of us."

Reuben smiled. "That sounds good."

They sat down at one of the table and chair sets in the store-front, close to the window. The sun shone in, warming Abigail's black *kapp*. They only had about an hour and Abigail wanted to ask him everything, but where to start? The silence was deafening.

Finally Reuben put his sandwich down. "Tell me, Abigail.

How is it that a beautiful young woman like yourself isn't married?"

Abigail could feel the heat in her cheeks. She supposed when you got to the old maid stage there was no time left for small talk. It was an intense way to get to know each other, but she appreciated that he was so straightforward. She took another bite of her sandwich, trying to form an answer. Did he really just call her young and beautiful? "No one's ever asked me," she said finally.

"No one?" He sounded surprised.

Abigail shook her head then remembered the letter. Well, she hadn't meant to lie and she certainly couldn't explain it now. She took another bite of her sandwich. She supposed if he was going to ask the tough questions, then she could, too. "Why haven't you married?"

"It's a long story." He frowned a little.

"We've got about an hour." She smiled, glad the focus was on him for a bit.

He took a deep breath. "When I was sixteen I left the community with the intentions of never coming back. I was young and didn't want to listen to what my father had taught me. I didn't want to end up with the same life as my father had. So I went to school, got a job and an apartment and for over fifteen years I lived like an *Englisher*."

It was surprising but it made sense. He didn't talk or act like most Amish men.

"Go on."

"I never really fit into their world. It was always too loud, too fast. No one understood me. I went on dates but *Englisher* women are very…different."

Abigail laughed. She knew how different *Englishers* could be from working at the woodshop. She couldn't imagine trying to court an *Englisher* man.

"I knew it was time to come back to the fold. I wished I would have done it years sooner, but I know I wouldn't have learned as much."

"Was it difficult, coming back?"

"The church welcomed me, but I'm not exactly treated the same as everyone else. I tried to court a widow last year but it turns out she didn't trust me with her children, having lived an *Englisher* life so long."

"And the men?" Abigail had to ask.

He gave her a questioning look.

"None of the women here treat me as equals." She lowered her head, staring into her lap.

"Ah, yes. I've been called an 'old boy.' To them, you're not a man if you haven't yet married, no matter your age. Beards weren't that popular in the *Englisher* world, so I never worried about not having one. And just coming back into the community I didn't want to raise a fuss about it. It is definitely more humble for me to shave—but I didn't realize it would be quite so *humbling*."

Abigail hadn't ever thought about a man having the same feelings of isolation as she had. *A kindred spirit.* He was very open, so unlike talking to the Schwartz brothers—even David.

"I pray you find everything you're looking for here."

"Oh, I think I may have found everything I needed already."

Abigail cleared her throat and then took another bite of her sandwich. Kindred spirits had to stick together, right?

It wasn't until Reuben returned to work and Abigail was once again alone in the storefront, faced with the pen and pad of paper, that she remembered the letter. She would need to write a response to John, but whatever would she say? She sat down in her chair with the pen to the corner of her mouth. She couldn't believe this was happening to her.

Merciful heavens.

How did she go from believing she'd be an old maid forever to having two suitors on the line in a matter of two days?

Abigail watched the mailman stop at the mailbox outside. What must the poor man, John, be thinking? That she'd strung him along all this time, not giving him a straight *ja* or *nay*? And her good friend Bertha had arranged for them to write. What would she think if she knew? Surely she would have mentioned it by now; they wrote letters to each other weekly. Maybe it was God's doing, keeping that letter from her all this time. Maybe Reuben was the one she was supposed to be with. It was bothersome though, that he'd been living in the *Englisher* world for so long. What had he been doing all that time, and what had he experienced that Abigail hadn't?

But he'd come back and joined church. Should he be punished for his past?

Which man would be the best *vater* to her children? Abigail tried, but she simply didn't know enough about either one of them to make any kind of decision. Would she end up casting lots?

Lands, what a way to pick a husband.

She hoped it didn't come to that, but if it worked for preachers and bishops maybe it would help her find true love. She owed John an answer and as soon as possible.

CHAPTER 3

$\mathcal{I}$t had taken John Reuben Miller most of the day to travel to the Swan Creek Swiss Amish settlement. Luckily, Mountain Woodworks furniture store was on the main highway, close to town. He checked the address on the envelope again. Yup, this was the place. He took a deep breath. With any luck, he'd come out engaged—if Abigail Lengacher was willing, that is. He still couldn't understand why she hadn't responded to his proposal letter. Had he moved too quickly for her? That had become a fault of his, but he figured at their age, she would be just as eager to marry as he was. He hopped down from his buggy and stood as tall as he could, stretching his muscles after a long buggy ride. He felt nauseous, but this was no time to give in to nervousness. He tried to picture his father in this situation. He'd never seen his father nervous in his life. It was now or never.

In the parking lot, a young Amish couple stood close to a buggy. It was easy to see they were in love just by their body language and how closely they stood. He prayed for the same for his life; if it only be God's will, he knew it would be so. He entered the door, causing a bell to sound. Inside, a man and woman stood close, his hand holding her arm. They were engaged in serious conversation. The man turned to leave, his beard full, and the young man from outside came in.

"Are you being helped?" the young man asked.

"I'm looking for Abigail Lengacher," John Reuben said.

"Well, you're in luck. She's right here." The young man motioned toward the married woman and then disappeared into the back.

"What can I help you with, sir?" She walked behind the counter and stood.

"You're Abigail?" Had she married? Was that why she hadn't responded to him? But why wouldn't she have written to say so?

"*Ja.*"

This must be some mistake. Could there be another Abigail Lengacher working here? Had Bertha mentioned anything about what she looked like? He tried hard to remember.

"Abigail *Lengacher?*"

"*Ja.* Do you have an order with us?"

"No. I was told…" He couldn't ask her now. What kind of fool would he be to ask a married woman to marry him? But why else would he be here?

"*Ja?*"

"I was told you may have work available here. I'm looking to relocate from Gawson's Branch. I'll be in the area a couple weeks to decide." At least that part was true. He did want to move to Swan Creek settlement.

She nodded. "There have been several families to move here from Gawson. It seems we have the only land available for a hundred miles." She was beautiful. He had certainly missed out in marrying her.

"Do you have a large family?" she asked.

She thought he was a widower. *Because I don't have a beard.* "No, ma'am, I'm the only one."

Her eyes changed shape immediately, pain behind them. "I'm…I'm so sorry for your loss. It's heart wrenching enough when a man loses his wife, but to lose all his *chinda* as well? What a terrible tragedy."

"No, ma'am, you misunderstand. I'm not a widower. I've... never been married." Oh, he had hoped this would have played out differently. If only she weren't married herself, then he wouldn't be so embarrassed by it.

Abigail's mouth dropped open. "I do apologize, sir. I...I shouldn't have pried. I...I think we may have a job opening." She cleared her throat. "Wait here. I'll go get David."

Her eyes held pity for him. He could see it. He watched her disappear behind a door at the back of the store room. It was a mistake coming here. He thought for a moment about just walking out the door and not looking back.

It was several minutes before she returned with the young man he'd seen outside. He hardly looked old enough to work there, much less to be the one to make all the decisions. He introduced himself as David Schwartz and led John Reuben in the back to meet his brothers. They asked him about his district and he had to explain that he had recently come back into the fold and joined church. In the *Englisher* world they would have asked him about his work experience, but not here. They spent the rest of the time until lunch showing him how to spray varnish on a table top evenly, so it didn't run, and so there were no bubbles.

"Thank you," John Reuben said, shaking David's hand as he came back to the front. He had to admit, it was nice to have a job without filling out three pages of paperwork front and back to get it.

"Was David able to help you?" Abigail stood in front of him.

"Yes, thank you, Abigail." He'd almost forgotten why he was there in the first place. To ask Abigail to be his wife. Only he was too late.

"I didn't catch your name, sir."

"Reuben, Reuben Miller." He only went by John Reuben because there were already two men named John in his family.

Most of the Amish men he knew didn't even have middle names, only the initials of their parents. It made him feel like a boy anyway, and this trip was about changing the things he didn't like about his life. He stepped forward and shook her hand, trying to keep the look of disappointment off his face.

"It's nice to meet you. So you'll be working here for a few weeks?"

"I was told to take an hour for dinner and come right back." He forced a smile.

"Oh, that's wonderful. I'm...so glad we could help."

The young woman from the parking lot entered with a bag from McDonald's.

"I think they just quit for dinner break," Abigail said to her. "You can go on back."

"*Danki*," the young woman said, her accent, he couldn't quite place.

Abigail waited until she closed the door behind her before speaking again. "Would you like to get some dinner? I mean...or I could bring you something back from town. The guys usually bring something with them or go home, but my house, my *vater's* house, it's too far away for that."

Why was she so flustered? "You won't be having lunch with your *beau?*"

"I don't have a *beau*. Or a husband. I'm not married, is...is what I mean." She cleared her throat.

Not married? He tilted his head and gave her a long stare. Maybe God *had* brought him here for a good reason. "I guess we could get some lunch together, then." Reuben held the door open for Abigail, the hope within his heart restored.

They rode together into the town of Asheville to a little café, just down the road from the furniture store.

"Do you live far from here?" Reuben asked at the table.

"About two miles. It's not a bad drive, except in the winter."

"Did you get much snow?"

"It only snowed once all winter, on Christmas day."

"What a blessing," Reuben said, watching Abigail's eyes twinkle. The soft brown freckles on her cheeks brought out the brilliant blue in her eyes.

The waitress came and they each ordered a light lunch of soup and salad. It was difficult to talk to Abigail and not reveal what was really on his heart, but he would have to speak openly if he wanted this to work. It was important to let her know everything. He would have to tell her the truth, that he was the man who proposed marriage to her foolishly in a letter. But not just yet. He had come on too strong last time and scared her. He was lucky to be getting a second chance at all.

CHAPTER 4

he next day Reuben prayed for God's hand in his relationship with Abigail and for the strength to tell her the truth as soon as he could. But as he walked in and saw her standing there, he froze. "It's beautiful weather for this time of year, isn't it?" was all he could say when he looked at her pretty face. Oh, why did he always have to talk about the weather when he was nervous?

Abigail nodded. "*Ja*. It is."

How would he ever be able to tell her the truth?

"Were you able to find any properties yet?"

"What's that?" He pretended he couldn't hear her, buying him some time to form a response, and turned his ear slightly toward her.

"I thought you were looking for land to buy, so you could move into the district."

"Yes. I am. But there are other things I'm looking for as well." He caught her gaze. *Say it now, while we're alone.* He opened his mouth.

The door jangled and Asa and Joe Schwartz walked in. "Well,

Reuben, are you ready for another hard day's work?" Asa slapped Reuben on the back.

"Yes, sir." Reuben smiled as they ushered him into the back.

It wasn't long until lunchtime. He found Abigail alone in the store front. "Would you like to go to lunch with me today, Abigail?" he asked.

She put her hand over her mouth. For a moment, he imagined she was already his wife. He stepped forward and held out his hand to her, pulling her upright to stand before him. He imagined kissing her, but knew better than to try it. "We could walk to the restaurant down the street or I could hitch up and we could go somewhere further into town."

"I brought dinner today," she said.

"Oh." He hadn't planned on that.

"But I brought enough for both of us."

Reuben smiled. She was already thinking of him. That was a good sign.

CHAPTER 5

*A*bigail fretted until closing time. She would need to figure all this out and quick. The only way she could think of was to invite Reuben for supper, even if she knew she'd regret it. For her family to know all her business would be beyond embarrassing, but what could she do? She had to get to know him—fast. It wasn't long before he opened the shop door.

"Would you like to join my family for supper?" Finally, she was able to get out a sentence without tripping over it.

"I'd like that."

"*Guete*. If you're ready, you can follow me home." She knew her whole family would be surprised that a man was showing interest in her, but she hoped they wouldn't embarrass her too badly.

THERE WERE twelve in the house for supper that night. Abigail and her sisters set up a smaller table to the side for the youngest family members. *Vater* sat eyeballing Reuben as *Mueter* lightly bounced the baby in the crook of her arm.

"So, Reuben," her *vater* began. "What kind of work do you do?"

"I want to start a buggy shop, and if the Lord be willing, I'd like to do it here, in Swan Creek settlement."

Buggy making? What was he doing in the woodworking shop if his trade was buggy making?

"A business man, eh?" *Vater* said, looking somewhat impressed.

"I've found it's too hard to make a living working for someone else."

"That's smart, boy."

Abigail remembered what Reuben had said about always being treated like a boy instead of a man, but if he was bothered by the comment, it didn't show.

Her *vater* took a roll from the plate that was passed to him. "So, how's Abigail going to come into all this?"

"*Vater*," Abigail said. "Reuben is our supper guest, nothing more." She could feel the heat rising in her cheeks.

"I'd like to hire some hands at first, but eventually I'd like to find a partner or two to expand the business. I wouldn't trouble my wife with any of it. I'm sure she'd be too busy with her own work." Reuben never even looked Abigail's way.

"Well, Abigail is a hard worker. She's worked for the Schwartzes for six years now, and still helps with the chores 'round the house." *Vater* scooped a big helping of mashed potatoes onto his plate and passed the bowl to his right.

"*Ja*," *Mueter* spoke up. "And she's a fine cook, too. If you marry her you'll be well fed, that's for sure."

"*Mueter!*" Abigail said between gritted teeth.

Reuben smiled. "Do you know of any houses for sale, big enough for a family? I'd like to settle somewhere I'd never have to move again." Reuben took a bite of fried fish, rubbing his fingers together above his plate, as little bits of cornmeal fell.

"I think there's a real nice place over on Buster's Fork that might still be for sale." *Vater* began eating, but his eyes were on their supper guest.

Reuben looked up from his plate. "It wouldn't happen to be near any good fishing holes, would it?"

"It would. You fish?"

"Who doesn't?" Reuben gave a half smile.

"Abigail can clean a mess of fish faster than any woman I know," *Vater* said.

"Is that right?" Reuben's eyes opened wide at Abigail, who was shrinking in her chair.

"Uh, huh," he said.

"I'll keep that in mind." Reuben took another bite, his mouth beginning to curl up on both corners.

"I'll tell you what," *Vater* said. "If you take her off my hands, I'll give you two horses for a wedding present. That oughtta' sweeten the deal." His eyes squinted. Abigail knew what he was doing. He was trying to see what Reuben was made of. She'd seen it happen just this way before, with her sisters' guests.

"Some of the finest horses in the country," *Mueter* added.

"*Vater!* Please." Abigail put both hands over her face.

Reuben laughed a little, but then with a fairly straight face said, "I think if you'd throw in a half dozen laying hens we might just have ourselves a deal."

Abigail wanted to crawl under the table.

When *Vater* finally finished eating he stood behind Abigail's chair, resting his hand on her shoulder. "Yup, he'll do," he said quietly and then disappeared outside, leaving Abigail with her head down.

Abigail walked with Reuben to his buggy after dark. "I apologize for my family. That's just how they are. If my siblings had been allowed to speak freely at the table it would have been much worse."

"Your father's a hoot."

"An old goat, you mean." She would have words with him about it later.

"Just because he tried to pay me to take you off his hands, after boasting of all your wonderful merits?"

Abigail closed her eyes, wishing she hadn't invited Reuben over in the first place.

He patted the horse's nose. "I enjoyed your family, very much."

"Well, they certainly liked you. They only tease the ones they like."

"I'm glad. I think we all know why I'm here, Abigail." His face was suddenly serious.

"What do you mean?"

"At the end of the week I'm going to ask for your hand in marriage. I hope you'll accept."

The end of the week? Abigail swallowed hard, unsure of how to respond. As badly as she wanted to be married at last, she couldn't help but feel pressured at how fast everything was moving. She watched as Reuben stepped up into the buggy. He tipped his hat to her. "Good night, Abigail." He clicked his cheek and the horse and buggy hurried away.

CHAPTER 6

*R*euben kept the horse at a steady pace. He regretted the way he'd left Abigail. He shouldn't have pushed her like that. It was his forwardness that had scared her away the first time he tried to propose to her. He got the feeling that her family would accept him readily. It was Abigail he was worried about. She liked him, or the best he could figure, she did. But why had she not answered his letter? He would have to tell her eventually, that he was the same man who had written to her. But what if telling her ruined everything? What if he had somehow messed up everything by something he wrote in the very beginning? Maybe he needed an answer first. The end of the week was coming. He'd have it soon enough. Then he'd tell her the truth.

"Morning, Abigail," Reuben said to her as he came through the door on Thursday morning.

"Morning." Her head was lowered, but there was a smile on her face.

What must she be thinking? "Are we on for lunch today?" he asked.

"Of course." Her voice was soft. Reuben wondered if she'd ever whisper loving words in his ear. Had he been wrong to give her a time limit? Why couldn't he have just told her he was moving either way, and that he wished to court her properly? Oh, but he'd wasted his time before with several failed relationship attempts. He was done with courting and if Abigail Lengacher didn't want him then he was done with women altogether. He could build a little house at the furthest corner of the settlement and live out his days alone.

Oh, but her skin looked so soft. He longed to touch just one freckle and call those bright blue eyes his. If it was God's will, she would be his wife soon enough. He nodded to her respectfully before entering the workroom door.

ABIGAIL HELD her breath as he left the room and let it all out at once when the door at last shut. He was a *guete* man—a forward man—but a *guete* one as well. She'd save them both the anxiety and give him an answer at dinner today.

But he hadn't actually proposed yet.

Did that mean she'd have to wait for him to ask formally? She wasn't sure. Well, maybe she couldn't give an answer to a question that wasn't asked, but she could definitely express interest. Abigail's heart was running a race inside her chest. There was just one thing she needed to do first.

She had to write a letter to John. It was only right. He'd asked first and he deserved an answer. She did hope her friend Bertha would understand. Maybe she'd write her as well. Abigail got out the pen and paper and began. It was difficult to put into words, but she knew he would appreciate her honesty. She was glad, when she tucked it into the little envelope and placed the stamp on the front, that it was taken care of at last. She hurried it out to the mailbox, and with the raising of the flag she felt a sense of freedom and excitement. She was free to marry Reuben...when he asked. Oh, she hoped the time would pass quickly.

REUBEN WASN'T sure just what it was about Abigail, but something was different. He watched her eat spring greens and cubes of cheese with her fingers. She was more open, meeting his eyes boldly, rather than looking away with shyness. It was very... encouraging. He was almost certain if he asked her right then she would say yes, but he'd given her till the end of the week and he needed to keep his word. He'd rushed her much more than he should have already.

One or two more days won't change anything.

Abigail tilted her head and the sun's rays from the large storefront window caught the edge of her *kapp*, lighting up her whole face. "You're quiet today," she said, with a glow like an angel.

Had he been quiet? "Maybe I'm usually quiet and I've just been chatty since I met you." Reuben took a bite of his lunch.

"And why would that be?"

"Because I was nervous to meet you." It was true. He remembered the nausea he was faced with when he walked into the store for the first time.

"I don't believe that," she said. "I see you as rather bold—not at all timid."

It had taken a lot of courage to walk in that door. "You've made me bold. Otherwise I wouldn't be."

"It doesn't matter," she said. "I can see inside your heart, Reuben Miller. You're a *guete* man—an honest man. What's more for a woman to want?"

Was she hinting? He hoped so, but he hadn't been completely honest with her. Not like he wanted to be. He frowned, wanting to blurt it all out right then, but he couldn't. Not without messing everything up. "You're the bold one, Abigail."

"How so?"

"Well, for one thing, you went out on a limb for me to get me this job. And you didn't even know me." He watched her cheeks grow a few shades darker. He'd guessed correctly. Why had she done that if not because they were both unmarried?

"Well, how is it that you came to the woodshop in the first place, if your profession is buggy making? And who told you to see *me* about a job opening?"

She was onto him. "I...don't recall."

"It seems you have in mind a pretty bold question to ask of me in the next two days. That leaves very little time for wasteful chatter, don't you agree?"

"I do." He liked where this conversation was going.

"All right then. Name one thing. Ask anything of me, bold or otherwise and I'll do my best to answer." She sat up straight and expectantly.

She was challenging him. He liked that in a woman. A touch of orneriness sprang up inside him. He leaned forward and whispered, "I want to know how long your hair is, when you brush it down at night, and no one is there to see but you and the lantern."

She put her head down and cleared her throat loudly.

"Don't answer that. I shouldn't have said it, and anyway, I'd rather be surprised." She'd wanted boldness; that sure stopped her questions. He finally caught her eye, her cheeks coloring fiercely, but a slow smile formed nonetheless. So she wasn't totally put out with him. That was a relief. He would need to behave himself if he didn't want to scare her away. He ate the rest of his lunch in silence.

CHAPTER 7

The *Englisher* woman bent over, looking under the dining table in the storefront. The heavy purse on her shoulder slid around and almost hit her in the head before she caught it. "So it's solid all the way through—no laminate?"

"Of course, ma'am. All of our furniture is made here in the woodshop by Amish craftsmen, out of solid wood." Abigail had several lines she'd made up and memorized for the benefit of *Englisher* customers. She hoped the woman would leave soon. It was obvious she wasn't planning on buying anything today, and it was almost time for dinner break. Unfortunately, they never kicked anyone out just because it was time for dinner.

This could be the day, Abigail thought to herself. Friday was the end of the week for a lot of people in the world—mostly *Englishers*—but still, Reuben had spoken so openly with her yesterday that she felt in her heart he was going to ask her today to be his wife. She was ready to say yes. She didn't love him, but she knew she easily could, and the whole thing had felt God-ordained from the very beginning. They were both alone in the world without a helpmeet and God had led them to each other for a reason.

"Do you ever run sales on any of your furniture? Like a spring clearance or a summer blowout?"

Abigail stared at the woman. She didn't have a line ready for that one. "*Nay*, ma'am." Abigail wouldn't miss working in the furniture store, not when she had a house to keep of her very own. *Soon,* she told herself. *Soon.*

Just then the door jangled again.

Oh great, more customers.

She would never get a dinner break at this rate. Abigail turned her head. "I'll be right with…" She stopped at the sight of a familiar face. "Bertha?"

Her old friend gave a silent little wave from just inside the door, her wrinkled smile a welcomed sight. Bertha's dress was nearly identical to Abigail's, only a brighter shade of tan than was usually seen in Swan Creek Settlement, her gray eyes friendly and bright.

"Excuse me, ma'am," Abigail said as she hurried over to Bertha. "I didn't know you were coming. It's so *guete* to see you."

Bertha took Abigail's hand in hers. "I just wanted to come by and let you know I'll be in the area for a while. My cousin is having a big work frolic and I offered to help her with the food. I can see you're busy here, so I'll leave you be. We can get together some other time."

"Don't be silly. It's almost dinner time and we'll be closing up shop for an hour. Did you get my letter?"

"Not for a week."

"Well, there's someone here I want you to meet."

The shop door opened and out stepped Reuben. Abigail took Bertha's arm and led her to him.

"John," Bertha exclaimed. "I'd wondered when you were going to visit."

"John?" Abigail searched his face, guilt written all over it.

"I can explain." Reuben shook his head tightly, his hands held up between them in defense.

"How do you know Bertha?" Abigail tilted her head to one side, trying to organize her thoughts. Then it came to her. "John Miller? You're my penpal?" She threw her hands over her mouth with a gasp. "Why didn't you tell me?"

"Well, dear, who did you think he was?" Bertha's voice was high-pitched.

Abigail turned around, still covering her mouth with her hands. The *Englisher* woman was staring, causing Abigail's blood to run hot. "What are *you* looking at?" Abigail yelled, and watched the woman scurry out the door. Then Abigail turned back to Reuben. "Who are you?"

"I'm John Reuben Miller," he said slowly.

"Why would you deceive me like that?" Abigail's voice was an angry whisper.

"How did he deceive you, dear?" Bertha asked.

"I didn't know he was the same man who proposed to me in a letter."

"He proposed?" Bertha's face lit up in delight.

Reuben's jaw dropped. "So you *did* get my letter. I waited over a month for you to answer. That's why I came."

"Then why did you lie to me?" she asked.

"I...I thought you were married."

Abigail tried to bore a hole into his eye sockets with her stare. Was he trying to make a fool of her, making her think she had two suitors? She'd worried so much about John's feelings when all the while he was standing right in front of her, lying about who he was. "Why would you think I was married?"

He took a breath. "When I first saw you, you were having an intimate conversation with a man."

Abigail thought back. "That was my brother."

"I'm sorry. I never meant to lie to you and I was going to tell you."

"This doesn't feel right, Reuben...or John. I don't even know

what your name really is. I thought this was God-led but now"—
she shook her head—"I don't."

Bertha let out a whoop, breaking the tension. "Could
someone please start at the very beginning for me? I haven't
followed any of this." Her face drooped wearily from trying to
figure it all out.

"I can. Come on, Bertha. It's dinner time." She took her friend
by the arm and led her outside the store, leaving Reuben standing
there with his mouth open.

IT COULDN'T HAVE ENDED any worse than this. What had he done?
Reuben paced the empty storefront. Had he really managed to ruin
his last chance with Abigail? He rubbed at the tense muscles in the
back of his neck. Why hadn't he told her the truth from the very
beginning? He took a deep breath to fight off the urge to slam his
fist into something. It was a stupid thing he'd done, but maybe he
could fix it. It was only lunchtime. She'd be back to finish the day's
work and he'd straighten everything out with her then. He sat down
at the table by the window, and listened to his stomach growl.

Reuben prayed that God would give him the words he needed
to make things right. An hour later, Abigail returned. She came in
the door, causing the bell to sound. Thankfully, Bertha wasn't
with her. She stared at him like a deer would, in the headlights of
a car. He thought for a second she might even run out again.

"Please, Abigail. Hear what I have to say." He stood close to
her and dropped down to his knees, taking her soft little hand
into his. "I'm sorry. When you didn't answer me I felt like…like I
was a failure. I didn't know why you rejected me, but I still felt
like we belonged together. So I came. And when I thought you
were married I was going to walk away and not look back. And
then I was given a second chance. I hoped you'd agree to marry

me before I had to tell you. It was wrong and I'm so sorry. Please forgive me."

He watched as she seemed to ponder his words.

"I forgive you."

Thanks be to God. He let out a tired breath. "Abigail, will you be my wife?"

She nodded, a thin smile on her face.

"Yes?"

She was still nodding. So why did he feel so uneasy about it?

"I<small>F YOU WANT A FAST WEDDING</small>, we should do it while Bertha is still on frolic, it'll save her the trip." Abigail sat with her feet propped up in the dining room chair under the solid oak table on display in the storefront. The sun was starting to set. She wondered if she should return to work at all. She guessed one more day wouldn't hurt, to finish out the week. It would make payroll easier...for someone. They would need to finish up details as it would be too dark to see soon, and they didn't keep any lanterns at the store. Besides, *Mueter* and *Vater* would worry about her if she was too late.

"You really don't care anything about a big wedding?" Reuben asked.

"*Nay.*" There were so many more important things than big weddings.

"Come on. Every young woman dreams of a big wedding."

"I think you've watched too many *Englisher* programs on television, and I'm not exactly a spring chicken." Abigail wondered what else he'd watched on television.

"Well, if you're sure. I just want you to be happy." He took her hand on the table top and held it. She pulled it back slowly and took her feet down from the other chair.

"What's wrong?"

"Nothing. It's just been a long, exciting day is all." She hated that it had ended this way. Why did he have to lie to her? Things were moving along perfectly until then. If she had only received the letter on time she would have agreed to marry him sight unseen. She didn't know why it mattered if she planned on marrying him anyway. This morning she was going to marry Reuben because she felt it was God-led. Now she was going to marry him because she knew if she didn't, she'd be an old maid forever. She knew the outcome was the same, but she felt cheated, somehow.

Reuben stood and pushed his chair in with a scraping sound on the hardwood floor. "You'd better get home before your family starts to worry. We can work out the details tomorrow."

She locked the door and he helped her hitch up her buggy.

"Good night," he said.

"Good night, John Reuben." Abigail cued the horses and took off toward home.

CHAPTER 8

$\mathcal{R}$euben paced back and forth in the parking lot, the morning sun still low in the sky, waiting for Abigail to arrive. He had hoped she would be at work early today so he could talk to her. He'd barely slept all night in his rented bed in town. The look on Abigail's face when she'd left him and the way she'd called him John Reuben haunted him well into the night.

He let out an anxious breath as Abigail's buggy pulled in and he watched her hop down. "Can I help you with that?" he asked.

She motioned for him to go ahead. He took the horse while Abigail headed to unlock the front door. A few minutes later he met her inside, thankful no one else had arrived yet.

He held his hat in his hand. "Abigail?"

Their eyes met, sending a shock through him, causing him to speak boldly. "I know you don't love me yet, but I love you."

She snickered softly, looking away, her tone almost mocking when she said, "You don't even know me, how can you possibly love me?"

He took a step closer. "The Bible teaches that love isn't just a feeling we have about one another. It's an action. Something we're commanded to do. It says we should love our wives and I choose to love you."

"Do you really think God put us together?"

"I know it in my heart. Do you?"

She shook her head silently. "I thought I did."

Reuben's heart broke all over again. "Then I release you from your promise. You're free to marry another." His worst fears had come true. She'd met him and didn't want him. It had nothing to do with anything he'd written in his letters.

"You know there is no other. Unless I want to marry a widower, or a man half my age, which I don't."

Her words cut him deeply. "Then you're stuck with me, is that it?"

"I didn't say that."

"But you were thinking it." A tense silence followed. Did he want a wife who didn't want him? He hated to admit it, but he still felt they belonged together. Was it God or was it because it was his last hope, too? "Marry me, Abigail, and give me half a chance. I'll do my very best to make you happy."

Another long moment passed before she nodded silently. Reuben knew in his heart they were meant to be together, but he was still a long way from convincing Abigail. He was just glad she was going to give him the chance.

ABIGAIL SLIPPED the new dark blue dress she'd made over her head, and Bertha helped her tie on her special "marryin' apron." She'd spent a lot of time over the last week perfecting every stitch, wanting to think she'd have a wonderful, happy life with John Reuben, but there was something still nagging at her. Abigail stretched her shaking hand, which held a tiny mirror upward, to see her hair being wrapped in a bun. Larger mirrors were seen as vain and hanging it on the wall would be downright sinful. Abigail was glad Bertha was here to help her pin her hair securely—and to offer emotional support.

"Bertha, what if I'm not doing the right thing?"

Bertha took a deep breath and shook her head. "No one is perfect, dear, but you know he's powerful sorry about what happened. I thought you'd forgiven him."

"I have," she said. "But still, how do you know this is God-led?"

Bertha smiled. "God knew you were both unhappy being alone and He brought you together through all three of our prayers. Didn't you spend countless nights praying for the right man to come into your life? I prayed that prayer for you, too. And John Reuben prayed, and I expect every caring person in the community prayed it as well. How do I know this was God-led? Because I know John Reuben, that's how. That *man* is God-led. And you're promising before God to serve each other the rest of your lives, however long that may be."

Abigail sat in silence, soaking up the wisdom in her friend's words, remembering why she always went to the older woman for advice.

"You may not be head-over-heels, crazy-in-love with each other yet, but when God brings His children together like this, you can bet there's going to be a blessing waiting for those who are faithful and serve Him. That, my friend, is God-led."

Abigail thought a moment and then threw her arms around her. "You're a true friend, Bertha. I love you."

"I love you too, dear. Now let's get that *kapp* straight, so we can get you a husband today. Does that sound *guete*?"

"*Ja.*" Abigail wiped the tear from the corner of her eye. "I'm gettin' a husband today." Abigail's eyes widened at the realization of her own words.

REUBEN WAITED PATIENTLY for the service to begin. It wasn't out of superstition that he hadn't seen Abigail, but of sheer lack of time. There had been so much to do before the wedding. They still couldn't take possession of their new home for two more weeks. But if they'd gone with a traditional wedding in the fall, they would probably live with Abigail's parents until sometime in the spring anyway. He had hoped to talk to her once more before making her his wife officially, but it was too late now. It was eight thirty in the morning—several hours before he'd get the chance to speak to her privately.

He watched Abigail enter her father's living room and sit down on a bench with the rest of the women for the opening sermon. He caught her eye, and the smile she sent across the room set his mind at ease.

Soon the bishop called them to their places before him, and a moment later they promised to love and serve each other for all their days according to the scriptures in the Bible. After the blessing and the final prayer they were dismissed.

It was official. Abigail was his wife. It had taken hours, but still it happened so quickly.

People scattered in all directions. Women were in the kitchen, serving food, and the men were moving the long benches around.

Other than sitting next to Abigail during the noon and evening meals, he really didn't see her. It was well after ten that night before things had wound down and people began to leave. He found Abigail sitting on the porch and sat down beside her. "How are you, Mrs. Miller?" He wasn't just making small talk, he really wanted to know how she was doing.

"I'm exhausted. You?" She was so beautiful, and now she belonged to him. He loved her already as he'd spent many years entertaining the idea of her, but would she ever love him the same way?

Several men were suddenly in front of them. "Let's go, Reuben."

"Where to?" he asked.

"Time for a good old fashioned shivaree," one of them said, picking Reuben up. He struggled as they carried him off the porch and through the yard. But there was no getting away from a shivaree, and as long as he played along, he knew he probably wouldn't be hurt. He heard one of them unlatch the gate to the pasture.

"Where we goin', guys?" he yelled as the lights from the house started to grow smaller and smaller. He was starting to panic a little. He hoped they weren't going to tie him up and leave him in the woods. He'd forgotten to put a pocket knife in his new trousers.

"Not much farther," one of them yelled, nearly out of breath. They took him by the arms and legs and swung him as they counted off, "one...two...three!" Reuben flew through the air and he braced himself to hit the ground hard. Instead, he hit the cold water with a terrible splash. He sprang up quickly, gasping for air. Finally, he got his footing and stood. Swan Creek didn't run this far south—he was in a pond. A cow mooed in the distance. It was a cold, wet walk back to the house.

ABIGAIL WATCHED as her brothers and cousins carried her husband away. She figured he'd end up in the pond. At least she hoped that would be the extent of their orneriness. Her cousin, Jeb, was the only one she worried about taking it too far, but he'd calmed down quite a bit since he started running around with Emma Wittmer.

Abigail went inside and filled the water tank on the back of the wood stove to prepare a hot bath for her new husband. It was going to be a long night.

Abigail awoke to the sun shining through the bedroom window. She'd only laid down a moment while she waited for

John Reuben to take his bath, cleaning off all the smelly muck from the pond. Only it had been more than just a moment.

Where was he?

She changed out of her wedding dress and apron. The dress would now be used only for the most special occasions and the apron would be carefully packed away in her hope chest. Dressed in her "everyday" clothes, she went downstairs to find her new husband, the man she'd barely spoken with since she'd agreed to marry him.

She found him outside with some of her siblings, cleaning up the yard from the all-day celebration. They were laughing and carrying on while they worked. It was a beautiful thing to watch, a sight she never thought to even wish for, but a blessing all the same.

She went into the kitchen and found the breakfast her mother had left for her on the table. Apparently, she was the last one to rise. After a quick breakfast she joined her mother in cleaning up the inside of the house.

"There you are," *Mueter* said from the hallway, a broom in her hand. "I wondered when you'd re-enter the land of the living."

Abigail held the dustpan while her mother swept a pile of dirt into it. "It was a rough night," Abigail said. She still couldn't believe she'd fallen asleep waiting for her new husband to take a bath.

"Well, we missed out on a family tradition and I'm sorry about that."

"What family tradition?" Abigail stood with the dustpan in her hand.

"I've always taken you girls aside before your wedding and told you about the birds and the bees, but I expect you've done figured it all out on your own by now."

Abigail raised her eyebrows. She covered her mouth with her other hand, trying not to laugh at her *mueter's* plan to educate her. Doubting she'd missed anything useful, she waited for her *mueter* to finish.

"Just don't get your hopes up too high at first or you're apt to be disappointed. You've got your whole lives to get it right, that's what I've told every one of your sisters before they left home."

Abigail cleared her throat. "Thank you. For that. *Mueter.* That's very...*guete* advice. If you'll excuse me."

Abigail emptied the dustpan and brought it back. "I'm going to go help outside for a while," she said and hurried out the door, her cheeks burning. She ran around the back of the house and doubled over laughing. She knew her *mueter* didn't mean it to be humorous, as her family often did, but Abigail couldn't help herself. She laughed till her sides hurt, then she thought about her *mueter's* words again, and started analyzing them to bits. What had she meant about being disappointed?

*a*fter family Bible reading that evening, Reuben lit another lantern and took hold of Abigail's dress sleeve, gently leading her upstairs to their bedroom. He shut the door behind them and locked it, then set the lantern on the bedside table. He kicked off his boots and threw himself down onto the bed. It was so quiet he could hear Abigail's breathing across the room where she stood. He patted the bed beside him. Reluctantly, she obeyed.

"Are you okay?" he asked when Abigail didn't look up.

She nodded silently.

He could see she wasn't ready to be intimate. "I don't expect anything of you, Abigail."

She turned to face him, chewing on her bottom lip. "You don't?"

"No. We're not exactly a normal couple. We don't have to work on anyone's timetable, and who's to know?"

"You mean that?"

"Yes. A little progress now and then might be nice though."

One side of her mouth turned up along with one eyebrow.

"I'm just saying." He shrugged his shoulders, hoping to further dissolve the tension in the room.

Abigail stood once again. "I need to change into my gown."

"I can turn my head. Will that make you feel more comfortable?"

"*Ja.*"

He turned his head and when she finally gave him the okay, Abigail stood in front of him in a long gown and her *kapp.* She untied the strings and pulled it off her head. It took her a minute, but after an inner layer and removing many hairpins, her long blonde hair came tumbling down, some in the front and some in the back, like streams of gold, pouring over her shoulders and down past her waist to—how far? The lantern light wouldn't tell him. He drew in a sharp breath.

My stars, I've married Rapunzel.

She ran her fingers through it, shaking her head gently, and then climbed into the bed, under the covers beside him, and laid her head down.

He wanted to kiss her on the mouth, but he knew she wasn't ready for that. He would wait patiently. Leaning over, he kissed her forehead, taking in the sight of her, hoping to capture the image to form his dreams with, then blew out the lantern. "Good night, Abigail," he whispered.

"*Goot nacht,*" a sweet voice returned, reminding Reuben that the lonely nights he'd wrestled with all those years were now in the past.

ABIGAIL AWOKE TO AN EMPTY BED. She'd always been so good about waking without an alarm clock—until now. Her family must think she was up with her husband all night. Her face got hot and she tried not to think about it. It was difficult not to be self conscious though, especially with a family like hers, who would say anything for a laugh, no matter who it embarrassed. She prayed they would behave. It would be much easier once she and Reuben were in their own home, but then she'd be alone with her husband all the time and, of course, he'd expect things from her. Her pulse sped. She wished they could get it over with so they could start living down the disappointment her *mueter* had warned her about. Did every married woman go through this much stress or was it just her?

It was Thursday, the first open market day since it'd closed last fall. Reuben and Abigail followed her parents in their own buggy to the open field of tables, ripe with goods to sell, just outside of town. It was time for people to start seeing them together. The wedding had happened so quickly and they'd only invited close family and friends, so she knew it would come as a shock to some. Abigail counted on it. She kept close to her new husband, not letting him get out of her sight.

Abigail stopped at a table filled with canned foods. She picked up a large Mason jar of pickled okra. They would be visiting relatives for several weekends, receiving wedding gifts from them, and she knew some would give them canned foods for the pantry. She looked forward to when her own garden would produce enough to start canning.

"Doesn't your *mueter* grow okra every year?" Ethel Graber asked from behind the table, her wrinkled face a good match for her hard, wrinkled heart. She was always making snide comments to Abigail.

"She certainly does, but I'm buying for my own pantry today." Abigail handed her the money.

Ethel laughed.

Abigail's face flashed hot as she cradled the jar in the crook of her arm. "What's so funny?"

Suddenly Reuben was at her side, putting an abrupt ending to Ethel's mocking.

"Are you ready?" he asked.

Abigail gave Ethel one last look as she took her husband's arm and walked away.

That certainly shut her up.

"Is there anything I can buy for you?" Reuben asked, not seeming to notice the exchange.

"I have money." She thought about it a moment. "I guess it's our money now. I bought you some pickled okra."

"I didn't mean for the house. I meant just for you. I haven't bought you a wedding gift yet."

"That's really sweet of you, Reuben, but you don't have to. You've bought me a house. That's a present enough. I can't wait to see it."

"I guess it does kinda beat pickled okra to pieces, doesn't it?" His cheeks rounded as he smiled, making Abigail almost want to pinch one.

She laughed. They had strolled to the end of the aisle. Only one more left and they would have seen everything. There would be more vendors each week, as gardens and pantries overflowed, and as nice weather drove more people out of their homes and into the sunshine.

Reuben walked with his hands in his pockets. "A man back there tried hard to sell me his goat. I think he only had the one."

"That was Ebby. I don't want to care for a goat, do you?"

"No. What I want is to get the buggy shop going." He kicked at the ground in front of him.

"What do you need to get started?"

"Well, the house has a shop building and it will work, with a few modifications. What I really need are a few men who want to work with me."

"That shouldn't be too hard." Abigail smiled.

He raised both his eyebrows.

"*Mah.*" A little boy from the corner of Abigail's eye pulled at his mother's skirt. "What happened to that man's beard?" he asked a little too loudly.

She watched Reuben hang his head and walk a little faster.

"John Reuben," she said, pulling at his arm.

He stopped and turned to her, his face darkened with anger. "It's just Reuben," he said sternly, then took off again, leaving her standing there alone.

REUBEN SAT with his head in his hands. He couldn't even help his new wife into the buggy; he was too ashamed to look at her. Why had he taken his anger out on her? She sat down beside him and he grabbed the reins. The horse knew what he wanted without him even saying so. In a few moments they were outside of town, driving back toward Abigail's parents' house.

She hadn't made a sound since she sat down. Finally, he dared to look at her. She sat tall, facing forward, tears staining her cheeks, her mouth stiff. What had he done? He pulled the buggy down a dirt road he'd never seen before and stopped it close to the ditch where several sycamore trees slanted toward the creek, a long rope hanging from one the tallest, nearly touching the water below.

"Abigail, I'm sorry. I shouldn't have spoken to you like that. It wasn't your fault."

"I'm not crying because you raised your voice to me." Her high-pitched voice a stab at his heart.

"Then why?"

"Because I know how much that hurt you." She dabbed at the corners of her eyes with her sleeve.

"Then you're not mad at me?"

"*Nay*, J—Reuben. My *vater* yells all the time, but we know he still loves us, and our *mueter,* too. I can handle your temper." The look she gave him melted his heart.

"I don't usually have a temper. Only when it comes to that."

"*Guete.* Then we won't have to worry about it in a few weeks, then will we?" She smiled softly, her eyes puffy and red.

He wanted to kiss her. She was beautiful, inside and out, and she understood him so well already. She loved him, very much. He could see she did. She was loving him already with her actions. Such a gentle soul who cared for everyone. She just didn't know how to show him with affection yet.

ABIGAIL UNDERSTOOD the need for Reuben to do man's work that afternoon, she just wished he wasn't alone with her *vater* so long. There was no telling what they were talking about, out at the barn.

Unable to take it any longer, her curiosity led her to the back of the barn where, if she guessed correctly, she might be able to hear their conversation through a crack in the barn wall—if she listened hard enough. She'd eavesdropped there a time or two before. It was where *Mueter* and *Vater* came to escape their eleven *chinda* when they had serious, private matters to discuss. It wasn't a habit of hers, by any means, but she had learned that *Mueter* sometimes came up with the punishments for her unruly *chinda* and *Vater* merely handed them out. It was clever parenting Abigail would file away in her mind for later use, if need be. She wondered what kind of *vater* Reuben would be. The thought of what it would take to *get* children flashed in her mind and she shook it out of her head quickly. Reuben was an attractive man, but she was not looking forward to that first awkward encounter. They hadn't even kissed yet.

She heard the sound of them mucking out the horse stalls. A peek through the crack revealed it was Reuben working and *Vater* was watching. Reuben needed to work off some "man steam" anyway.

"So, how's it goin', son?" Abigail heard her *vater* say.

"It's okay," Reuben said quietly, seeming to be more focused on the work in front of him.

"That bad, huh?"

"I didn't mean it that way." He looked up at *vater*.

Vater was catching Reuben in his words. This wasn't going well.

"I know it can be hard living under another man's roof. It's not much different than having eleven *chinda,* if you catch me."

Reuben stopped and rested his arm on the handle of the pitchfork. "No, sir. I don't believe I do."

"Well, there's no privacy. But that's okay 'cause I'll tell you what I'm gonna do. I'm gonna let you use the barn here, any time you need it, after evening chores."

Vater! She wished she could yell at him. If *Mueter* were here, she'd do it for her.

"I don't think that's necessary…"

"Sure it is." He slapped Reuben on the back. "Now, you're getting a late enough start on your brood. Take my advice. Why, our last three *chinda* got their start right there in that hay loft. Abigail's *mueter* never had any complaints, and what's good enough for the goose is good enough for the goose's daughter, you catch me?"

"I…I catch you." Reuben wore a goofy grin.

Abigail had heard enough. *The old goat.* Couldn't he mind his own business? Butting into the intimate parts of her marriage. Of course, there were no intimate parts to their marriage—yet. But that still didn't give him the right.

After supper, Abigail's *mueter* dismissed her from kitchen duty. "You'll have piles of your own dishes to do up soon enough. Take a rest."

Her *vater* stood leaning against the doorway between the kitchen and the living room. "I believe Reuben could use your help straightening up the hay loft for me, though."

One of her little brothers spoke up. "I can do it for you, *Vater.*"

"*Nay,* son, this is man's work. Reuben here can handle it."

"But why's Abigail goin' if it's man's work?" He scrunched his nose up at *Vater.*

"She's got to go along and make sure he does a *guete* job of it. Now don't let me hear any more lip from you. Go on."

The boy left the room in a hurry and *Vater* slipped a fast wink Reuben's way. Reuben opened the kitchen door for Abigail. If only her *vater* hadn't said it was *man's work* she'd have fled before he'd gotten the rest out. As it was, she had to go along. Her husband's dignity was at stake.

*R*euben took Abigail's hand in his when they were safely outside the house. He knew no one would be disturbing them, his new father-in-law would see to that. "I'll explain everything, once we get to the barn loft."

A few moments later Reuben held his hand out to Abigail at the top of the ladder.

"So, you were going to explain everything?" She took his hand and stepped up into the loft beside him.

He pointed his finger in the direction of the house. "Okay. Your father…and your mother…hmmm. How do I put this?"

Abigail laughed. "I know what my *vater* wants us to do up here."

"You do?"

"It's my *vater* we're talking about."

Reuben breathed a sigh of relief. "Well, from the looks of it I'd say your mother might have been in on it, too." He knew their plan wouldn't work on Abigail, but he admired their spunk about it anyway. His own mother and father were quite the opposite, always serious about everything. He wondered if Abigail ever appreciated her parents' playfulness.

"It wouldn't surprise me. I'm going back to the house." Abigail turned toward the ladder.

"Now, wait just a minute." He took hold of her hand, pulling her back.

She gave him a hard look. "You don't think we should…"

"No." He shook his head. "I mean…unless you want to…" He cocked his head to the side and leaned down to see her better.

"In the hay loft? Really?" She scrunched up her nose at him.

"Well, where do *you* want to start our family? I know you want children of your own. I can see it in the way you look at your baby sister."

Abigail got quiet.

"What'd I say?"

"I've never held her." She stared at the floor.

"What?"

"I've never held her."

"She must be what…eight months old or more? How is that even possible?" Reuben sat down on the floor of the loft, making himself comfortable on the hay, stretching his legs out.

"I went to work and my sisters help my *mueter*."

"But why?" he asked. He'd not met an Amish woman yet who didn't want kids of her own.

"It just…became too painful."

She thought she'd never have her own. Reuben's heart ached for her. "Did you tell your mother?"

"*Ja*, but she was the only one I told."

"I'm sorry, Abigail. I didn't know it was that bad." He wanted to hold her close and tell her everything was going to be all right, but she wasn't comfortable with him. He thought he'd been patient, but maybe he was still pushing her too hard.

Abigail sat down on a haybale beside him.

"Thank you for sharing with me. I think we grow a little closer each time we share. Have you noticed that? I tell you what.

I want you to tell *me* when you're ready. It won't always be this way, but for now, I'll just wait a little longer."

"Do you mean that?"

"It won't be forever. At least I hope not. Not if you want kids before we're too old to have them."

Abigail laughed.

"There it is. That's what I was waiting for. Come here."

She gave him a questioning look.

"I've seen you give your adult brothers more affection than me. No wonder your father's trying to help. I just want to hold you. Will you let me hold you?" Reuben held his arm out and patted his chest. "Come on."

She got down on the floor and sat close to him. Then she laid back with her head on his chest. It was a start. She was a good woman, but for some reason still hesitant. He hadn't even kissed her other than on the forehead before bed. He wondered how long it would take for her to warm up to him.

ABIGAIL LAID her head on Reuben's chest, wrapping her arm around him. She couldn't believe she was laying with her husband in the hay loft when they could be in the house getting ready for bed. But if they didn't play along her *vater* would only come up with worse ideas. She could hear Reuben's beating heart mixed with the faint sound of his breath. It was a strange, yet relaxing song. The warmth of his body placed a feeling within her she knew too well—longing. She longed to be close with him the way a wife is with her husband, only not here. Not in the barn or in her *vater's* house. Only in the privacy of their own home, and only when she knew she could trust Reuben not to laugh at her for being as old as she was and not knowing the first thing about what to do. For a moment she wished she had lived with the *English* all the years he had.

The next thing she knew she was awakening to total darkness. She remembered being in the hayloft. "Reuben?" She was starting to panic.

"I'm right here." His voice came from the darkness beside her. She felt a hand land on her arm. "Oh, merciful heavens! What have we done?"

"We just fell asleep, it's all right."

"No, it's not all right. Now it's too dark to get down. I can't even see the ladder."

"Well, we'll just have to wait till morning then."

"I don't want to sleep in the hay loft. It's cold out here. And what will everyone think?"

"They'll think we're a regular old married couple. Come here." He pulled her toward him, hugging her tightly. He was warm. It still felt strange to be so close to a man, but it was nice. His even breathing calmed her down. He was right. This was what they were supposed to be doing, they were married after all.

The next thing she knew, one of her little brothers stood over them. The light of day shone through the cracks between the boards. "What are you two doing sleeping in the barn?" he said, clearly amused.

A few minutes later they walked into the kitchen. The whole family was seated at the table, eating breakfast.

Vater smiled and said, "And what's good for the goose is good for the gander, ain't that right, son?" He slapped the table and his laugh echoed off the hardwood floor.

REUBEN SHUT the bedroom door behind them, a smile still on his face.

Abigail gave him a wicked stare.

"You have to admit, that was funny."

"Try it for thirty years and then we'll talk."

"Point taken." He tried to wipe away his smile. She *was* cute when she was angry, though.

"I can't stay here, not with the way they're all looking at me. Not today." Abigail was pacing the bedroom floor.

"Well, where do you want to go?"

"Home. Our home."

Reuben sat down on the bed. "I'm sorry, Abigail. We don't take possession of the house for another eleven days."

"Well, can't I at least see it?"

"I guess I could take you by there. An *Englisher* family owns it. They'll probably be moving all week."

"Can we go now?" Her eyes were big and pleading, like a little puppy.

He sighed loudly. "I'll get my hat."

*T*he house was white. At least they wouldn't have to paint it right away. Abigail couldn't believe she was looking at her new home. There was a shop for Reuben to work on his buggy business, a shed, and a huge backyard, the perfect spot for a garden.

"Well, what do you think?" Reuben asked as the buggy slowed near the house.

"I love it. Look, the *Englishers* are there, moving boxes." A man was walking with a large box in his arms toward a truck parked in the driveway. He set the box down and walked back into the house, the screen door closing behind him.

"*Englishers* are a curious bunch, aren't they? Look at all that stuff." She stopped herself. She'd forgotten her husband lived like an *Englisher* for over fifteen years.

Reuben drove the buggy up into the yard and hopped out.

"What are you doing?" she asked.

"Don't be shy. It's just like talking to the *Englishers* in the furniture shop."

That was what she was afraid of.

"Hello there. I'm Reuben Miller, the new owner." He shook

hands with the man as soon as he set his next box down in the truck.

"Well," the man said, "I'd heard it was an Amish couple that bought it. I'm Jim Mason. Good to meet you."

"Could I give you a hand?" Reuben asked.

"I suppose you're wanting to move in pretty badly, then?" The man was older, probably in his late sixties. Abigail got down from the buggy and came up to where the two men stood.

"I was just offering to be neighborly, but yes, my wife and I are very excited to move in."

"Well, I have some heavy furniture that I could use some help with. It might help us get out of here a little faster."

"I'd be glad to help you any way I can. We're free all day, isn't that right, Abigail?"

Abigail nodded.

"This is my wife. We were married just last Tuesday."

Abigail smiled politely. She was surprised at the way Reuben spoke to the *Englisher* man. She had been taught not to associate with *Englishers* unless she had to, and she certainly would never volunteer information the way he just did. Many people from the community had an *Englisher* friend or two, but they didn't go out of their way to make new ones.

A woman came out of the house wearing a light blue jump-suit, holding a lamp. She gasped when she caught sight of them.

"This is my wife, Helen," the man said.

Helen rushed up to them. "How do you do?" She shook both their hands while they exchanged names, looking positively delighted to see them.

Reuben followed the man into the house, leaving Abigail with Helen. It looked like they were going to be here for a while. Abigail decided to take Reuben's lead and offer to help. The sooner these *Englishers* got out of their house, the sooner they could move in.

"Is there anything I could help you with, Helen?"

Abigail soon found herself packing shelves and shelves of books into boxes. She wondered if Helen had read them all. She couldn't imagine having that much time on her hands to read all day, but then, working at the woodshop she would have. She wondered now why she hadn't thought of it before. It was hard to find appropriate books, but she heard Ruth was going to try to stock some in her new store. But she wouldn't have the time now, she could see this house was going to be a lot of work.

The carpeting would need to be replaced with a hard floor and they would have to put in a wood cookstove, install a hand pump for the well, build a chicken coop, an outhouse, and a place for the horses. The way it looked, they'd be living with her parents till summer. Abigail frowned.

"That there's my favorite book," Helen said.

Abigail looked down at the book in her hands, the one Helen was referring to. It had a picture of a woman with a lot of makeup, wearing an Amish dress and the see-through kind of *kapp* they wore in Pennsylvania. She was looking longingly at a man with a baby-face, dressed in a straw hat and suspenders Abigail knew no Amish district in the state would ever approve of. Wisps of her hair and the strings from the woman's *kapp* were blowing in the wind.

"It's about an Amish couple who fall in love, only their bishop doesn't think they should be together. So they decide to run off and be Mennonites, only he gets amnesia and can't remember who she is, but if she takes him back home they'll both be shunned."

"It sounds…lovely." Abigail handed her the book, not sure if she wanted it packed in the box or if Helen wanted to sit and read it to her. She hoped it would go in the box.

Around noon, Helen fixed ham and cheese sandwiches and some potato chips on paper plates. "I'm so embarrassed," she said, "but I already packed away the good plates."

"There's no need to be embarrassed. We all use paper plates from time to time," Abigail said.

"You do?" Helen's eyes were wide.

"*Ja*. We have a lot of gatherings where there'd never be enough dishes if we didn't."

"I hadn't thought of that." Helen pulled out cans of soda from the refrigerator.

Abigail wondered at Helen. How did the woman think they lived?

"Remind me after lunch and I'll show you where all the flowers are. Only some of them have come up and you may want to keep them. I planted a beautiful snowball bush that will bloom sometime next month."

"Thank you. That would be lovely." Abigail was glad they'd offered to help. She was able to see their new house and learn more about it, and the best part, they didn't have to spend the day at her parents' house.

It was getting along toward evening when she heard Reuben talking to Jim, "Would you mind if we went ahead and started working in the yard tomorrow? It's going to take a while to get the garden ready and we should have started planting it two weeks ago."

"You want a garden, huh? Well, I could get the tractor out and plow you up a spot. Wouldn't take more than twenty minutes. If that's allowed."

"The reason we don't use tractors is because it keeps us from relying on our neighbors for help. It gives us a sense of community that way. I think that would be a right neighborly thing for you to do for us. We'd appreciate it very much. And I can be around all day tomorrow if you need any more heavy lifting done."

Jim nodded and headed for his tractor, parked in the field behind the house.

Abigail and Reuben decided how big they wanted the garden

spot to be and a half hour later it was plowed. Abigail stood with her hands covering her mouth.

Reuben spoke, "Do you feel bad about it? I should have asked you first. He offered and I didn't want to refuse."

"No, it's not that." Abigail wiped her eyes on the sleeve of her dress.

"Are you crying?" He stooped over to see her better.

"Ja."

"Are they...tears of joy?" He sounded unsure.

She nodded.

"Huh," he said. "I did something right." His words were spoken matter-of-factly, but still she wondered about the meaning behind them. What made him think he wasn't doing things right?

DAYS PASSED. Reuben worked hard to get things set up at the new house. He didn't care what he had to do, they were going to sleep in their own bed the night he first held the front door keys in his hand. He hadn't asked for help, telling himself it was because the house wasn't really theirs yet, and he didn't want to bother Jim and Helen with a work frolic in their yard. But really, he knew he hadn't yet made friends with anyone but his wife's family.

When Sunday finally arrived he was ready for a day of rest.

Reuben sat in the third Lengacher home of the day and watched as the women all doted on Abigail. Her family presented them with dishes, towels, canned foods from their own pantries, tools, and much more.

Realizing all the men had left the room, he stepped out onto the porch where a young man stood. Well, he'd found one of the men at least. He leaned against the porch rail. "I remember you," Reuben said. "You were one of the guys who threw me in the pond, right?"

"That was me." The young man with hair almost the color of Abigail's stepped forward to shake his hand. "Jeb Lengacher."

"Nice to meet you. What kind of work do you do, Jeb?"

"Aw, about anything and everything." His voice was low and he had more of a southern drawl than a Swiss German accent.

"A jack of all trades and a master of none, isn't that what they say?"

"That's me." He laughed.

Reuben pulled at the growing hairs on his chin. "So tell me, Jeb, what do you know about building buggies?"

ABIGAIL RAN Reuben's shirt through the ringer, squeezing all the water back into the washtub. Her mother and two of her sisters were helping with the wash, but she wanted to make sure she was the one to wash her and Reuben's clothes. It would be fast work when she moved out, only having to care for the two of them, instead of thirteen—fourteen if you counted Reuben. The clothesline was already full; the rest would have to go on the front porch.

"Yoo hoo," a voice called from around the corner of the house, and a moment later Ada Hilty appeared with a blue bundle in her hands.

"How are you, Ada?" *Mueter* asked.

"It's a beautiful day and I'm done with the wash, if that doesn't tell you anything about how I'm doing then nothing will."

Mueter chuckled.

"I brought something over for Abigail."

Abigail dropped the trousers she was holding when she heard her name. Ada walked over to her and held out the bundle. A new quilt.

"For me?" Abigail asked. No one but her *mueter* had ever made her a quilt before. She wiped her hands thoroughly on her apron and carefully took it from her. She never thought she'd see the day when the ladies made *her* a quilt. It was from Ada's quilting bee that met weekly with all the ladies in the neighborhood. She unfolded it and noted a lovely triangular pattern in three shades of dark blue, framed in black around the border. Big enough for two people.

"It's beautiful. Thank you, Ada."

"Well, it was about time you got yourself hitched. Perhaps now you'll find time enough to join us for a quilting frolic now and then."

Abigail's eyes were misty. She was being accepted at last. "I'd like that."

*T*hat night, Reuben went to bed before Abigail. When she came in he was turned away from her. "Are you asleep?" she asked.

"No."

It didn't even sound like Reuben. "What's wrong?"

"Just tired." His voice was gruff, but she didn't sense he was angry with her.

She knew it was more than just being tired. She'd heard from *Vater* that there was still much to do before they could move in and only he, Reuben, and Jeb had worked on the place today. Tired was a good feeling; her husband was discouraged. She knew everyone in the community would help out if they only knew what Reuben wanted. But it seemed that he found it easier to talk to *Englishers* than to his own people. She hoped it was because he was new to the area, not because he'd spent so many years living in the *English* world. That concern had been on Abigail's mind a lot lately. She prayed that God would send her husband help in the form of *guete* friends. That He would lift his spirits and show him he was accepted, and loved.

REUBEN PRAYED that today would go better than yesterday. Jim and Helen had turned over the outbuildings to him and given over the whole yard. It should have been a productive day, but nothing went right. After two trips into town for the right supplies and still no progress, Reuben was ready to call it a day. They spent the rest of the afternoon cleaning up the yard and picking rocks from the garden—women's work.

Abigail rode beside Reuben in the buggy. He hoped she wouldn't see him fail again today. All he wanted was to get them moved out of her parents' house to make her happy. Maybe then they could spend some time working on their relationship.

There were several buggies parked in the yard when they pulled up. His father-in-law had with him two of his married sons. Jeb was also there with his father, and a couple of his brothers. A few minutes later, David Schwartz arrived with Asa and Joe. Reuben hadn't asked any of them, but somehow they knew he needed the help. He praised God for answering his prayers. He was finally being accepted into the community.

About one o'clock Abigail pulled up in her father's buggy. Reuben hadn't even noticed she'd gone anywhere. She brought out sandwiches for everyone and cups for water.

During the next few days they were able to build "his and her" outhouses, a chicken coop with a run, horse stalls, and make some modifications to the shop. He would be able to start his buggy business at last. Each new day brought different people to help and he was glad for them all.

AFTER A LONG WEEKEND of visiting more relatives, receiving more gifts, attending church, and even more visiting, Abigail was exhausted. She would be glad when they'd made it around to all their relatives and could spend their weekends restfully. All the outside work at their new house was done, thanks to all the help from the community, and Monday was spent working in the garden. Tomorrow morning they would get the keys and the house would officially be theirs. Abigail peeked in the window. It was just before sunset and they hadn't seen the *Englishers* all day.

"I wish we could get in now. I really want to walk through it empty." She frowned at her reflection in the glass.

Reuben walked around the house to the window and peeked in. He jiggled the screen.

"What are you doing?" she asked.

"Well, it's been pretty warm this week. I wonder if any of these windows are open enough I can get through."

"You mean break in?"

"Uh, yes." He went down to the next window and jiggled it to see if the screen could be popped out easily.

"What if someone sees you?"

"You think we're going to get into trouble for breaking into our own house?" He laughed.

"Well, it still doesn't seem right." Her heart rate sped up.

The screen came loose and he slid the window up. "Got it."

She watched his upper body disappear as he climbed inside, his legs hanging in mid air for a moment. She ran to the window, then looked around in every direction to make sure no one had seen.

"Reuben?" She waited for an answer but there wasn't one. "What do you see?"

Suddenly he was behind her, his hand on her back. She jumped, turned, then slapped him in the chest. "You scared me."

"Sorry." His eyes met hers. She carefully slowed her breathing back to normal.

"We're in. Come on."

She followed him through the front door.

They walked through each room, describing what would

probably go where. Abigail chose the biggest upstairs room to be their bedroom for now. She'd slept upstairs her whole life and it wouldn't feel right not to now. They could always change their mind as their family situation changed. When they came back around to the living room again, Abigail stood looking up the stairs. Feeling Reuben's hands at her waist, she turned around. The warmth of his touch soaked through the fabric of her dress, causing her to breathe in sharply.

His tall body leaned over and he caught her eyes once more. "Well, what do you think?"

"I think it'll do nicely." The realization that she was married to the man before her hit once more. He had every right to kiss her, and she knew he wanted to. She wanted to kiss him, too, but what would happen if she did? Would he think she was ready for everything? Was she? She put her head to his chest, a safe place she'd been before, holding him close.

CHAPTER 13

*R*euben smiled wearily at his beautiful wife as they stood in the yard of their new home, reflecting on all the work it had taken to get here. The day had finally arrived. They had left Abigail's parents' house early that morning, hauling a load of their belongings with them. Then he left Abigail to work in the house while he went into town to pick up the keys from the realtor at ten. When he got back, two of the Schwartz brothers were unloading furniture from their buggy, and half a dozen laying hens were already in the chicken coop, a gift from Abigail's father. Reuben was thankful for his new family and friends. It seemed they had everything they needed to get started and he knew they'd manage the interior soon enough. It would give him and Abigail something to work on together over the next few months. He spent the rest of the day installing the hand pump for the kitchen sink and setting up the new gas-powered refrigerator.

"Your cookstove isn't ready to be picked up yet and there's still a lot to do in the house, but if you want, we can make do here. Are you ready to move out of your father's house?" Reuben wiped his dirty hands on his trousers.

She clasped her hands together. "You better believe I am."

"All right. We'll go back for one last load and eat supper, then we'll come back."

"And spend our first night in our own home," she said, finishing his sentence.

"Yes."

She threw her arms around him, and he held her carefully. He looked forward to having some privacy. He hoped it would make a difference in Abigail.

THE EVENING AIR was warmer now. They didn't even need a blanket in the buggy anymore. "Well, I hope you ate a good supper at my *mueter's* house," Abigail said as they rumbled down the dirt road. "I'm not sure what we can fix up without a cookstove."

"We'll build a fire outside if we have to. I want to sleep in my own bed, don't you?"

"*Ja.*" She wondered just what he would be expecting and how quickly, causing her palms to sweat just thinking about it.

"I saw you holding your little sister this evening."

She remembered the feel of her soft skin and the sweet baby smell. "It's so much different now, knowing I could soon have one of my own."

He laughed. "Well, if you want a baby, that's going to require a lot more work under the covers than we've been doing."

"Reuben," she said with a low voice, heat stealing into her face. "We've been married for over a week now, can't I talk to my wife about sex?"

"Merciful heavens, I can't believe you just said that." She uncrossed her legs and then crossed them the other direction, away from him in the buggy.

"What? Sex? It's not a dirty word."

"Keep your voice down," she said, repressing a smile.

He laughed again, clearly amused. "There's no one out here for miles. Who's going to hear me? Sex," he yelled loudly. She quickly put a hand over his mouth. He pulled her hand away, laughing. "Sex is the best wedding gift a couple will ever get and it's given to us by God Himself. He wants us to enjoy it and not just for making babies."

"I've been in church my whole life, Reuben Miller, and I've never once heard a sermon on...that."

"In *Englisher* churches it's more common. You won't really hear whole sermons on it, but it comes up in Bible studies from time to time. It's a shame it's not talked about more."

"And what else would you have them say of it?" She challenged, folding her arms tightly to her chest, the heat burning in her cheeks.

"That wives should listen to their husbands when they talk about sex." His eyes were so wide his forehead wrinkled.

"Will you stop saying that...that word?" Abigail put her head down, smiling.

"What did your mother tell you about sex? Come on. Out with it."

Abigail wondered how he could be so calm and confident talking about this. "Do you mean before marriage or after?" she said finally, hardly believing they were talking about it in the open like this.

"I'm very surprised there were either. Let's start with before."

She thought a moment. "When I turned sixteen and started going to singings, she told me to keep my skirt down when the boys were around. It was sort of a rhyme around my house. That was all that was said."

"Uh, huh. And what about after you were married?"

Abigail inhaled deeply. "She said...not to worry if it was a disappointment at first, that we had our whole lives to get it right." There, she'd said it.

"Uh, huh. Well, we'll just have to see if that proves true."

"You don't know?"

"How would I know?"

"I just...assumed."

"Ah, I see. You figured since I lived as an *Englisher* for half my life that I'd experienced all the world had to offer? Is that why you've held back?" He shook his head. "I thought..."

"What?"

"I thought you didn't find me attractive." He shrugged his shoulders.

"Reuben," she whispered. He was a very attractive man. She was sorry she'd hurt him that way. She didn't realize all this time she'd been hurting his self-esteem. She had only wanted to get away from her *vater's* house so she could feel more comfortable with him.

He sighed. "Listen, we have a long road to travel together. Promise me you'll never be afraid to talk to me about anything. Even if it's embarrassing."

"*Ja*, okay." She wondered if any other Amish women were as lucky as she was. His *Englisher* years had served him quite well. She doubted all Amish men could speak so freely with their wives. What an unexpected blessing.

He cleared his throat. "So how many women do you assume I've been with?"

She slapped his arm. Was he going to keep on, just like *Vater* would?

"No, if we're going there, I want to know that you really think of me. How many women do you think I've been with in my lifetime?"

"I don't know. Three or four?" She held her breath for his answer, hoping it wasn't more than that and not sure if she wanted to know at all.

"None."

"None?" She hadn't expected that.

"I could have. I had chances. But I'll bet you did, too. Am I right?"

He was right. The *beau* she'd had for so long—the one she thought she'd marry, till he dumped her suddenly—had kissed her a lot during buggy rides home. Once he'd suggested they drive down past Buster's Fork, all the way to Swan for a midnight swim. She'd known what he really wanted to do. She'd said no and it wasn't long after that he broke ties with her. She was so glad now she hadn't said yes. Many times after that she had wondered what would have become of them if she'd gone.

He bumped her arm with his. "I wanted to wait for you. And if it takes a lifetime to get it right, that's okay by me."

"Ja?" Her cheeks were still warm from the conversation.

"Yes. But if it's going to take that long to get it right, we may want to get started pretty soon. Neither of us are getting any younger."

She elbowed him again.

He laughed and it suddenly reminded her of the way her *vater* always joked lovingly with her *mueter*.

ABIGAIL STOOD in her own kitchen, staring at the oak hardwood table. She ran her fingers over it lovingly, just like she had so many times before when it sat in the storefront. It was finally hers and so were all the dreams she'd had about it. All she'd ever wanted was here: the house, the furniture, a handsome husband who loved her, the hope of children to come. She was finally ready to start her new life. Her pulse sped at the thought, faster and faster, warming her cheeks. Soon it felt as if Abigail's heart would break free from her chest, it was beating so hard. She found herself pacing back and forth in the kitchen, waiting for Reuben to come inside. He had to unhitch the horses and feed and water them. He was certainly going to be surprised when he figured out what she had planned...if she didn't chicken out first. Her stomach turned a little. The door opened and suddenly there he was. The man God had given her for a husband. She puckered her lips.

"What's wrong?" he said immediately.

"Nothing." She tried to say it casually, fiddling with the strings on her *kapp*. Was she giving the wrong impression? She tried giving him the look all the *Englisher* women wore on the magazine covers in the supermarket checkout lines.

"Are you all right?" His eyes narrowed in on her curiously.

"I'm fine." She cracked a smile at herself. Was she not even capable enough to let her husband know it was time? She walked up to him. She could kiss him, but he was too tall to reach. Should she asked to be kissed? Stand on a chair? This was getting embarrassing.

Oh, merciful heavens, why is this so hard?

Then she had an idea. She took his arm in hers and pulled him toward the living room.

"Where are we going?" he asked.

"Upstairs," she said quietly.

"What for?"

She looked him dead in the eye.

He stopped. "Don-don't tease me, Abigail." He shook his head tightly.

She put her hands on his shoulders and stared up at him, hoping her confidence would hold.

He put his arms around her waist and leaned down, her whole body softening at his touch. She felt an eager affection coming from him and suddenly an overwhelming urge to draw closer. Heartbeat throbbing in her ears, she met his lips with hers, finally ready to submit herself to her husband, heart, body, and soul. The awkwardness had suddenly disappeared into flames of desire. They locked eyes again, breathing in unison, their faces inches apart. She could hear him swallow.

She took hold of his sleeve and tugged him toward the stairs.

His voice cracked slightly as he began to speak. "You're serious? This is the signal?"

She nodded with a faint smile.

"I just want to be sure I'm not misreading something here."

She lifted one eyebrow, and with the most confident voice she could manage she said, "Are you coming or not?"

He jumped like he'd been shot, then scooped her up into his arms, carrying her up the stairs. She couldn't help but laugh, wrapping her arms around his strong neck. Reuben paused at the doorway to the bedroom, taking her mouth once more, sweetly draining all her doubts and fears. Then he closed the bedroom door behind him with one swing of his boot.

REUBEN AWOKE to golden streams of Abigail's hair flowing across his chest. She pulled it away from her face as she sat up, hugging the covers tightly around her.

"I think the time for shyness is over, don't you?" He watched her dress quickly, not letting him see more than she had to. He felt a little orneriness coming on and before he had time to think it through he said, "So, was it as good for the goose as it was for the gander?" He braced himself to be slapped, but he knew it would be worth it.

She just shook her head at him and sighed. "Merciful heavens, I've married my *vater*."

He laughed. He was going to enjoy a whole lifetime of teasing that woman. Life was good.

"I'm going to try to make breakfast," she said sleepily.

He could tell she was holding back a smile. "Good luck. The woodstove won't be here for another week."

"Ever tried a pickled okra sandwich?" She wound her hair and stuck pins in it all over. Then pulled her *kapp* down tightly on top.

"I'll be down in a minute and we'll figure something out."

She left him in bed, closing the door behind her. As he dressed for the day he noticed the letters on the chest of drawers. He thought back to the courage it took to write to Abigail for the first time and how he'd soon after declared his intent to marry her. She had received that letter late, causing him to have to be even more brave, but it was all a part of God's plan. He picked them up and studied each one.

Thank you, God, for Abigail. She's a good woman and everything I prayed for. You promised if I'd come back, You'd bless me for it, and You have—a hundred fold.

Tucking them neatly under his socks in his drawer, he couldn't imagine any possession in the house ever being more dear to him than the reminder he had of answered prayers—Abigail's letters.

THE LONG WAY HOME

"I do not frustrate the grace of God: for if righteousness come by the law, then Christ is dead in vain." Galatians 2:21 KJV

CHAPTER 1

$\mathcal{H}$e had kissed her once before, the summer she had turned fourteen. Anna May Shetler could still remember that hot day when the sun beat down so hard on Abner Schwartz's cornfield it'd nearly melted them all. Overcome with the heat, her older sister had become weak and was taken inside with the rest of the women. There they took care of the smallest of the children, shucked corn, and prepared supper for a frolic that had lasted two days longer than it should have, and the end was still nowhere in sight. With three-quarters of the last ten-acre field left to go, the community labored on, helping Abner to bring his harvest in before the sun scorched it all.

Anna May's *vater* had commended her for not becoming discouraged, and for helping with the harvest just as hard as any of her brothers.

She had worked hard all right, picking corn faster than a chicken after a junebug to keep up with Jonas Hilty. It had taken her all afternoon, but she'd finally made it to the end of her row before he had finished his. She crossed the narrow path to stand beside him, a moment's rest her reward.

"Well, what do you think, Anna May?" Remembering the way

he said her name so low and confident made her draw in a sharp breath. "Will we finish before the week's end?"

She had hoped they would never finish, that somehow she could watch Jonas pick corn in the row beside her for all eternity. "If we work hard and don't get discouraged," she said, borrowing words from her *vater*.

Jonas dropped an ear of corn into the basket near his feet, took off his straw hat, wiped the sweat from his forehead with the sleeve of his upper arm, then returned his hat to his head. Then his eyes beheld her as if he'd never seen her before in his life. He was tall for fifteen, and more muscular than most. She had hoped she didn't look like a little girl to him.

"If we weren't standin' in a cornfield right now, I might just have to kiss you," he'd said softly.

Time stood still.

Her sister had said she'd have to wait till she was sixteen to be alone with a boy, but there they were, hidden in the cornstalks with several thick rows standing between them and the rest of the volunteers.

"You got something against cornfields?" she'd asked.

He leaned in and kissed her right on the mouth, the edge of her *kapp* bumping his hat brim, knocking it out of place. It was over quick-as-a-wink and then he pushed his hat back down and said, "Not a thing, Anna May. Not a thing."

The next row and all the rows after that had felt like recess at the one-room schoolhouse.

It had been five years, but the memory was still as fresh as Saturday's pie. Anna May wondered what kissing Jonas would be like now. She'd spent the last three years trying to find out and was beginning to get discouraged. At this rate, she'd be an old maid and still wondering.

It was time for boldness. She, and others, were gathered around a long wagon in the barnyard. It was used to transport hay, lumber, and other items too big to fit in a buggy. They had all heard that Jonas could lift the back end of it all by himself, but Anna May wanted to see it with her own eyes. It was considered prideful by most, but she supposed someone had asked him to do it anyway.

Jonas had grown much taller. His shoulders widened and chest filled out, making him and his brother the largest, and undoubtedly the strongest, unmarried men in Swan Creek Settlement. His light brown eyes shone in the moonlight, soft waves of sandy blond hair, a few shades darker, protruded from under his straw hat. Rolling his sleeves up past his elbows, he said, "Stand back, ladies. I don't want to see anyone get hurt."

The crowd took a step back, anxiously awaiting Jonas's next move. Perfecting his stance with the shuffling of his boots, he took hold of the wagon, just under the frame at the backside, and heaved. The two back wheels slowly rose off the ground. He held it up in the air a couple seconds then carefully lowered it back to the ground, muscles bulging.

Elias Hilty, Jonas's twin brother, shook his head and walked away. Anna May figured he could probably lift the wagon as well. After all, they both worked with their *vater,* doing heavy farm work on a regular basis. Once, she'd seen Elias, with very little effort, hoist a whole bale of hay onto his shoulder to lift it over the horse stall, rather than simply opening the door and walking it in at his side, like she'd seen every other man do.

Becca Lengacher, Anna May's best friend, thought Elias was the best looking of the two. It was obvious to anyone they were brothers, but they weren't identical, and besides that, their personalities were nothing alike.

Jonas was outgoing and fun. He wasn't full of idle talk, but when he spoke, everyone paid attention, wondering what he might say or do next.

Elias was quiet, reserved. He seemed to spend all his time trying to get out from beneath his brother's shadow. They were only minutes apart in age. The story was that Elias came out first, but only because Jonas pushed him out with his feet. Anna May remembered hearing their *mueter* complain about their fighting, even taking them to Bishop Amos once for reprimanding. That was only after they were too big for their *vater* to correct them with a belt across their backside.

The crowd had dwindled down to three girls, including Anna May, and then Jonas. She anticipated his next move, slipped away, and hid herself behind the old oak by the barn. Hoping no one had seen her, she peeked around the large tree, waiting for Jonas to walk by on his way to the drink table. In a moment, he was there, and just as she'd prayed, he was alone. Her heart lodged in her throat as she tried desperately to think of something clever to say to him. Should she compliment his strength? *Nay,* the others had done that already, and with little effect.

He had given Miriam Wittmer a ride home a few times last fall, but other than that he rarely asked a girl twice. Anna May wondered if he was trying to give each girl a ride, to see what he thought of them all. If so, she would see to it that it was her turn tonight. Only she knew once he kissed *her* again, he wouldn't ask another. She was determined to make Jonas Hilty hers, no matter what she had to do.

The sound of Jonas's feet set her mind into action. She pushed down the lump in her throat and stepped around the tree, suddenly face to face with him, just as she'd planned.

"Anna May." He tipped his hat, no doubt wondering where she had come from.

"Jonas," she said, trying desperately to smooth the nervousness from her voice.

"What have you been up to tonight?" he said with his usual playful tone.

"I just came back from a little stroll. The stars are right pretty tonight, don't you think?"

He eyed her keenly, then looked up at the stars overhead. "Not half as pretty as you are, Anna May."

"That's nice of you to say. There are a lot of pretty girls here tonight." She fixed her eyes on his, hoping he'd say she was the prettiest.

He took off his hat. "You know, Anna May, I seem to recall a young boy flirting with you in a cornfield one summer. You wouldn't remember any such foolishness, would you?"

He remembered. Everything was going according to plan. She could tell she had his interest, she just had to keep it; his lips were so nearly hers. "You may be right. It was such a long time ago..."

He stepped forward and leaned in toward her. Sensing his intent, she closed the rest of the distance herself. His pouty lips met hers with purpose. Gone was the boy she'd kissed before. His mouth moved over hers the way the water smoothed the stones in Swan Creek. Warmth from his hand on her cheek—

This was even better than she'd planned. She ached when he finally broke free.

"I promised I'd take Beth home tonight, but now I wish I hadn't," he said under his breath. His eyes connected with hers in a way she'd only seen in married couples. "Maybe next time?" he asked.

She gritted her teeth. Soothing her aching pride, she decided she'd received something a lot better than a ride home from Jonas. He would be hers eventually. She just needed to keep her wits about her to make it so. "I already have a ride home tonight, too. But *ja,* maybe next singing. We'll just have to see." She stepped around him, close enough that her arm brushed his, making sure he would remember the encounter vividly this time, just as she would. Her cheeks warmed as she walked.

Now she needed to find a ride home, and quick.

Anna May patrolled the barn lot, circling the perimeter, looking for someone, anyone who hadn't paired up yet. She knew she could get a ride from her cousin, if she had to, and her house wasn't that far away if she needed to walk, but her pride needed a man to drive her there, a man that would set Jonas to thinking on what he missed out on. A man like—

"Elias Hilty?" A man with his back turned stood by his open buggy, ready to step up into it any second. He had wide shoulders, and as her brothers would say, he was built like a brick outhouse. Only he and Jonas fit the description well. Turning around, he confirmed her suspicions.

"What are you doing out here all by yourself?" Anna May asked.

"Just heading out."

"So soon?" she asked, trying with difficulty to give him the same eyes she gave his brother only moments ago.

He tilted his head at her curiously. "You lookin' for a ride home?"

"That's kind of you to offer. I accept." She climbed up into the buggy before he could get another word out, not even waiting for him to give her a hand up.

As he climbed in and took the reins, Anna May spied Jonas and Beth down the driveway. How Beth had bested her, she didn't know. Ever since church that morning Anna May had been careful to keep an eye on Jonas. The only time she let him out of her sight was when she'd went to the oak tree.

No matter.

When he saw her riding away with his brother he wouldn't put her off so quickly. She just needed to make sure Jonas saw them together. As long as *someone* saw them her plan would work, but she would take much more satisfaction in seeing the look on his face. She smiled to herself.

"Did you enjoy the singing?" Elias asked.

Anna May turned her attention to her companion for the remainder of the evening. "I thought it was just lovely. Did you?"

"Oh, I think singings are the best part of Sundays. Everybody getting together, the praise hymns, the yodeling. I hate to say it, but I like it even better than church."

Of course he liked it better than church. Two hours of singing or three hours of listening to the preachers and the bishop drone on and on? It was an easy choice for Anna May.

Elias turned the buggy onto the main dirt road. Jonas and Beth weren't too far ahead of them.

"Me, too." Anna May placed her hand on his upper arm. She knew it was wrong to pretend she was interested in Elias only to get to Jonas, but surely Elias would appreciate the flattery. She squeezed his arm. "I bet you could lift a wagon just as well as Jonas."

He bristled at her words. "It was a prideful act."

"Maybe. But you could, couldn't you?"

He hesitated. "*Ja.* I lift the back end of an empty wagon a few times a week to build strength."

"And that's not prideful?"

"*Nay.* You never know when you'll need more strength." His voice was low and quiet for a man so big, and not nearly as commanding as Jonas's.

They were nearing her road, the turn just ahead. Jonas and Beth had already passed by it. Her house was only minutes away. "Hadn't thought of it like that. I never knew you were such an interesting person, Elias. It's a shame we don't have a longer ride."

"And I've enjoyed your company as well, Anna May. I agree, it's a shame." In the light of the full moon overhead, Anna May could make out a smile on his face.

"Well, I guess if you wanted, we could take the long way home. We could cut around on the other side of Buster's Fork. It would only be a few more miles, and I would delight in talking with you further."

"I'd like that," he said, not slowing down as they neared her road on the left hand side.

Anna May commended herself for a plan well executed. Beth's

house wasn't too far ahead, and Jonas would surely see them as they drove by.

"You know, it's been a while since I gave anyone a ride home." Elias adjusted his legs, which looked too long to ever be comfortable in the buggy.

Anna May pretended to be surprised. "Why, Elias, a big, strong man like you?" She squeezed his arm again. "I figure you could have your choice of any of the girls in Swan Creek Settlement." He wasn't Jonas, but he was handsome enough, and a strong, hard working man was readily sought after among the women. Elias was just too picky. After keeping company with her friend Becca Lengacher a few Sundays, Elias had practically ignored her since. And Becca was one of the prettiest girls Anna May knew.

He laughed. "I think you have me confused for my brother Jonas. He's the one all the ladies are after."

He was right. The competition was fierce.

He continued, "But luckily, I'm not looking for the same kind of lady as he is."

"What kind of lady is he looking for?" Anything Elias could tell her about how to snag Jonas would make the whole evening that much more worthwhile.

"I can't speak for him, but I think he's still got his head in *Rumspringa*. I'm looking forward to joining church this fall and settling down with a lady after my own heart. One who loves God and is committed to His ways."

Beth's house was just around the corner. Anna May hoped to be carrying on merrily as they drove by. The thought of it thrilled her to no end. When Jonas saw her holding Elias's arm he'd be sorry he put her off. He might even come calling before next church day to make sure she didn't agree to spend time with someone else first.

"*Ja*, I know what you mean," she said.

"You do?"

"*Ja.*" What had he said? Anna May couldn't recall. "I think we all want the same things in life, don't you?"

"Not everyone is as committed at our age. And so many are leaving the community. It's becoming a big problem. We need to find out why and reach out to them."

"*Ja.*"

There it was, Beth's house. But wait. Why wasn't there a buggy parked in front? The realization soaked through, clear to Anna May's bones. They had gone on by. Jonas was taking her joy riding. So much for regretting giving Beth a ride. She clenched her jaw.

"You don't know how much good it does my heart to hear you say that."

What had she said? She smiled and removed her hand from his arm. Anna May knew that if Jonas and Beth were joy riding they could have turned down any number of dirt roads or even onto the highway that would be devoid of cars this late on a Sunday night. They'd never catch up to them now. Gone were her plans of besting Beth. Now she was stuck with Elias. It was only a few more miles around Buster's Fork and she'd be home. She would try to remain pleasant until then. She could let her anger out into her pillow soon enough.

Elias stopped the buggy at a closed gate. He hopped down and opened it wide. The pasture behind it belonged to Reuben Miller. He had relocated from Gawson's Branch recently and had opened up a buggy shop on the property next to the house. He made a road along the fenceline of one of his fields and spread word that anyone who wanted could use the road as a shortcut to avoid a stretch of highway up ahead with a dangerous intersection. It was also a good way for him to get more people to pass his buggy shop and Anna May had heard his wife, Abigail, was selling chicken eggs as well. He only kept the gate shut to keep out *Englishers*. Elias shut the gate once they were through.

Being so private, the road had also become popular with the

youth, who used it to sneak in a kiss before returning to the main road on the other side. Anna May hoped Elias wouldn't try anything like that. As he climbed back up into the buggy and smiled warmly at her it put her mind at ease. He was more like a gentle giant, seeming to know his strength and guarding it well. She couldn't imagine him being anything less than a gentleman, yet his strength and size carried with it the potential to do anything he wanted.

She'd only known of two of the male youth in the community who ever stole kisses and one of them had just recently been forced to marry when the gal he'd been keeping company with was found to be with child. The bishop had allowed them both to join church in the spring, rather than fall, conducting the baptismal classes at her parents' home just before they wed. Anna May was glad she'd never accepted a ride home from him. The couple seemed happy enough, but being forced to marry wasn't in her plans, neither was joining church any time soon—unless Jonas did. To be with Jonas she'd join without hesitation.

They drove slowly down the path made from the wheels of many buggies driving over the grass repeatedly.

"Do you like spring mushrooms?" Elias asked.

"*Ja*, who doesn't?" She figured the time would pass faster if she kept the conversation going.

"I was wondering if you'd like to join our family for a mushroom hunt later this week. We've heard they're bringing in sacks full now."

A mushroom frolic? Elias sure hadn't invited Becca to do anything with him. Would she be surprised. And there was a chance she'd see Jonas, but, *nay*. She couldn't. There was no harm in accepting a ride home from someone, but going further wouldn't be right by anyone's standards.

"That's really sweet of you, Elias, but…"

"Do you hear that?" He turned himself halfway around to see behind them, where another buggy was approaching quickly.

"I wonder who it is," Anna May said.

"I don't," Elias said under his breath.

Suddenly Matthew was pulling up beside them. He was riding with Rachel Wickey.

Elias groaned.

Anna May and Becca had always thought of Matthew as Elias's sidekick. He was thin and wiry with thick glasses, and in his straw hat he looked like a boy instead of a sixteen-year-old youth. Elias was nearing twenty. Together, the two of them looked like the lion and the mouse from the story they'd read in school.

Elias pulled back on the reins and the buggy came to a stop, Matthew's buggy beside them. "Wanna' race?" Matthew asked with a sly grin.

"No thanks. I was just taking Anna May home."

Anna May gave a little wave.

"Hey there, Anna May." Matthew waved back.

Elias cleared his throat. "Well, I guess we had better be heading out."

"What's your hurry? Come on. Let's show these gals what we can do."

Anna May eyed Elias curiously. "Do you usually buggy race?" It didn't sound like something he would do.

"Sure we do," Matthew said. "Let's show 'em."

"We haven't raced in over a year and you know it," Elias said. "And besides, we're both keeping company." He raised his eyebrows, no doubt, a signal for Matthew to let it go.

"All in good fun, *brooda*," Matthew said. They weren't brothers. Anna May didn't even think they were cousins, but she'd heard Matthew call some of the young men that.

"I won't even razz you when I win."

"Are they both race horses?" Anna May asked. Most of the horses the community members had were bred locally, but sometimes an *Englisher* would purchase several at the race track auctions and bring them to their part of the country to resell.

"*Ja*, they're both retired race horses, only mine's faster." Matthew clicked his cheek, causing his buggy to pull ahead of them, then pulled the reins to slow it back down.

"I'm not racing you, Matthew," Elias said. "It was foolish when I did it a year ago and I certainly won't do it now."

"Come on, Elias. Just to the end of the field."

Rachel sat beside him, looking eager to do anything Matthew did. Anna May didn't really care either way. The faster they traveled through the field, the faster she'd reach home, but it wasn't up to her. All eyes were on Elias.

"Give me a moment to consult with the lady," he said. He turned to Anna May, whispering close to her ear, "I'll let him pick up some speed, then I'll pull back. Maybe he'll think he's won and then we can continue our conversation."

Anna May laughed. She couldn't help it. It was funny he was letting Matthew have control of him like that. She figured if Elias had just raised his voice a little it would have sent Matthew on down the road, never to bother him again, but Elias was too concerned with his feelings for that.

"All right. Are you ready?" Elias asked.

"To the end of the field?"

"To the end of the field."

"All right," Matthew said. "Hang on, Rachel. This could get bumpy."

Knowing Elias's plan, Anna May didn't worry about hanging on. She'd ridden in a fast buggy plenty of times, often when her family was running late for church.

Matthew counted off. "Ready, set, go!" he shouted, and both buggies leapt forward. It took a little distance for the horses to realize what was going on, but when they did, they came to life, beating their hooves against the pasture in thunderous stomps.

The buggy hit a bump and Anna May held onto the bench

seat. The pasture was much rougher than the road to church. They were still gaining speed. Just when she was beginning to get a little anxious, she saw Elias pull back on the reins to slow the buggy. She hoped Matthew wouldn't realize he'd been tricked and want to race all over again.

The buggy started to slow and Matthew's pulled ahead. As soon as he was past, Elias pulled on the reins again to bring them back to a normal speed.

Another big bump sent Anna May off the bench and back down again hard. The horse veered to the left suddenly, away from the buggy. It had broken free of the hitch. Anna May drew in a sharp breath.

"Hang on," Elias yelled. Anna May started to cry out but instead shut her mouth tightly, bracing herself as they hit another bump. Her eyes wide, she watched Elias pull the brake. The buggy bumped again and into the air it flew.

A weightless feeling before her body smashed hard into the ground.

In the darkness, a voice called out her name, or was it Miller they called for?

CHAPTER 2

"*A*nna May, can you hear me?"

Anna May opened her eyes to a bright light. What a strange dream. Who was this person in white supposed to be? A sharp pain ran through her lower abdomen, her head heavy.

"You hit pretty hard. Do you remember being in an accident?" a man asked.

The last thing she remembered was being in the buggy with Elias. And all those bumps. Weightlessness. She took in a breath. "Ah, it hurts." Talking intensified the pain and she cried out again.

"Just try to relax." The man was touching her stomach. How awkward. Where was she?

"Don't try to move unless I say. Can you wiggle your toes for me?" His voice was calm.

Anna May wiggled her toes. "They feel numb."

"But they're moving, so that's normal. You hit your head pretty hard, probably on a rock and you've broken your pelvis."

She knew her pelvis was a bone down low somewhere, but she wasn't sure exactly where. "How bad?" she whispered, surprised at the effort it took.

"You were lucky. Especially since the accident happened in such a remote area. I heard it took a while to call for help. You're going to need surgery, but we plan to fix you up good as new."

The doctor turned to another person in the room and whispered something she couldn't make out. "These ladies will take good care of you. I'll see you before surgery in the morning." He patted her arm and left the room.

Anna May's head was spinning. How did she get to the hospital? She couldn't remember a thing. Had Elias brought her? "Elias," she said out loud. What had happened to him? If he didn't live… The weight of Elias's blood on her hands turned her stomach. Eternal damnation awaited those who shed innocent blood. Had it not been for Anna May's jealousy, Elias would never have taken her home.

One of the women fluttering about the room stopped. She was dressed in pink, her blonde hair was in a little knob on the top of her head. With a look of sympathy and a quiet, high pitched voice she said, "There's someone outside waiting to see you. We can send visitors in one at a time if you'd like, but not for long. You need your rest."

Anna May lifted her arm. It was bare. Where was her dress and what was she wearing? She felt the fabric, which was more like paper than cloth. She touched her head. Her *kapp* was missing as well, and only part of her hair remained in the bun she'd twisted that morning.

Or was it a new day already?

She pulled out one of the remaining pins, letting it fall where it wished. A strand of brown tumbled down, the length of her arm.

Everything hurt.

The door opened. Anna May wondered who would see her half dressed first. Elias appeared, his hat in his hand.

He was alive.

Maybe she wouldn't burn in Hell after all. His eyes showed her how bad she looked. According to him, she was a wreck.

"How are you feeling?" he asked.

"Did the horse run over me?" she asked quietly.

"*Nay.* You were thrown from the buggy."

"It feels like the horse stepped on me."

"I bet it does." He knelt down on the floor by the bed, much closer now to her face, the humiliation of what she must look like burning her cheeks.

"Where are *Mueter* and *Vater?*"

"I'm sure they're on their way. Reuben Miller rode to the telephone down the road and I stayed with you, till the helicopter came to get you."

"Helicopter?" She'd flown in the sky? An eerie sensation coursed through her veins. It wasn't natural to be in the air. Would God judge her for that, too?

"They wouldn't let me come with you. I wanted to…" Elias began to tear up. It must have frightened him badly. Anna May wondered if he had been hurt at all. Why was she in the bed, broken, when he didn't seem to have a scratch on him?

"I am so sorry, Anna May." He took her hand, tears falling with near silent sobs. "This is all my fault." His hands on hers brought further humiliation.

Anna May was still too stunned for tears. She'd never intended to let Elias hold her hand, not in the buggy and not now. "How did you get here if my parents haven't made it yet?"

He sniffled and his crying calmed enough to speak. "One of the first responders on the scene gave me a ride to Wayne Stevens's house. I woke him up and begged him to bring me. Reuben Miller said he'd let everyone know and arrange for them to get here as soon as possible."

So not much time had passed.

"Please forgive me, Anna May. I never meant for any of this to happen." Elias was starting to cry again.

One of the nurses tapped him on the shoulder. "Sir, she really needs her rest. If there are any other visitors tell them to be quick."

Elias stood and wiped his eyes on his shirt sleeve. "I'll go check the waiting room to see if they've made it yet." He gave her one last solemn look and walked through the door.

"He's been so worried about you," the nurse said. "He must care for you very much."

She must have thought Elias was her *beau*. If only she knew that was the furthest thing from the truth.

ANNA MAY STARED at the ceiling from her bed, now situated in the living room. She wasn't allowed to leave it for a long time. The doctor said it would be nine to twelve weeks before she was healed, and each day felt like an eternity. How would she make do like this for months?

The ever-present pain was pressing deeper. Anna May took the little white pill from the side table. The glass of water *Mueter* had left for her felt too heavy to lift without causing even more painful pressure below. After a moment to think on it, she opted to choke it down dry. She had only been home from the hospital two days—or was it three? The monotony of her new schedule already threatened to break her.

There were pills for pain, pills for inflammation, and then antibiotics, all given at particular times around the clock—times known only by *Mueter*. Ice packs twenty minutes on, twenty minutes off. She was told to drink lots of water, but that only led to more pain when her bladder needed emptied. She was told to move as little as possible, but every other hour her *mueter* or sister would move her legs around to prevent blood clots. And a few times a day her wounds would need cleaned and dressed. If none of those events were occurring, she stared at the ceiling.

Anna May couldn't do anything for herself, and although someone sat in the chair beside her at all times, she felt completely alone.

Englisher doctors didn't understand. Amish women couldn't stare at the ceiling all day without going mad.

A tapping at the kitchen door sent *Mueter* hopping. The people of the community had been sending over sunshine baskets since she'd been released from the hospital. They were made to cheer her, but each one was just a reminder of how many people knew about her situation, further embarrassing her.

"Anna May will be thrilled to see you," *Mueter* said from the kitchen. Anna May wondered who it was she'd be so thrilled to see. She hoped it was Becca, the only person in the world she felt she could be herself around. The only one who wouldn't quote scriptures in an effort to "help."

"How are you feeling, Anna May?" Elias Hilty asked as he entered. His presence made the whole room feel smaller.

She looked around, but he was alone. It would have embarrassed her to no end if Jonas had come, too. She looked a fright, her *kapp* barely on, and not even tied. "Like death," Anna May whispered.

Her mother let out a little gasp. It wasn't something nice young ladies said, but in her condition, who was there to reprimand her? No one knew what it felt like but her.

"I'm sorry, *Mueter*. It just hurts so much." Her eyes closed partway.

"Maybe I should go," Elias said.

"*Nay.*" She was tired of the way her *mueter* watched her, as if expecting her to fall to pieces at any moment. Anyone was a welcomed visitor at this point.

Mueter nodded. "I'll be just outside if anyone needs me." Anna May's younger brothers and sisters were out in the yard, playing in the warm sunshine of May. In a few hours, her older sister would come by to help out.

Elias sat down in the chair beside her bed, facing her. Silence followed. It was odd to see such a big, strong man sitting idle in a rocking chair on a beautiful day. He should be out working the fields with his *vater* or caring for the family's new colts.

"Is there anything I can get for you?" he asked.

"*Nay.*"

"I'm so sorry, Anna May." Elias started to tear up but calmed himself. "I'll do anything to help you through this. You just tell me what you need and I'll do it."

"There's nothing anyone can do but wait for me to get better."

"And that's the hardest part, right? I know everyone wants to help any way they can, but me especially. This was all my fault, Anna May. It never should have happened and I take full responsibility for it."

Anna May didn't answer. She guessed he was right. Buggy racing was a bad idea, but how was he to know the hitch would break? She saw the pain in his eyes and felt sorry for him. He was kind and gentle, never causing anyone any harm. *Nay*, this was God's judgment on her, not on him.

"The Lord giveth, and the Lord taketh away," she said. It was true. One never could tell when they'd kindle the flame of God's wrath, and she had. She only hoped it was over soon and could avoid His anger in the future.

She'd only wanted to get closer to Jonas. Weren't they allowed some concessions while still in *Rumspringa*? She would have joined church eventually, married Jonas and bore him many strong sons and daughters. She would have been a *guete* little wife, just like her *mueter*, and her *mueter's mueter* before her. She'd only gone wrong when she'd brought Elias into the mix. She shouldn't have used him to get to Jonas. This was God's way of telling her she'd crossed a line and He'd made his point clearly.

"You're a strong, faithful woman, Anna May. You'll get through this just fine. But I still want to be here to help."

Anna May understood his guilt. She'd felt the same when she

thought he had been killed in the accident. If he had died, she would be doing everything she could to make it up to his family. "I forgive you, Elias. You don't need to do anything to earn that." Her eyes felt like they were made of lead. She struggled to keep them open.

"I know, Anna May. The Lord has already forgiven me, and I'm so glad to hear you do, too. Now we just have to get you better."

We? Just what was it he planned to do to make her better? And how forward of him to presume to know the mind of God. Anna May closed her heavy eyes just for a moment.

She awoke, wondering how long she'd slept. A glance at the clock on the wall said nearly two hours. Elias sat slumped in the chair with his long legs outstretched, crossed at the ankle.

"Why didn't you wake me?" she asked, slurring her words.

"Why would I? You're supposed to rest."

"I'm not very good company." She tried to decide if it was sweet of him to watch her sleep for two hours or rather forward. Her head hurt. She put her hand to it, knocking her *kapp* to the floor. Elias quickly picked it up and handed it back to her. She fumbled with putting it back on, while Elias reached out repeatedly in an effort to help, drawing his hand back each time, and never actually making contact with her *kapp.*

Once she had it situated he said, "I told your *mueter* I'd tell her when you awoke. She's been doing housework."

Anna May wondered what day of the week it was. She knew she'd missed wash day and ironing day already, but she wasn't sure what chores she would be doing right then if she hadn't been in the accident.

"I'll tell her on the way out."

He was leaving. It was for the best. She wasn't able to keep a conversation going anyway. She'd hoped now that he'd visited and she'd forgiven him he could return to his life as usual. Then she wondered if *her* life would ever be normal again. How many girls would Jonas drive home before she was able to attend another singing? The thought almost brought on tears.

"Thank you for visiting, Elias. I'm sorry I wasn't better company."

"No need to apologize, Anna May. I'll be back tomorrow to check on you."

He smiled at her one last time before leaving.

Tomorrow?

Surely he wasn't going to make visiting a habit.

THE NEXT DAY Elias brought in a sunshine basket just before dinner time. He set the basket on the side table by the bed. "My sisters picked out most of the things, but the card is from me."

"*Danki,*" Anna May said. She could see a small square box of tissues, some long colorful drinking straws, and some notepads with a pen. She had helped put together sunshine boxes many times before, but this was the first time she'd ever had them given to her, and there were so many. Everyone in the community was trying to care for her in some way. The embarrassment Anna May had initially felt was starting to dissolve as each new box arrived.

Elias sat down in the rocking chair. "I brought your *mueter* some mushrooms to fry up for dinner. I remembered you said you liked them." He lowered the hat in his hand gently to the hardwood floor beside him.

"That's really nice of you, Elias, but you didn't have to." He was being too nice. The last thing she wanted was to lead him on any further and have God strike her down again. She envisioned a bolt of lightning coming down from the sky and through the window to where she lay.

"Well, I figured since you couldn't come with us to gather them I should bring them to you."

She had forgotten he had invited her to hunt mushrooms with his family before the accident.

Elias was a handsome man with many of the same features Jonas had. His eyes were darker brown though, and his hair dirty blond, where Jonas's was a bit lighter. Their builds were very comparable. She'd once thought Jonas to be the stronger of the two, but after spending some time with Elias, she wasn't sure. They were both *guete-looking* men, but still, Elias was no Jonas. He lacked the confidence Jonas had, and the sense of adventure. She could tell Elias was all about rules, wasting his *Rumspringa* with ideas of community outreach. Jonas was the kind of man who would meet her at Swan Creek for a secret swim if she asked. Just being around him made Anna May feel more alive.

"Elias, I should tell you something."

"What is it?" He looked eager to jump from the chair and do her bidding.

"I think you're a very nice young man."

"Well, I think you're a fine young woman yourself, Anna May." He relaxed a little in his chair.

"You didn't let me finish. I'm…" How could she put this? "I'm not sure with everything that's happened I'm ready to court anyone right now."

"Of course not. I just want to be your friend, Anna May. I figure you could use a *guete* friend after all you've been through, right?"

She nodded her head, glad for his understanding in the matter.

"*Guete*. I'm just here to help cheer you while you get better, nothing more."

She wondered now if he had been drawn to the house once again by sheer guilt or if he wanted there to be something romantic between them. No matter. She'd let him know she wasn't interested. As hard as this time was, a friend might be just what she needed, especially if it helped to get her *mueter* to stop hovering over her all the time.

CHAPTER 3

"$\mathcal{I}$s it almost time for supper?" Anna May asked as she opened heavy eyes. She must have fallen asleep again. The pills the doctor had given her for pain put her to sleep not long after taking them. Without them, the pain was unbearable, with them, only manageable.

"Almost. Elias hasn't made it yet," *Mueter* said. She walked around the bed and pulled back the sheet.

"You asked Elias to supper?" Anna May flinched as *Mueter* grabbed her leg and began stretching and bending it to prevent blood clots.

"Well, he's been helping your *vater* with a lot of things around here lately and you seem to enjoy his company. Is there a problem?"

"*Nay.*" She didn't know he'd been helping *Vater*. All she knew was that he visited every day and was okay with just being friends. She was thankful. Time passed much faster when he was around and the sooner she was better, the sooner she could pursue Jonas. She hoped Elias would make a *guete* brother-in-law some day.

Each evening her supper was served to her in bed in the living room. One or two family members would take turns eating in the chairs beside her while the rest of the family took their usual place at the long table in the kitchen. Sometimes her *mueter* would eat with her, other times, her *vater*. One of her siblings waited on her, bringing her anything she asked for quickly. Mealtimes were one of the only things she had to look forward to anymore. With each meal served she knew she'd made it through another part of the day. After three, she'd be on to the next day. Still, at this rate nine to twelve weeks seemed like an eternity.

A few minutes later she heard Elias speaking with her *vater* in the kitchen about the north pasture. She hadn't even heard him knock. Anna May wondered if he was planning to help *Vater* with more work around the place.

Mueter entered with a plate of food and handed it to Anna May. "I'll bring you something to drink. Elias will be keeping you company tonight." *Mueter's* eyes held the smile her mouth did not. Did she think Elias was her *beau?* "Do you need anything else, dear?"

"*Nay. Danki.*"

Elias entered the room with two glasses of sweet tea and set them both down on the side table. "How are you feeling, Anna May?" He put his hands in his pockets and waited for her to answer.

"Every day is still a hard day," she said quietly. It wasn't something she'd feel comfortable saying to her *mueter* or to *Vater*. They would accuse her of not trusting God for her healing and go on some long sermon about it, but she knew Elias would listen.

He frowned. "I'll be right back." He walked into the kitchen and came back in a moment with a plate of food. He sat in the chair with the plate on his lap and bowed his head. "Dear merciful Lord, the time has come once again to thank You for Your many blessings and for the food we're about to receive. You've given us so many wonderful things, Lord. Thank You for this food and for sparing our lives, so we may serve You another day. We ask You, oh Lord, to give

Anna May strength and relief from her pain. That You wouldn't withhold any *guete* thing from her, as Your daughter that we know you love. We thank You for working all things out for the good of those who love You. Amen." He lifted his head and began to eat.

Anna May wondered at the way he'd spoken to God. She supposed someone like Elias, who always did right, could ask anything they wanted of Him boldly. She hoped Elias's prayers would reach Heaven. She still had many *guete* deeds to do before any of hers would. "*Danki*," she said.

He gave a thin smile as he lowered his head. "You're welcome. I pray for your healing daily, but if you'd like we can pray together when I come by to check on you."

Anna May nodded.

"I hate it that you'll be missing church," he said. It had been nearly two weeks since the accident.

She would be missing more than just church. The singing that followed was supposed to be the evening that Jonas finally drove her home. Her heart ached more than anything else in her body for the first time in many days.

Elias eyed her curiously, perhaps waiting for her to speak. "Can I get anything for you, Anna May?"

"*Nay.*" She was tired of hearing that question from everyone. People were even saying it in her dreams.

"Well, you're getting better every day, I can tell it. Your color is much better today." He took a big forkful of peas from his plate.

"I wasn't aware my color was off." How hideous must she have looked in the past days since the accident?

"Well, it just wasn't your usual glow, but now it's back." He smiled carefully.

"I have a glow?" Anna May raised an eyebrow. Was he being serious or just trying to make her feel better?

"Usually."

She couldn't keep the smile from growing on her face. "Like... what kind of glow?" It wasn't often she was close enough to hear a man's honest opinions of her.

His eyes caught hers. "Like the soft glow of a lantern just before dark. Its purpose is to bring peace about the darkness to come, rather than to give light, but its presence is just as comforting." Elias went back to eating as if he'd just said it may rain tomorrow. It was a beautiful compliment. And knowing Elias wasn't trying to court her made it all the more heartfelt. If Elias saw little things like that about her, she wondered what Jonas noticed.

∽

"Ouch," Anna May said, as her oldest sister, Regina, pulled the hairbrush through her knotted hair.

"Well, if you'd of let me brush through it yesterday, it wouldn't be in such a mess, now would it?" The brush stopped abruptly about three-fourths of the way down, causing her to remove it and start again from the bottom.

It had only been a few minutes, but to Anna May it had felt like an hour of torture. "It's exhausting. You have no idea. I've a mind to shave it all off."

Her sister gasped. "Don't go doing anything stupid like that. You'll be well soon enough." She brushed through the tangled section and then started on another. "It would be funny though," she added quietly.

"What?"

"To see the look on Elias's face on your wedding night, when he pulls the *kapp* off for the first time and finds you bald." Her bubbling laughter echoed off the hardwood floor.

"Elias is not my *beau*, for your information."

"Sure he isn't."

"He's not." Anna May turned her head, pulling the hair from Regina's hands.

"I'm not here to argue with you, *schweshta*. I'm just trying to make you look nice for company."

"Who's coming this time?" So many people had come to visit in the last week, but none had announced it beforehand. They would drop in anytime after breakfast and before supper, talking with Anna May a while and then helping *Mueter* in the kitchen or with tidying up and then they'd be on their merry way. If they were too boring, Anna May would pretend to sleep and they'd leave sooner, or at least take their conversation with *Mueter* into the kitchen.

"The Hilty brothers are helping *Vater* in the north field today. They should be coming in for dinner any time. I just hope *Mueter* fixed enough food for them. It'll be like feeding a couple oxen."

"The Hilty brothers?" Elias had several brothers of different ages, but when someone said *the Hilty brothers* they meant Jonas and Elias. Together they could get the work done faster than anybody. However, it was difficult to get them together. They didn't often show up for the same frolics anymore. She wondered what made them want to work together today with *Vater*.

"*Ja*, and if you'll cooperate I'll have time to set the table for *Mueter*. So do you want me to help you with your hair, or would you prefer me to sheer you like a sheep? Because either way I was told to help you get that *kapp* on your head."

Anna May laughed at her sister's attempt at being stern. "All right. Carry on." Of course she wanted her hair up if Jonas was coming. It would be no *guete* for him to see her like this. She pinched her cheeks. Was she glowing?

She felt her sister's fingers move nimbly around her hair. She'd made a good tight bun, not the loose kind like *Mueter* would have done for her. But *Mueter* was still afraid to do anything that may hurt her. If only she knew that the pain was severe enough at times, she longed for her bun to be too tight, if only to distract her from pain elsewhere. Her sister pulled the *kapp* down and Anna May tied it in the front in a neat bow.

"There. I'll bring you a plate soon."

"*Danki,*" Anna May said.

She couldn't believe Jonas was going to be in her house. She straightened up the covers and tried her best to look presentable.

In a few moments she heard the men enter through the kitchen, boots shuffling on the hardwood floor, and *Vater* thanking them for their hard work. Anna May listened hard, hoping Jonas would eat his dinner in the living room with her. Chairs scraped against the floor, and in a moment everything was quiet.

Anna May frowned. Had even Elias forgotten she was bedridden in the living room?

Footsteps grew louder and her sister appeared with a plate of food in her hands. "*Mueter* and I will be in to sit with you in a moment," she said, handing her the plate.

Anna May tried not to look disappointed. In a few moments her *mueter* and sister were both seated with their food and drinks and they bowed their heads for a silent prayer. Anna May thanked God for the food and begged God to send Jonas in to talk to her. She knew she had no right. God didn't owe her any special favors, but she promised she'd find someone in pain as soon as she was healed and do her best to help them through it in return. She hoped it was enough. She hadn't seen Jonas since she kissed him under the big oak at the singing. She hoped he was thinking of her all this time, just as she was thinking of him.

After her sister took the empty plates to the kitchen, Anna May heard chairs shuffling again. The men were finished eating, too. She supposed they were *Vater's* company, not hers, but she still wished for a word with Jonas. She could hear heavy footsteps approaching.

Jonas and Elias entered the room. Anna May held her breath for Jonas's reaction.

"Hey, there, Anna May," he said.

"Jonas." She smiled.

His eyes held pity, making her wonder if maybe it would have been better not to be seen by him yet. The brothers stood close to her bed, the two of them towering over her like grain silos.

"I'll be in the kitchen if you need me, Anna May," *Mueter* said, walking away.

Jonas and Elias each took a seat, one on each side of her bed.

"So, how are you feelin'?" Jonas asked, leaning back in *Mueter's* rocking chair, his straw hat hanging on his knee.

"Much better today," she said with a smile.

"That's wonderful," Elias chimed in. "I'm so glad to hear it."

Anna May smiled, suddenly remembering she had two visitors, not just one. "So what have you been up to lately, Jonas?"

"Chores, mostly. There's been a lot more work around the house the last couple weeks."

Anna May thought for a moment. *Ja.* That was a stab at Elias for being away from home so much. It hurt to think she wasn't worth it to him, but perhaps it was just jealousy.

"Well, I hope I haven't caused you too much trouble," she said.

"Oh, no, it's not your fault, Anna May. If my clumsy oaf of a *brooda* had been more careful you wouldn't be lying there in the first place."

"It was an accident," Elias raised his voice a little, further defining the tension that was building in the room.

"*Ja*, an accident," Anna May said, trying to cool them both. "I could have ridden home with anyone that night, and the result could have been just the same." She hoped she'd been successful in making him feel sorry he hadn't taken her home. She hadn't planned on laying a guilt trip on him. It wasn't Jonas's fault the hitch on the buggy broke, but if he would have taken her instead of Beth, none of this would have happened.

Jonas's eyes scanned her up and down. "Well, you look real good, Anna May." Did he mean she didn't look as broken as he expected or did he find her attractive? "When is it they think you'll be out of the bed?"

"I don't really know. The doctor said it would be nine to twelve weeks before I'm healed completely, but surely he can't expect me to stay in bed all that time. The surgical screws they put in are supposed to help me to heal faster."

"Do they take them out?"

"*Nay*, they're with me forever." The realization that even when she fully healed she'd still have the metal inside her made her feel a bit sorry for herself. Like she'd never be perfect and whole again. Still, it was her own fault. If she hadn't been trying to make Jonas jealous, this never would have happened.

"They've got a lady coming out to check on me next week sometime."

"Well, I can't wait till you can come back to church and singings." Jonas's eyes met hers. Was he trying to communicate something he didn't want Elias to hear?

"I'm looking forward to it myself."

He had been thinking of her. The kiss she'd left him with was enough to carry them both through. She was determined to get better and meet Jonas for a Sunday singing.

CHAPTER 4

*T*he August heat bore down hard on Anna May's head, threatening to bake her in the dark blue dress and black *kapp* she wore.

"Do you want me to wheel you back inside?" Elias asked, wiping the sweat off his forehead.

"*Nay*. I've missed out on too much nice weather already," Anna May said.

"Well, you're getting around so much better now. I'll bet the doctor will tell you to get rid of the wheelchair altogether." Elias sat on the grass in the front yard beside her.

Anna May hoped so. Her appointment was in a few days. She hoped he'd tell her she was good as new and ready to do anything she wanted. *Mueter* wouldn't let her out of the house for church or a singing until he did. Kathy, her physical therapist, had worked her hard to get her to this point. Anna May would still need to keep up the exercises to build her strength and endurance, but she'd come so far in the past months. She only used the wheelchair because she still tired so easily. She felt God was finally smiling down on her again. After reading her Bible and praying with Elias each time he came over she certainly hoped He was. She would need God on her side if she was going to get Jonas Hilty to ask her to marry him.

"Where is the next singing, anyway?" she asked.

"I believe it's at the Wittmer's."

According to the rotation that would mean Rachel Wittmer. She had two marrying-aged daughters, Emma and Miriam. They would be the ones organizing the games and the singing in the evening. Anna May wasn't close with either of them, but it wasn't the women she was interested in visiting with anyway.

Elias adjusted his long legs, stretching them out on the lawn. "The bishop passed around the sign-up sheet for fall baptismal classes."

"Already?" It was difficult to think of fall classes and marrying season when it was so blamed hot outside.

"It's just around the corner."

Anna May twisted carefully in her chair. "I can't believe I practically missed the whole summer."

"I wouldn't call it missed, you just spent it a little more restfully." Elias always put a sunny spin on everything. "Are you going to sign up? For the classes?" he asked.

"I hadn't thought about it," Anna May said.

"Me either, until Jonas and I saw the sheet."

"Jonas?"

"*Ja*, he and I were some of the first to sign."

So Jonas Hilty was finally joining church. This was good news. That meant he was ready to settle down. And settling down meant choosing a life mate.

"I believe it's high time for me to join church too, Elias. Do you think you could put my name on the paper for me? I'm sure the doctor will release me at my next appointment." She could just as easily do it herself, there was plenty of time, only she wanted Jonas to see her name listed, as close to his as it could be.

"Sure thing, Anna May." Elias grinned from ear to ear.

She hoped he didn't get the wrong idea. Elias had been a *guete* friend to her while she healed. In the beginning he'd come to check on her most every day. And after she started therapy he came at least a few times a week. They had played board games, talked about most everything, and he read the Bible to her at times when she thought she couldn't bear the pain any longer. But it was just that—a friendship. It was Jonas she wanted, it always had been, and she'd done her best to be honest with Elias ever since the accident. She feared God's wrath and Hell fire if she didn't.

Elias was still smiling. It would be difficult, but Anna May would tell him again if she needed to. She'd know after the next singing.

THE ROOM WAS UNNATURALLY cold for the heat of summer. Anna May shivered a little, but it might have been more from excitement. It was almost over and Anna May couldn't wait. She'd spent weeks learning to walk, at first on crutches, and doing stretches and exercises to build strength and flexibility. This was the appointment she'd been waiting for; the one where the doctor would check her and say well done. Where he would tell her it was okay to do all the things she wanted to do again, like attending church and singings.

She sat in the tiny room in a wheelchair, waiting with *Mueter* and *Vater* for the doctor to come in and explain to them what he saw on the X-Ray they'd just taken.

Her regular doctor couldn't make the appointment. He'd had his whole day rescheduled, and the receptionist couldn't reach Anna May, so another doctor was filling in. She hoped the outcome would be the same. As long as he told her she could attend the next singing, it didn't matter to Anna May.

There was a knock at the door just before it opened. "Anna May Shetler?" the doctor said, his perfect teeth shining in a bright smile. He had dark brown hair, cut short and arranged perfectly.

Anna May nodded as he stuck out his hand to each of them in turn.

"Hi, I'm Richard O'Dell. I'm filling in for Dr. Combs. Actually, you're my only appointment for the day. That's why I'm in such a good mood, I get to play golf the rest of the day. You like to play golf, Anna May?"

She shook her head.

"You guys play a lot of volleyball though, right? That's much better exercise than golf anyway." He laughed as if he'd just told a joke. "Well, I've got your X-Ray here." He rammed the film upwards into the black frame hanging on the wall and flipped a switch. The light came on, showing a picture of Anna May's fragile bones. "The dark spots are the pins they put in." He pointed to the film as he spoke. "It looks like everything is healing beautifully. Have you had any trouble?"

"It still hurts sometimes, but not nearly like it did." Anna May rubbed her hands together, trying to warm them.

"Yes, pelvic fractures can be very painful, and as the bone rebuilds itself it can continue to cause pain. Do you still have prescription refills?"

"Ja."

"And are you keeping up with your therapy exercises?"

"Ja."

"Good. Those will help." He took a deep breath. "Well, I don't know what restrictions Dr. Combs placed on you, but I'm going to say you're ready to slowly and gradually start building up to doing all the things you did before—minus the flying out of buggies." He stopped, waiting for Anna May to smile along with him.

She loosened up a little, glad he was giving her good news.

"You should refrain from doing any strenuous work or exercise for a while, until you've gradually worked up to it. No jogging, lifting heavy weights, that sort of thing, but light house-work will be fine and walking as far as you're comfortable. You just don't want to push yourself too hard at first. Take your time."

"Is there any long term damage we should know about?" her *mueter* asked.

"Well, it's difficult to say. Fractures like this usually come with a high likelihood of fertility issues, and if Anna May is able to conceive, childbirth could prove difficult. I would recommend a hospital delivery, rather than a home delivery with a midwife. Most likely you'll be looking at a c-section. Does that answer your question?"

"Wait," Anna May said. "You mean, I can't have children?"

"I didn't say that, exactly. Many women with pelvic fractures as severe as yours have trouble conceiving, but it's not impossi-ble, and a good fertility doctor may be able to help."

"We leave issues like that up the Lord," *Vater* said with a stern look.

"I understand," the doctor said, pressing his lips together.

Anna May understood all right. The Lord wasn't done punishing her yet.

"Can I answer any more questions?" the doctor asked.

Anna May could tell he was wrapping things up, no doubt ready to be on his way to play golf.

"I was wondering if I could…" Why couldn't she find her words? Would she really not be able to bear children of her own?

"You're clear for all kinds of low-impact activities, including with your husband, if that's what you're asking."

Anna May blushed. "Can I ride in a buggy to church?" she asked quietly.

She knew she could, she just wanted *Mueter* to hear it from the doctor's mouth, so there would be no arguing about it later.

"Yes, you may want to sit on a pillow if it's bumpy and do be careful. It can take up to a year to fully recover from this kind of injury."

The doctor shook everyone's hand again and told them to have a good day. *Vater* wheeled Anna May out to the van where their hired driver awaited.

It was as if someone had pulled the life out of Anna May. A silent tear escaped. She'd tried so hard to do what was right; why was she still being punished?

MUETER AND VATER went out as soon as they arrived back home, telling the whole community what the doctor had said. They asked everyone for continued prayers, but Anna May had given up on that. The Lord was still angry with her and that made her angry with Him. He knew how much she wanted to be with Jonas. Now how could she? Jonas wouldn't want her, nor would any other man in Swan Creek Settlement. The doctor had said it was possible for her to have children, but not likely. Only the hand of God could make it so, and He wasn't going to. Was there nothing to help her find favor with God?

Anna May sat at the kitchen table, cutting up onions to help *Mueter* with dinner, when Elias walked in.

"How are you feeling, Anna May?" It was the first thing he always said to her upon arriving. Today, she wasn't sure how to respond.

"Let me know when you get those onions chopped, dear. I'll be outside." *Mueter* shut the big door behind her when she left, something they didn't do during the day this time of year.

"What's wrong?" Elias asked as he took a seat next to her.

"I suppose you'll find out soon enough. The doctor said I may not be able to bear children." It was embarrassing and forward of her to say to Elias, but at least it was out there. Now maybe he'd stay away from her and she wouldn't have to tell him she wasn't interested.

"Anna May, I'm so sorry."

She looked at him and his eyes welled up with tears. The sight brought an outburst of her own. Sliding the cutting board out of the way, she put her head down onto the table, cradling it with her arms and sobbed. Had she been that bad a person that God would do this to her? Weren't there others out there He could exercise His wrath upon? How could one all seeing, all knowing, able to do anything for anyone at any time, leave her broken forever? It would have been better if she'd died in the buggy accident than to never be able to marry and bear children. What kind of life would she have now?

When her tears were spent, she remembered Elias was in the room with her. She raised her head slowly, peeking up at him. He had his head down, too, praying. She should tell him he was wasting his time, that God had no intentions of helping her, but deep down she hoped God owed Elias a favor, and that he'd be able to bargain for her.

WEEKS PASSED. Elias had tried countless times to tell her that God was in control of her future, but that was what Anna May was afraid of. She had missed a singing night already because she didn't know what to say to everyone and she refused to miss another.

Church had been difficult to sit through without the wheelchair. The hard pew was torture and she refused to sit on a pillow in public. Still, all eyes were on her. Her name even came up in the sermon once or twice when the preacher talked about having faith. Anna May was glad when church was over. It was the singing and youth games, held later in the day, she had come for, when she'd finally see Jonas away from her *Vater* and *Mueter* and hopefully find out what he thought of her.

After dinner on the grounds, some of the youth set up the volleyball net. By then, Anna May was feeling the effects of sitting on the hard bench. She ached deep. The pills she carried in her dress pocket made her sleepy and this wasn't the place to be sleepy. She wanted to be alert and say all the right things when she was finally able to speak to Jonas.

Anna May sat in a lawn chair not too far from the volleyball net as she watched Emma Wittmer approach.

"Anna May, can't I get you anything? How 'bout a pillow?"

"*Nay*, that's nice of you, Emma," Anna May said.

"Well, how 'bout some sweet tea?"

"Sure," Anna May said. She watched Emma rush to get a drink and wondered why her friend Becca didn't like Emma. She seemed sweet as pie. Anna May could get around pretty well now, she really didn't need anyone bringing her pillows and sweet tea all the time, but she sure was hurting now.

Each person that walked by gave her a smile that read pity. A flock of girls had surrounded her to keep her company. They told her how nice she looked and how nice it was to see her out. None of it mattered, though. There was only one person whose opinion mattered to Anna May.

By the time the singing was done, the pain was nearly unbearable. Still, she'd waited so long for this, how could she leave early and wait two more weeks for the next singing? She walked slowly out of the barn doors into the night air. Suddenly, she was face to face with Jonas.

"Hey, there, Anna May," he said.

"Jonas."

"That sure was a nice singing," he said.

"*Ja*, it was," Anna May said, trying to hide the pain. She forced Jonas's eyes to meet hers.

There it was. Pity.

Her heart sank. She'd hoped seeing her out of bed would change things. Was there any hope at all? "Would you like to take a walk, Jonas?" She smiled her best.

"I don't know, Anna May. Maybe you should take it easy for a while." His tone wasn't playful anymore, but serious. Had so much changed between them since he'd visited her after her accident?

"I heard you signed up for baptismal classes," Anna May said.

"*Ja*. I figured it was time." His eyes darted about.

"Me, too. I figured it was time to put away childish things and think on settling down." That was what he wanted, wasn't it? Someone to settle down with?

"That's real nice, Anna May. I'm happy for you."

A stabbing pain in Anna May's heart matched the one she felt in her broken bones. He was happy for her? Those weren't the words she'd waited so long to hear. Her breathing began to be labored. Suddenly she felt a larger than average presence beside her.

Elias.

"You look like you're hurting again, Anna May. Can I take you home?" he asked.

Jonas tipped his hat and walked away. She wanted to scream at him to stay, but it was no use. He saw her differently now. She was broken beyond repair.

A LANTERN WAS LIT in the kitchen when they arrived at her home. *Mueter* had waited up for her, breaking the unspoken rule. The adults weren't supposed to know which youth was seeing another. And when a youth attended their first singing, a sibling or cousin would instruct them never to tell any of the adults who they saw riding with whom. It was up to the couple if they wanted to keep it a secret or not, but when she'd had the accident everyone in the community soon found out she was riding with Elias. Since then everyone had the idea they were a couple. Elias knew better, though. She had told him so. She had tried telling her *mueter* and sister but to no avail. They hadn't believed her.

The way Elias hung around during her recovery, why would they? So here *Mueter* was, sitting at the table waiting for her to arrive.

"Well, how'd it go?" she asked when they were safely inside the kitchen.

Elias was still at Anna May's side. "I'm going to head on out. I'll be over Wednesday to help your *vater*. I'll check on you then?"

Anna May nodded.

"You don't have to be in a hurry, Elias," *Mueter* said quickly. "I was just worried about Anna May. I'm going up to bed right now, though. You two sit and talk as long as you'd like." *Mueter* smiled and hurried out of the room. She must have known she'd crossed a line she shouldn't have. Still, it was very trusting of her to leave them alone when it was obvious *Mueter* wanted more than anything for her to have Elias as her *beau*.

"Do you need a pain pill?" he asked.

She nodded. "I have one in my pocket."

He fetched a glass of water and sat down at the table beside her. "Why didn't you take it before?"

"They make me sleepy," she said, popping it in her mouth and washing it down quickly.

"Well, it was a big day for you. Sleep is what you need right now."

"Thank you, Elias." Anna May stared down at the table.

"You're welcome."

But Anna May hadn't meant for the water. "Thank you for being my friend," she said. He had been a better friend to her all this time than her best friend Becca. It was only now she was seeing it. Elias took her hand in his and it reminded Anna May of waking up in the hospital and seeing Elias crying by her bedside.

He was here because he felt guilty. She looked into his eyes, so much pain behind them. How much more guilt had he felt after hearing the news? He'd broken her beyond repair. She knew he was sorry but it was what it was. She wanted to blame him for it, to hate him even, but he had been much too good to her for that.

He sighed and the flame in the lantern flickered. He leaned forward. Was he going to kiss her? How would she tell him not to? She sat still as a stone. His lips met hers but only for a second.

"Elias, I…" she shook her head.

"You need your rest, Anna May. I'll see you Wednesday." Elias rose and quietly let himself out the kitchen door.

CHAPTER 5

*A*nna May had never agreed to have Elias as her *beau*, but as time passed, she wondered if maybe he was. *Mueter, Vater,* and her sister all believed it, as did most of the community. She wondered if Elias believed it, which would leave her being the last to know. Anna May walked through the garden trying to think back to all the signs she'd somehow missed. He came over all the time to help *Vater* or just to check in on her. She was well now, and they both knew there was no need.

He was a regular visitor at the supper table and *Mueter* adored him, always telling Anna May what a handsome young man he was. But the most interesting part was how she couldn't get any of the eligible men to speak to her at singings or in town. Were they rejecting her for her brokenness or did they fear the wrath of Elias? Anna May chuckled to herself. She could never imagine Elias angry, much less a threat to anyone.

Baptismal classes would soon be over and she'd be expected to take a vow before the church. Elias and Jonas would be taking it, too. It was the only way a community member was allowed to marry. After joining church, they would pair up quickly and start families of their own. Anna May was still holding out hope that maybe, somehow, she could do so with Jonas Hilty. Only it would be impossible with his brother acting like her *beau*. What could she do? With the marrying season fast approaching, she would need to think of something quick. She didn't want to hurt Elias, but it would hurt him more if she didn't tell him.

Mueter had invited him to supper and Anna May decided she'd take him aside after that and let him know where things stood between them. He was a gentle soul, and she prayed that God would help her find the words to say to him.

"You love him, Lord. For his sake, not mine, help me to say the right things." She figured God would hear that prayer, since it was meant so unselfishly. God might still be put out with her, but Elias He'd found favor with. She could see it in the way Elias talked.

That evening after supper, Anna May asked Elias to take a walk with her. They strolled around the barn lot, Anna May waiting anxiously for God to deliver the words that so desperately needed said. "Elias," she started, finally willing to venture with or without God's help, "I need to talk to you about something."

He stopped walking and turned to face her, his form a mountain that moved slowly.

"Maybe we should sit," Anna May suggested.

"Are you not feeling well?" he asked, scanning her face as if to gauge her well-being.

"I'm fine," she said, finding a grassy spot to sit.

Elias sat down on the ground beside her. "What's wrong?"

"Elias, I'm never going to be like other women in the community."

He cocked his head to one side. "I believe God created you unique, that's true."

"You know what I meant by that. I won't be the wife that most men will want. I may not be able to bear any children at all, much less the usual eight or ten."

"That's up to the *guete* Lord, not the doctors."

"Either way," Anna May said. "I've told you before, but I think it needs repeating. I forgive you, Elias. It wasn't your fault any of this happened. If anything, it was mine. You don't owe me anything and I don't expect anything from you. You can stop coming over all the time, and I'll find my own ride home from singings. You're joining church soon, and it's about time you found yourself a *guete* woman to wed."

He eyed her curiously. "I think I've already found the woman for me, but she's telling me to go away. So what am I to do?"

"Just go, Elias. It's for the best."

Elias stood to his feet and reached his hand down to her. She took it and he carefully helped her to a standing position. "I'll see you tomorrow, Anna May," he said and kissed her softly on the cheek.

Anna May replayed the whole scene in her mind, wondering what must be going through his head. Had she still not gotten her point across? What more could she say without being outright mean?

IT WAS hard to get away from Elias, but somehow she had. Anna May found herself hiding in the dark behind the same oak tree where she'd kissed Jonas Hilty back in the early spring. Now it was fall, marrying season, and today's baptism had made her and Jonas both eligible to marry. She hoped she could once again catch Jonas unaware on his way to the drink table and not attract anyone else's attention in the process.

The night air was crisp and cool but Anna May's palms were sweating. She wiped them on her dress as she saw him approaching. Her heart sped like a race horse as she stepped out from behind the tree. "Hello, Jonas," she said.

"Anna May, where did you come from?"

"Oh, you know how I like to look at the stars," she said with a hint of dreaminess in her voice.

"Well, it's too cloudy to see any tonight," Jonas said, looking up.

"That's why I came back." Did she have to spell it out for him? "You know, it seems like we've been here before…"

Jonas smiled. "*Ja*, we have. But that was before you started seeing my *brooda*."

Anna May took a step closer. "Elias is bound to me by guilt—nothing more. I've tried to tell him to let it go but he won't."

"You mean there's nothing between you two?"

"*Nay*." Anna May gazed longingly at Jonas's mouth. When he didn't try to kiss her she said, "You know, if I remember right, I believe you promised me a ride home, that is, if you're not already taking Beth home tonight." Anna May knew he and Beth hadn't been seeing each other. She'd had Becca keeping an eye on who Jonas left with for some time now.

"I believe I'd be afraid you might break, Anna May," he said nervously.

"The doctor said I wouldn't, I asked." She made eyes at him, hoping he would understand.

His hesitation angered her. She took a deep breath. "It's because of what the doctor said, isn't it?" she asked.

He shook his head. "*Nay*."

"You know, Jonas Hilty, I thought we had a connection. I thought you might be the only one to tell me the truth about how people see me now. But maybe that's what you're doing."

"There's something you should know." Jonas swallowed hard. Suddenly Naomi Byler appeared and took him by the arm. "I've asked Naomi to marry me," Jonas said.

Naomi pushed his shoulder with hers playfully. "I thought we were going to wait for it to be published before we told anyone." She giggled.

"Well," Jonas said, "Anna May knows how to keep a secret, don't you, Anna May?"

Anna May nodded absentmindedly. "I'm so…happy for you," she choked out.

"Thank you," Naomi said. "Come on, Jonas, we've got so much planning to do." She ushered him away and with that, any hope of ever marrying Jonas walked away with her.

~

ANNA MAY LAY on her bed, staring at the ceiling for the fourth day in a row. She had her mother in fits worrying about her, but it couldn't be helped. She hated God for doing this to her. She understood needing a whipping when you'd done wrong, but this? It was too much to bear. God had taken from her the only thing in life she ever truly wanted. And now there wasn't even any hope of getting it back. She had laid in bed all those months and now she was content to lay in it for all of eternity.

Suddenly, there was a knock on the bedroom door. "I'm not feeling well, *Mueter*. Please leave me be," she said.

The door opened and her *mueter* peeked her head in. "I was just checking to be sure you were decent. You have a visitor. Her head disappeared and the door opened completely. Elias stood on the other side of it, *Mueter* could no longer be seen. Elias walked in, ducking under the door frame, and sat on the side of the bed.

"What are you doing in my room, Elias Hilty? Have you no decency?" she spat out.

"Your *mueter* is worried about you and so am I. She asked me to come up and talk to you."

Well, that explained it. Her *mueter* was so eager for her to marry Elias she'd sent him to her bedroom. How forward of them both. "Well, what is it you plan to say to make everything better?"

"Marry me." He looked her dead in the eye, waiting for a response.

"What?" Anna May's voice softened. "Elias, I thought we talked about this." She sat upright.

"You talked, now I'm having my say. I want you as my wife, Anna May Shetler. I want to take care of you and love you the rest of my life. Will you be my *fro?*"

She knew why he was asking. He broke her and there was no fixing it. No one else wanted her to be their wife, so it was up to him to take responsibility. Anna May hung her head in defeat. He would care for her for life, working away the guilt year by year. She didn't love him, not the way a girl should love her *beau*, but she knew he'd make a *guete* husband. She'd tried to get him to see he didn't owe her, that he was free to marry another, but his guilt kept drawing him back. Everyone already thought they were together, they might as well make it official.

"You know you don't have to," Anna May said. "It would be best for you to find another."

"Anna May…" He shook his head.

"But I know you won't. So I accept."

Jeb Lengacher and Emma Wittmer stood before the church congregation and Bishop Amos declared them to be husband and wife. It was a beautiful wedding. Anna May could hardly believe hers would be next. Jeb and Emma looked so happy together as they sat down to dinner with friends and family gathered all around them. David Schwartz held a chair out for Ruth and Anna May envied the way he looked at her. They were together because they wanted to be, not because of guilt or a sense of responsibility. The way, she was sure, Jonas would have looked at her if she'd never been in that horrible accident. She still longed for Jonas, even though she knew he'd never be hers. How long before that went away?

Anna May was tired of feeling abnormal. She was different than all the other women in the community and now her marriage would be different, too. Forever she'd be known in the minds of the community as the gal Elias Hilty had to marry out of a sense of duty. But it was he who'd made the decision. She'd tried to talk him out of it. It was his fault he was going to be bound to her for the rest of their lives. She only hoped he didn't regret it.

~

On her wedding night, Anna May had done all the things that were expected of her as a *guete fro*. Then, late into the night, after Elias was out cold, she'd cried herself to sleep. She didn't love him and he didn't love her. She was sure things were supposed to be different in a marriage. They hadn't been married but a few hours and she was already miserable. How long would she have to endure God's displeasure of her?

~

Being married while still living in her *vater's* house was beginning to feel like serving two masters. Not that either of them were the least bit cruel, but they both had different ideas about what Anna May should be doing. *Vater* told her to rest and to take it easy, while Elias told her to get out in the community more. Anna May was glad they were moving out. Elias had built them a new home during the winter and it was finally ready to move into.

It was moving day, only no one would let her move a thing. Not one box. And she wasn't allowed to carry anything down the stairs, either, lest she fall and break her bones all over again.

Although the thought had crossed her mind a time or two, her family was being ridiculous. She wasn't made of glass and doing nothing was causing her more harm than good.

She struggled with her frustration as she sat in the living room, watching the rest of the family flutter about busily. She thought about going back to bed, only her bed wasn't hers anymore. It now belonged to her younger siblings. Elias had purchased a new bed for them, already set up at the new house.

The sound of Elias's boots coming near didn't phase Anna May. He sat down beside her. "What's wrong?" he asked.

"Nothing. Unless you count the fact that no one has let me lift a finger all day to help with my own things. Even my underwear in the drawer were moved out from under me." Anna May crossed her arms.

"That was probably your *mueter*. I didn't touch them, I promise." His eyes were big, like he didn't want any trouble from her.

"I figured as much."

"Well, things will be different after today, you'll see." He took hold of her hand. It still felt strange for him to touch her. They'd been married months now, but he still felt like a good friend rather than a husband. And oh, how awkward the nights could get. He was a *guete* man. He deserved better. At least someone who wasn't still pining away for his twin brother. Anna May was ashamed of herself, but what could she do about it? Elias had said it would be different in their own home. Anna May certainly hoped so.

"I HEAR Aunt Ada's having a quilting bee this afternoon. You should go." Elias sat at the kitchen table, eating his eggs and toast.

"I'd rather not," Anna May said, staring out the window above the sink.

It was summer, over a year since the doctor's news had shattered her life. Broken bones she could handle, bedrest for months, constant severe pain, and people taking pity on her as well, but when he'd said she couldn't have children, that was the breaking point. A year of not being with child told Anna May it was true. God didn't love her. She wondered why He made her in the first place, if not to torment her. To dangle Jonas Hilty in front of her face and then snatch him away. And ruining any chance she had at ever being a *mueter*. She was married to a man bound to her by pity. And it was all "in God's will."

Everyone had prayed, Elias the most, but what *guete* had it done? Nothing had changed. She was still miserable and childless, and married to the wrong man.

"You really need to get out of this house," Elias said. "It's not *guete* for you to be shut up in here all day by yourself." He pushed his plate away when he'd finished.

"You don't know what it's like being around the other women. I'd rather just stay home." Anna May still looked longingly out the window instead of at Elias.

"Babies are a gift from God, given in His own time. We must be patient and not lose hope."

The chair scraped against the floor, then Elias stood behind her with his hand on her shoulder. "Look at me," he said.

Anna May turned and faced her husband, looking straight up at him. He put his finger under her chin. "I love you, Anna May."

Sure he did. In a world where love meant being responsible for. It was the same way she "loved" doing the wash. It was her responsibility and she wouldn't let anyone do it for her, but she didn't really love it, as much as she tolerated it. It was hers all the same, though.

She turned around and pumped out a glass of water. Reaching into the cabinet by the sink she pulled out a little amber bottle.

Elias put his hand on hers, closing it around her hand and the bottle both. "Do you really need those, Anna May?"

The doctor's office wouldn't give her any more of the *guete* pills, the ones that helped her forget about everything and just sleep. They prescribed her antidepressants instead. She felt weird with them and more weird without them.

"*Ja.*"

"Pills are supposed to help you get better and I don't think those are doing their job," he said softly.

"Then what will, Elias?"

He took the pills from her and set them down on the counter. "Only God's healing."

"It's been a year. This is all the healing I'm going to get." She avoided his eyes.

"I meant in here." He placed her hand on her heart. She sighed. He was going to preach to her again. She used to be able to talk to him about anything, but now, every time she did he would start belting out a sermon louder and longer than Bishop Amos on church day.

"I think I'll go lie down." Anna May sidestepped Elias and went into the bedroom, curling up on the bed. She listened for him to leave the house. She knew he had work to do, she just hoped it was enough to keep him out of the house till supper. She hated it when he was there and she hated it even more when she was left alone, but going anywhere was out of the question. She didn't know how to talk to anyone anymore, not even her own family and friends.

CHAPTER 6

A knock at the door awakened Anna May. "Just a minute," she yelled from the bedroom. She glanced at the clock on the wall.

Two in the afternoon.

She straightened her *kapp* just before she opened the door. "Becca? What are you doing here?" she asked.

"I hadn't seen you around in a long time and thought I'd pop in. So what are you up to today?" Becca stood just inside the kitchen door, looking around.

"I was...just tidying up."

Becca eyed her suspiciously. "I don't think you were," she said slowly, peeking into the bedroom. Leave it to Becca to forget good manners and snoop. The bed wasn't made.

"Okay, I was just lying down a bit. What's it to you?" Anna May was glad it was her friend and not someone else who had caught her slacking on her chores.

"You need to get out more." Becca pointed to Anna May as she spoke.

"You sound like Elias," Anna May said, sitting down at the

table. She wondered how she could be so tired even after a long nap.

"Well, maybe he's smart as well as handsome, ever think of that? And what's this?" Becca rushed over to the sink. "Are these breakfast dishes?" She scrunched up her nose as she picked up a plate.

Not caring anymore what Becca found, Anna May made no effort to get up. "Elias said he wasn't coming home for dinner, so I figured I'd get to them later."

"Anna May, really? Come on, I'll help." Becca started pumping water and moving dishes about. Anna May got up and fumbled around like it wasn't even her own kitchen they were in. In a little while they had things back in order.

"There now, isn't that better?" Becca asked. "Now we can sit and relax a spell."

Anna May was glad for it. She was exhausted. She led her friend into the living room and sat down.

"So," Becca said, "tell me what it's like being married to one of the most handsome men in Swan Creek Settlement."

Anna May should have expected—since it was Becca, and since they were all alone in the house—not to count on ordinary polite conversation. "Why do you ask? Are you still upset he stopped asking you to ride with him?"

"Lands sakes, Anna May." She laughed nervously. "What a thing to say. Of course I'm not pining away for your husband. I've been riding with Sam for a while now. We'll probably get hitched this fall."

All Anna May's friends were grown and getting married. Where had the time gone? "I'm happy for you."

"I just asked because sometimes I wonder if you know what a *guete* feller you ended up with."

Anna May nodded. She knew Elias was a *guete* man and a *guete* husband. She just wished her heart knew it as well. Anna May debated about whether or not to tell Becca what was really on her mind. She decided not to. Even being close friends, it wasn't appropriate to say out loud. And how could someone like Becca understand anyway? She had always thought the world of Elias.

"So you're joining church this fall, then? I wondered if I'd ever see the day."

Becca laughed. "We're a sight, aren't we? Remember when we were twelve and made a pact never to join church?"

Anna May slowly rocked in the rocking chair. "We were going to wait until we were so old they tried to make us and then build a cabin on the other side of Swan Creek and live out our days in the woods."

Becca laughed. "I can just see how well that would have turned out. That was before we were interested in boys, though."

Anna May rested her head against the back of the rocker. "Maybe for you. I was born interested in boys."

"I think you're right. Didn't you chase some boy around in the second grade, trying to kiss him on the playground, and Emma Wittmer ran and told on you?"

Anna May nodded. "I'd forgotten about that." All this reminiscing was starting to make her feel sad. Were the best days of her life behind her already?

"Emma's always been a know-it-all tattle-tale."

Anna May felt a stab in her heart. It was something she knew Becca would never say to anyone but her. She didn't know Emma very well, but from what she could tell she was a sweet-heart. She wondered why Becca would say something like that, especially about her own sister-in-law. The whole conversation was suddenly uncomfortable for Anna May. The last thing she needed was for God to make her life worse for participating in gossip. It was time to take the conversation in a new direction.

"How's Jeb doing with the buggy business? I heard he was working for Reuben Miller now."

"Not *for* him, *with* him. They've become partners. And it really seems to be taking off."

"I'm glad for him. What about Sam? What kind of work does he want to do?"

"Sam's into horses. He wants to breed and train them."

"Sounds like a good business. He might want to talk to Elias. The Hiltys do some of that along with farming."

"*Ja*, I heard Jonas and Naomi were raising horses."

Another stab in Anna May's heart. Now she remembered why she never asked anyone over for company. "Would you like some tea, Becca? I believe I'll make some for myself." Anna May stood and walked into the kitchen.

Becca followed. "*Nay*, I'd better be running along. *Mueter* will be wanting me to help with the canning."

"Well, it was *guete* of you to drop in. We'll have to get together more often." Anna May tried to fake a smile as she said goodbye to her lifelong friend, maybe for always. She didn't intend on visiting with her anymore than she had to. It was just too painful.

"So how was your day?" Elias asked at the supper table.

"Same as always," she said. Every day seemed the same to Anna May—miserable.

"You didn't do anything exciting today?" he asked.

What was he getting at?

"*Nay*. Becca came to visit, but other than that it was the same as yesterday and the day before that, as far back as I can remember." She pushed her food around on her plate.

Elias dropped his fork to the table with a clank. "You mean after the accident."

It sent a jolt through Anna May. "You know I don't blame you for the accident," she said quickly, her head down.

"Sometimes I wonder," he said quietly.

A tense moment of silence passed.

"So how was your visit with Becca? Did you two catch up on old times?" Elias began eating again.

"I suppose."

"Well, was it a *guete* visit or wasn't it?" His brows were lowered, eyes focused firmly on her.

Why was he being so grouchy? "*Nay*, for your information, it wasn't."

"Why not? I thought she was one of your closest friends." Elias's tone had changed into one of compassion and understanding again. It was the Elias she was used to, though the grouchy Elias had been making appearances more often lately.

"Because Becca hasn't grown up yet. She was talking about Emma Wittmer—I mean Lengacher—and I didn't like it. Emma's a *guete* person; it's a shame Becca can't see that." Anna May pushed her plate forward. She'd only eaten half of what she thought she would when she'd fixed the plate.

"Perhaps it's time to make new friends," Elias said carefully. At least he wasn't being pushy.

"Perhaps."

ANNA MAY WAS EXHAUSTED. Between the housework and all the visitors she'd been getting lately, she just couldn't get enough rest. At least the house was staying cleaner. She feared if she didn't make up the bed someone would find out and she certainly couldn't let anyone see her with breakfast dishes in the sink at two in the afternoon. The days were passing by faster, but she wondered how long she could continue painting on a smile to keep other people from knowing what was really going on inside her.

She had just sat down when she heard a knock at the door. For a moment she thought about not answering it. She wondered if they'd believe she wasn't home. Elias would have a fit if she did, telling her how rude she was.

"I'm coming," she yelled as she made her way to the door. They'd wait for her or they wouldn't; she wasn't going to rush. She opened the door. Jeb's Emma stood on the other side.

"Emma, come in. What brings you around my way?" Anna May asked. It truly was a surprise. Emma had never visited her before, and they certainly hadn't been close during *Rumspringa*.

"I was just passing through and thought I'd invite you over to Ada Hilty's quilting bee tomorrow. The ladies have a real *guete* time and I'm sure you'd enjoy it." Emma looked around the room. "What a pretty place you got here."

"Thank you. I don't know, Emma. I hadn't thought about a quilting bee. What time does it start?" Anna May knew if she asked the time, Emma would at least believe she was considering it.

"It's at two, or just whenever you get dinner over with. Some of us are later than others." Emma's face shone with goodness. She was the kind of person Anna May wanted to be.

She'd spent too many years with Becca complaining about everything and everyone. Emma had God's favor and she was happy. Anna May wondered what that would be like.

"I don't know, Emma. I'll talk it over with Elias and think on it. Thank you for inviting me. Would you like some tea?"

"I would, but I've got to get back and get supper started for Jeb. But I bet you know how that is." Emma smiled and said goodbye, leaving Anna May to wonder the rest of the evening what errand could have Emma "just passing through" this far north in the settlement.

～

"How was your day, Anna May?" Elias asked at supper. "Did you have any visitors?" He avoided eye contact as he ate.

"Oh, just Jeb's Emma." Anna May took a big bite of food.

"And how'd that go?" he asked.

She chewed a bit, making him wait for her response. "Fine." Another big bite went in.

"So you had a *guete* visit then?"

Anna May nodded.

"Well, did she have any reason to come all this way or did she just want to talk?"

"Mmm, she wanted to invite me to a barn raising frolic tomorrow at two."

"A barn raising? I thought it was a quilting frolic. Who's getting a new barn?"

"I knew it." She slapped the table. "You sent Emma over here just like you sent Becca and everyone else in the community I've been entertaining for the last two weeks. Do you know how exhausting it is having company every day? It's all I can do to get my chores done."

His eyes flashed hot. "Well, if you'd leave the house now and then and get out into the community I wouldn't have to send the community to you."

"I don't feel like it, Elias."

He raised his voice. "You're going to the quilting bee tomorrow and that's final."

"I'm not."

"You're my *fro* and I say you're going!" Elias slammed his fist down on the table causing everything on it to jump.

Anna May's heart stopped. She ran into the bedroom and slammed the door behind her, throwing herself onto the bed in a flood of tears.

ANNA MAY DIDN'T WANT to leave the house and she wouldn't have if it hadn't been for the fact that Elias stayed home to see that she left. She knew her husband had told her to go to Ada Hilty's quilting bee and sit with the ladies for a couple of hours. She also knew the scriptures said she was to submit to her husband's wishes. Anna May had feared God's wrath if she didn't. But while driving her buggy down the road it occurred to her that there was nothing left for God to take from her except her life—a life she no longer cared about. She turned the buggy around, knowing full well that Elias wouldn't stay home all day. He'd wait for her to leave then go on to work. It was a *guete* plan, except she forgot he would ask a hundred probing questions till he got the truth out of her at supper time.

She pulled into the drive with a sick stomach and a guilty conscience. Should she turn around and just go? Emma had said some came late. And it wouldn't matter how long she was there as long as she'd shown up.

She turned the buggy around, but as she did she noticed Elias's buggy was still parked in the back with another buggy she didn't recognize. She couldn't help herself. She put on the emergency brake and hopped down, trying to form some excuse about something she'd forgotten to bring to Ada Hilty's quilting bee. She stepped into the house quietly, tiptoeing into the kitchen with bare feet.

"I just don't know what to do," Elias said. "I'm starting to think it's not just the accident."

"What do you mean?" another voice said.

Bishop Amos?

"I think she may have spiritual issues I didn't know about."

Was he telling all their problems to the bishop? How humiliating.

"Well, she's a member of the church. I baptized her myself."

"*Ja*, I know. But something's not right with her. I've tried everything. Maybe it's me she doesn't like."

"If you're doing your part, it's not you."

"She's starting to try my temper, Bishop. I don't know why God is testing me so."

"You wouldn't..."

"Hit her? Never. But still, it's building up inside."

Anna May had heard enough. She didn't want to find out what kind of temper her husband had by getting caught eavesdropping or disobeying his order to attend the quilting bee.

Anna May cried all the way to Ada Hilty's. She knew there was something wrong with her, it just knocked the wind out of her knowing her husband and everyone else probably did, too. She couldn't back out now, though. Elias was expecting a quilting bee report at supper time.

She walked in and sat down. Every married woman in the neighborhood sat in Ada's living room. Ada was passing around a plate of cinnamon rolls. Anna May wondered how long she'd have to stay to be able to prove she was there. A couple ladies greeted her, but most kept right on talking and laughing. Anna May had forgotten how to laugh.

Abigail Miller was cutting up to Emma Lengacher, "He gave me twin boys for a wedding gift and all I gave him was a jar of pickled okra." The room erupted with laughter.

"How are you, Anna May?" Emma said when the room quieted down some.

"I'm just running late today, sorry."

"No need to apologize. We haven't gotten much quilting done today, anyway. No wonder the men call it a hen party. Are we going to quilt or ain't we, ladies?" She laughed.

"As soon as I finish this cinnamon roll," Ada Hilty said, plopping herself down in a chair.

Anna May had been to a few quilting bees before she was married. This one wasn't much different. It was a chore staying alert enough to answer everyone's questions, but Anna May did her best.

Soon, the ladies were helping Ada clean up and heading to their buggies to rush home and fix supper for their families.

"It was *guete* to see you here, Anna May. I hope you'll come back next week," Emma said as Anna May headed for the door.

"*Ja*, maybe." Anna May didn't look back as she walked to her buggy, afraid of catching anyone else's attention. She'd thought Emma had wanted to be her friend. Only now she knew Elias had asked her to visit. At least she could say she'd attended the quilting bee. That was what he'd wanted. Maybe it would cure his temper.

"How was the quilting bee?" Elias asked as he sat down for supper.

Anna May set a plate in front of him. "Fine."

"Fine, meaning you went, right?"

"I did." Anna May prepared a plate of her own from the food sitting on the counter.

"Well, how was it?"

"I told you, it was fine." She sat down with her plate beside him and waited for him to say grace.

When he'd finished, she began eating, silently.

"Will you go back?" he asked.

"If you want me to, I suppose I'll have to, now won't I?"

"Don't be like that, Anna May. You know it's for your own *guete*."

"You're right."

He wanted her to be normal just as much as she wanted to feel normal. At least he would have his way. They ate the rest of their supper in silence.

CHAPTER 7

A few weeks had passed since Anna May attended the first quilting bee.

"Where's supper?" Elias asked as he sat down.

"It won't be ready for a bit. We're waiting on our guests to arrive."

"Guests?" he asked, wide-eyed.

"*Ja.* I've invited Jeb and Emma over. Is that okay?" Anna May was dicing tomatoes and avoiding eye contact with Elias. Anna May did her best to give the appearance of being normal for Elias's sake, and it seemed to be working. At least someone in the house was happy.

"Well, *ja.* Of course." His whole tone changed. "That's great."

She could feel his eyes on her, no doubt wanting to know what had gotten into her. Anna May hated having company, and she'd told Elias so on a regular basis.

A few moments later Jeb and Emma stood in her kitchen, Emma's dress starting to protrude a little in the middle. They had married the same week as Anna May and Elias, only now they were going to be parents, something she and Elias may never get the chance to experience.

"Let me help you, Anna May," Emma said.

"*Nay*, everything's ready to go. You both sit down." Anna May brought the food to the table, dish by dish. Finally she sat down and signaled Elias to say grace.

Supper went well. Anna May worked hard to smile and laugh at the right times and say the right things. She almost fooled herself into thinking she was having a good time. She wanted Elias to be proud of her for her effort, and not tell all their problems to Bishop Amos anymore.

After dessert and a long chat in the living room, Jeb and Emma headed home. Anna May let her shoulders relax as soon as the door closed. It had been exhausting putting on a show for so long. She went straight to her room and changed into her nightgown. Elias would have to shut up the chickens before he could come to bed.

He stood in the doorway. "Are you going to bed already?"

"*Ja*. Do you need me to do something?" she asked.

"*Nay*, I just thought we might talk."

"What do you want to talk about?" Anna May took off her *kapp*.

"I don't know. Anything."

"I'm kind of tired, Elias." She got into the bed and pulled up the covers.

"So you can talk with Jeb and Emma but not to me? Is that it?" The temper she once thought was impossible for Elias to have was again threatening.

She sat up in bed, alert. "I'll talk to you about whatever you want to talk about." She didn't want it to be her fault he was upset.

"Nevermind. I've got chores to do." The sound of Elias's boots could be heard going through the house and out the kitchen door.

～

IT SEEMED NO MATTER what Anna May said anymore, it set Elias to stomping out the door and across the property to the horse stalls. She tried to guard her words well, carefully weighing each one before she let it out of her mouth. It was a tiresome game she was sick of playing with him. A game she could never win. Had she said the sky looked like rain he would accuse her of not being optimistic enough. Or if she said the dish she'd prepared could use some work he would say she was just fishing for compliments. Once, she'd told him the corn wasn't growing very well and he'd said, "Of course not, Anna May. With faith like that, why would it?"

So when he sat on the edge of the bed one night just after she'd crawled in it and asked, "Why do you hate me, so?" Anna May was afraid to answer.

It didn't matter what she said, it wasn't going to end well. Anna May quickly tried to weigh her options but only came up blank. She didn't hate him, and it surprised her that he thought she did. She'd tried hard to be a *guete fro*, and do the things she was told, the things that were expected of her. They never argued in front of anyone, always keeping their personal problems private. She obeyed him and did everything he asked of her without complaint. She wasn't sure on what he based his reasoning that she hated him.

Not wanting to anger him by making him wait any longer she opted for the simplest answer, "I don't hate you, Elias."

He stared at the floor with his head down for a moment.

"Then why does it feel like it?" he whispered.

They sat in silence a long while. Anna May didn't know what to say. Then he got up and walked out the bedroom door.

IT WAS wash day and Anna May was out of soap. She stood in Ruth's store admiring the fine things for sale, the soap she'd came in for in her hand. Ruth was chatting up a storm, speaking their Swiss German dialect so fast Anna May could hardly keep up, when the bells on the door jangled and Naomi Hilty walked in. She was beautiful and she looked so happy.

With a husband like Jonas, why wouldn't she be?

Anna May shook her head, trying to dislodge the corrosive thought. Jonas was not hers and never would be. If she could just get over her anger about it, maybe she could remove the wedge that had been driven between her and Elias and then work on the one between her and God. She did her best to smile politely at Naomi. Not realizing a smile might not be enough for Naomi, Anna May cringed as she approached.

"Hey there, Anna May. I haven't seen you since second Christmas. *Vee bish do?*"

"*Guete, danki*, and you?" It surprised Anna May when the urge to wring Naomi's neck was absent. She knew Naomi had nothing to do with her own circumstance, but the thought of violence had crossed her mind during the holidays.

"Fine."

Anna May's eyes were drawn to Naomi's now swollen midsection.

Was everyone having a baby?

"Well, we need to get together more often, Anna May. Ain't it a shame our husbands are *breada* and they don't see each other for months at a time?"

"It is." Anna May couldn't imagine not seeing her brothers or sisters for that long, even though some of them could be difficult to be around sometimes. "How about you and Jonas come over for supper tonight. We'd love to have you both."

Naomi smiled brightly. "That's a great idea. We'll see you this evening."

Anna May paid for her soap and took one more look at Naomi before leaving the store. Naomi had something Anna May wanted. Not Jonas, for she knew that would never be, but happiness. Anna May doubted Naomi had to put on a fake smile and pretend to enjoy company. The woman had God's favor and Anna May wanted that, too. If it were at all possible, Anna May would find out her secret. It would be a difficult evening for sure, but the chance at being as happy as Naomi was too tempting to resist.

∼

"YOU DID WHAT?" Elias huffed. "How could you do that without asking me first?"

"I didn't think it was a big deal. You're always trying to get me to have company over. How was I supposed to know that didn't include your own kin?" Anna May stood at the sink, trying to wrap her mind around what she'd done wrong this time.

She could feel him approaching, towering over her at her back.

"You could have invited anyone in Swan Creek Settlement and you chose Jonas?" His volume was unnerving, especially at this distance. She spun around to face him. Elias slammed his fist down hard on the counter beside her, sending Anna May cowering.

A few tense seconds passed. She could hear his breathing slowing back down to normal. He reached for her. "I'm sorry, Anna May," he said, much calmer now. "You know I'd never hit you."

She'd never thought so before, but now, well, he was just so angry and unpredictable. Sidestepping him, she went outside for some fresh air. He'd scared her and he was sorry. At least it got him to calm his temper for the moment.

∼

THE SIGHT of Jonas and Elias together in the kitchen made Anna

May's stomach turn. She hated that she was still drawn to Jonas like flies to butter, but she'd hoped having him over would somehow help.

The tension at the supper table was as thick as the chocolate cream pie Anna May had made for dessert. Elias's eyes were stone cold toward her, and the looks passed back and forth between him and his *brooda* were even less friendly. What had Anna May done inviting them here? Naomi and Anna May exchanged several apologetic looks. Anna May could tell Naomi was just as surprised as she was at the discontent between the twin brothers. They'd shared their *mueter's* womb but they couldn't break bread at the same table? Had they put on an act at past social gatherings, or did they mind their manners better with their *mueter* and *vater* around? It was a concept Anna May was still having difficulty comprehending.

"So, your Aunt Ada said you've got some colts on the way," Anna May looked at Jonas as she spoke. "Were you planning on selling them or keeping them?"

"Keeping them. They're from some of *Vater's* finest." Jonas shoveled in the casserole. Anna May had made two of them, knowing how much Elias ate and thinking in doubles.

When Jonas didn't go on, Anna May continued, "Well, you're lucky, Naomi. It would be nice to play with baby colts. We never had any young horses growing up."

"Horses must be trained right from the beginning." Elias took a drink of sweet tea from the glass in front of him. "They're not to be fooled with or you could spook them and they'd never make a *guete* team horse."

Anna May lowered her head at his tone.

"It all depends on how well you train them," Jonas said. "You can't send a clumsy ox to train a colt, that's for sure." The glance Jonas sent toward Elias was accusing.

Why would he call Elias a clumsy ox? Elias had successfully trained as many of their *vater's* colts as Jonas had, maybe more.

Elias set his glass down hard, causing some of the liquid to fly out into a little puddle on the table. Jonas took another bite, acting as if he hadn't said anything wrong.

Naomi cleared her throat. "You've built a lovely home here, Elias. It's very cozy."

She means small.

Elias had called it their starter home, promising to build on when they needed to, but Anna May knew it would probably never come to that. She doubted Naomi meant any ill will in her comment, though.

"*Danki,*" Anna May said, answering for her husband, "Elias worked very hard building it. Did you see the cabinets he made?" She pointed to her kitchen cabinets, made of solid oak, varnished and polished to a shine.

"They're very nice," Naomi said. "Well, aren't you all glad cooler weather is on its way? I do love the fall season, don't you, Anna May?" Naomi was fidgeting with the cuff of her dress sleeve on top of the table, having already finished eating.

When there's nothing else, mention the weather, Anna May thought. "I do," she said, nodding her head. She wondered how to get the couple out of her house as quickly and politely as possible. If the men would finish eating, she could at least invite them into the living room, getting them away from the closeness of the kitchen table.

"This is very *guete*, Anna May," Jonas said, gesturing toward the casserole. "Naomi, you should make something like this sometime."

Naomi sat up straight as if someone pinched her. Was cooking a sore spot with her? Anna May began to watch the body language between Naomi and Jonas. The tense glances she sent her husband indicated things weren't as perfect as Anna May had pictured. Maybe being married to Jonas wasn't much different than being married to Elias. A comment like that would have pricked at Anna May, too, if Elias had been the one to say it. She was thankful he was more considerate than Jonas in front of company.

Anna May eyed Jonas, shoveling in the casserole with the table manners of a potbellied pig, his upper body hunched over the plate as he rested his elbow on the table. She'd certainly married the more mannerly of the two. Watching Jonas eat and pass snap judgments on her husband made Anna May begin to be thankful she hadn't married Jonas after all.

Elias caught her eye. She hoped he wasn't still sore with her. She smiled at him carefully, hoping he knew she was sorry.

CHAPTER 8

*T*hat night, while Elias was shutting up the chickens, Anna May changed into her nightgown, but left her prayer *kapp* on. She wanted to pray and know the Lord was hearing her. She was thankful God had opened her eyes to what a life with Jonas would have been like and with the wedge between them gone, she hoped she could be close with God in the way Elias and all the happy people in the community were.

Come to think of it, Elias hadn't been very happy lately. Had she caused her husband to sin, provoking him in his anger? It was difficult to please the Lord. Anna May wondered how any of the women in the community managed it, but somehow she knew they did. She could do it, too. With Jonas gone from her mind she could. Her husband deserved better. She would be the wife Elias needed, finally earning herself favor with God.

Anna May dropped to her knees beside the bed and made promises to God she truly hoped she could keep.

ANNA MAY THOUGHT hard about what to put in the sunshine box.

Its recipient was an elderly woman in the community who had fallen and broken a hip. Anna May remembered how painful broken bones were, and how long it took to recover. How much harder it would be for an eighty-year-old woman. When she finished, she sealed up the box and admired it. She'd made three this week alone and had already hand delivered two of them. If she left now she could get the last one out and be back before too long. She quickly scratched out a note to Elias, telling him she'd be home late.

She had a lovely visit with Edna Schwartz. What a dear old woman she was, but knowing Elias would be waiting for her, Anna May hurried back. She found him sitting at the kitchen table when she walked in.

"I'll have your supper ready in two winks, I promise." Anna May pulled out pots and pans and began throwing a meal together. She worked quickly and soon they were sitting together with food in front of them. It was then she realized Elias hadn't said a word to her since she came in. The note was still lying there on the table. Surely he'd read it and knew she'd been doing a good deed.

"Edna Schwartz is a dear soul, isn't she?" Anna May asked, trying to put the focus on the good she'd done during the day.

"*Ja*, she is," Elias said wearily.

"Did you…have a *guete* day?" she asked carefully.

"The same as yesterday, and the day before that, and every day as far back as I can remember."

She suspected he meant since he married her. Couldn't he see she was trying? That she wanted to do right? It wasn't that long ago he was practically trying to push her out the door to get her to leave the house. Why was God allowing him to act this way toward her when all she wanted was to serve him?

DESPITE THE WAY Elias spoke to her, it made Anna May feel *guete* inside to do nice things for people in the community. She didn't have children and probably never would. Maybe this was what God wanted her to do with her time. It was better than lying in bed all afternoon. It made her feel like she finally had a chance to earn God's favor.

All week long she'd helped out at the home of Sarah Cobb, who'd speared her foot with a pitchfork the week prior. Sarah had no daughters, only sons, and they were too young to help with the cooking. After dinner, Sarah had sat with her foot propped up in a chair, directing Anna May how to make her special lemon pudding pie for supper that evening. Anna May put together a salad for them to have with their supper; a casserole her neighbor had sent over. It'd be easy enough for Sarah's husband to reheat.

In the evenings, after making supper for Elias, Anna May would sit at the kitchen table and study the Bible until Elias would come in from evening chores and then they'd do their Bible devotions together.

She avoided gossip with people like Becca Lengacher, paid attention in church, volunteered every chance she could to help with a work frolic, and never said a cross word to Elias, no matter how much she wanted to. She even threw out her antidepressants in a bold step of faith. And for the most part, it was working. Gone were the days of feeling sorry for herself and her situation. She never sat with idle hands or dark thoughts and she knew it was only by the grace of God she was able to do that. But still, it was difficult. Each day was hard work, but she knew the reward in Heaven would be worth it.

The only problem was Elias. It seemed the harder she worked for the Lord the more put out with her he was and Anna May couldn't understand it. Back before they'd married, and Anna May gave little thought to pleasing God, Elias had his heart all for Him. Was he jealous of the time she spent with God? Couldn't he understand she needed to do these things? That God *wanted* her to do these things?

The kitchen door opened and Elias walked in, his boots muddy from the fall rains. He kicked them off by the door, and Anna May hopped to clean the wet spot they made in the floor.

"Sorry," he mumbled as she took the boots into the wash room and cleaned them enough they wouldn't leave puddles. He sat down at the kitchen table.

"You're a bit early for supper. Can I get you some coffee or something else to drink?"

He stared at the wall, not speaking.

"Are you okay, Elias?" His blank stare had Anna May beginning to worry.

"Did you ever love me?"

Her heart stopped. "Lands, what a question. Why are you asking me that?" Anna May sat down beside him.

"Because sometimes I wonder." His gaze wandered from the wall to Anna May, then down to the floor.

It broke Anna May's heart. He was a *guete* man, and she was trying so hard to do right by him. But she wasn't loving him the way he'd expected. He was still disappointed in her. But didn't he know from the beginning?

Courage and maybe frustration moved her to speak. "You're unhappy with me. Elias Hilty, I *begged* you to find another, but you refused." Anna May's heart thumped wildly. "I told you not to marry me, that I didn't want anyone to marry me for pity. But you wouldn't hear of it." Her hands shook. She had dug up bones she should have left buried. Her conscience pricked. Was she provoking her husband to anger? Was it a sin to speak this openly with him?

"You think I married you out of pity?" His anger-laced voice was deceptively quiet.

"Well, didn't you? I know you always felt responsible for the accident but I forgave you. I released you to marry another and you didn't. I am what I am, Elias. I have no secrets. You knew all about me when you married me."

"No secrets?" His voice rose. "You mean you weren't in love with Jonas when you said you'd marry me?"

Anna May was stunned, caught like a rabbit in a trap.

Elias leapt from his seat at the table and began pacing the kitchen floor, clenching his fists. "I saw the way you looked at my *brooda*—a little too late, but I saw. It was *him* you wanted all along, wasn't it? Not me. It was never me." Elias slammed his fist on the countertop, vibrating even the floor beneath Anna May's feet.

She held her breath.

With a red face he let out a deep roar that filled the room then slammed his fist into the kitchen cabinet, breaking its door in one huge crack. He roared again, and with one swipe of his arm, all the canisters on the countertop were dashed to pieces upon the hardwood floor.

Anna May's body trembled, her heart nearly stopping with each of his actions before beating wildly again. All this time she thought he'd never hurt her, but now she wondered. Was she even safe to sit at the table? What was she to do?

"I loved you, Anna May. I didn't marry you because I pitied you. I married you because I *loved you*. And I thought you loved me. But you never did." He panted wearily, giving her sad eyes that communicated his deep hurt. Perhaps he was calming down and they could talk about it. Then, all at once, he took hold of another cabinet door and pulled it off its hinges with a heavy grunt.

Anna May leapt from the chair and bolted out the kitchen door. She ran all the way to her buggy, quickly hitching up her horse.

Elias had gone off the deep end, and it was all her fault.

She needed help.

She drove her horse as fast as it would go to the only place she could think of—Bishop Amos's house.

ANNA MAY JUMPED out of the buggy when she arrived. She ran up to the door just as Bishop Amos was coming out.

Abner Schwartz followed close behind him. She hadn't expected him to have company. Abner, along with John Miller, and Amos made up the three preachers in the district. Technically, John was just a deacon, but he filled in when Amos or Abner were away, providing the second sermon of the day on church Sundays.

"Anna May, what brings you here?" the bishop asked.

"I need to talk with you, in private," Anna May said, her still-shaking hands behind her back.

"Well, then you'll need me to stay," Abner said. "For a witness."

Any woman who needed to talk with the bishop had to bring her husband with her or have a witness present. Women were encouraged to make an appointment for this reason. Anna May hadn't, and her husband was at home destroying the house he built with his bare hands.

A strong feeling came through Anna May, telling her not to allow Abner to be the witness in their conversation. "Where is your wife, Bishop?" Anna May asked.

"She's gone to check on Sarah Cobb. I doubt she'll be back for a while; she left just a bit ago."

The feeling grew stronger. Anna May knew she couldn't go home—not yet anyway, and she couldn't allow Abner Schwartz to be the witness. Perhaps she could go find the bishop's wife over at Sarah's.

Just then a buggy pulled in the drive. "Well, there's Mary now," Amos said. His eyes narrowed in her direction. "I wonder why she's back so soon. Well, anyway, thank you, Abner, for coming. I'll see you on Sunday and we'll talk more then."

Amos shook Abner's hand and Abner got into his buggy.

Amos went to his wife and held out his hand for her to jump down.

As he ushered her into the house she said, "It was the strangest thing. I got just down the road and the wheel on the buggy started making the most peculiar noise. I turned around the first chance I got and drove it home, but as I came up the drive it sounded fine."

"I'll take a look at it later, dear. Right now there's someone here for counsel. We need you to provide a witness so Anna May and I can speak." Amos turned toward Anna May who was following close behind them both. "And depending on the subject matter, you may be able to offer better counsel than I could, anyway. What seems to be the trouble, Anna May?" The bishop motioned for her to sit in the living room with them.

Where should she start? Her whole life was a mess.

"Bishop, I want a divorce." The words surprised Anna May as much as they probably did Amos and Mary.

"A divorce?" The bishop huffed, eyes wide. "Now, Anna May, don't you think you're overreacting a bit? You know we don't allow that."

"*Nay*, Bishop. My husband's a *guete* man. He's kind and gentle and he loves and fears God...at least he was all those things before I married him. He deserves someone who will love him, someone far better than me."

The bishop exchanged glances with his wife then back to Anna May. "You're saying you care for and respect your husband, but you don't love him?"

"Not the way I should. You see, Bishop, we married for all the wrong reasons. Actually, we never should have married in the first place. We're nothing alike. I thought all this time he only married me because of the accident. Because he thought it was his fault and couldn't let the guilt go unless he did. Turns out I was wrong. He did love me. But I didn't love him. I was in love with Jonas." Anna May put her head down and began to cry. She never meant to share so much with the bishop. She'd only come to ask him to go talk to Elias and calm him down. But now that she was here she felt the sudden urge to let it all out and cleanse her guilty conscience. Maybe if she confessed every wrong thing she'd ever done, the bishop could pray for her and then she'd feel like she was supposed to—like everyone else.

She opened her mouth again and like a dam bursting, all her sins came pouring out. When she was done she sat quietly, watching the faces of Amos and Mary, who now knew how fake she really was. It was *guete* to get it all out, only now she was left feeling empty and void. Was it a mistake coming here? Maybe she'd only managed to make everything worse, telling the bishop and his wife all their problems.

"Anna May," the bishop started, "there's only one thing that can fix your problems, and that's Christ."

"I know that, Bishop, and I've been trying. I've gone over to help Sarah Cobb all week, I've been reading my Bible for hours each night, I've—"

"But have you asked Jesus into your heart?" he interrupted.

What a fool question. Of course she had. She'd asked Him to come and fix her problems every day for years, but she couldn't seem to get her prayers to reach Heaven.

"What he means, Anna May," Mary said, "is have you confessed your sins to Jesus, asked Him into your heart, and proclaimed faith in His righteousness and mercy? Have you been saved?"

"I…I don't know. How can anyone know for sure?" she asked.

"You can know for sure, Anna May. If you trust the Bible is true, you'll find everything you need written inside. We'll show you." Bishop Amos motioned for Mary to bring him his Bible. He opened it up and began to share verse after verse that spoke of

God's love for each person and how with Jesus' death and resurrection people were freed from the law that once bound them.

When he'd finished, Amos said, "So, the real question, Anna May, is do you believe the Bible is the true word of God?"

"I do, Bishop."

"Every word?"

"*Ja.*"

"Then do you believe we can know we are saved?"

Anna May hesitated. She'd never heard this in any sermon before. Abner Schwartz would preach that it was high-minded to presume the mind of God. It went against everything she thought she knew about everything. But there it all was, in black and white in the same Bible she'd been reading every night. "*Ja,*" she said finally.

"Then let us pray."

Anna May bowed her head, but as soon as she asked Jesus to forgive her of all the sins in her life she knelt down in the floor beside the chair. Tears flowed from her eyes, and soon she was bent over with her face nearly touching the floor.

Why would You save me, Lord? I know that You will if I ask, because it says so, right in Your word, but why?

Because I love you, Anna May. And true love is never earned, only given freely.

Anna May shook at the words God had spoken to her. When she finally rose from the bishop's living room floor she felt clean and whole. She'd finally found what she'd been missing for so long. The secret others held but she didn't. She'd found the Lord.

CHAPTER 9

*I*t was after dark when she returned home. She was full of hope and joy and wanted to share it so badly with Elias. She wondered if he knew of the verses Amos and Mary had shown her. Then she remembered how angry he'd been when she'd left and Anna May wondered how much damage he had caused to the house in his fit of rage.

Unable to find her way through the dark kitchen on account of overturned chairs, she went back to the buggy and got out a lantern.

Back inside the house, she gasped. The kitchen looked as if it'd been hit by a tornado. She went into the living room. Thankfully, the furniture was all intact.

There wasn't any sign of Elias, so she figured he'd gone on to bed. A pang of guilt for not fixing him any supper went through her. It was well worth it, though. She was even glad he'd destroyed her kitchen. If he hadn't, she'd still be trying to carry burdens too heavy for her to handle alone.

She peeked into the bedroom, but the bed was still perfectly made.

Where was he?

She breathed a sigh of relief that he wasn't home, but still, she worried about him.

She had no idea he was capable of such anger. Anna May turned the chairs upright, swept the flour and rice off the floor, and went to bed, praying for Elias the whole time.

~

TRUE LOVE IS NEVER EARNED, only given freely.

The Lord's message to Anna May hung in her mind all morning. Suddenly the conversation she'd had with the bishop made more sense to her. She did love Elias. He was a *guete* husband to her, and her best friend. At least they had been best friends before they married. He had always been so kind to her, even before the accident. And afterwards he hardly left her side as she slowly recovered. She wondered now how she ever would have gotten through the whole ordeal without him. Then, when she spent months wallowing in self-pity he had done his best to lift her up, sending friends over to talk to her.

How had she been so blind? It was all her fault they'd been more like strangers ever since they married, barely talking at all. She had been waiting around for a feeling like the one she had for Jonas when she was fourteen, a feeling that made her want to do things against God's will. That wasn't the kind of love God wanted for her marriage, and now Anna May knew it. She was to love him freely the way he had loved her once.

And love him she would.

Anna May finished cleaning up the mess in the kitchen. At least three of the cabinet doors were ruined and would need to be replaced. Everything else was put back in its place, and Anna May started breakfast.

She hoped Elias was as hungry as she was after missing supper last night. Maybe his stomach would draw him to the table. She waited as long as her hunger would allow, but he didn't come. She ate breakfast by herself and threw the half dozen fried eggs she'd fixed for Elias out the door, setting her hopes on dinner at noon.

When he didn't show up for dinner, Anna May decided to wait until supper. If he didn't come home by then, she decided, she would ride over to Bishop Amos's house and they'd likely send out men to find him. She prayed nothing bad had happened to him.

Early that evening she fixed supper, keeping her eyes on the windows the whole time, hoping he'd come in the kitchen door any moment. She set the table and when he didn't show up after two hours she decided it was time to ride over to the bishop's for help. She had hoped it wouldn't come to this.

She put on her coat, as the fall evenings were getting cooler each week. She went to the horse stall to hitch up her horse. That's when she saw him, lying in the extra horse stall on a bed of hay.

Anna May gasped. "Elias Hilty, I was worried sick about you." She opened the stall door and ran to him, kneeling down in the hay beside him.

His face was hard, indicating his heart probably was, too.

"I was about to ride out for the bishop to help me find you. Where have you been?"

"Anna May, I'm leaving." He spoke but didn't move from where he lay.

"What do you mean?" Her voice shook.

"I'll send you money, and you'll live here just fine. But I can't stay here. Not anymore."

"Elias, please. Don't leave. I love you."

"It's okay, Anna May. I forgive you. But I can't stay and let my anger get the best of me. I won't." He stared up at the tin roof.

She had pushed him too far. "You don't have to, Elias. I was wrong. I did love you all this time, I just didn't know it. You've been my best friend and I love you, for no other reason than I just do. Please don't leave me, please. I'll do anything you say, just don't go." A tear slid down Anna May's cheek.

"That's the problem, Anna May. I shouldn't have to tell you to love me."

"Supper's on the table, Elias. Please come inside. We'll talk about it."

"*Nay*. I'm staying out here, where I can't break anything if the mood strikes me."

She wiped her eyes on her sleeve. "Then I'll be back." Anna May got up, went into the house, and packed up the food into a large basket. She hurried out to the horse stall to Elias. She handed him a plate of food and a fork. "You must be starving. Have you eaten at all today?"

He took the plate. "A man can only take so much, Anna May," Elias said between bites.

He was eating the food she fixed. That was a *guete* sign. Anna May took a deep breath. If she could only get him to come inside.

He looked at her and then at her plate of food. "Why aren't you eating?"

"I just...missed you so much, Elias." She had. If only she had realized how much he meant to her a little sooner.

He set his plate down when he'd finished and she took hold of his right hand. He winced. His knuckles were swollen.

"Did you hurt your hand?" she asked.

He didn't answer but Anna May knew he had. She brought it up to her lips and kissed it. "You are precious to me, Elias." A tear escaped the corner of her eye. "I didn't know just how much, but now I do. I'm sorry about the past, and I'll spend the rest of my life making it up to you, but I do love you, right here, right now. And someday I hope you'll love me again, too." She held his hand to her cheek and shed another tear.

"I don't know, Anna May."

"Come inside, Elias."

"*Nay*, I think I need to be out here tonight."

Anna May reluctantly released his hand. "Very well."

She collected the dishes and carried them back to the house. Taking a few bites off her plate and leaving the rest on the table, she thought quickly. She changed into her nightgown and grabbed a thick blanket from the closet. Then she put on her boots and carrying the blanket, made her way back to the horse stall.

"What are you doing?" he asked when he saw her approaching.

"If anyone needs to sleep out here, it's me. Scoot over."

He crossed his arms in front of him. "Anna May, I don't think you understand the reason for me sleeping out here in the first place. It's to put some distance between me and you."

"If you want distance, Elias Hilty, you'll have to go in the house. I'm sleeping here tonight."

"I'm not leaving you to sleep in the horse stall!"

"That's what I figured." She laid down beside him and spread the blanket over them both. "Good night, Elias. I love you." Anna May knew with God on her side, she'd win him over, she just wondered how long it would take.

Sometime deep in the night, Anna May awoke to Elias carrying her inside the house. He laid her gently in the bed and covered her up. She grabbed hold of his arm as he tried to walk away, and pulled him back toward her. She scooted over in the bed, giving him room to lay beside her. Reluctantly, he laid down with his back facing her. She stretched her arm out around him and buried her face in his shirt. She wasn't letting him go.

Not ever again.

Morning came. Anna May got breakfast ready and did the dishes from the night before. Not long after, Elias came in and sat down at the table. She set his plate in front of him and fixed another one for herself. Then she waited for him to say grace. When he didn't, she began, "Oh, merciful Lord, thank You for loving me so freely. I pray that love spreads through this whole house. Thank You for the accident that led me to Elias, who never would have become my husband any other way. Thank You for the broken kitchen that led me straight into Your waiting arms, oh Lord. And thank You for giving me a husband I can love more and more each day. You truly have blessed me. Now we thank You for the food we're about to receive. May it nourish us and give us strength for the work ahead. Amen."

Elias simply stared at Anna May.

"I hope you like pancakes." Anna May had made him one in the shape of a heart. She smiled, hoping he'd accept her gesture.

"*Danki*," was all he said.

"So what kind of work are we doing today?" Anna May asked casually.

"We?" Elias squinted his eyes.

"I'm not letting you out of my sight, Elias Hilty, not till you know how much I love you."

*A*nna May sat on the ground not far from the stump where Elias stood chopping their winter's wood. She was seeing him with fresh new eyes, as if for the first time. She'd always known he was a handsome man, but seeing him there, working hard, she began to truly desire him.

All day she had filled her mind to overflowing with the way he used to be. All the things he'd done for her and said to her. Things she'd pushed aside, thinking he was just trying to be nice. He really did love her all that time, and she was such a silly girl not to know it any sooner.

How long, Lord, before he loves me that way again?

Anna May couldn't wait to read more of God's word, not because she had to, but because she needed to know more about a God who loved her so much He would send His own son to die for her. There were things hidden in the Bible she wanted to look for, like searching for a lost treasure. But God was telling her that her place was with Elias for the time being. She had hurt him so badly. Anna May wondered if she'd ever be able to repair their relationship.

Elias set another chunk of wood on the stump. "Don't you have chores of your own to do?"

"Not till dinner. Do you wish to get rid of me that badly?" she asked.

Elias didn't answer. Instead, he chopped harder.

When he couldn't chop anymore for need of a rest, Anna May stood and brushed off her backside. Then she began gathering all the wood pieces he'd strewn about and stacked them neatly in a wall Elias had already started. Elias sat on the stump rubbing his sore hand.

"Do you think you might have broken a bone? We could go to the doctor in town."

"*Nay.*" He watched her work a moment. "Shouldn't you be visiting someone in need?"

She kept on working. "I am. Right now my husband needs me, and I need him."

How many times had she run off to do "God's work" when her husband was begging for her attention at home? Her place was with him, wherever that led her that day.

ANNA MAY'S hands worked fast to bring supper to the table. She'd spent another day following Elias around, hoping he'd realize she was sorry for hurting him, and take her into his arms. She longed to be held by him. As it was, she could barely get near without him giving her the cold shoulder.

She set two plates of food onto the table and waited for him to say grace. When he had finished, they heard a knock at the door.

"Bishop, *vee bish do?*" Anna May asked, letting Bishop Amos in.

He took off his hat and held it with both hands. "I'm just fine, Anna May. I just came to check on the two of you, and see how you were getting along." He eyed the cabinets, still in a state of disrepair.

Anna May's cheeks warmed. She was suddenly ashamed of all the things she'd told Bishop Amos when she'd met with him at his home. "We're doing just great, Bishop." She wondered if it would make Elias even more angry with her if he found out.

"What about you, Elias?"

Elias hesitated, then locked eyes with Anna May. "Fine, Bishop." He nodded his head.

"Well, I hope so. I've got high hopes for the two of you." Thick tension clouded the room and an awkward silence followed.

"Will you stay for supper?" Anna May asked.

"*Nay*, Mary will be waiting for me." He turned to go but then he turned back as if just remembering something. "You know, sometimes we get off on the wrong foot and we do our best to make it better when maybe what we really need is to agree to start over."

"*Danki*, Bishop," Anna May said as he walked out the door. She hoped Elias took those words to heart. That was exactly what she needed, a chance to start over. She smiled tensely at Elias before sitting back down at the table where they ate the rest of their supper in silence.

THE NEXT DAY, Elias set to work on fixing the kitchen cabinets. Knowing he would be in and out of the house, Anna May caught up on the wash and house cleaning she'd neglected all week. She was starting to feel sure he wouldn't leave, but she knew she still had a long way to go toward making him love her again.

With the wash on the line, Anna May picked up the empty laundry basket and carried it in through the kitchen door. Walking by Elias in the kitchen, she stumbled and almost fell, catching herself just in time. She looked down to see a small can of varnish turned over on the hardwood floor. Elias grumbled, and Anna May threw the basket aside and ran out to the line to fetch some towels. They weren't very absorbent since they were half soaked with water already, but they removed the puddle of varnish from the floor. Left behind was a dark stain the size of a dinner plate.

"I'm sorry," Anna May said. "I didn't mean to."

They were both on their knees now, staring at the huge spot on the floor. His hard face softened a bit as she began to cry. "We'll just have to sand it down is all. Nothing to cry about," he said gruffly.

She cried harder, letting it all out now. "I'm so sorry, Elias."

"I know," he said.

He patted her on the back. She looked up at him and sniffled. Was he finally starting to forgive her?

He stood. "I'll ride into town and get some more varnish and some sandpaper. We're going to have to fix the floor now, too."

Anna May sulked. She wanted to go with him, but she was in the middle of all her chores, and there was a pot of beans boiling on the stove she couldn't leave.

He reached out to her, helping her off the floor. "I'll be back."

"Are you sure?" she asked. She knew if he said he would be back, he would, but she wanted to hear the words all the same.

"I never leave a job half finished," he said, and out the door he went.

Anna May spent most of the time Elias was gone praying for his safe return. When he came back it was dinnertime. They sat at the table together but Anna May couldn't eat. She only stared at the mess she'd made in the floor.

"It's okay," Elias said finally. "Really."

"Do you mean the floor, or us?" she asked, hoping for a positive answer.

Elias sat silent a moment, his brows lowered in frustration. "How could you possibly have ever thought I didn't love you?

Was it my fault? Did I not make that clear enough? Was I not a good enough husband to you?"

Anna May took a cleansing breath, trying not to cry. "I was a fool. That's all the excuse I have. I didn't want you to marry me because I thought you were just feeling obligated."

"Because of the accident?"

She nodded. "And when I realized no one else wanted to court me I figured I should let you."

"Because I broke you, is that it?"

"Because you *thought* you broke me. But now I know the truth. It was all part of God's plan."

"For us to be miserable?" he said under his breath.

"*Nay.* For us to be happy and blessed. We can't go back, Elias, only forward. And I go forward loving you freely. I didn't know how to love you before God changed my heart. I didn't know how to love God or myself, either. I want to grow old with you and serve the Lord beside you. If you'll just give me another chance." She reached across the table and placed her hand on his, waiting for an answer.

Elias nodded his head, tears in his eyes. Anna May went to him and threw her arms around his neck. He pulled her into a tight embrace, his warmth filling her with peace.

"I love you, Anna May," he said.

"I love you, too, Elias. More than you'll ever know."

THE FOLLOWING DAY, Elias finished fixing the kitchen cabinets and began sanding the varnish spot on the floor. Anna May had finally caught up on the housework and had made a large roast they would eat for dinner and supper. It was the simplest thing she could think to cook, to keep herself out of Elias's way while he worked, and still have their meals on time.

"The food is ready, whenever you want to eat," Anna May said as she stirred the large pot she'd pulled out of the oven.

"I want to finish this. You go ahead. I'll eat later." Elias pushed the sandpaper around the spot a few times, then blew a quick breath on the floor, wiping the dust off with his hand.

Anna May sighed. "Is there anything I can do to help you?"

"*Nay*," he said.

Anna May hung her head. The anger and resentment was gone from their relationship, but it was still going to take a lot of work to be close like a married couple should be. Anna May wondered to herself how long it would take. She turned to go sit in the living room and wait for him.

"There is one thing."

Anna May glanced over her shoulder at Elias, still kneeling in the floor looking at her. "*Ja?*"

"I could use someone to keep me company." He gave a little smile.

Anna May carefully sat down on the floor beside him, stretching her legs out straight. She quietly watched him work, noting each line in his face and how they grew deeper when he concentrated. She wanted more than anything for him to pay attention to her. She wondered how many times he'd hoped for the same thing. The thought brought tears to her eyes. She had hurt him so badly.

"You're not saying much," Elias said, looking up once more.

Anna May turned her head, but not in time.

He scooted closer, nudging her chin with his finger to make her face him again. "Why are you crying?" he asked.

Anna May shook her head.

"If we want this to work we need to be open with each other, don't you agree?" His tone was kind, but serious.

She nodded.

"Then tell me what you're thinking." He pushed the sandpaper aside and slid even closer to her.

How could she share what she was thinking? She studied the lines in his face again. Could it even be put into words? Brushing the hair behind his ears with her fingers, she wondered what to say; he was still waiting for an answer. But she'd already spent too much energy worrying about always saying the right thing and had become exhausted from it. He was her husband and he loved her; she would show him.

Leaning forward, she put her lips to the middle of his forehead and then between his eyebrows. She kissed the crease of both his eyes and then the lines around his mouth. The feel of his soft breath, followed by his hand on her cheek, encouraged her to keep going. Her lips touched his, but Elias was holding back. In her frustration she started to speak but stopped herself.

"Just say it," Elias whispered. "Don't be afraid of me."

She swallowed hard. If she didn't say it she knew she'd just end up in more tears. "Love me." She lifted his hand up to her lips and kissed it. "I know I don't deserve it, Elias, but forgive me, and love me anyway."

His eyes locked with hers and suddenly his whole demeanor changed. He kissed her full on the mouth, his desire for her evident. She wrapped her arms around his neck and he shifted his weight, scooping her up into his arms and carrying her into the bedroom.

CHAPTER 11

*A*nna May watched as David and Ruth vowed to love and serve each other the rest of their days. It was a beautiful wedding held at the Wittmer house, and it meant so much more to Anna May now that she understood the goodness of the Lord, how He put couples together to love and care for each other for the rest of their lives.

Anna May sat in the back of the room. Behind her, an *Englisher* man and woman dressed in fancy clothes with perfect hair. The whispers had confirmed what Anna May thought. It was Ruth's *mueter*. She hoped they had reconciled now that Ruth was grown and marrying.

Ruth was a sweet girl. Anna May loved to chat with her when she made a trip to Ruth's store, and she'd spent a lot of time with her the week Elias helped them to build on an addition for Naomi, David's *mueter*.

Anna May prayed they would have as much happiness in their home as she had had with Elias in the past year. It was hard to believe they had been married for two now. The only thing they lacked were children.

Anna May tried to push the thoughts of children aside. She

wouldn't allow herself to get her hopes up, but she knew it was possible she was with child. She was beginning to feel nauseous at times, but that wasn't enough to prove anything. She wished she would have kept track of her days better. It had just been so difficult to watch each month's hopes get dashed time and time again.

The Lord had been *guete* to them. They went out and visited with the youth who hadn't yet decided to join church, showing them the verses in the Bible that Bishop Amos and his wife Mary had shared with Anna May. Verses that had changed her life and her marriage forever. Sometimes they shared their story with them, so they might understand God's goodness as well.

If God didn't see fit to give them children, Anna May knew God still loved her and simply had other plans for her. Still, it hurt. She saw the way Jeb and Emma's baby girl looked up at them and smiled for no other reason than she was being held by someone who loved her. And she knew it wouldn't be long before David and Ruth would probably have little ones running about the store.

Bishop Amos said a prayer and the wedding was over. Anna May went outside to get some fresh air and to calm her stomach. She leaned over the porch rail with her head low.

"Are you all right?" Elias asked.

"*Ja.*" She looked up at him. His beard had grown so full now, making his face look even larger than what it already was. She reached up and patted him on the cheek. "I'm fine."

He eyed her suspiciously. "You're looking a little pale."

She raised an eyebrow. "*Danki*, Elias. I appreciate the compliment."

"I didn't mean you don't look beautiful. I was just saying you look like you may be coming down with something." Leave it to Elias to sense something like that.

Another wave of nausea rolled past, making Anna May feel almost light headed. "Now that you mention it, I don't feel all that well." She leaned over the rail again, holding her head with her hands.

"How long have you felt poorly?" he asked.

"About a week."

"I think that's enough time to get you to the doctor. If we go now, we can make it before they close." He held his arm out for her and reluctantly she took it.

She did her best to appear like she was fine as they headed off to the buggy. As Elias hitched up the horse, Anna May saw Emma walking by, carrying her little one on her hip.

"Are you leaving so soon?" she asked.

"I'm not feeling very well. Elias wants to take me to the doctor. It's probably just a stomach bug. Would you tell Ruth and David we're sorry to have left so early?"

"Sure thing, Anna May. And I'll be prayin' it's *guete* news." She smiled knowingly and strode toward the house. It made Anna May a little uncomfortable that Emma knew what she was hoping for. Chances were it was just a stomach bug and then she'd have to tell Emma and be disappointed all over again. She wished she hadn't told Elias she was feeling sick in the first place, although it was becoming harder to hide.

Down the road they went, and before long the bumps of the wagon wheels on the gravel made Anna May feel even worse. She leaned against Elias. "I don't think I can make it to town. Maybe you should just take me home."

"You're scaring me, Anna May. I think you should see the doctor." He made the horses go faster with a slap of the reins.

Her stomach was rolling again. Finally Anna May yelled for him to stop. The buggy came to a halt and Anna May jumped down and bent over the ditch-line, losing her breakfast in the tall weeds. A few minutes later she climbed back in and sat down beside Elias. He just stared at her.

"Well," she said. "What are you waiting for?"

Elias motioned for the horses to continue on.

"We can go home or even back to the wedding, if you'd like. I feel much better now."

"I don't think so, Anna May." He shook his head. "That's not normal. You're going to the doctor."

Not long later, they arrived at the doctor's office. In the waiting room, Anna May completed the paperwork on the clipboard the best she could. She came to some checkboxes; one asked if she were pregnant. Anna May checked no. Of course God could allow it to happen. It *was* possible. That was when she began to hope.

When a young woman with another clipboard in hand called her name, Anna May turned to Elias. "I'll just be a few minutes. I'm sure it's nothing." She knew what the doctor and his assistant would be thinking and it wasn't anything for Elias to be involved in. They were going to test her and if it was negative he'd be disappointed, too.

The tiny hope she had turned into nervousness when she was asked to take a pregnancy test. What if she wasn't with child? Then what? But a little voice inside her said, *What if you are?* She held onto that tiny voice for fifteen minutes while she waited for the doctor to enter the room.

"Anna May Hilty?" he asked.

"*Ja?*"

"Well, yours is an easy diagnosis. You're pregnant. Congratulations." He smiled and waited for her response.

Anna May looked down at her lap. She was with child? Was it really happening? Her hands trembled.

"Are you all right, Ms. Hilty?" the doctor asked.

She put her hands over her mouth, speechless.

"You are happy, right?" he asked. "I've never seen an Amish woman who was unhappy about a pregnancy."

"I was told," she got out in one breath, "that I might not..."

"Yes, I have your history in my file. It looks like you'll need to have a hospital delivery via c-section. Did they tell you that?"

"*Ja.* But what about the baby?" She sucked in a tight breath after the word baby. This was real. She was talking to the doctor about a baby of her very own.

"I don't think you'll have any trouble carrying a child despite your injuries, but delivery could be an issue."

"I'm going to have a baby," she said quietly.

"You're going to have a baby." He smiled, shaking her hand. "Congratulations."

ANNA MAY TRIED to wipe the look of shock off her face as she entered the waiting room where Elias sat. He rushed across the room to her. "Well, what did he say?" he asked quietly.

How would she tell Elias with all these people around? "Pay the bill and I'll tell you all about it on the way home."

"You're scaring me, Anna May," he whispered, his eyes searching her face.

"It'll be okay, just pay the bill."

Outside in the parking lot Elias helped her up into the buggy. He got in beside her and again asked, "What did he say?"

"Just get us out of town and I'll tell you all about it." Anna May was still trying to wrap her mind around the events of the day. She knew she should just blurt it out, but how would Elias react? Would he laugh or cry? Would he even be able to keep the buggy on the road? Anna May knew she wouldn't be able to drive a buggy at that moment.

"Do you need any medicines?" he asked as they pulled onto the main road.

"*Nay.*"

"Why aren't you talking, woman?"

"I..."

"Are you feeling sick again?" he asked when she didn't finish.

"Just pull over on the first dirt road outside of town," she said finally.

Elias's growing anxiety was evident in the tension of the reins as he brought them down on the horse again, causing the buggy to fly through the busy street. Anna May held the buggy seat tightly with one hand, but her other was lightly on her stomach, the realization that someone was growing inside there was something she couldn't get past. A tingle went down her spine. How long had the little one been in there? How long had she been a *mueter* and not even known?

The buggy came to a stop suddenly. The sound of Swan Creek overflowing its banks into a grove of sycamores hypnotized her.

"Anna May, I want you to tell me exactly what the doctor said. Whatever it is, we'll deal with it. Now, what did the man say?" The frustration in Elias's voice was evident.

She took a deep breath. "He said we're carrying an extra passenger in the buggy today." She stared up at him blankly, waiting for his response.

His eyebrows scrunched together in thought. "You're?" He pointed to her stomach.

"*Ja.*" She nodded.

"So that, back there in the weeds?"

"*Ja.*" Anna May was finally smiling after being in shock so long.

Elias's breath became fast and short, his face scrunched up tight. With the fingers and thumb of one hand he rubbed both his eyes. "The Lord is *guete*," he whispered, then nodded his head. "The Lord is *guete*."

Then he began to cry it out louder to the sky, "The Lord is *guete*." And as he looked to the heavens the tears came streaming down.

~

A FEW MONTHS PASSED. The smell of corn and grease filled the kitchen. "How are you feeling, Anna May?" It was something Elias asked her every day, and each time it reminded her of the way he cared for her while she had recovered from the accident.

"I'm fine, Elias," she said as she turned the cornbread frying in the pan on the stove. "The morning sickness only lasted the first few months."

"I worry about you," he said.

"Well, you don't have to." She pulled two plates out of the cupboard and set them on the table, looking forward to the day when she would set out three.

"Do you need any help cooking?" He sat at the kitchen table twiddling his thumbs.

"If I did, who would you get to help?" Anna May raised her eyebrows and turned the corner of her mouth up, waiting for an answer.

"I can cook eggs," he playfully offered.

She laughed. "And that's the only thing I can't stand to eat right now."

"Is there anything I can do? Anything at all?" He threw his hands up and then tucked them under his arms.

Anna May thought hard. He needed a project to keep himself busy. But what? "You could make the baby a bed."

"A bed?"

"Well, *ja*, a baby has to sleep, right? And you did such a *guete* job on the cabinets. I know anything you could come up with would be beautiful." She slid a piece of fried cornbread off the spatula and onto the plate in front of Elias.

"You're right. I could make a bed. I'll get right on that." Elias stood, the chair beneath him scraping as he got up.

"Sit down, Elias." Anna May pulled his arm till he sat. "You have a few months to work on it. No need in letting your supper get cold."

He smiled at Anna May.

"What?" she asked when he kept smiling at her.

"You're going to be a *guete mueter.*"

"You think so?" she asked. It wasn't something she would ever admit to anyone, but sometimes she wondered.

"I know so." Elias pulled Anna May over to sit on his knee.

She giggled. "And that's another way to let your food get cold."

"I don't mind," he said, drawing her in for a kiss.

She melted in his embrace, the heat rising in her cheeks. She pulled away. "I didn't work this hard in the kitchen to let you eat cold food, Elias Hilty. You're going to sit here and eat."

She finished filling the plates on the table and Elias said grace. Anna May never felt his eyes leave her the whole meal. The closeness with him she'd prayed so much for was now a reality.

Danki, God, for bringing Elias into my life. I didn't understand Your plan for me back then, but I'm ever so thankful for it now.

*T*he snowball bush in the yard had finally bloomed. Anna May stood beside it, the fragrance blowing toward her with the wind. The sky was growing dark, another storm approaching. She held her heavy stomach with both hands as the cool breeze pushed on the brim of her *kapp*. In two more days they would travel into the city and come back with a little one in their arms.

The doctor had said the surgery would be quick and that Anna May wouldn't feel a thing, although she'd be awake the whole time. She thought back to the surgery she had after her accident. The pain had lasted for many months after.

Help me to be brave for my little one, Lord.

Anna May knew she could get through it with the Lord's help, but still it nagged. As scary as another surgery was, she was glad for it. She remembered her own *mueter* struggling for days to have her youngest *brooda*.

She could only imagine how much more complicated having a baby would be with bones held together by screws from the buggy accident. At least with a c-section it would be over quickly. The doctor had told her the procedure would take less than two minutes if it were an emergency. It was hard to believe anything could be done that fast, but he didn't seem to be exaggerating when he spoke of it in his confident, yet unattached tone.

"Are you trying to give me a heart attack, woman?" Elias called from behind her.

Anna May turned around, her protruding midsection now pointing at her husband, who watched her with wide eyes.

"I've been looking all over for you," he said.

"I just took a little walk down the road." Anna May's back ached as she started toward the house.

"Well, you could have told me." He held the front door open for her.

"You were out in the field. How was I to tell you?"

When she was safely inside, Elias shut the door and wrapped his arms tight around her from behind, placing both hands on her round middle.

She sighed. "You worry too much."

"Well, what would you think if two-thirds of your family suddenly went missing?"

Anna May laughed. "I'd think they got tired of sitting around the house doing nothing and went for a walk, that's what."

"Just a few more days," he promised.

"Do you really think you'll stop worrying and being so protective as soon as the baby is born?" Anna May knew better.

"Probably not, but I don't want you overdoing it. We're a long way from the hospital, you know." He sat down in the living room and pulled at Anna May's arm to sit with him.

"I can't," she said. "I've got to get supper on."

"I'll do it."

"You know, today I'm tempted to let you."

"Are you feeling bad?" he asked, inspecting her for some evidence of it.

"*Nay*, I just wonder how bad you'd burn the eggs." She snickered.

He pointed his finger in her face. "Just for that, I'm going to do it, and you're going to have to eat whatever I cook. Sit down."

Anna May shook her head. She was feeling fine, better than usual even. It seemed the air was easier to breathe and she had more energy, only now her back hurt. Maybe she shouldn't have taken that walk after all, but she couldn't let Elias know or he'd be rushing her off to the hospital.

"You just rest. I'll take care of everything tonight." With that, Elias disappeared into the kitchen.

"Just don't burn the house down," she called after him. She could hear him chuckle as she propped her feet up on the coffee table. He needed something to do to keep him from hovering over her, anyway.

The rain began to thump on the tin roof, quietly at first, then louder. She smiled. It was just what they needed to get the garden off to a good start. A few minutes passed, and soon the rain was coming down so hard she couldn't see out the living room window. She hoped it didn't beat the young tomato plants to death.

A thin fog began to fill the room before Anna May could even smell it. "Need some help in there?" she called.

"*Nay*, everything's fine. Just a little smoke."

A little smoke?

The living room was filled with *a little smoke*. The kitchen had to be overflowing with it. Anna May started to go help when she felt the twinge in her back that sat her back down in her chair.

Carrying this baby so long has given me back problems.

A few minutes later, in walked Elias with a plate of eggs and the look of a major accomplishment.

"Did you have any trouble?" she asked as she took the plate from him. Her eggs appeared to be cooked properly.

"Not at all." He smiled and walked back into the kitchen. He returned with his plate, a half dozen burned eggs and toast.

It was all Anna May could do to eat her supper with a straight face.

∽

IT HAD BEEN difficult to get to sleep that night, but the sound of the rain on the roof finally made it happen. The next morning the rain was still coming down in buckets.

"Where do you think you're going?" Elias asked as Anna May headed for the kitchen door.

"To the outhouse."

"Not today, you're not. I'll get you a chamber pot. You'll slip in the mud and hurt yourself."

Anna May huffed. "Will you listen to yourself? Have a little faith in God, won't you?" All at once another pain went through her back. This time it radiated completely around her body. She winced, holding both hands to her back.

"What is it?" Elias asked, walking all the way around her.

"Nothing. Just my back."

"How long has it been hurting you?"

"Since yesterday."

Elias looked her dead in the eye, silent.

"My back hurts me sometimes. That's normal." She shook her head softly.

Elias got his hat and boots. "We're going into town."

"It's nothing," she said, louder now.

"Then we'll be that much closer for the appointment tomorrow. Besides, with all this rain I don't want to worry about us getting stuck in the mud. Do you have your things ready?"

Maybe Elias was right. The last pain was much worse than all the others. It would make Anna May feel better being close to town, too. No harm in being prepared.

She got her bag and jacket and in a few minutes they were on their way.

Elias formed a tent over them with the tarp he kept in the buggy for when it rained. Anna May could sense Elias's fear. He was good at talking to people about trusting God and pointing out the appropriate Bible verses. She believed he did trust in God during the good times, but when things went bad he could quickly fall to pieces. It was up to her to keep it together, which was exactly why she hadn't mentioned the pain before.

Soon they pulled into the driveway of Elias's friend, Matthew. "What if he's not home?" Anna May asked.

"Then we'll see if his *vater* will ride with us." Elias jumped out quickly and ran for the house. They would need someone to come with them to bring their horse and buggy back since there was no way of knowing how long they would be away. Whoever it was could also spread word to Elias's family, so they could take care of the chores a day earlier than planned.

Anna May watched Matthew push his straw hat down on his head before leaping off the porch in his rain boots. Elias followed. Matthew sat down on the other side of Anna May and covered up with an edge of the tarp. He tipped his hat, his thick glasses dotted all over from the rain. She hoped his presence would help set Elias's mind at ease somehow.

A pain shot through Anna May and she cried out, grabbing Elias's arm. He gave the command and the horses went faster, each bump reminding Anna May of the night of the accident. She wanted to keep calm for Elias's sake, but the fear was growing. It started in her chest, but soon threatened to consume her.

What if they didn't make it in time? Would she lose the baby? How could she face another day if that happened? Would she ever be able to forgive herself for not telling Elias sooner?

"It's going to be okay, Anna May," Elias said, his voice steady. "We're not that far from town."

He meant Asheville, the small town nearest to the Swan Creek Amish settlement. It was where the clinic was, but not the hospital. It was a forty-five minute drive from there by car.

Another bump sent a pain in her back that burned like fire. Elias pushed the horse even harder. Thoughts of flying out of the buggy into total darkness came back to her. "Please slow down, Elias. It hurts."

Reluctantly, he slowed the horse some. The rain began to slow a bit too, giving Anna May encouragement. God was looking down on them, and would help them get to the hospital in time, she just knew it. The clouds ahead were lighter.

As the rain came to a stop and the sun peeked through the clouds it quickly became warmer. They pulled the tarp off them and Matthew helped her remove her light jacket. For a second she felt relaxed, hopeful.

Then she saw it.

Up ahead, a large tree lay across the road. There was no way the buggy could get by it, and even with the strength of ten men they'd never be able to move it.

"What now, big guy?" Matthew asked as they came to a stop.

Elias jumped down to look at the fallen tree. He climbed back into the buggy and turned it around. "Can we borrow some tools?" he asked.

"Sure thing, *brooda*."

"*Guete*. I want you to ride out and fetch Jonas. Tell him to bring tools and bring back every able-bodied man you see along the way. I'll ride back and get started." The horse and buggy made a huge circle in the road and in a moment was headed back faster than ever.

Anna May suddenly felt nauseous. She gripped the seat of the buggy with both hands and winced at every big bump. She wanted to tell Elias that there was no time, but she didn't know how. This baby was coming, tree or no tree.

CHAPTER 13

*a*nna May got out of the buggy at Matthew's house while Matthew and Elias loaded the buggy with tools. She didn't want him to leave her there, but he wouldn't be of any help now.

"I can't ride any longer, Elias."

"Stay here. I'll be back for you. I won't take long, I promise."

Her heart sped as he readied to leave. She tried to hide the pain she was feeling and the pressure she felt down below. Matthew's *mueter* had several *chinda*. Surely she would help.

The doctor's words went through her head. *No homebirths.* But what choice did she have? Even if Elias rode out to the nearest phone for help, she doubted there'd be time to make it to the hospital now.

Anna May prayed hard, harder than she'd ever prayed for anything.

Dear God, please take care of us. I couldn't live another day if anything happened to my baby.

Then God spoke, *Who knit you together in your mueter's womb?*

You did, Lord, she answered.

Who put you back together when you were broken?

You, Lord. Tears welled up in her eyes.

What makes you think I couldn't do it again?

She drew in a sharp breath. *Nay, Lord. Please, anything but that.*

As Elias turned to leave, Anna May began to cry. The Lord wanted her to trust Him, and as hard as it was, she had to. He was right. He held her and the babe in His strong hands and she must accept His will.

"It'll be okay, Anna May. I'll move the tree with my bare hands if I have to." He took hold of her shoulders and stooped down to look her straight in the eyes. "Trust me."

"I need you to pray, Elias," she squeaked out.

"Of course, Anna May. I have to go now. I'll be back before you know it."

"*Nay.*" She took hold of his arms while they were still on her shoulders. "I need you to pray that God's will be done—not ours."

"Everything will be—"

"You don't know that, Elias, and neither do I. Promise me you'll pray for God's will and not your own." Tears streamed down Anna May's cheeks. It wasn't the prayer she wanted to pray, either, but she had been convicted by God Himself.

Elias frowned.

"Promise me."

"I promise," he said finally.

She nodded for him to go, and as soon as he was out of sight she sank down onto the porch steps in tears.

Please, God, help me to accept Your will.

One of Matthew's little sisters came out the door. "Are you okay?" she asked.

Anna May quickly wiped her eyes on her dress sleeve. "Of course," she said, faking a smile.

Then Sylvia, Matthew's *mueter,* stood in front of her. "Come on, dear." She held her hand out and helped Anna May up. As she escorted her into the house, she told her children to go outside and play.

"Where are you going, *Mueter?*" one of them asked.

"Upstairs."

The little girl scrunched up her nose. "What for?"

"I'm going to show Anna May the new curtains I made, and then we're going to visit a while. I want you to play outside till your *vater* comes home. Do you understand?"

"*Ja.*"

"Good girl." Sylvia patted her on the head as she walked by. She had done a good job at convincing her children there wasn't a thing in the world wrong. Anna May wondered how she did it so easily.

"You're close, aren't you?" she whispered when the door to the upstairs bedroom was shut and locked.

"I'm so sorry. We were on the way to the hospital. I'm supposed to have a c-section in the morning, but there was a tree in the road and Matthew was only supposed to bring the buggy back—"

"You mustn't wear yourself out explaining things to me. Just lie down." She pointed to the bed, neatly made up for company.

"I don't feel like lying down." Anna May shook her head. She shouldn't be here. If anything she should be home or at her own *mueter's* house, but not here in Sylvia Miller's spare bedroom.

"Then don't," she said softly. "I had most of my *chinda* upright. It can be easier that way."

Just then, pressure like a ton of rocks pushed on her pelvic floor, and a familiar pain she'd had off and on since her accident. She squatted down on the floor and tried hard not to cry out.

Sylvia ripped the covers off the bed and threw them on the floor. "You're closer than I thought." The words sent Anna May to shaking all over.

A moment later Sylvia said, "Come on, I'll help you get those shoes off and we'll try to get everything else in place before the next wave comes."

Anna May sat on the edge of the bed and let Sylvia pull her

shoes from her feet, dark thoughts surrounding her once more. "Do you think the baby has a chance?" Anna May said quietly.

Sylvia's face fell. "Merciful heavens, what kind of question is that, Anna May? Of course your baby has a chance. If it's God's will, this baby will be born safe and healthy, and from the looks of it, very quickly."

"But what if it's not God's will?" Anna May held her breath.

"Then the *guete* Lord will still be holding your hand the whole way. Yours and your little one's. That can be hard to accept. I've lost two of my little ones, but I know where they are, and I have peace about it. Either way, it'll be okay, Anna May. Just have faith."

Anna May didn't know Sylvia had lost two of her *chinda*. Until you held a healthy baby in your arms it simply wasn't talked much about, leaving the ones who lost their babies to grieve alone, something Anna May never thought much about until now.

She realized there wasn't anything she could do. Just like the tree in the road, she had no control over what happened to her or her baby. It was time to trust God and let Him take care of it.

The pressure was back now, stronger than ever. "Mmmm," Anna May grunted. She squatted with her arms on the side of the bed, gritting her teeth.

"Don't tense up. Just let it all go. You must clear your mind to clear your body."

As the pain subsided, Anna May opened her eyes.

"You're going to need to rest between or you'll wear yourself out. I only made that mistake once." Sylvia stacked pillows behind Anna May and had her sit on the edge of them. "Now, tell me when you feel it and I'll pull your arms."

"It hurts," she cried.

"Don't view it as painful. You must think of it as pressure only and it will be."

Anna May tried to clear her mind.

My life is Yours, God. Do with me what You will.
She breathed deep.
And this babe was never really mine, anyway. I place him or her back in Your hands. I know You love me, and I know You love this little babe. I trust you, God.

Another wave swept over her. Sylvia pulled her arms, rocking her forward into a squat. Anna May imagined the pressure as a wall that stood between her and the Lord. She pushed against it and in her mind the wall moved a little. Then she released into a rest.

This happened over and over. How much time had passed, Anna May didn't know, but her legs were heavy and shook when she put any weight on them.

"I can see the top of the baby's head, Anna May," Sylvia said. "You're doing fine. Just relax till you feel you need to push again."

She panted. "It feels like I need to keep pushing all the time."

Sylvia gave her a tense look. "Then take a deep breath and don't stop till the baby comes out." Sylvia's even tone encouraged Anna May. She caught her breath and the image came again. This time the Lord was on the other side of the wall holding her little one. Anna May cried out with a push and the wall broke free, allowing her to step over to the other side.

Sylvia put the baby in her arms and Anna May laid back on the stack of pillows.

～

"ANNA MAY," Elias called out from downstairs. Sylvia got up from the edge of the bed where Anna May and her new baby lay. She unlocked the door and called for him to come on up.

"Hurry, Anna May, the road will be clear enough for us to pass by the time we get down there." He stopped suddenly in the doorway at the sight of her.

"Elias," Sylvia said as he slowly entered. "Come meet your son." She smiled and shut the door behind her.

"A son?" he asked. His shirt was stained with dirt and sweat. He removed the hat from his head and dropped it on the floor beside the bed. "Is he?"

"He's sleeping." Anna May smiled wearily.

Elias's face creased into a tight frown, his eyebrows slanted. "And you?"

"*Ja.* Everything's fine, Elias." Her voice was soft.

He got down on his knees beside the bed and began to cry, bringing to Anna May's mind when he cried beside her hospital bed after the buggy accident.

"*He's been so worried about you,*" the nurse had said. "*He must care for you very much.*"

Anna May knew it to be true this time. He bowed his head in silent tears, no doubt thanking God for the way the day turned out. Anna May ran her fingers gently through his hair. How had she ever doubted his love for her?

"You're going to be a *guete vater*, Elias. I can already tell."

She thanked God for His mercy and kindness, for helping her see His ways above her own, for her newborn son, and for bringing her the long way home.

ABOUT THE AUTHOR

Tattie Maggard lives near Swan Creek, just south of a Swiss Amish community in rural Missouri. When she's not chasing black bears from her yard, she's writing Amish romance, homeschooling her daughter, or playing an old tune on the ukulele. The Amish of Swan Creek is Tattie's first Amish series.

Sign up for Tattie's newsletter for updates and to get a free short story, Mending The Heart, sent straight to your inbox. Visit www.TattieMaggard.com for more info.

Thank you for reading and reviewing. God bless!